IN DIFFERENT SKIES

REBECCA WILBY

SKYLIGHT
PRESS

First published in Great Britain by Skylight Press,
210 Brooklyn Road, Cheltenham, Glos GL51 8EA

Designed and typeset by Rebsie Fairholm
Printed and bound in Great Britain

www.skylightpress.co.uk

ISBN 978-1-908011-02-2

In memory of Zoë Barnes,
still blazing on the inside.

I saw his round mouth's crimson deepen as it fell,
Like a Sun, in his last deep hour;
Watched the magnificent recession of farewell,
Clouding, half gleam, half glower,
And a last splendour burn the heavens of his cheek.
And in his eyes
The cold stars lighting, very old and bleak,
In different skies.

— *Wilfred Owen*

Chapter One

The first time it happened was in Tewkesbury Abbey.

There was nothing to forewarn of its coming, no trigger or invitation. It just came out of a silence, an embodied silence which leaves the air tingling. Katherine, in a church for the first time in years and bored witless, had no thought whatsoever of opening up a gap in the surrounding reality and gazing, tube-like, through time.

For a moment, the absence of the choir's voice was as tangible as its presence had been, vibrating the hollow fabric of the abbey with lingering purpose. The silence swelled against the walls, was forced up into the high gallery with its long row of stone arches, rushed into the hollow spaces and then faded to reveal only the low hiss of the gas heaters.

Katherine looked down at the sheet she had been casually crumpling, a cheap photocopied Order of Service on canary yellow paper. She was trying to work out how much longer it was going to go on for, and aware that her friend Mike was trying to read it over her shoulder.

'What now?' he whispered softly. 'Is it finished?'

'I think that bloke is going to do another stint.'

'Oh no.' He sank in his chair.

She settled back in her seat and focused on the head of the old lady in front of her. It was a strange thing to see a stranger so intimately close, and yet all she could see of her was a row of white curls poking out from a mink-coloured nylon fur hat, a pearl earring clipped to a crinkled ear and a sagging, magenta-flushed cheek. When the woman moved her head a sweet violety smell asserted itself over the general frankincense fug. Katherine hoped the old lady couldn't hear the sniggered sarcasm which she and Mike had been exchanging for the past half hour.

After a bit of shuffling a man with thin greasy hair and spectacles sprang to the pulpit and folded his arms on the front edge. He looked like such a stereotypical vicar that Katherine felt herself switching off before he'd even said anything. He cleared his throat too close to the microphone, sending a guttural boom through the church building. He had a folded piece of paper in front of him, half concealed, which he glanced down at frequently.

'Wake me up if anything interesting happens,' she whispered.

Mike made a quiet affirmative noise and began idly inspecting a wad of crumpled sweet wrappers which he'd found at the bottom of his pocket, unfolding and smoothing each one in turn.

Remembrance Day was imminent; the speaker went into a sentimental speech about the war dead. Patronising epithets of sacrifice and duty were dredged up for their annual outing. Katherine, who had only gone along to listen to the music, tried to detach her mind from the stream of words and retract into her own mindspace. The prime reason she liked the sound of choral voices in a large abbey building was because of her synaesthesia. She'd had it all her life, an overlapping of sensory boundaries which brought bursts of colour into her field of vision whenever she heard music. It happened quite spontaneously and she had no control over it. Sometimes it was textural and liquid, other times solid and static, sometimes overwhelming but always interesting. In a setting such as this she could get total submersion; the choir's voices became a radiance of purple, shimmering with individual tones, in which she could almost lose herself; oceanic waves from burgundy to indigo in which every voice streamed an individual trail of tones. Her colour sensation in live choral music was the nearest she could get to a religious experience. But she wasn't so keen on sitting through the religious service that went with it. Her spirituality could never relate to deity or dogma. The colours were slack and dead as the slow, reverberating drone of the man's voice made her ache with boredom and she shifted uncomfortably in her seat.

Mike leaned across again, ever solicitous.

'Are you all right?'

'Numb arse,' she whispered.

'Who's a dumb arse?' His brow furrowed.

'No, numb arse. What I've got.'

'Oh.'

They were sitting at the back of the abbey where several rows of foldaway wooden seats had been put out – needlessly, as it turned out – to supplement the usual pews. The nave was lit primarily by a large cluster of candles, which left the western end of the building almost in darkness. Only the far end was brightly illuminated with a golden radiance off the stonework and the rich reds of velvet drapes; the tall pinnacles of stained-glass were grey-black against the evening sky.

She wondered if she could simply drop off to sleep. Would anybody notice? She tried for a bit, but couldn't keep her eyes closed for more than about ten seconds without feeling self-conscious. She tried to pull the colour visions back into her mind, but they were empty without the music. All she could do was shut out the speaker's monologue, her attention momentarily snapping back into focus every now and then to catch a few words, meaningless without a context, before drifting back into a daydream state.

They were sitting next to the war memorial which was just visible in the gloom. A nondescript wooden panel with a few columns of names, too dimly lit to be legible, set into the wall with a plain altar rail at the front underneath. It was already swamped with poppies, lots of identical mass-produced wreaths, plus one or two simple wooden crosses with paper poppies in the centre.

Katherine gazed at it idly. The whole thing had a slightly sinister look in the near-darkness, the poppies like blotches of blood on the flagstones. It seemed to radiate silence. She felt her mind drawn into it. It was detached from the droning clergyman as if it inhabited an existence of its own. Her thoughts were blank but she tried to project herself into that silent space as if the whole universe had contracted into it and it was now the only point that really existed. She felt a cold tingling sensation in her arms which came and went in small waves.

Then she saw a man's face staring back at her. It came and went almost too quickly for her brain to register it, but its impact gave her a jolt. It was the face of a young soldier with a moustache and uniform.

She saw his features quite clearly, or at least sharply enough to leave an imprint in her mind. It wasn't a face she recognised. A rounded face, sad and serene, with clear eyes. The one unsettling impression that remained with her was the look of surprise – almost fear – that had spread across the man's face in that fraction of a second. It sent a cold rush of adrenalin through her. Not only had she seen him, but he had seen *her*.

'You asleep?' Mike whispered, leaning over to see.

'No.' The feel of her own voice moving up her throat came as a shock.

'Yes you were,' he jibed. 'I saw you jump when you woke up.'

'No I wasn't. I'm just – I felt a bit strange for a minute there. Really strange. I'll be all right.'

'Are you not feeling well?'

'I'm fine. Just forget it.'

The choir began again at the far end of the abbey, an isolated female voice at first in bright azure points of light, gradually augmented with purples until the hissing gas heaters were drowned out by voices and colours. Katherine took several deep breaths and looked up at the ceiling, where she could just make out the detail of the roof in the low light. It was high vaulted in criss-crossed sections with the tracery picked out in gold. There were dozens of carved bosses on all the joins with different figures and faces, from the angelic to the blatantly pagan. She focused on their chiseled details, afraid that if she let her mind wander off into a daydream state again she might find herself confronted with more faces from nowhere, and that frightened her because she didn't know who the man was or how she could have seen him.

She focused her attention on the grinning face of a green man high up in the centre of the ceiling, a fissured, half-human head spewing out a voluptuous posy of chiselled leaves. His mouth was stretched with mirth and abundance, and the leaves merged into his chunky curls of hair. Full of the joys of spring on a dark November evening.

Once she had relaxed a bit her fear faded out and was replaced by curiosity. Then she wished she *could* see the man again, to get a better look at him, to get some idea of who he might be, and where he was, and whether he could see her as well. The music and the colours continued, but she was barely aware of them now.

After what seemed like an interminable shuffling queue for holy communion, the concert was over. She waited until the collective scrape of chair legs on the flagstones had mostly subsided then stood up and put on her coat and scarf. Mike, who had little faith in the efficacy of church heating and hadn't bothered to take his coat off in the first place, edged into the stream of parishioners which had already bottlenecked in the north door. Katherine tugged at his sleeve.

'Just a minute. I want to have a look at something before we go.'

She gestured for him to leave her to it, and shuffled the other way towards the war memorial to get a closer look now that some lights were on. The names of the local war dead were painted in columns of gold script down the tall panel. Around and in between each name the wood was worn shiny-smooth by years of polishing. It was difficult to imagine the names were real people; they were flat, glazed with age, and unfamiliar. At the top of the panel was a carved image of Christ on the cross with the two Marys gazing up at him miserably. A Latin quotation looped along the bottom edge.

Hanging from a long pole at the side of the memorial was a large tricolour, whose colours had faded to something closer to a homogenous grey. Katherine reached up and rubbed the edge of the red area between her fingers. It felt rough, heavy and unspeakably ancient. Its smell was a mixture of dust, mildew, potting sheds and old sacks.

On the other side a wooden cross was pinned to the wall, age-darkened and pocked with woodworm. The bottom was ragged, as though it had originally stood in some soggy place and had rotted right through. A small brass plate explained that it had been a battlefield grave marker for local man killed in action in 1915, and had been sent to his widow after the war when it was replaced with a proper headstone. The widow had asked for it to be kept in the abbey, and now here it was.

The name of Gunner W. Roberts was still fairly legible in the original lettering, tidily painted in black. He was one of a multitude, singled out only by the presentation of this surviving stump. But the curiously disturbing relic didn't help Katherine to imagine Gunner W. Roberts as a real person – living in this very town, probably walking dozens of times over the same spot on the same flagstone where she now stood, except of course there wouldn't have been a war memorial back then. She could just about conjure up an impression of the widow, and empathise with the sharp rush of horror the woman must have felt every time she looked at the wooden cross. She had probably struggled with the opposite problem – equating the man she knew and cherished with this sterile piece of wood. And now the sterile piece of wood had outlived them both.

Katherine leaned over the altar rail and peered into the luxurious mass of poppies. They were cheerfully mass-produced from coloured paper, machine crinkled and stapled on with a black plastic button. Yet somehow they had an extraordinary dignity. She could not bring herself to touch one – it would have been a violation of something. A row of small poppy-centred crosses had been arranged along the front of the memorial, made from white new wood, each with 'Remembrance' stamped on it in black.

The annual ritual of decorating memorials with plastic poppies had never appealed to her much, but she could hardly bear to take her eyes off them. She slowly drew away from the altar rail and noticed it had another inscription carved underneath: *More things are wrought by prayer than this world dreams of.* The stillness and poignancy of this little shrine seemed to prohibit any attempt at prayer. She listened as the silence settled on the abbey like a comfortable overcoat.

On the Tuesday following Remembrance Day, Joe Waldron sat on the stone bench inside the abbey porch and watched the dying leaves whip round his feet in persistent circles. The wind caught, snatched, fretted and withdrew. It held his attention for a couple of minutes, then he returned to his crossword.

'Five down, arched recess in church. Well, that's appropriate. Four letters, A-something-S-something.'

He flexed his back to relieve some cramped muscles, pressing his spine against the cold stone wall, and refolded his newspaper as the wind began to agitate and tease the corner. He was sure it must be a word he was familiar with. It was mildly annoying that he was sitting in the porch of a church looking up at an arched recess, and it wasn't giving him any help whatsoever. The only words for architectural bits and bobs he could think of were complicated ones. Tympanum. Presbytery. Nothing that was A-something-S-something. He looked for another word that might intersect it and give him another letter, but nothing else was joined to it. After some hesitation he gave up and wrote 'ARSE' in the grid.

Arched recess. Arse. That was good enough.

'Hello there. It is you, isn't it?' A female voice.

He looked up and saw one of his ex-students from a long ago sixth form, now very much grown up.

'Well I never. Katherine, isn't it? From A-level English. Blimey, it has been a long time.'

'Ages. Are you still teaching?'

'Oh yeah. Be teaching till I drop dead, I reckon. But it has its moments. I wouldn't want to do anything else.'

Katherine smiled. He had aged a bit from what she had in her memory, including a curious greying of the eyebrows. She couldn't remember whether his hair had always been flecked with grey or not. There was something unfamiliar about his familiar face, partly the fading and puckering of age and partly because she was seeing him out of context. She remembered him in a lofty room with formica-topped tables forever rocking on not-quite-matching legs, and a herring-boned parquet floor, with scuffed books, and biros that had got clogged up with grit and dog biscuits (that bit was just a phase) from the bottom of her school-bag. He taught her English in the sixth form, enthusing about Robert Graves and William Blake and pretending to enthuse about D. H. Lawrence. His wife had been an art teacher.

'What brings you here?' she asked. 'I seem to remember you lived in Cheltenham.'

'I do. I'm collecting my daughter, who does some sort of Art Therapy course in Tewkesbury. I've got an hour to kill, so I thought I'd come and spend some time in the abbey.'

'Oh. If you're going in, is it all right if I tag along?'

He sat up and folded his paper. 'Yes, if you like.'

They made their way into the building. There was a lingering autumnal darkness inside, which lifted gradually as Katherine's eyes got accustomed to it. It was a truly huge building, so sturdily put together that the walls had been squeezed outward by the weight of the stone piled above them, and leaned uneasily against their buttresses. Joe Waldron was something of an obsessive when it came to local history; he had a great knowledge of Tewkesbury Abbey and was really in his element.

'There was a terrible battle just outside here in 1471. I always remember the year of the Battle of Tewkesbury because it's the same as the number you dial to find out who your last caller was. Useful, that. The defeated soldiers fled to the abbey for refuge and were just hacked down in the aisles here. The abbot had to come down here himself and intervene. That would have been Abbot Strensham, who had a service station named after him on the M5. If you can imagine it, all these walls were originally covered with paintings, beautiful medieval paintings, every inch. The Victorians thought they looked a mess and scrubbed them off.'

'That was a silly thing to do, wasn't it?'

'They didn't think so. Tastes change.'

He showed her the dip in the floor which marked the point where the abbey had once been divided in two, half for the monks and half for the people, and pointed out the chunks of pale stone spiralling round the pillars where there had once been a staircase. In the tracery of a tomb, he showed her a tiny carved figure of a monk standing on a vanquished devil, and the sacristy door which looked normal on this side but was fortified on the other side by bits of hammered-out armour from the battlefield. He pointed out a linear pink stain on the stonework where the monks had most likely set fire to a bookshelf, and a little fragment of wall painting in a chapel which was the only bit the Victorians had missed.

Katherine was quite entertained by now.

'How come you know so much about it?'

'Oh, I'm big on local history. Not just the abbey, all sorts of stuff. It's mainly the first world war I'm interested in at the moment, its effect on the area, that sort of thing.'

Katherine felt her stomach turn over.

'That's funny. I'm kind of looking into the first world war myself. Just idle curiosity though, I don't know anything about it.'

'What is it you're researching?'

Katherine wasn't ready to confide. She had been pulled back there today by a fierce magnetism that wouldn't let her alone, and had felt she might find some closure by going back to where it had happened. But it wasn't something she could explain to anyone else.

'I'm not sure what set it off really. I was here a few nights ago at a concert, one of these Music in the Abbey things. I was sat next to the war memorial and – um – just started thinking about these people and what they must have been through.'

'Yeah, that's pretty much what set me off as well. We ought to have a good look at the war memorial while we're here.'

Since her recent visit someone had put a wreath of white roses in front of the memorial, but apart from that it was swamped with poppies, layer upon layer of red paper poppies. Joe reached down and stroked one, moving from wreath to wreath, turning the labels to read them. Some were personal, for never-met great-grandfathers, some were to soldiers in various wars, presented by local organisations.

'This area did suffer badly in the Great War,' Joe said. 'It doesn't look too bad on that list, but the death rate was about one in four for the blokes who joined up around here. That's pretty devastating for any community.'

'Why did they enlist? I mean, it must have been obvious that a lot of them were going to get killed.'

Joe shook his head. 'Nobody really had any idea what it would be like. It was unprecedented at the time, and people weren't savvy about war like they are today. A lot of men from Cheltenham went into the 10th Gloucesters. Then came the Battle of Loos and most of them were wiped out.'

Katherine swallowed. 'I didn't know that.'

'These weren't even soldiers,' he said, gesturing to the panel of names. 'They were farmers, shop-keepers, bus drivers, *schoolboys* some of them. It's so depressing.' His eyes glazed over as he withdrew to the trenches and craters and barbed wire of his imagination.

The more she looked at the memorial the more she felt a connection with it, though not an entirely comfortable one. There was something amiss, or disrupted, somewhere at the back of her mind, where she was aware of it but not quite conscious of its true shape. The history of war bored her, and the violence of it repulsed her, but something irritatingly vague on the edge of her consciousness kept her coming back to it. She felt an urge to move on, and began to walk back up the transept towards the lady chapel. Joe followed, and was silent for the first time.

'What's this then?'

Katherine was drawn to a door sized opening in the wall, but which didn't go anywhere. It was about the size of a wardrobe, with nothing in it except an ancient floor of medieval glazed tiles and a hanging votive lamp. Just an empty space with no obvious purpose.

'Ah, that.' Joe's interest snapped into gear. 'I'm glad you spotted that. It's a magical doorway.'

She looked at him to see if he was joking. 'What do you mean?'

He shrugged. 'Go and stand in it.'

'Do you think I'm allowed to?'

'It's fine, nobody's looking.'

Intrigued, Katherine stepped into the alcove. There was immediately a tingly rush of adrenalin inside her which forced her to take a deep breath. It was like stepping into a forcefield.

'What am I supposed to be looking for?' she asked, trying to be normal.

'Well, you can see it used to be a doorway, can't you? See there's a bit of metal sticking out of the back wall which looks like part of a hinge. It originally led to the old cloister when it was a monastery, though there's nothing much left of that now.'

'The Victorians again?'

'No, Henry the Eighth. He had all the abbey buildings smashed up except the church.'

'Silly sod. So what happened to the door?'

'It was blocked up centuries ago because it doesn't go anywhere any more.'

'And why did you call it a magical doorway?'

Joe grinned. 'Can you not feel it?'

She instantly felt light-headed and put a hand on the wall to steady herself. There certainly was a beautifully warm sense of power in this recess as if it was somewhere detached from the rest of the abbey, and its intensity made her skin tingle. Then as she looked at the wall where the doorway had once been her perception shifted and it was as if she was looking right through the stone at an image projected on a screen somewhere beyond. She saw the same face as before, the same man. The impression was even stronger this time. As clear as daylight. His eyes met hers directly and gave her a zap in the pit of her stomach. He looked like a first world war soldier.

Shivering, she made a rapid exit from the alcove and felt a muscular spasm along her spine as the vision left her. Its departure was instant and she was relieved to be back in the normal world.

Joe knew something had happened and was looking at her expectantly.

'Well?' he asked. 'What did you feel?'

She smiled resolutely. 'Nothing much. Sort of peaceful.'

'Well, I have to go now I'm afraid.' He scribbled down his address and phone number on the back of one of the till receipts that perpetually haunted his coat pockets. 'If you want to have a chat about the first world war any time give me a call. In fact, if you can come over on Thursday evening I'll show you some of the research I've done.'

'I'd like that,' she said. 'Yes I'll give you a ring.'

He turned to go and tucked the newspaper under his arm. The arched span of the apse soared above his head and brought his mind slapping back to his unfinished crossword.

'Arse. Apse. Oh sod it.'

Chapter Two

The shape of the arch skewed in and out of focus like an image in a disturbed pond. When it fragmented and dissipated it was a frightening sensation, losing the edges of the image in a dark unconscious. But always it lurched back into tangible form, and every now and then it snapped sharply into terrifying clarity.

What distressed her most in it was the black. Thick, creeping, stifling black. There was a wire mesh grille holding it back, but the raw chasm behind the flimsy screen tapped into a primordial fear which came at her in shuddering waves.

She tried to rationalise it. Was she afraid of something coming out of the darkness? Or was it more a fear of being dragged into it? Was it simply that she couldn't see through it, and its menace was unknowable? No particular fear stood out, it was somehow a conglomerate of them all, an archetypal knot of fears. It put a cold weight in the pit of her stomach and a rush of static over her skin. And the *noise* was something else again.

It was a hollow booming vibration that seemed to exist only within her own skull and rumbled and reverberated with unrelenting intensity, like a recording played in a loop.

As the scene became clearer she saw that the archway with its black opening was a few feet above her. Her lower body could not move, trapped in some confined space which she was aware of but couldn't see. Her head, shoulders and right arm were free but the rest of her was pained with cramp. The forced inertia, in a vacuum of inner panic, was unbearable. It pushed her again and again to the brink of unconsciousness.

She could see at the mouth of the arch that a sticky line of dark detritus had run from the corner and streaked its ugly way down the wall. The bricks were grey-white, shiny ceramic like in an underground station, and smeared with filth. Sometimes it appeared to be liquid which made dark lines down the wall. Sometimes it was sticky and got caked up on the edge. It caught in the wire of the grille, already black with rust and soot.

Sometimes if she made the effort to stare hard into the recess she could see earth behind it, as if the ground banked up sharply on the other side. Facing the blackness head on like this seemed the only thing to do, but each attempt brought the terror up to the surface like an electric shock. There was a half remembered image underlying the fear – something she had seen. Something that had tumbled out of the black and been caught up against that grille. She had an abstract awareness, nothing more; the memory itself was absent and had merely left its ugly hole.

The terror surged upward again and her whole body reviled against it, mentally pushing it away, forcing it back behind the grille.

For the first few seconds after she woke up Katherine thought she was going to be sick. The darkness continued to swim and sweep in front of her eyes. Gradually it stabilised into the familiar reality of her bedroom and the dark folds of the curtains tipped with streetlight orange. With a substantial effort of will she pulled her mind out of the black recess and back to the real world. She wanted to get up and go to the toilet but a lingering panic hovered over her and she couldn't get out of bed. She lay in a semi-daze, waiting for it all to go away.

She was too tired to face going to work the following day, so she called in sick and took herself on a walk into town.

The Promenade was heaving with people, as it always was. She craved the presence of people, ordinary people doing banal mundane things – it made her feel connected to reality again, although also strangely alienated as she passed unheeded in the throng. She walked slowly past the shops and stared in the windows. A posh woman in beige slacks buying shoes, the shop assistant kneeling in supplication among boxes and tissue paper. Teenage girls, gum-masticating, flicking sharply through rails of trashy clothes without really looking at them. In a tea-shop, tourists pursing scalded lips on the rim of an overpriced coffee. At the periphery of her vision some generic dance music pounding from a shop made pinpricks of off-yellow light in her synaesthete senses.

She strolled down the almost imperceptible slope which had once been, she knew, a Regency promenade, and whose double line of trees had presided over two centuries of pedestrian life. Before that, although it was difficult to imagine, it had been a swamp. The elegant sweep of uphill Regency allure at the other end had once been accessible only by a plank bridge. Now it was cut off by the snarling inner ring road, following the course of the buried river.

She veered away from the shops to the other side of the street, where there was a long terrace of voluptuous Regency houses, once occupied as private homes but now, through an unlikely conjunction of circumstances, used as municipal offices. The white-painted railings were hand-wrought, topped with twirling decorative urns. At one time the terrace had had its own communal garden and a long sweeping driveway for carriages; the latter was now used as a pay-and-display car park. The gardens survived as a municipal showpiece, bereft of the railings which had once made them private, now cut with strips of flower bed where frost-nipped petunias clung to a slightly sagging life in purple and yellow drifts. The benches were all too wet to sit on so she just kept walking.

And then her eye was caught by a mass of bright red flowers, though these were synthetic ones. Poppies. She found herself standing in front of the town's war memorial.

How could she have forgotten it was there? The white obelisk of Portland stone was conspicuous enough. It stood on a large stone base whose surface was inlaid on all sides with names in leaded letters. Far bigger than the Tewkesbury memorial. Far more names. She felt that the unknown man in her vision had done this deliberately, brought her to this spot on purpose.

'Well come on then,' she said under her breath. 'I've seen you twice and I know you've got something to do with war memorials, so you might as well introduce yourself.'

There was no response. She was only aware of the wind in the trees and the drone of traffic. She walked away along the edge of the garden, down the old avenue of trees over a guano-spattered pavement. There was a stall at the far end selling second hand books and old postcards. It caught her eye first of all because it was unusual to see a market stall in this part of town, and then her attention was pulled towards a sepia-printed postcard sitting conspicuously among the gaudy 1970s beach scenes in a cardboard box. She went over for a closer look and was confronted with an image of the Menin Gate in Ypres. She wasn't sure what that was, but it looked like a rather chunky mausoleum with a river flowing round it, all printed in muted brown tones which obscured the detail. She turned it over and read the bland holiday message on the back, which was scrawled in brown ink and notable only for its dullness. It had a Belgian postage stamp and had been franked in 1934. She was about to put it back when she saw the small text at the bottom: Menin Gate. Memorial of British Heroes.

'Another bloody war memorial,' said Katherine to herself, shaking some coins out of her purse with a sense of grim inevitability. 'And probably a waste of eighty pence.'

But she did feel it was the response she had just asked for, and so it was necessary for her to have it.

Unknown to her, at that same moment Joe Waldron was under siege.

He had wandered in all innocence down to the verdant cool at the bottom of the garden, where it was peaceful and sheltered. It almost had its own microclimate, fenced in by a tangled screen of raspberry canes, barbed stems still heavy with berries, which separated it from the rest of the garden. Joe cultivated fruit, vegetables and marijuana in this private plot. It was his particular pleasure to select his dinner-time menu from the garden rather than the larder. Always a good way to amuse guests, to ask them what they wanted to eat and then say 'right, I'll just go and dig one up', as long as they were spared the sight of him slicing slug tunnels out of potatoes and picking aphids off the undersides of basil leaves. The vegetable garden was his special joy, and he did at least know what had been sprayed on it.

Joe was a firm believer in organic gardening, though the belief came easier than the practice. Snails were the cause of evil temptations. In the early part of the season he would spend hours mixing up bucketfuls of soot, crushed eggshells and dog hair (product of next door's labrador) and distribute it meticulously between his rows of lettuces and beans, to deter mollusc marauders. His principles were tested to the limit when all his seedlings were reduced to mangled stumps and he was seized with the temptation just to blitz the slimy little bastards with pellets, but generally he managed to stick it out.

The marijuana harvest was almost over, and he only had one plant left now, six feet tall with fluttering green fingers like palm leaves and drooping, sticky buds. It gave him great joy to have grown such a beautiful plant, and he ran his hand through the leaves to fill the air with its spicy and herby sausagemeat smell.

'Oi, come out! I want a word with you.'

Joe froze. The shout came from the direction of the house but he wasn't aware that anybody could see him down here – it was supposed to be his secret garden. And the tone of the voice was not pleasant.

'Come on! I know bloody well you're in there.'

Shit. He unbent his knees slowly and peered in the direction of the voice. Through the raspberry entanglements he could see Jeannette from two doors down leaning over the low fence into the garden next to his; leaning very carefully, because the fence top had just been painted and had barely had time to dry. She shifted her posture impatiently, and yelled again.

'Oi, you fat old cow, get out here.'

'Oh thank God,' muttered Joe to himself. 'It's not me.'

A window scraped open in one of the bedrooms of the house next door and his neighbour, Alison, appeared.

'Are you talking to me?'

'Yes I am. Get your fat arse out here now.'

Joe, trapped and cowering in his vegetable patch, unable to move without being seen, could hear the rhythmic thump of feet on distant stairs and after a pause the figure of Alison appeared through the French windows at the back of the house. There was nothing he could do except stay put, or it would just look like he was lurking in the bushes.

Jeannette was flushed and excited, enjoying the confrontation like a drug-rush. She was a small wiry woman in her early sixties, twice divorced and now retired – though from what nobody knew, because she had told different neighbours at different times that she was a teacher, a journalist and a solicitor, and Joe doubted that any of them were true. She could also be an atrocious flirt, and wore the sort of clothes which are usually best left to teenagers. Her hair was grey and white, in an almost military short-back-and-sides which sprouted a tufty bit at the back, and her face was puckered into a lemon-sucking mask of permanent disapproval.

She rapped the fence with a stump of garden cane, the first hint of a threat of violence. 'This is my fence,' she announced crisply.

'It's a shared fence,' replied Alison calmly. And from what Joe could remember of the Land Registry plans for these houses she was quite right.

'Don't be stupid. You don't get shared fences, otherwise there'd be bloody *arguments* about who gets to paint them. This is my fence and that one's yours.' She gestured towards the sagging partition that adjoined Joe's garden. 'I won't have you painting your bloody shitty colour all over my fence.'

Now Joe understood what the argument was about. Alison, treating her side of the fence with a chestnut brown preservative, had painted the little strip of wood that ran along the top, which had formerly been a forest green colour which matched Jeannette's side of the fence, and Jeannette was paranoid enough to think it was an insidious ploy done solely to spite her.

Alison shook her head. 'You're off your bloody trolley, you are. I painted the top of the fence, so what?'

'Because it's not your fucking property. It's criminal damage.'

'You want your head seeing to, duckey. I've got every right to paint that fence and I'm not going to be intimidated by a mad old bag like you.'

'And I'm not taking any shit from a fat ugly cow like you. Look at you,' she sneered, 'with your dumpling face and dumpling body.'

Alison stood silent for a moment while she took in the full force of the comment. It was meant to hurt, and realising that it did, Jeannette carried on.

'It's disgusting. You've got six sodding chins. You look like a fucking Rottweiler.'

Alison swelled up to her full height. 'At least I don't go poncing about in the garden with no effing clothes on.'

'What?'

'I've seen you out there, flopping all over the place with everything hanging out. It's disgusting.'

'I'll sunbathe nude in my own fucking garden if I want to.'

'Deadheading the flowers with your tits hanging down to your waist – it's a bloody disgrace, at your age.'

'I can't help it if there are *perverts* leering out of their windows–'

'Some pervert, to want to look at a dessicated old bag like you.'

Jeannette's voice reached squealing point. 'Oh yeah, and what about you and your bloody thong knickers? I see them out there on the washing line, and the thought of your big blubbery arse in a G-string makes me want to *puke...*'

'You're a fine one to be eying up undies on other people's washing lines, you daft moo.'

'I don't give a fuck about your bloody washing line, but when there's a pair of bloody thongs on there, I mean, God...'

'Yes you do, you spend your whole life staring out of that window. You know exactly who's been here and how often I go out, and what all the neighbours are doing, because you're sat there in your sodding window all day spying on everybody –'

'I don't know how you get into them.'

'What?'

Jeannette's face lit up as a new thought struck her. 'I bet you don't wear them at all, do you? You just put them out on the line to make people *think* you can get into them –'

'You're a fucking nutter, you are.' Alison had had enough now.

'Oh-ho!' squealed Jeannette gleefully, 'now we can see what a foul-mouthed cow you really are. That's lack of breeding, that is.'

'That's a bit ripe coming from someone who goes around dangling her crabby old tits over the rose bushes. You should see what it looks like from behind, it's bloody disgus–'

'Mm, this fence is nearly dry,' she said blithely. 'I'll fetch my green and re-paint the top in a minute.'

Alison slipped into the trap.

'Don't you *dare* touch this fence or it'll be the last fucking thing you do, you slagging-cunting-pissing-turdface-bollocking-fuckbag.'

'Right. That's it. I'm going to call the police. I'm not going to have abuse shouted at me.'

Jeannette turned and went calmly back into the house, closing the door with a soft clunk.

'You're just frustrated, you are,' Alison shouted after her. 'That's your trouble. You're frustrated because even the *perverts* don't want *you.*' She flounced back into her house, slamming the French doors and making the upstairs windows shake.

Joe gently released himself from his pins-and-needles crouch behind the foliage. He felt an almost physical distress at the barrage of obscenities. It buffeted his sense of decency, and it was quite unsettling to be its unwilling witness.

When he was sure it was all clear he made a bee-line for his own back door and found his daughter Judi in the kitchen scrubbing carrots.

'That old nutter from two doors down is at it again,' he said.

'I thought I heard her shrieking out there. What's the matter with her this time?'

He gave her the gist of what had happened.

'Oh for God's sake, it's a shared fence, isn't it?'

'Do *you* want to go and tell her that?'

Judi threw the carrots vindictively into a colander.

'She pisses me off, that woman. She told me she can hear loud talking from next door late at night but I never hear anything. I reckon she must be sitting there with a glass pressed against the wall.'

'I wouldn't be surprised. I mean, she's got binoculars on her front window sill and nothing else to do all day. I've a good mind to go out there with my binoculars and start peering through *her* window –'

'You always tell me off for winding her up, Dad.'

'That's different. Do as I say, not as I do.'

'You can stuff that.'

Chapter Three

10th Glos. Bttn.
B.E.F. France
Monday 23rd August 1915

Dear Hugh,

Good God, I bet the weather in Egypt isn't as hot as it is here. We're all roasted, and my own discomfort is compounded by the men grot-bagging about their itchy uniforms. I can't let them even undo the top button, much as I would love to tear off my own collar and tie and sling it onto the dungheap, which incidentally occupies a glorious position outside my window.

We've now been out here for two weeks. Seems like forever, as one monotonous day blends into another. We've just got back to camp after a brief stint at the Front – yes, after all these months of waiting I really have been out there in the 'firing line'. To be perfectly honest it wasn't all that exciting, aside from one or two singular moments. Most of the time it involved standing around for hours in a smelly trench. There seems to be something of a 'live and let live' arrangement in this sector, whereby we don't bother to shell the enemy and they don't bother to shell us, apart from a few token rifle bullets to keep up appearances. I haven't seen any Germans at all yet.

One thing which was not for the faint-hearted, though, was the march up to the line on Thursday night. We had to go up there under cover of darkness for obvious reasons and that meant absolutely *total* darkness. There was a guide in front of the platoon who knew his way, and the rest of us followed by clinging on to each other's back-packs. I had the unenviable task of bringing up the rear, which was an alarming experience. We were in single file because the road was badly chopped up and full of holes (though nobody fell in, by some miracle). The communication trenches, when we got to them, were horribly narrow.

The worst enemy I've faced so far has got to be the telephone wires. They're just tacked to the trench wall and then as soon as it rains the blasted things sag and get caught round every part of your anatomy as you try to pass by. Every now and then you come across one that's fallen down completely in a great treacherous loop round your feet. There is a temptation just to rip them out of the way and be done with it, but they are the most important means of communication we have out here. There may come a day when one's life depends on the wires being intact. Needless to say a lot of them are damaged and broken by shell-fire and suchlike, which only adds to the general tangle. The men soon learned that the only way to negotiate these obstacles in the dark is to pass a message back down the line. When the guide says "mind the wire", the chap behind him passes it back and it goes on down the line of men. In the communication trenches we were walking along duckboards; even in this blistering summer the trenches fill up with sticky mud. I was rather tired by this time, and when the man in front of me leaned round and said "gap in the boards – pass it back" I instinctively turned to repeat it to the person behind me. Before my brain could register that I was at the back and there wasn't anyone behind me, my right foot disappeared down a hole in the duckboard and plunged into a pool of mud that came well above my ankle. Fortunately my injuries were limited to a loss of dignity, compounded by having to march the next half mile to the rhythm of left-squelch, left-squelch.

We did have a few hairy moments on our first day at the Front. The Boche were evidently using our section of trench for rifle target practice. Every now and then there was a flurry of pings and snaps as the bullets hit our wire and sandbags. My instinct was to throw myself on the floor and pray for deliverance, but then a rather surly walrus-whiskered sergeant from the regulars explained in a patronising tone that "if you hear the bullet come over then the b— thing's missed, sir, hasn't it?" Even so, I couldn't help ducking every time I heard a ping.

Apart from that we just stood around, or slept. Overnight accommodation consisted of large holes dug into the side of the trench, with the modest privacy of a hessian curtain. Mine had a sort of chicken-wire hammock arrangement, which seemed to keep me awake no matter how tired I was, and I was cordoned off from the outside world by a cut up Post Office sack. It had 'NOT TO BE TAKEN AWAY' stamped across it, which I feared might be a liability if anyone came looking for it. The hovel lacked a

27

surface on which to safely place my oil lamp, but since there was also nothing it could possibly set fire to if it fell over I just stuck it in the middle of the floor. I'm told the dug-outs are deeper and more comfortable in the support trenches further back. Maybe next time.

During the day I just had to try to keep the men occupied and out of mischief. Mostly it was a routine of breakfast at eight, rifle and equipment cleaning till noon, "lunch" (by which I mean soggy black tinned potatoes and hardtack biscuits), and trench repairs and inspections in the afternoon. After a general "stand to" at dusk (am I giving away any military secrets here?!) the nightly patrols went out, though that was mostly left to the regulars, as our chaps currently lack confidence and experience. For the moment they stay behind and hone their killer instincts by swatting mosquitoes.

The trenches we had were solidly built and well revetted – much better drained than the communication trenches we came through on the way up. Also they haven't taken much Boche shelling so they were in good condition. There wasn't a lot we could do with them other than sweep the duckboards.

After a couple of days we were taken out of the line and marched back to our billets. And here we are. I wish I could tell you the name of the place – I don't see that it would cause a major catastrophe if I mention the name of the town – I mean, I presume the Germans do know that the town exists and that it's occupied by us, so they won't learn a lot if they intercept this letter – but I'd better bow to the wishes of His Majesty's Censor. Suffice to say we're in a pleasant, jolly town, and I'm billeted in a respectable Victorian house with roses in the front garden and fruit bushes in the back. I've lost count of the number of raspberry crumbles I've had since arriving in France (it is the only dessert our cook knows how to do, and we've given him permission to pillage the garden accordingly). I'm sharing with three other officers but they are all pretty decent chaps (apart from Nowell and his confounded socks) so we get along all right. We're still pretty close to the Front but the town itself still has an air of normality. There's been hardly any shelling here so it's relatively undamaged – unlike some of the villages we came through on the way up.

Unfortunately the battalion suffered its first casualties last Wednesday. Not during our sojourn in the trenches, but while we were here in the 'safety' of this town. It seems that some men from the 10th Gloucesters were resting out in the fields when an aeroplane flew over quite low. Since most of them have never seen one before they just sat there, gazing up in idle curiosity. A couple of the lads said that when the plane was directly above them they actually saw the pilot lean over the side and throw out a bomb, by which time it was a bit late to do anything about it. One artillery chap was killed and several wounded, including two from the 10th. Nobody from my platoon.

The worst ordeal for my men was the train journey from the coast, when we first arrived in France. They were packed into cattle trucks, forty men to a truck. I can assure you they were not amused. Then when we got to our destination we had a two mile march in full kit in the blazing sun. It wasn't so bad for me because I was able to commandeer a horse, but it was purgatory for them, and the camp we ended up in had a serious shortage of clean water. I need not expatiate on the effect this had on the sanitation.

Something happened last night which I've been dying to tell you about. I went for a drink in the aforementioned jolly town (which still has most of its civilians and therefore a thriving trade in ardent spirit and other pleasantries). One café-estaminet in the market square has become a very fashionable haunt, and I got into conversation there with some officers from another regiment. One of them was called Kipling and I asked, in jest, whether he was related to the Kipling who writes all those wonderful stories. He said, rather sheepishly I thought, that he was his son. I was in half a mind about whether to believe him, but I thought I could see some resemblance – at least he had a moustache and pebble glasses, if you call that a resemblance. He was a pleasant chap with a lively – if somewhat immature – sense of humour, and I must say he looked incredibly young. I asked him whether he was aspiring to be a writer and he said he couldn't even spell, let alone write, so I wished I hadn't asked. Apparently his 'Daddo' is only about twenty miles from here at present, working as an authorised journalist. I must admit I wasn't fully convinced by his story until I told Nowell about it later on, and he said he remembers reading in the paper that Rudyard Kipling has a son serving in the Irish Guards – which was indeed this young chap's regiment.

The night skies are still providing me with something pleasant to look at. I got an exceptionally good view of the Perseid shower this year, mainly because it peaked during the dark phase of the moon, which allowed even the most subtle of meteors to stand out beautifully. Not that there is much need of shooting stars out here at the moment; the artillery gunners on both sides are making plenty of their own.

I trust this letter will find you in good health and high spirits, as I am; subject to the Will of God and the Army Postal Service.

Your affectionate cousin,
Richard

Chapter Four

'You see, George, the trouble with Field-Marshal Haig was that he was out of touch. He never came into direct contact with soldiers at the Front and he hadn't a clue what was going on. He'd served in a few imperial campaigns where the enemy had been a bunch of tribesmen hopping up and down with spears. He understood angry native people with spears. What he failed – one might say *refused* – to accept was that modern weapons were changing the whole business of military operations. He was convinced that the way to duff up the Germans was to get the cavalry to gallop over and pike them – which they may well have done, if they'd been able to get there without being shot to bits. He couldn't accept that a couple of blokes perched on the trench with machine guns could mow down an entire wave of cavalry like a child kicking over a sandcastle. He thought machine guns were over-rated, newfangled modern rubbish, and didn't change his mind until the day the Germans gunned down 60,000 British men on the Somme.

'But what really gets me about Haig is his shameless racism. He would put in the colonial troops whenever he was expecting heavy casualties, because he felt they were more expendable than British-born men. I mean, he knew Gallipoli was going to be a hellhole, so he sent the Australian and New Zealand troops to deal with it. Then there were the Canadians at Vimy Ridge, who also bore the brunt of the first poison gas attack at Ypres. He pitted the Ulster Division against a fiercely defended fortress on the Somme, and the South Africans to one at Guillemont, the Australians at Pozières, the Indians and Sikhs at Loos. George, you're not listening, are you?'

The guinea pig made no response, being concerned with the more immediate issue of grappling with a slice of tomato. Joe watched the animal's head quiver in time with its rapid irregular munching, and he stroked the soft crinkly ears with his finger. He had become very fond of the two guinea pigs that Judi had bought a few years ago, then got bored with, and left for him to feed and clean out. They had become his regular companions when he was reading or studying, and he found it very relaxing to watch them waddling around the room making clucking noises, their clumsy three-toed feet scrabbling uneasily over the carpet pile. George was secretly his favourite, a gingery brown one with a gloriously pointless rosette of white hair on top of his head, and ears that looked like poppadoms.

Joe took a sip of tea and realised as the soggy bulk slapped against his upper lip that he had forgotten to take the tea-bag out. He salvaged it with two fingers and a biro, and tossed it as far as he could out of the open window. It was technically possible to throw tea-bags and apple cores onto the compost heap from here, but it required a steady hand and on this occasion the tea-bag veered too far to the right and stuck, impaled, in the upper branches of a rose bush.

He cursed mildly and turned back to the book he was vaguely reading before he had distracted himself with his lecture to the world in general. After half a page or so he felt a sudden, very localised heat spread across his leg. The guinea pig had widdled on his trousers.

The doorbell rang just as he was about to shout some abuse, and the guinea pig, startled into panic, jumped onto his shoulder with unexpected agility and burrowed down the neck of his jumper. He thought it best to ignore the front door, did his best to edge out of the armchair without dislodging the guinea pig and groped towards the supply of kitchen roll on the desk. His hand caught the cup of tea that was perched on the edge and sent a slop of it across the polished wood. Cursing slightly less mildly this time, he grabbed the kitchen roll and mopped at the tea while the guinea pig slid down his back, still inside his jumper. He felt its claws lightly scoring his skin as it went down, part-painful and part-ticklish.

The door was suddenly open and Katherine was there, taking a brisk step into the room and then hesitating to take in the sight of her former English teacher bent over with a twitching lump on his lower back, apparently talking to himself. There was a moment's pause.

'Hello Kath. I thought it might be you.' He gestured delicately towards a spare chair. 'Sorry I couldn't come to the door myself. If you'll excuse me, I just have to put away my guinea pig. Do take a seat.' He shuffled out, still bent double, with one hand cupped protectively around the bulge on his back.

Katherine moved towards the chair but stayed standing and surveyed the room. It was a Victorian house with a high ceiling and the room was chirpily decorated in a Regency yellow, with the part above the dado rail painted white. At least that was the general theme, but it was interrupted by two walls covered from floor to ceiling with well-stuffed bookshelves. On a niche by the window were framed pictures of Sir Thomas More and Socrates, and below them a sepia tinted photograph of a smiling young man in military uniform, leaning on a walking cane. There was a large antique writing desk under the window with a telephone half buried under a pile of messy papers. On the top was a framed photograph of Oscar Wilde and a saucer containing half a tomato and some dandelion leaves. On a smaller table nearby was a ghetto-blaster and a handful of CDs. Always curious about other people's music, Katherine leaned over and found Joni Mitchell, Jimi Hendrix and the Bonzo Dog Doo Dah Band.

Joe's book collection was incredibly diverse. It was neatly catalogued with sticky labels along the shelf egdes and had sections on medieval literature, local history, military history, gardening and poetry. There were also two or three shelves of what she would call weirdo books about psychic energy and star alignments. Another case was devoted to musty old hardbacks in varying stages of decomposition but meticulously ordered. It struck Katherine as odd that someone who kept their office in such a mess could be so obsessively tidy with their books.

'Sorry about that.' Joe reappeared and went over to his desk where he tore off a few sheets of kitchen roll and began scrubbing at his leg. 'Would you like some tea? I've asked Judi to put the kettle on.' He tossed the kitchen roll in the bin and sat down.

Katherine wanted to ask about the weirdo books, but it didn't seem appropriate to call them that.

'How's your wife?' she asked instead. She had been dreading the prospect of meeting her, since she had behaved so atrociously in her art class at school and couldn't imagine that she would ever be forgiven for it.

'Mrs Waldron,' he said grimly, 'pissed off with a hairy Irishman.'

'Oh. Sorry to hear that.'

Joe shrugged. 'I'm not that bothered.'

Katherine wasn't sure what to say to that.

'Well, it was a bit of a low point at the time I suppose, but it's done wonders for my bank balance. She isn't claiming anything, you see. Catholic guilt. She knows I need the money for Judi.'

'And Judi is – ?'

'Nineteen. She's got multiple sclerosis.'

'Oh fuck. Whoops, I mean I'm sorry. That must be hard.'

'It's OK, we don't bother with doom and gloom in this house. The MS comes and goes, and most of the time she can lead a pretty normal life. When it gets bad we get a nurse in, but she's been doing well for a while and there's a reasonable chance of it not getting much worse. But anyway, you didn't come here to talk about that.'

Katherine nodded towards the top layer of papers on the desk, which was scattered with photographs and notes. 'What's that you're working on?'

'Oh that.' Joe's eyes lit up with the delight of an obsessive who has found somebody to listen to him rabbiting on. 'This is my current big project, to photograph all the military graves in the area which relate to the 1914–18 war.'

He opened the top drawer of his desk and handed Katherine a photograph wallet. She flicked through the thick wedge of prints and saw that they were all pictures of identical white grave slabs.

'Since it was a nice day on Tuesday I took the opportunity to go over to Cheltenham Borough Cemetery and do the lot. Not all of them are war graves. If you look at the bottom of the pile there's a few civilian ones where people had the names of their lost sons inscribed on their own tombs. See this one...' he pulled out a print from near the bottom of the stack. 'This bloke died on the Somme and is buried in France, but his name and the details of what happened to him are on the grave of his father, who died in 1924. They just chiselled it down the side in smaller letters. It wasn't uncommon in those days, which makes my task more difficult because I have to walk round the cemetery and try to spot them. In a cemetery of that size it's no joke.'

Katherine tried to imagine how anyone could consider it fun to spend a day trekking round a suburban cemetery taking pictures of gravestones. And what would he do with them now? Stick them in an album and show them to guests?

'My other project revolves around this,' he bubbled, unfolding an enlarged copy of an old street plan with the streets coloured in with orange highlighter pen. 'This is what the town looked like in 1920. The streets marked in orange are the ones which lost at least one of their residents in the first world war.'

Katherine frowned. 'But they're *all* orange.'

'Not quite.' Joe scanned the map and found one that was still white, but it was difficult to spot them. 'It's pretty frightening, isn't it? What's worse is that I could have coloured in a lot of them several times.'

'How long did it take to research all that lot?'

'Ages. But not half as long as this.' He took out a fat ring-binder from the same drawer and spread it proudly on the desk.

'These are modern day street plans, a larger scale which shows the individual houses. I've collected the known home addresses of all the local soldiers lost in the Great War and checked to see whether their houses still exist. Those that do I've marked on the street plans. Then I go round town one area at a time and photograph them.'

His project, although very much unfinished, was quite an achievement. Certain houses on the street plan were shaded in and marked with the soldier's name and a page reference. The shading was colour-coded, red for Officers and blue for Other Ranks. The rest of the folder had photographs of houses, one on each page, with a short write-up about the soldier who had lived there. The colour codes, Joe explained, had been an afterthought, but he was really glad he had done it.

'It shows a very interesting trend, if you're familiar with the posh and not so posh areas of town. Almost without exception, the officers came from the big Regency villas and the private soldiers came from the cottages and artisan terraces. Which goes to show that military rank at that time was given on the basis of social status, not intelligence or integrity. There were a few low-ranking soldiers who had come from posh addresses but when I checked them out it turned out that most were just live-in servants.'

He left Katherine leafing through the project while he went to finish making the tea, and came back with an enormous mug and a few biscuits.

'I'm fascinated by some of those books over there,' said Katherine as he lowered the tea precariously towards a coaster. 'Can I have a look?'

'Of course you can,' he said, stuffing a biscuit into his mouth in one go. He was inwardly delighted that anyone would take an interest in his books, and stood up to see which ones she was looking at. She seemed to keep drifting back to the esoteric books, pulling them half way out to peek at their covers.

'Are you into all this?' she asked.

'Oh yes.' A glimmer of hope flared in his heart that he might have found a kindred spirit, someone who shared his interest in serious occultism, as opposed to the popular loony stuff. He dusted the biscuit crumbs onto the carpet.

'I used to read a lot of stuff like this a few years ago.'

'Oh yes?'

'I don't believe in any of it, but it's quite interesting.'

The light of hope was abruptly stamped out.

She took out a chunky paperback by Aleister Crowley and flicked through it, furrowing her brow.

'What's this about? Isn't this bloke supposed to be dodgy?'

'It's about sacred numbers and the Qabalah,' said Joe. 'And he wasn't as dodgy as he liked to make out, he just had a rather adolescent sense of humour. It's easy enough to see through the pranks in his books if you're sensible. It's usually the casual dabblers who fall foul of it.'

'And I presume you're not a casual dabbler?' Katherine put the book back on the shelf and waited for an answer, but he didn't say anything. She could hear him chomping another biscuit. She scanned along all the occult books and back again.

'You don't have anything about dream interpretation?'

It was half a question, half a disappointed statement.

'No. I don't.'

'Why not?'

'Because I'm not sure how much I believe it's useful. At least, most of my dreams are just turgid drivel, I couldn't be bothered to interpret them.'

She looked surprised. 'You don't believe in it?'

He shrugged. 'I don't doubt that some people have significant dreams, but mine don't seem to be, that's all.'

'Well, I would have said that myself until recently. But I've been having some really strange dreams lately, dreams that *feel* different, if you know what I mean. They're so vivid.'

'Been eating cheese at bedtime?'

Katherine made a dismissive gesture. 'Don't be like that. I'm serious. There's one where I'm pressed against a bank of earth face down with dirt in my mouth, too terrified to move because there are all these lumps of burning stuff coming out of the sky. Then there's one where I'm cramped in some sort of dungeon and there's this horrible arched window with a grille over it, like a church window except that there's some unseen terror behind it, and I can't see anything through it because it's all black inside but I'm so scared of it it brings me out in a sweat. I've had that one twice.'

'They're recurring dreams, then?' Joe was immediately more interested.

'Seem to be, yes. I've been getting them all week. Sometimes I have the same one twice a night. The one I had last night was different, but had the same feel to it.'

'What sort of feel?'

'Very emotional. Not necessarily any particular emotion, just a sense of this cloud of it hanging over me. I was standing in some sort of ruin – a house with all the walls fallen down and rubble all over the place, and there was a man lying in the middle of it. He was dead but there wasn't any blood or anything, there was nothing gruesome about it. It was just that he had this smile on his face. Very young and quite good looking. His eyes were open and glassy and he was staring into the sky with a rigid smile, and I just couldn't take my eyes off him, I stared and stared and stared for ages and it was – ' she saw that Joe was listening with intense interest '– totally horrible. And I was just wondering...' she swallowed. 'I think it's to do with the first world war.'

Joe picked up a biro and began absentmindedly sliding it back and forth between his fingers.

'And have you been thinking about war recently? Something that might have set your imagination off?'

'No, not especially.' She thought for a moment. 'I've only been dwelling on it to the extent of buying a poppy, like everybody does.'

Katherine gulped down her tea. She desperately wanted to find an explanation for the dreams, which were unpleasant and exhausted her, but at the same time she was afraid to dig too much in case the truth was something she didn't like.

'So what does it mean? Any ideas?'

'Well,' said Joe, sucking his teeth in a grotesque manner that Judi always told him was disgusting, 'the first dream you described sounds like a bombardment doesn't it? Sometimes soldiers had to lie flat against the trench praying that they wouldn't get hit by shrapnel. That's horrible stuff, little balls of metal, each about the size of a marble. They used to pack a few hundred of them into a shell with some explosives, and they would burst in mid air over the enemy's trenches. All the metal balls would fly all over the place, and they'd be red hot. A marble-sized blob of molten metal just dropping on you out of nowhere.'

'Yeah, that does sound very like it,' Katherine said grimly. 'But why the hell am *I* dreaming it?'

Joe opened his mouth to say something, then snapped it shut. 'I don't know.'

'It's a bit frightening. Don't you think?'

A soft, concerned look spread across his face, and now she felt confident that she had been right to trust him.

He said: 'Let's go for a stroll in the garden, if you've finished your tea.'

In the crisp outdoor air Katherine felt more at ease. She immediately liked Joe's garden. It had a Victorian wall on one side, with a white salty bloom on the brickwork and the twiggy remains of a clematis sagging on a trellis. The sky was crisp and sunny, which gave the garden a vibrant glow even in its damp and leafless season. There was a pool of green water under a terracotta water spout, which had been cleverly built into the wall to integrate with the older features. The lawn, speckled with blotched auburn leaves, had the flatness and springiness that comes only from a century of regular mowing. The air felt cold and clean as she breathed it in, and smelled of English autumn.

'So what is it,' Joe asked, 'that really sets these dreams apart from ordinary dreams? How do you know when you have one?'

'Oh I don't know. It's a subtle thing. I don't know.'

Joe could see out of the corner of his eye that the dreaded Jeannette was watching from her upstairs window, no doubt on the offchance that something gossip-worthy might happen. He thought it wise to ignore her.

'When did they start, these dreams?'

'The first one was after that concert I went to in the abbey. You know, the day I saw the man.' She stopped, and Joe saw the embarrassment flush across her face.

'Man?' He tried not to make it sound like a prying question, and failed dismally.

She swallowed a couple of times, momentarily distracted by the inexplicable presence of a tea-bag, crucified on the thorny stalk of a rose bush. She looked down at the grass.

'Do you believe in ghosts?' she asked.

'Yes.'

'I don't.'

Joe could tell she meant it. Or thought she did.

'But?' he ventured.

She sighed.

'But – I saw something. A man's face.'

'Where?'

'In the abbey. Or in my head. I don't know.'

'You saw this in the abbey during the concert?'

'Yes. That's why I was back there on the day I met you.' She ran a hand over her hair in a repetitive gesture. 'It started last week. I went with a friend to one of those music recitals they have in the abbey from time to time. Choral stuff.'

Joe nodded.

'It was getting quite near the end, and to be honest I was bored with the vicar rattling on, because I was only there for the musical bits. I know it was a service for the war dead and all that, but I'm not very religious. I was staring into the darkness, and all of a sudden I saw this bloke's face looking straight at me, clear as anything. He was as surprised as I was.'

A similar look of surprise struck Joe's face.

'He saw *you*?'

'Yeah. I'm sure of it.' She thought for a moment, analysing the memory. 'I saw his eyes suddenly widen, and I almost felt his gut reaction. It was like a mutual shockwave. That sounds weird doesn't it?'

'Well, don't worry about that. What did he look like?'

'I don't know really. It happened so quickly, and I'm not that good at describing people. I'd say he had brown hair, and pale grey eyes. And a small moustache. He had quite a nice face, a caring sort of face, but not a great looker. Fairly average kind of bloke really.'

'Did you see what he was wearing?'

'Not really, it was like seeing a close-up photograph of somebody. I didn't see the rest of him, only his face. And as I say, it was over in a second. I get the impression he was wearing a soldier's uniform but with a shirt and tie, he was quite smart-looking, but I'm not definite about that.'

'This may sound like a funny question, but did you *see* him with your physical eyes, or was the image inside your head, like a daydream scene?'

Katherine was unsure and tried to recall the experience, to no avail.

'I've no idea whether I actually saw him or not. To be honest it felt like a bit of both. Like the synaesthesia I get, where I see colours and they're kind of real and objective but on the inside, so I can tell them apart from the colours in the real world.'

'Synaethesia? That is interesting. So, did he say anything?'

'No. But I got the impression that he would've liked to.'

'You said you had a friend with you. Did the friend see anything?'

'No. I didn't tell him about it either. It was obvious he hadn't seen anything. He asked if I was ill.' She sniggered.

'Not much use there, then.'

'I think there was some connection with the war memorial,' she said. 'That's what I was vaguely looking at when it happened.'

'And the dreams started the same night, did they?'

'No. God, no. It was much more spooky than that. I saw the man again. He came back big-time.'

She related briefly what had happened when she stood in the alcove in Tewkesbury Abbey.

'It was the same man?'

'Definitely. His presence was incredibly real. It was like he was right there.'

'That is a bit spooky.'

'Yes, but there was nothing evil or frightening about him. I remember not feeling particularly scared, just a bit unsettled.'

'Then maybe he's just a nice person just trying to make contact. I don't think it's necessarily anything to worry about.' His hand dangled into a nearby flower bed and absent-mindedly stripped the seed-heads off a crocosmia stalk. 'Some people have an ability to communicate with people on what you might call the inner planes. A lot of them don't even know they've got the ability until something like this happens.'

Katherine shook her head as if to clear it.

'So this guy is the spirit of somebody who's died, or something.'

'That'd be my guess, yes.'

'I'm sorry Joe, but I desperately want to believe that's a load of crap.'

Chapter Five

My Filthy Hut
"Somewhere In Egypt"
26th August 1915

Dear Richard

So much for the postal service being irregular in our time of national distress. Your letter reached me within three days. It must have come over with a consignment of spare camels or something.

You are right about the heat. It is beastly hot, and there's precious little we can do about it. You would think that being born in India I might be able to cope with it better than most, but I fear I have acclimatised to English weather too well. We are permitted to wear shorts, but the loss of dignity involved scarcely seems worth it. My knees are certainly not fit for public display and I prefer to keep them to myself. Captain Stockwell is currently the only officer who has chosen to 'go legless', and it is quite enough to put everybody else off it.

I have devastating news. I AM WOUNDED! Alas! How ironic that while you're out in the front line battling with the Hun, it's *me* who gets wounded first. I blush to confess that I was bitten by a horse. I don't expect any sympathy from you whatsoever, but it is actually a pretty nasty one and I am obliged to keep my whole hand bandaged up until it heals. At least when you chaps at the Front get wounded you can parade around and get sympathy from French girls. Out here there is nobody for me to parade in front of except horses, camels and a few (male) natives.

Unfortunately the bite is entirely my own fault. We were shifting some heavy building materials up to the place where we were working, and this little bay horse got the wind up his tail. He's a bit of a blighter, I suspect his previous owner was relieved to be rid of him when he was called in for war service. Anyway, he started carrying on, trying to buck and kick his way out of the harness. I daresay you would have dealt with him in two seconds flat, but the young soldier who was leading him also got the wind up and just let go of him! So I went after the horse and the young soldier legged it over the sandhills. I cornered the horse against a wall, and as I grabbed the bridle he lunged out and bit me, right in that fleshy bit between thumb and forefinger. It swelled up like a golf ball, so I had to go to the medical orderly. He wasn't very sympathetic, but he said it was quite a deep bite and I had to keep it clean and cool until the swelling goes down. I have to say, with all the unpleasant diseases floating around in this country I'm not inclined to ignore his advice, so I've got it well wrapped up. At any rate the swelling prevents me from using my fingers – they just won't move.

The inconvenience of having only one useable hand is far greater than I would have bargained for, especially as it's my right hand. There are certain things that one simply cannot do one-handed or left-handed, such as wipe one's behind (don't tell Aunt Ginny I said that) or button up one's shirt. For the first four days I was unable to write because I couldn't hold a pen, and had to chase my dinner round the plate until it got cold. The swelling is much reduced now; that is to say, it looks rather more like a hand and less like a lump of pastry dough.

I must admit I envy you your ability to get stuck into some Hun-thrashing. The level of anger one feels out here for the enemy so far away is immense. Out here, there is one devastating and invincible enemy: SAND. The wind whips it up and carries it into every imaginable place. It gets into one's dinner, pyjamas and revolver. It itches down the back of one's shirt collar. The men find it in their packs and mess-tins. It really is a most abominable menace, with no means to avoid it. It's in the air we breathe, it stings our eyes and throats. It is a devil of a job to make it go down the plug-hole after a bath (not that baths here are as frequent an occurrence as one would like).

The other day-to-day menace is the hostility of the natives. They consider it their God-given right to rob us at every opportunity, and the lengths that they will go to are horrendous. Our men live in tents, basically a canvas structure on a concrete base with a low perimeter wall, the whole thing propped up with a central pole. They soon learned that they cannot leave their packs unattended unless they are tied firmly to the tent-pole. Anything left lying around is routinely stolen. There have even been incidents where the natives have come in with a knife and slit the kitbags open, stealing as much from them as they can carry. This causes a great deal of anger and resentment among the men, who would readily lynch any culprit if he could be caught. The men are also obliged to sleep with an arm (or a leg) hooked through their rifle sling, as the natives' desire to steal weapons is great enough to bring them sneaking into the tents at night when the soldiers are asleep. If a thief is really determined there is nothing to stop him. In another camp a few miles away, two natives sneaked in and cut the men's throats in order to get at their rifles. Despite the pontifications of the colonel the following day, the culprits haven't been caught. In desperation we have now set up a sentry post, to range a searchlight over the camp all night.

Having said all that, I have a share in a servant who is a native and he is a jolly fine fellow. His name is quite unspeakable – that is to say, unpronounceable – so we just call him Sambo. His English is rather sparse, often comically so, but he takes care of us with great pride and assiduity, and acts like a guard dog to prevent our being burgled. The other day when I was walking along the main road I got swamped by fruit sellers. It's just like India in that the locals waste no opportunity to get money out of you, whether it be stolen, wheedled, or traded for dubious goods. The people here sell nothing but fruit and souvenirs, with a persistence that is little short of assault. I ignored the first two or three that approached me but soon there were half a dozen of them. Sambo, a tiny chap and the very model of humility, suddenly began yelling at them in his own language. I have no idea what he said, but they all scattered instantly, and one woman burst into tears. In situations like these, having a servant who is a native is a major advantage.

It is inadvisable to buy anything from street vendors, because the moment one of them sees you handing over money the others descend like vultures. Also, the fruit they sell is usually dirty. We have told the men a hundred times not to buy dirty-looking fruit, but when they've been on a route march in the sun it's a great temptation for them. The message seems to have got through now, thanks to the down-to-earth approach of one of our sergeants. I overheard him lecturing his men thus: "The natives here is disgustin'. They wipe their a— with their hand and then go out and pick fruit! Of course it's b— dirty!" Ah, if only we had such a way with words.

I hope this letter finds you as it leaves me. In good health and high spirits, I mean, not one-handed. Give Fritz a round of bullets from me.

Yours in Hun-bashing fraternity,
Hugh

Chapter Six

Little was needed to put the finishing touch on a miserable day, but the crowning glory, when it came, did have a tiresome inevitability about it. Striding home along the darkening rain streaked pavement in woefully inadequate shoes, her head still swimming with the anger and frustration that had become a frequent part of her working day, Katherine had bumped into her former boyfriend with his new girlfriend, and when they had asked her to go for a quick drink with them she had felt unable to say no. She soon lamented her spinelessness, because the girlfriend had turned out to be even more insufferably boring than she remembered. Emotional prejudices aside, she had tried very hard to like the girl, who was very young and grinned ingratiatingly from behind rectangular glasses. But she only ever wanted to talk about herself, and whatever Katherine tried to contribute to the conversation it seemed the girl had already done the same thing, but better, or in a more interesting way, and would interrupt a story so that she could share her own superior anecdote. Katherine bristled. The boyfriend gazed at the girl in doe-eyed adoration. After half an hour Katherine got fed up with being interrupted and began to interrupt back, until they were both defiantly talking over each other, not daring to leave any pause for breath for fear that the other would talk into it. Eventually Katherine stood up and said she had stuff to do and walked off. It probably appeared horribly rude, but as far as Katherine was concerned the girl was about as deep as a puddle of piss on a parquet floor, and she couldn't be bothered to be polite any more.

So now it was late, and raining harder as she walked home, hungry and fed-up. She began to chant a mantra under her breath, 'bas-tards, bas-tards, bas-tards' in time with her footsteps.

When she got back to her flat she saw that the security light still hadn't been fixed and she had to make her way down the weatherworn basement steps in the dark. There was a narrow passageway leading round to the back garden at the bottom, filled with sinister darkness and a row of shrubs heaving and creaking in the wind. The security light had been put up after a neighbour had a man lurch out at her from that shadowy recess, though he turned out only to be a passing drunk who had wandered down there for a slash. Katherine walked stealthily up to the communal door and rammed her key in the lock as quickly as she could against a mounting tide of fear, tempered by a simmering resentment that solitary women were so bloody vulnerable.

In defiance of the dark she did not bother to put the light on when she reached the safety of the entrance hall, but stumbled through the blackness to her front door. She found the keyhole with her fingers and guided the key into the lock. At that moment she was struck by an incredible wave of misery and grief. Nameless grief, without a focus. She thought of her boyfriend and the twisted look of embarrassment on his face when he had dumped her, but found that just for the moment she didn't give a toss. This was grief for something else, something unspecified, and felt like a block of concrete wedged over her shoulders.

She was not someone who was normally prone to depression. She got angry with things, and got upset about things, but the demoralising black stodge of depression rarely troubled her. She quickly put the light on, and heard a howl of greeting and a dull thud as her cat launched himself from his customary position on the kitchen work top and trotted out to meet her.

'Hello Raoul,' she said miserably, as the cat smoothed himself across her lower leg. She ran her hand along his back and down his tail and he gave her an expectant glance and slinked back to the kitchen. She followed him and slopped out half a tin of what appeared to be abattoir floor sweepings into a dish, and watched him wolf it down with a loud open-mouthed purr.

She wandered through to the living room and scrabbled through a pile of old bus tickets and till receipts for the piece of paper she knew she'd stashed there last week, found it, and tapped the number into the telephone.

'Hello?' A male voice.

'Hi Joe, it's Katherine. I'm sorry to bother you but I think I need to have a talk with you.'

'What, you mean it's to do with –'

'All that *stuff*, yes.'

'Still being visited by the soldier chap?'

'Yes. The thing is, Joe, it's really doing my head in. I need to know what this is I'm dealing with here.'

There was a moment's pause.

'Do you want me to come round now?'

That hadn't actually been her intention, but the thought of having some company and someone to talk to suddenly seemed like a welcome proposition.

'Um – that would be a great help, if you're not busy. I don't want to put you out...'

A strange sarcastic laugh came down the line. 'No, you're not. Not at all. Give me about twenty minutes.'

As soon as she put the phone down she realised what a mess the flat was in and went into a brief cleaning frenzy, while the cat stretched along the back of the sofa with his claws casually hooked in the curtains. She threw the more obvious junk into drawers and swept the carpet with a dustpan and brush, and then began to worry whether her bookshelf looked intellectual enough. She pulled out a stack of trashy novels and hid them in the bedroom, then scraped together enough poetry and classics to fill up the gaps just before the doorbell rang.

Joe was wearing what seemed to Katherine a bizarre combination of trendy jeans and a schoolmasterly tweed jacket. She ushered him into the living room.

'I hope you don't mind cats. Watch he doesn't moult all over your jacket. You need to wear ginger clothes when you come round here.'

Within ten seconds of him sitting down the cat was spread out on Joe's lap, grimacing with pleasure and flexing his claws in a slow, blissful rhythm.

'He's lovely,' said Joe. 'What's his name?'

'Raoul.'

'That's unusual.'

'Yes. Why is it that I still keep wanting to call you "sir"?'

Joe smirked. 'You can if you want.'

Katherine settled herself in a chair on the other side of the table, which gave the proceedings a kind of interview atmosphere. She cleared her throat decisively.

'Look. I don't know what this is all about, this weird dream business, and there's a part of me that doesn't really want to know. But supposing you were right about it being a contact of some sort. If so, is there anything I can do to stop it?'

'Well, sort of.'

'What do you mean, sort of?'

Joe paused for a moment, caressing the cat's head.

'I could probably teach you to control it. Then you could switch it on and off at will.'

'I can't just get rid of it?'

'Well, yes, you could. But you might find it keeps coming back. Not necessarily the same stuff, but other things.'

'*Other* things?' Katherine was horrified.

'You know, other communicators. Or you might pick up bad vibes in someone's house or somewhere, and not be able to control it.'

'You know all this is completely new to me, don't you? I've never even met anyone who's had this sort of problem.'

'You have, actually. At least one person.'

'Who?'

'My ex-wife, Pat. She went through the same sort of stuff you're going through, in a slightly different way.'

'What happened?'

'She was exceptionally sensitive to bad vibes. Or black pancakes, as she called them. She'd go round to somebody's house for a social and practically run out screaming. It was so embarrassing.'

Katherine studied her fingernails. There was no sound except Raoul's slow purr and the tick of the clock on top of the television cabinet. Raoul shook his head vigorously, spraying Joe with cold dribble.

'Look Joe, I'll come to the point. I'm a sceptic. At least, I want to be a sceptic. But I've got to the point where I have to admit defeat and ask for some help, because I don't know what the hell is going on.'

Joe leaned across and rested his elbows on the table.

'I might be able to do something about it,' he said slowly. 'But you'll have to really trust me.'

'I do trust you.'

'No you don't.' He smiled and shook his head. Her face turned to a look of annoyance and frustration but he shook his head again.

'You probably trust me enough to do what I tell you, on a superficial level. That isn't enough. I'm asking you to *believe* what I tell you.'

'How can I?' she protested. 'I can't choose what I believe and what I don't. I'm not deliberately trying to be obstructive, I just need to see some kind of *proof* –'

'That's where you're going wrong, you see. It's not a case of believing it when you see it. It's a case of seeing it when you believe it. You'll get your proof, but the first steps have to be taken in faith, or you're wasting your time. And mine.'

Katherine sensed that she was up against a brick wall.

'All right, I'll try. I really will try.'

'OK then. If you wouldn't mind fetching me a cup of tea, we'll make a start.'

She decided to drag out the special teapot, and checked her jar of loose tea to make sure it hadn't got mildewed. She found some reasonably edible biscuits in the cupboard which she arranged carefully on the plate so that the staler ones were on the side where Joe was less likely to pick them up. When she went back into the living room he was writing something on a note-pad.

'I hope you don't mind if I jot a few things down,' he said. 'Might be helpful to us later on.'

'No,' she said, although she actually found it a bit intimidating to think that her words might be written down and scrutinised. But he didn't seem to write down very much, and kept the notebook within her view so that she could see all his comments.

'To start with,' he said, 'let's decide where we stand. You don't believe in ghosts, I think you said.'

'That's right.'

'Not even in the light of recent events?'

'Not really, sorry.'

'There's no need to be sorry. And you haven't had any experiences like this before?'

'No. I don't think so.'

'Apart from synaesthesia.'

'Oh that. I've always had that. I just see colours when I hear music.'

'Where do you see the colours?'

'Well, kind of in my mind's eye I suppose. But they are real enough. They just come up spontaneously and I have no control of it. It's very consistent, so if I listen to a piece of music several times I always see the same colours.'

'And you see this soldier man's face in your mind's eye, the same way you do with the colours?'

'Yeah I s'pose.'

'OK. So what about life after death?'

'Well, I don't go in much for the pearly gates and all that. But I'd like to believe that something carries on after you snuff it. Otherwise it all seems a bit of a waste of time, doesn't it?'

Joe chewed the end of his biro thoughtfully.

'Are you still getting the same dreams?'

'Yeah. Not every night, but most nights. Last night I had the one about being down in the cellar looking up through the grille. I hate that one.'

'What about the visits from your young man?'

'Yes, once or twice.' She hesitated, feeling stupid for talking about it. 'It isn't always quite the same though. Last night while I was drifting off to sleep I saw this dark chamber. It was some sort of church basement or something, because it was very dark. I was stood at the back and the man was kneeling down in front of the altar, praying. I couldn't see any detail of him at all, he was shadowy and had his back to me, but I know it was him. Just a gut feeling, but I'm sure of it.'

'Right. Can you remember what the room looked like?'

'Dim. Dingy. A lot of rubble lying about. I get the impression it was underground, though that's just a gut feeling as well. I don't think there were any windows, not that I could see. There was one candle on the altar and not much else. A grotty old cross, I think. And a dark wooden statue in a recess behind – I think it was a female statue but I couldn't see it very well. The walls were built from rough stone, and there were large alcoves all the way round, tall ones with arched tops, quite odd-looking. And a couple of stone pillars in the middle of the room.'

'Did you recognise it?'

'No. I'm not big on dingy cellars. It definitely wasn't the same place I see in the other dreams, if that's what you mean. It had a totally different feel to it. Not sinister at all. Quite peaceful, actually.'

'Peaceful?'

'Yes. It was like a sanctuary.'

'Thank you,' said Joe, smiling. 'That's very helpful indeed.'

'Joe… if this *is* a real person I'm seeing…'

'Yes?'

'Who the hell is it?'

'I don't know. Hopefully we might find out soon.'

'Do you think it's a dead person?'

'I don't know. Probably.'

'I don't think I want to talk to dead people.'

Joe toyed with his pen, flicking the lid on and off. Katherine waited silently for a response.

'Look, I tell you what. I'll give you two sets of instructions, one for developing this psychic ability –'

'Don't use the word "psychic",' cringed Katherine. 'It makes me think of goggle-eyed women with tie-dye skirts and dangly earrings.'

'All right – one for developing your sensitivity and helping you to communicate with this person in a controlled way, and one for banishing him altogether. Then you can choose which one you want to use. Right?'

'Agreed.'

'Right then, I want you to set aside fifteen minutes every evening and sit yourself in a straight-backed chair, like the one you're on now. Then close your eyes and breathe very slowly and deeply until you're nice and relaxed, and imagine you're enclosed in a sphere made of white light. It's your own private space where nothing unpleasant can get inside. If any images spontaneously come into your head then let them. You won't get any nasty images, not while you're inside your sphere. Don't force it, just let it happen, and jot it down when you've finished. Then ring me up and tell me about it.'

'What if nothing happens at all?'

'It's more than likely that nothing *will* happen, for a while. It needs practice, like anything else. But I still want you to write it down. Even if you only sat there feeling bored, it needs to be recorded.'

'OK. And what if I decide to banish him? How do I do that?'

Joe leaned forward with a conspiratorial expression, almost dislodging the cat.

'I can let you in to the secret of the most powerful exorcism I know. More effective than all the Latin stuff with the bell book and candle and what have you. Words that are guaranteed to banish the most horrifying of visions, instantaneously.'

'Yes please.'

'You won't be offended if I tell you?'

'Oh, pack it in. I'm only interested in whether it works or not.'

'Oh it works.' He grinned. 'You tell the vision to fuck off.'

She scowled for a moment, assessing him.

'I don't believe that. You're winding me up.'

'Well you'd better start believing, hadn't you, if you want to get this sorted. The thing is, it works because you really bloody mean it. It's no good reciting a lot of Latin that you don't understand. It's your intention that makes an exorcism work, not the actual words.'

'Are you seriously telling me that if I tell this man to eff off he'll just go away?'

'Absolutely. If you really want to make sure, you can follow it up with something positive and physical. Even if it's just to stomp around and crash something and make a lot of noise. Or stuff yourself with something nice from the fridge.'

Katherine could see the sincerity and enthusiasm in his face and wondered who was more loopy, him or her. Raoul, oblivious to it all, stretched out a paw and sank his claws affectionately into Joe's knee. Joe extricated it without flinching.

'And is this what Mrs Waldron did when she had the same trouble?'

'Oh yes. Apart from the time she was staying with her sister who came in and saw her shouting "fuck off" into a wardrobe, it saved a lot of social unpleasantness and worked a treat.'

'If I went to my GP and said I was seeing strange visions, she wouldn't prescribe this as a solution, would she?'

'No. She'd suspect that you were either deluded or that you'd been making use of illegal substances. Neither of which would be as helpful as the suggestion I've just made.'

'Maybe I am deluded.'

'Maybe. But there's only one way to find out isn't there?'

He ran his fingernail along the length of his biro and flicked the cap into the air with such a perfect trajectory that it landed with an exquisite plop in Katherine's cup of tea.

'Touché,' she said.

Chapter Seven

10th Glos. Battalion
B.E.F. France
Thursday 9th September 1915

Dear Hugh,

Since my last letter I have been getting a taste for what this war is really about. No, I haven't been back in the line, I've been moved to some perfectly disgusting billets in a nearby village. My 'home' is an abandoned farmhouse with the east wall blown clean out. Needless to say nobody occupies the two rooms that are fully open to the elements, but my room is adjacent, and I can look through a hole in the bottom of the fireplace straight over the fields towards the German line, or – more immediately – straight down into the midden heap in the farmyard. No change there, then.

The accommodation here is severely cramped, not least because we are sharing it with a Scots battalion. Most of the officers are billetted three or four to a room, but there are only two of us in the top room because it is about the size of a broom cupboard, and, of course, exceedingly draughty. My companion is a Scots medical officer who appreciates privacy. I eventually discovered the reason for this, and for his guilty expression whenever I entered the room, when I observed him one night taking a swig from what appeared to be a pair of field-glasses. Needless to say he was keeping a secret reserve of whisky in the leather case, which he didn't want to have to share with anybody, despite the copious supplies sent out to him by his family. Apart from this forgivable weakness he is an agreeable fellow, and I have spent two or three evenings playing cards with him while the sweet aroma of compost-heap-cum-latrine drifts up through the holes in the wall. We thought we were lucky to get a room with decent beds, but the mattresses were so infested with nasty itchy bugs we had to discard them, and so we sleep on a couple of blankets draped over the bare springs. It is not comfortable, but better, I have to remind myself, than what the men have to endure outside. They are crammed into a couple of barns and a stable block, and sleep on the animals' bedding. Their food and sanitary conditions are an abomination, but there's precious little we can do about it. The so-called drinking water has to be boiled before use. Several of my men have complained that their Scotch companions have filthy habits. When I tentatively passed this on to my fellow officer he said that the Scottish lads had been complaining about the filthy habits of the English men.

Whatever their behaviour in sanitary matters, and the indiscretion of the kilt in certain blustery weather conditions, these Scots are far more experienced at soldiering than we are, and are respected for it. They are also by nature some of the toughest and most loyal fighters.

One area in which we do excel, however, is the use of the new cricket ball bomb. You'll have read in the newspaper that the cricket-loving British Tommy supposedly has an advantage over the Boche when it comes to bomb-throwing. The men have had some rigorous training with these devices, and are enjoying themselves. I have to admit that I'm not entirely convinced of the safety of them. The 1st Gloucesters had a nasty incident on the training ground when one with a defective fuse simply blew up. It's one thing to die fighting for your country, it's another to be pointlessly killed by dud equipment.

Whatever the hardships though, I would quite readily spend the duration of the war in these conditions. We hear the shells at night, but generally only in the distance. We have only had one come down near us so far, which hit an outhouse on a neighbouring farm. Fortunately it was one of the only buildings in the area that was uninhabited (on account of having already lost its roof during an earlier bombardment) so there were no casualties. I just lay in bed and listened to the gentle patter of wood and dust falling on our roof.

Apart from that, there is very little activity in this sector at the moment. We see the ration carts and occasional ambulances going up to the Front, and we see the very tired and dirty battalions coming down from it. But the shelling is generally remote. Last night I stood in the farmhouse kitchen (which is now open-air of course) and watched the curious mixture of colours in the sky. There is an almost constant glow of eerie orange, with occasional arcs and flashes of intense white. It's like watching the birth of the stars. Not that there are many real stars to be seen out here in the man-made sky; my astronomy notebooks remain in my kitbag, unopened. But the artificial sky has an allure of its own, in a strange way. It was hard to imagine that every one of those bright bursts was raining down death, it was so beautiful. Even the infernal snoring in the barn next door seemed half a world away.

One of the other inconveniences of this billet is that there is no mess hut, so we cannot eat here. We are obliged to take a walk of almost a mile through thick mud (and worse) to dine at Company H.Q., which is currently based in some wretched café run by a fiendish landlady, one of the only civilians left in the village, who evidently feels that extorting cash from the British is worth risking a few bombs for. At any rate she has plenty of poor quality food, which is just about edible, washed down with warm and watered-down ale. There's nothing else to be had for miles around, but my diet is supplemented by the cakes and chocolate Louisa sends over to me. I find myself eating them sneakily in the dark while my equally sneaky companion quaffs his whisky. We never seem to share anything.

Louisa tells me she has enlisted with the Red Cross for some voluntary nursing work. They have opened a V.A. hospital at the Abbotts in Cheltenham, and she's hoping to give her services there. She's a brave girl, but I'm afraid that she might find the work distasteful. I don't think she has much of an idea what the war is really like. Nobody at home does. Probably just as well.

I trust that your unfortunate wound is on the mend. I expect I would have got myself bitten too if it had been me. When I see some of the poor equine wretches plodding around out here, underfed and frightened half into fits, I thank God I didn't follow my original intention of enlisting in a cavalry or horse transport brigade. I couldn't bear to watch them suffer day in, day out.

Well, I must away; the joys of the foot inspection await me in my platoon's pig-sty.

Yours, Richard

Postscript: I daresay you think I'm joking when I say my platoon lives in a pig-sty.

Chapter Eight

∼

'Fuck off!' shouted Katherine, and the dimly lit chamber with its praying figure vanished abruptly. 'Fuck off, fuck off, *fuck off!*'

She sat up in bed. The room was quiet, empty, normal.

'Well there you go,' she said to herself. 'It does work.'

She settled back down and slept uninterrupted for the rest of the night.

Her meditation sessions, after a week or so of tedious repetition, had begun to produce a few spontaneous images but nothing that had any obvious significance. One thing that annoyed her was that whenever she visualised a sphere of light around herself there always seemed to be a wooden chair in the middle of it. Just a plain one, empty. It wouldn't go away, no matter how hard she tried. Then one evening she found it occupied by the soldier figure. He sat there quite silently, smoking a cigarette. Her immediate response was indignation that he had the nerve to smoke inside her sphere of light, which she felt ought to be a no-smoking zone, and she banished the image with some annoyance and never saw it again.

Having now learned how to get rid of her uninvited visitor, though, she found herself becoming curious about him to the extent that she no longer felt alarmed by his presence. In fact, despite herself, she found that she was getting to like him.

She began to make deliberate attempts to visualise his face. It seemed that the harder she tried the more difficult it was to see any visual image, but what she got in its place was a stronger sense of his presence. She noticed she could either see a clear image of his face or have a strong awareness of his presence, but not both at the same time. Sometimes she felt as if he was standing just behind her.

On Joe's advice, she got into the habit of going to sleep with an A4 writing pad and a biro beside her on the bedside table, and a low wattage bulb in her lamp which gave just enough light to see the paper. The room had a slightly frightening appearance in this near-darkness, so she didn't make use of it very often. But it was at this time of night, just as she was drifting off to sleep, that the strongest sense of his presence came through.

Then one night she woke up with an absolute conviction that the man had just been talking to her in her sleep. She opened her eyes in the dark and reached out to him mentally. He was still there, she could feel it. Should she go back to sleep and hope he carried on? Or should she try to write it down? Reluctantly, she switched on the lamp and propped herself up in bed with the writing pad in front of her. Yes, he was still there, and she had a nervous tingling feeling inside. She picked up the biro and wrote: 'I can feel your presence. Is there anything you want to say to me?' She put a dash in the margin of the line below, to mark the start of his answer.

She sat there feeling stupid, with the pen poised above the line. She wasn't sure if she was waiting for a voice to boom out of the ether or a mysterious ghostly hand to grip the biro. Nothing happened. After a few minutes she slung the writing pad on the floor and went back to sleep.

She dreamed of a night sky, full of stars. She was lying back in an open space – a garden, she thought – looking up at the stars, which were so beautiful she could almost believe they had been put there as a special display just for her. There were lots of constellations she couldn't identify, but she recognised Orion, stretching up from the horizon, and the fierce twinkling splendour of Sirius, the bright star just below Orion's feet, which flashed with shades of red, green and white. She turned to her companion, whose face was angled towards the sky with a serene expression, his eyes catching an occasional glint of the moonlight. He was leaning his head against a kind of rucksack, and a tuft of his short dark hair was pressed against the coarse fabric. He had his hands folded over his chest, and was idly fidgeting with a lighted cigarette which only occasionally reached his mouth. She watched him in silence, taking in the detail of his tidy military uniform, and the shadows in his face. He was utterly absorbed in gazing at the sky, like a child watching a cinema screen.

'Quiet night,' he seemed to say, although he hadn't actually moved his lips or looked towards her. The words just formed in her head.

'What's your name?' she asked back in the same way. But he just watched the stars in silence.

A light suddenly burst across the sky, filling the whole area with a weird orange glow. The stars dissolved into it and vanished. She looked again at the man sitting next to her and saw his face partially illuminated, the shadows receding to one side. His eyes were intense and pale, as if the light now shining into them was being met by another light from within. There was no particular beauty in his face, but he looked kindly. He took a steady pull on his cigarette, blew the smoke away thoughtfully, and then turned towards her, fixing her in a bright gaze. It was as if he could see right through her and into her soul. In those few moments she felt an overwhelming sense of sadness, futility, and above all, loss. Gazing into his face, she could see all the pain which infiltrated his thoughts, pulsing out towards her like a searchlight seeking a focus.

The orange glow in the sky was slowly fading away. She wasn't looking at it directly but could tell by the shadows which were slowly creeping back into the contours of his face. But his eyes were still alight, still piercing the depths of her being.

She felt rather bereft when she woke up the following morning. The daylight trespassing through the gap at the top of the curtains brought with it an intense feeling of loss, as if someone she was very close to had been removed to somewhere totally unreachable. She wanted to cry, but her face was tense and dry as if there was nothing to cry with. The mood was very difficult to shake off. She spent ten minutes trying to pull herself together, then phoned her boss to say that she wasn't feeling too good and would be late for work. The one advantage of having a crap job, she reasoned, was that you could skive off, and lie to your boss, without feeling guilty about it. So she spent the next hour trying to write down her dream in as much detail as she could remember. It all looked a bit soppy in the cool light of day, but at least she now had something to show to Joe, who would probably say she was a loony.

'Right on,' said Joe. 'This is the sort of stuff I was hoping you'd get.' He put the guinea pigs down on the floor and they burbled away across the room.

Katherine sat in his office chair, swirling her cup of tea in nervous embarrassment.

'You think it really was him talking, even though the words were only in my head?' she asked.

'I don't see why not.' He brushed a couple of guinea pig hairs off the paper. 'I've known it to happen before.'

'Not very profound though, is it?'

'What do you expect? Not all communications have to be filled with arcane wisdom all the time.'

'It was a weird experience, because the words were just there in my head, it wasn't like a voice or anything. It was like there was someone else thinking with my brain. I know that sounds freaky, but it's the only way I can think of to describe it. Actually, I know what it reminds me of – you know when you're trying to learn a poem off by heart, and you say the words silently in your head? That's exactly it. My own internal voice, but unusually distinct and decisive.'

'Mm. Interesting.'

'It's a bit bloody pointless though, isn't it? How are we ever going to find out who he is? When I asked for a name it all went a bit blank.'

'There is actually a good reason for that. People scoff at psychic communication because it often doesn't give names or dates, not very accurately, anyway. But what people don't realise is that the communicator can only use words and concepts that are already in the medium's head.'

'Bit stupid then, isn't it? If you can only be told things that you already know?' She made a shooing away gesture at the guinea pig which was cautiously nibbling the sole of her shoe.

'Not at all. It's like an artist being given a palette of colours. He can use any of the available colours to paint a picture, and mix them together to get different shades, but he can't use any colour that isn't on the palette. So if the palette doesn't have red, he can't use red in the painting, can he?'

'I guess not.'

'But he might still paint a decent picture with what he's got. You get my point.'

'So, this bloke can communicate using words because I've got all the words in my head. But he can't tell me his name unless the name is also in my head.'

'Something like that, though I'm simplifying it a bit too much probably. The message comes through in an abstract form which is quite independent of language, and it's your subconscious mind that sorts it out into words and images. That's why you always hear it in your own language. If you had a contact with Socrates, say, he would appear to communicate in English, not ancient Greek. That's always a difficult thing to explain to sceptics.'

Katherine thought for a moment. 'But I'm sure I've heard of cases where people have come up with really specific stuff, that they couldn't possibly have known about. Stuff in foreign languages, with names. Is that all a load of bull then?'

'No, not all of it, but you're more likely to get that with trance mediumship.'

Katherine's face lit up. 'Oooh. What's that all about then?'

'It's where the medium goes unconscious and lets the contact take over. Sometimes you get much more detailed material coming through in trance, because it cuts down the amount of interference from your subconscious mind, mental blocks and what-not.'

'You mean,' said Katherine carefully, 'that if I were to go into trance I might actually be able to get this bloke's name and find out who he is?'

'Well I wouldn't bank on it. But it's possible, yes.'

'So why don't I do it then?'

Joe sat there blinking for a few seconds, then with a smile and a shake of his head began to stir the remains of his tea with genteel vigour.

'Well?' she insisted. 'I bet you know how to do it.'

He shrugged.

'And I'm happy to give it a go. What's the problem?'

He tapped the spoon on the edge of his mug and put it down on the saucer with self-conscious precision. 'I don't think I'd really recommend trance mediumship. Certainly not to someone who's sensitive and not very experienced. It tends to work best for those who can do it naturally.'

'Why? Is it dangerous?'

'Not dangerous, especially. Just a bit melodramatic and laborious. And you need to be very selective about who you allow in.'

'But if it's the only way to find out...'

'No, it's not the only way. If you carry on doing these meditations you may well get what you need sooner or later. It could turn up in a dream or a coincidental event any time. And even if you get into full trance, there's still going to be some interference from your subconscious mind, so it's far from foolproof. And if you've never done trance before it may not work at all. You don't go in and out of it by snapping your fingers like they do in films.'

She gave him her best persuasive look, honed from years of practice on aunties and boyfriends.

'It would be interesting to have a go though, wouldn't it? Even if it doesn't work. Please, Joe.'

He sighed impatiently, curiosity gradually edging out his reservations.

'Oh all right.' He put his cup down with a clatter which sent the guinea pigs scuttling under a bookcase. 'It might be interesting. Just don't blame me if you frighten yourself into a seizure.'

'I won't, I promise. Can we have a go now?'

'I guess so, if you can help me catch George and Ringo. I don't let them run around in here unsupervised, they eat things.'

They both set to it. Katherine managed to corner the chocolate brown guinea pig behind a waste paper basket, and Joe took them both back to their hutch while Katherine admired the view from the window. It was a lovely spot, overlooking lawns, gables, rooflines of Victorian terraces interspersed with trees, and the tall Gothic spire of Christ Church in the middle distance, with the hazy Cotswold ridge beyond it. She took a step closer to the glass to get a better view.

'Bloody hell!'

She stared first in disbelief, then embarrassment, and finally morbid curiosity. Joe came back into the room to find her frozen, open-mouthed.

'What's the matter?' he asked, alarmed. 'Is it the ghosty-man again?'

'No. No no no.' Katherine swallowed. 'It's your neighbour. She's dancing around her garden in the nuddy.'

Joe clapped a hand to his forehead. 'Not again.'

Katherine took another disbelieving look at the garden two doors away where a woman of mature years was twirling gracelessly across the lawn with outstretched arms, wearing only a wristwatch.

'She does this I'm afraid. We've tried to get something done about it but it's actually legal, believe it or not.'

'But Joe. It's *December*. Is she some kind of head case or what?'

'She's barking. But not quite mad enough to be carted off, unfortunately. She complains when people gawp at her, you know.'

'Why? If I had an arse like that I wouldn't –'

'No, quite. But to be honest, the *danse au naturel* is the least of our problems. She's a nightmare busybody who spends all day churning out threatening letters to all and sundry.'

'Blimey. And I thought this was a quiet neighbourhood.'

Joe twitched an eyebrow. 'You don't know the half of it.'

Chapter Nine

A Different Filthy Hut
Egypt
10th September 1915

Dear Richard

I have a few days' leave at the moment, so am catching up on a little letter-writing. I am now sharing a new hut (I mean 'new' in the figurative sense) with my old chum Skitford from school and another very jolly subaltern called Price. We're having a wonderful time at present. I've written you a poem. I hope you like it.

Here's a little ditty
From Hughie, Price and Skitty,
Who hope you have a jolly day
Blowing all the Huns away

Just give us bomb and rifle
And we'll thrash 'em in a trifle
And joyfully exclaim
That dearly loved refrain:
"Take me back to dear old Blighted…"

On second thoughts, it's pathetic isn't it?

We had a new draft into the battalion last week. Most of them very raw recruits from England who only enlisted in the spring. Some of them have only had about three weeks' basic training, and not a musketry course between them.

I am beginning to wonder whether it is army policy to put all the dimmest men in my platoon. It surely cannot be a coincidence that I always end up with them. I cite the following as examples among my ranks:

The man who tried to clean his rifle with Worcester sauce.

The man who paid a sergeant 2d. to chase away a ghost.

The corporal who gave the order to "unfire".

The engineer who asked whether one should start bricking up a well from the top or the bottom.

But then, I suppose it makes sense to put the clever chaps somewhere useful, where the need is greater, and the not so clever chaps in the supporting roles, like the engineering jobs. Most of the work in which we have been engaged so far amounts to nothing more than laying a few miles of water pipe across the desert, and it doesn't require much intellect to cement ceramic pipes together. It isn't generally a high risk occupation either, despite the occasional fright. The Turks are well out of our way, and the Australians are lumbered with most of the dirty work. We only have to contend with the sun and sand.

We all got invited to a ball at the colonel's place last weekend. It was an absolute riot. There were lots of local dignitaries there as well as military bigwigs. We all had to line up and shake hands with this frightfully distinguished nib who apparently owns most of the desert. Like the Egyptian equivalent of a maharajah or something. The trouble was, Skitford had dared me to turn up at this 'do' disguised as a native, and I jolly well did, just to see if I could get away with it. I often get mistaken for an Egyptian anyway, being naturally darker than average and I now have a suntan to go with it. So I borrowed all the clobber from Sambo – acres of white linen wrapped round me which kept getting caught on furniture and door handles. Would you believe it, not a single person recognised me! Skitford was going puce trying not to laugh. I kept getting saluted by officers because they assumed I must be somebody important who couldn't speak English. It would have been exquisite to go and shake hands with the maharajah-style chappy, but I just couldn't whack up the ginger to do it. I ended up hiding in the latrine until all the reverential bowing and scraping was finished.

I had a letter from Aunt Ginny yesterday. She said that Louisa has now taken up her post at the Red Cross hospital. Apparently it's the same unit that used to be round the corner from us, at Moorend Park. It transferred to The Abbotts a few months ago, which is a private house down All Saints way, recently vacated by its owner, who obligingly died just as the Red Cross were looking for new premises. I bet she looks a treat in her V.A.D. uniform, though I'd not care to have her come at me with a syringe.

Write soon, you old devil, we're starved of news out here.

Best whatnots,

Hugh

* * * * * * * *

In trenches.
10th Glos. Battalion
B.E.F. France
24th September 1915

Dear Louisa,
I would not worry you for the world, but you will already have discovered some of the truth about this war from your involvement with the Red Cross, so there is little point in my lying to you regarding my situation. I hope therefore that you will forgive the melancholy tone of this letter.

I have to tell you that we are going into a major 'push' tomorrow. I cannot tell you the details, but it's the biggest campaign that has ever been attempted and we are very confident that it will successfully break the German line. If that happens then the war will almost certainly be over very soon – hopefully before the end of the year. Therefore, whatever happens, I shall be proud to have taken part in it.

I'm not really sure what to feel about it. There is a pleasant excitement tempered by a cold creeping dread. I suppose that is inevitable when one has spent all these months training for this moment and impatiently desiring it, and now that it has arrived I can't be sure if I'm ready for it. Such a strange situation, I really cannot explain it. However, I don't want you to worry too much about me, because whatever will be will be.

To be frank, part of my anxiety at present is due to our position near the front line. The shelling is heavier than on my previous excursion to the Front, and although we have very few close calls, their constant chafing at one's nerves is something to be reckoned with. They make an appalling melancholy wail, like the screams of a lunatic. We are also living in the company of the dead, who lie unburied – and unburiable – on the other side of our wire. The impossibility of retrieving them means that they remain out there indefinitely. Right outside my own dug-out, in full view of my periscope, is a group of three men who have died upright, in a sitting position. They are huddled together cosily, and look for all the world as though they were about to take tea. Dreadful though it sounds, I pray for an enemy shell to come down and blot them out.

As if all this weren't dismal enough, my principal concern at the moment is Hugh. He sends me bright and exuberant letters and it really brings it home to me how young he is, and what little place there is for him in this muddle. I am terrified that he will be killed or maimed, when he is barely even out of school. He should be at home playing football and breaking windows.

Forgive me if I have made you feel depressed. I promise I shall be thinking of you while I'm out there in the heat of it.

For now, let us pin our hopes on 1916 as the Year of Peace.

God bless.

with best love,
Richard

Chapter Ten

Not everybody has the basement of their house converted into a ritual magic temple, but then it was becoming more and more apparent that Joe was not everybody. He had, in fact, really gone to town on it and had the floor carpeted with black and white contrasting tiles, the window covered by an embroidered diagram with Hebrew squiggles, and, most alarming of all, two tall temple pillars – one black, one white – which had evidently been home-made out of a length of plastic drainpipe with a lavatory ball-cock glued to the top. In the centre of the room Joe had placed a square coffee table, with a ceramic dish and a couple of candles. Katherine sat in the middle of all this and blew her nose ominously.

'Is this deco really necessary?'

'No. But it helps to set the right atmosphere.'

She was sitting in a wooden chair watching Joe trying to light a disc of charcoal from one of the candles.

'Are you a freemason?'

Joe looked down at his feet. 'Oh God, have I left that trouser leg rolled up again?'

'You are, aren't you?'

'This little set-up has got nothing to do with that. I have a Hermetic bent which is all my own.'

The charcoal disc suddenly erupted with fizzing sparks, and Joe quickly dropped it into the dish.

'You're ready then?' He poked the charcoal, which sent tiny orange sparks into the air around his finger.

'Yes. If you say it's not dangerous.'

'As sure as I can be. OK, here's what we'll do. I'm going to put the laptop on a chair next to you and it will record the proceedings for us. It will probably take you a while to go into trance though, so there's no pressure.'

Katherine watched silently as a fold of white smoke uncurled from the incense dish, and made as much effort as she could to reach out to her soldier friend, calling for him wherever he was. She had begun to form a firmer bond with him now, to the extent that she knew when his presence was imminent because she would feel a tiny loop and swirl in her stomach, followed by a cold feeling in her legs.

She was surprised to have this sensation almost immediately, but didn't dare say anything for fear of interrupting the fragile contact. The soldier's presence was as tangible as she had ever known it and she felt warmly confident that she was going to get something from this first attempt.

She began to breathe slowly on a count of ten, as Joe had asked her to do. It wasn't easy to keep it going, but there was no doubt that it made her relax a lot better. Then Joe started the laptop recording, and began to talk her through the next stage.

'I want you to imagine that your body is becoming lighter and lighter, and beginning to drift upwards through the air. See the ceiling getting closer as you move towards it. Now you turn round, and see that your physical body is still sitting in the chair, and that you are in a lighter form of your body, but firmly connected to the physical by a silver cord.'

Katherine visualised the sequence in her mind's eye, and had a disorientating sense of floating upward from her seat. With her eyes closed, she could clearly see herself sitting with her knees together in the wooden chair, and Joe sitting close by, lost in thought, with a fine silvery cord of light stretching out from her across the chequered floor. Weird, but at least she felt confident she was doing everything right so far.

'You are now standing in front of your body, knowing that it will be safe here if you want to leave it for a while. You go through the two pillars in the western quarter, feeling the texture of the carpet under your feet, and the smell of the incense. Now go up to the door, open it, and go out. You are at the bottom of the steps that lead out into the hallway. You go up the steps, walk past the telephone table and the novelty Oscar Wilde doormat, up to the front door and undo the night latch. See yourself slipping out through the door and closing it behind you. Now take a look at the street.'

Katherine saw a clear image of Joe's street, colourless in the twilight. There was the rose bush just inside the garden gate, a slightly run-down wall, and a light scattering of leaves over the brick-paved pathway. She went up to the gate and saw the pavement in detail, grit glinting in the cracks between the slabs, a solitary weed springing by the gutter, and a silvery Vauxhall with plastic wheel trims parked just along the road. She listened momentarily to the distant buzz and hum of traffic, and went out through the gate. As she turned towards town she had a sudden disorientating sensation like descending very fast in a lift.

'How was that?'

Joe's anxious face was the first thing that came into focus when she opened her eyes. Apart from an annoying feeling of having missed out on something, she felt extremely well, just a bit sleepy, with a very numb arse.

'It was fine I think,' she croaked. 'Did I go into trance?'

Joe made an incredulous noise. 'Not half!'

Katherine suddenly snapped back to reality. 'You're joking? Oh shit, did I say anything embarrassing?'

Joe grinned and shook his head. 'Does the name Monroe mean anything to you?'

Her stomach did a crashing somersault. 'Is that his name?'

'It's what he said. What *you* said.'

'Monroe? As in Marilyn?'

'Apparently. Would you like to listen to the recording?'

'I guess so. How long was I out for?'

'Only about five minutes. Long enough. I wasn't expecting you to go into full trance on a first attempt. I thought you'd stay semi-conscious the first few times.'

'Did my voice go all deep and scary?'

'Of course not, don't be silly. Now just listen to this.'

Joe pressed the space bar. Between long humming silences, and the occasional self-conscious throat-clearing, the audio track replayed Joe's voice giving instructions with what now seemed like painful slowness. Then, after a few minutes, her own voice appeared on the recording. It was just her normal, everyday voice, slightly soft but with nothing spooky or weird about it. Except that she had no recollection of any of it.

Kath: It's gone dark.
Joe: Where are you?
Kath: In a basement. A church basement. There's a candle but I can't really see.

Joe: Are you alone?

Kath: No. There's somebody else here, sitting on the floor in the middle. I've been here before.

Joe: Is it the same place you see in your dream?

Kath: I think so, yes. There are arches all around. It's an old place. Lot of dust. I can only see shadows.

Joe: What about the person in the room with you?

Kath: Yes, I know him. His name is Monroe. He comes from Cheltenham, like me.

Joe: What is he doing here?

There was a pause on the recording in which you could hear Katherine breathing.

Kath: He's in the Gloucestershire Regiment.

Joe: Is he the same man you saw in Tewkesbury Abbey?

Kath: Yes. I can only see his face when he looks up, but it's him.

Joe: Is he aware of you?

Kath: Yes, but he's busy. He's looking through a big notebook. There's not much light but he's got a lot of notes there. There's a candle on the floor next to him, and a small silver case.

Joe: Do you know why he's here?

Kath: This is the only place he can find to focus his thoughts.

Joe: Have you any idea where this basement is?

Kath: No. The village no longer exists.

Joe: No longer exists?

Kath: Only underground. It's only underground now.

Joe: OK. Is there anything more you can tell me about the place, what it looks like?

Kath: There's a wooden figure. Very dark. Some kind of goddess. I can see a crown of stars round her head, and a blue veil. Nothing else, it's dark and she's very black. Black face. There's a powerful atmosphere here. It's an ancient place, a channel for the underworld. The darkness is a part of the underworld, but it's a comforting darkness, not sinister at all.

Joe: What about Monroe? Can you speak to him?

Kath: He knows I'm here. That's enough.

Katherine was completely stunned that she could have given such a detailed description, and come up with such specific information, without knowing anything about it. Joe had told her what to expect, but it was still a shock. She didn't have any particular sense of having been unconscious or of losing five minutes of her life, though she obviously had. She knew there was no possibility that he could have faked the audio recording.

And yet the excitement at getting a result, actually getting a name for her visitor which might enable her to trace him, was incredible. She sat in the comfy chair in Joe's office stuffing herself with chocolate biscuits, which Joe insisted was a necessary part of coming back to reality. To be truthful she did feel extremely spaced out and light-headed, and somewhere deep inside her was a fear that this state might be permanent, and she might never get back to normal consciousness. But Joe wasn't worried. He was chewing enthusiastically on the end of a pen and poring over his notebook.

'How's it looking?' she asked. 'Have we got enough information?'

'Should have.' He took the pen out of his mouth. 'Assuming his name was Monroe, and he came from Cheltenham, and he served in the Gloucestershire Regiment, that does narrow the field down pretty well.'

'So where do we start?'

'Ah, there's the rub. We do have one vital element missing, and that's the date. We don't know exactly when Mr Monroe was around.'

Katherine frowned, and covered her mouth to avoid spraying Joe with biscuit crumbs. 'First world war, surely?'

'We don't really know that though, do we?' Joe threw down his biro. 'It could just as easily be the second world war, or the Boer war, or he might just have been a soldier during peacetime.'

'Yes, but –' She ran her fingers slowly over an Art Nouveau paperweight on the desk. 'It's the only time that fits. Firstly because it all started off with the first world war memorial in the abbey, and then I met you, an expert on the first world war. You don't think that's just a coincidence? And secondly, I just KNOW. I can feel it.'

Joe smiled, with a satisfied look on his face. 'You're beginning to sound like me.'

'But it's true,' she protested. 'I feel it in my bones. This is first world war stuff.'

'Mm. OK then. We'll work on the basis that he was around during the first world war. It's still going to involve trekking round a few museums and record offices though.'

'Fine. I'll take a couple of days off work. Again.'

The doorbell rang, startling them both.

'I'd better go and see to that,' said Joe.

He hadn't any idea who might be calling, but was startled to open the door to two rather embarrassed-looking policemen. One was quite chubby with black hair and a moustache. The other, slightly younger, had ginger hair and a moustache. Neither of them was smiling.

'Sorry to trouble you, sir,' said the chubby one. 'Could we just step inside for a moment?'

Joe felt a rush of fear, and was sure it must be showing on his face. He ushered them into the hallway and through to the living room. He could hear Judi shuffling about in the kitchen, and was glad she hadn't answered the door. He invited the officers to sit down, but they declined and stood in the middle of the room, where the ginger one gazed aimlessly at a nearby bookcase.

'We've just come from your neighbour's house, two doors away,' said the chubby policeman. 'Mrs Grady.'

'Jeannette, yes.' Joe tried to sound normal. It didn't help that the police seemed to be as nervous as he was.

The constable licked his lips cautiously. 'I'm sorry to ask you this, sir, but have you been squirting Mrs Grady with a water pistol?'

Joe was unable to suppress a nervous laugh.

'No,' he said, as sensibly as he could. 'No I haven't.'

'She says you have.'

'Well I haven't.'

'She claims she saw you.'

'Then she's mistaken.'

Or bloody lying more like, the barmy moo, he thought ungraciously.

The chunky policeman looked relieved. 'Well, if it wasn't you, sir, then we apologise for having troubled you. But if it *was* then I must ask you not to do it again.'

'It *wasn't* me,' protested Joe, annoyed at the suggestion that he might have done something which he knew he hadn't.

'She claims she was in the garden this afternoon and someone water-pistolled her from one of these windows here.' He indicated the general direction of the back of the house. Joe felt another urge to laugh but stamped on it hard. The policeman had an amusingly broad Gloucestershire accent, which didn't help.

'Forgive me asking,' said Joe, 'but is firing a water pistol actually a criminal offence?'

The constable took in a deep breath and looked even more embarrassed.

'That depends,' he said, 'on whether it was being used with intent to cause annoyance.' He obviously knew what Joe was getting at, because he added: 'We are obliged to follow up these complaints, I'm afraid, even if they do seem quite minor.'

Joe nodded, suppressing a sudden and uncharacteristic urge to run screaming round to Jeannette's house with a cricket bat.

'We are aware, sir, that Mrs Grady does make a lot of complaints,' continued the policeman with diplomatic understatement, turning to make his own way out to the entrance hall, 'but we do have to come and check them out.'

'That's fair enough,' said Joe, wondering if his face was as red on the outside as it felt. He could well imagine the shrill persistence with which this stupid woman must harangue the police station, badgering them with complaints about tea-bags and litter while stolen cars burned and fights broke out in other parts of town. 'Shall I see you out?'

'Goodnight then, sir,' said the chunky officer without a backward glance. His ginger colleague, who hadn't uttered a single word the whole time, produced an unconvincing smile. Joe hastily bolted the door behind them.

'Good God, what's the matter? asked Katherine, alarmed by the look on his face. 'Who was it?'

'You'll never believe it. A couple of coppers who thought I'd been squirting my neighbour with a water pistol.'

'Come off it. The police don't come out for things like that. Is this the neighbour who prances around in the buff?'

Joe nodded. 'She's always doing this. Making accusations.'

'And did you do it?' Katherine smirked.

'No, I bloody did not. Though I wouldn't rule it out in the near future. Anyway, let's draw up some kind of action plan for tracing this soldier. I need to take my mind off mad old bags.'

'Right. Well, I don't know where to start, so you tell me.'

Joe tore a page out of his notebook and began to make a list. 'There's the Public Record Office, but I don't hold out too much hope there. The service records for the 1914 war were bombed in the second world war, and they lost about 60% of them. Probably more useful to look somewhere else first.'

'OK. What about the county record office in Gloucester?'

'Yes, that might be worth a look. There's also the Soldiers of Gloucestershire museum, and possibly Cheltenham museum. Then we've got parish records, local organisations who may have kept old records, and possibly the census returns. The 1911 census will be useful, and the earlier ones might throw some light on who his parents were. It's a lot of work, but we just have to try every avenue, I'm afraid.'

'That's OK. I'm quite excited about it. It's like an Enid Blyton adventure.'

'Ha-aagh!' Joe leaped to his feet and rushed over to the bookcase. 'I've just thought of something.'

'What?'

'I've got a folder somewhere with a list of soldiers serving with the Gloucestershire Regiment during the first world war. I got it from a local history buff who's doing similar research to me. We might be in business.'

He found a black plastic ringbinder under a pile of magazines and began to flick through it. Katherine moved her chair round the desk so that she could see it too. It was a closely typed list of names, with ranks and addresses.

'He's not listed.' Joe leaned back in his chair and shut the folder with a snap, sending a small puff of dust into Katherine's face.

Her heart sank. 'Well I suppose it would be a bit much to expect to find him in the first place we looked.'

'Yeah,' Joe sighed. 'But we have to face the reality that trance communication is not that reliable, I'm afraid. We could be barking up the wrong tree altogether.'

'Or it could be that he doesn't exist and never did,' said Katherine, unable to disguise an aching disappointment.

Joe shrugged. 'That's possible too. But I think we just have to take it on trust for the moment.'

It was only when Joe found the pink and green plastic gun under a towel in the airing cupboard that the truth came out. He marched straight downstairs and confronted Judi.

'You're going to get me into bloody serious trouble, my girl.'

'What? Oh, that.'

'You know she went and called the bloody police over it?'

Judi shrugged disinterestedly.

'Well, she was sitting on a garden bench with no clothes on. Made me feel sick. I don't see why I should have to look at that outside my own window.'

'Yes, but there's a right way and a wrong way to deal with these things.'

'Oh yeah? Like when you wrote to the council, and it took six months and three follow-up phone calls before they'd write back to say there was nothing they could do?'

Joe was momentarily wrong-footed.

'Yes. Well. The point is – we need to be seen to be whiter than white, and not get caught stooping to her level, because as soon as the police start to think of us as trouble-makers we've had it. And it would really not have helped our case if they'd found *this*.'

'Oh come off it Dad, you know she deserved a good squirt. The police know it too. They were probably weeing themselves with laughter all the way back to the station.'

He held up the water-pistol, which made a sloshing sound as he moved it. It was comfortable to grip and made him feel empowered. He looked at it for a moment, unscrewed the lid of the water reservoir and peered inside curiously.

'Do you think we could get a cat to pee in this?'

Chapter Eleven

In the event of this book being mislaid, or the owner thereof being whooshed, crumped, whizz-banged, sniped, bombed, gassed or otherwise rendered napoo, please forward it to:

2nd-Lt. Hugh Crooke
Langford House
Charlton Kings
Cheltenham
Glos.

Introduction
I met a subaltern the other day whose task is to keep the official War Diary of the 10th Glo'sters. This involves keeping a sparse daily record (or almost daily) of excursions, objectives and casualties, and a brief summary of enemy activity. Each entry amounts to no more than a few lines and is devoid of detail, embellishment or human interest. I have therefore appointed myself as the keeper of an Unofficial War Diary for the 10th, which will fill in – albeit in a small and personal measure – some of the missing detail which is not deemed dull enough for the official diary. Due to time pressures it might be somewhat sporadic, but I shall endeavour to maintain it as efficiently as possible.

R.M.M.

15th September 1915
My starting point, therefore, is the flat, shattered wasteland of the Pas-de-Calais, and the ruined village of Vermelles; 'ruined' being the operative word. I doubt there is one building left unblemished, and among these architectural corpses we are obliged to make our home, taking great care to avoid moving around too much during the day, as we are very much within range of the German guns. My sanctuary is a small attic in one of the few houses which still has a roof (though the downstairs room has taken a direct hit

from a dud shell which remains embedded in the wall, its metallic nose watching serenely over us as we take our meals). As I write in my secluded room I look around at this most unreal of realities. A modern brick wall, bearing the rafters of a pitched roof – as yet unbreached. The rafters slope down to a low wall at about waist height, and the junction between the two creates a very useful shelf, partially stuffed with straw but still large enough for a few personal effects, such as cigarettes, chocolate, shaving things, and most importantly a photograph of Louisa, my best girl. A nail higher up in the rafters provides a convenient wardrobe on which to hang my trench-coat. I have been lucky enough to acquire a rather tasteful metal bedstead, decorated with curlicues and spirals. It is a cot-type bed with sturdy metal sides, so at least this prevents me from falling out during bombardments. From this cosy, temporary home I am preparing my men for the biggest battle of their lives.

The staff officers withheld the news of this impending 'show' for as long as they could, but we had been expecting it for at least a week before it was announced. All night and every night, we have watched increasing amounts of traffic streaming into the support lines behind us. Ambulances, and lorries full of medical supplies; wagons carrying heavy canisters; limbers loaded up with an enormous quantity of shells and other munitions; extra troops by the busload. All this and more has been trundling steadily along the shell-pocked roads which form the basis of our local transport network. In addition, the men of the 1st Gloucesters (who are stationed close to us) have been engaged in a spot of trench digging a couple of hundred yards behind the front line, and, rumour has it, even in No Man's Land beyond the front line. Trench digging is a necessary evil, but what doesn't seem to have been thought through very well is that the soil in this area is full of chalk, and the freshly dug earth glows with an extraordinary whiteness, especially when viewed from above. I saw an aerial reconnaissance photograph of the area, taken this week, in which the trench lines were thick white serpents springing over the landscape. I could hardly believe my eyes when the officer told me the photograph was 'as is', because they were so thick and white they looked as though they had been painted on. The Germans, for all their sins, are not stupid, and it is likely that they will have noticed the fresh white residue from this digging activity. It now covers several miles, and could only be interpreted as preparation for a major offensive.

16th September 1915
Today I was taken to a field in which a scale model of the surrounding area had been constructed, based on aerial photographs, which will supposedly help us keep our bearings when we venture out into No Man's Land. We were shown bricks representing houses, clusters of twigs representing woods, and scoops of coal representing slag-heaps. Trenches, ironically enough, were marked by lines of powdered chalk. I stood there stupidly, trying to take it all in, trying to visualise it in terms of the reality on the other side of the wire and commit the whole thing to memory. But it looked so irrelevant, so quaint, I was unable to do more than gaze at it blankly and put on a pretence of understanding.

However, I think my appreciation of it surpasses that of the pompous general who was in charge of this little toy battlefield. He sat on his horse like a sack of coal, an unnatural horseman, with his feet stuck forward in the stirrups, as if he were secretly imagining himself on a plinth in Trafalgar Square. If his horse had taken fright he would have ended up on his bott in the mud, but the animal stood quietly, too bored even to twitch its ears. When I spoke to the general later on he made no eye contact at all, and I could sense that he regarded me as his inferior in every respect. Afterwards I thought of him going back to his château behind the lines, easing his bulk into a gold-painted chair and tucking into a plate of roast beef, idly pondering the accolades he could expect when "his men" broke the German line, even as those same men squatted in holes in the freezing cold, without food or sleep. At that moment I felt more anger and hatred towards him than I have ever been able to summon up for the Germans.

On the way back to my billet I stopped to look at the château of Vermelles, a proud brick-built villa with its walls still mostly upright. No generals in residence here; it looked as though the German artillery had been focusing on it for some time, and there was no comfort or sanctuary within its smashed shell. I peered through the charred window-frames, now devoid of glass, and saw only piles of tumbled bricks and splintered timbers. Anything of value or human interest had long since been looted or blown to oblivion. Around the former château gardens there were broken walls and trampled shrubs, remains of earlier battles.

I had just begun to walk towards the chapel, a matter of yards away, when there was a series of ear-splitting crashes from the road on my left. The Germans were ranging along the main village street with heavy field guns, pounding the wrecked houses into more wreckage. A flash of fire appeared behind the windows of a cottage close by, and I frankly ran for my life. I had just enough sense to keep away from the château building, which was an obvious target, and made for a deep shell-hole on the other side of a garden wall, which had begun to fill in with brambles. I hopped over the wall with my heart practically in my mouth and ran for the hole. As I tore through the long grass my foot caught on something soft and heavy, like a ball of clay, and I fell flat on my face in the tangle of weeds. It seemed as safe a place as any, so I lay there for several minutes flat on the ground, feeling as though my heartbeat was shaking the earth beneath me more violently than the shell-fire. After what must have been about two minutes the bombardment abruptly ceased, leaving only a few clouds of smoke rising sedately from the village. I then realised that none of the shells had come within a hundred yards of me, and my panic had been an over-reaction based on inexperience.

I dusted myself down, and kicked the grass and weeds back to see what it was I had tripped over. It was a man's head. My foot had been caught on the corpse of a French soldier, probably left over from the fighting around Vermelles at the end of last year. His face was completely gone, but he still had an identity disc at the neck of his uniform. I felt too squeamish to try to decipher it or – heaven forbid – retrieve it, and turned away with a shudder.

I walked 'home' along the line of an abandoned and overgrown trench, littered with debris. Tin plates, water bottles, splintered rifles, twisted bayonets, crumpled and faded letters, German stick-bombs – all were scattered among the thistles in varying degrees of decay.

I passed a wayside madonna by the edge of the road, still largely undamaged due to her position within a small cluster of trees. She had a gaudily painted face like a chorus girl and her robe was spattered with bird guano. Someone was paying attention to her though, because there was a little bunch of dried weeds stuffed between her hands, a demure offering of cornflowers, buttercups and meadowsweet.

17th September 1915

This morning I went down to Battalion HQ with Lieutenant Nowell and some others, for a debriefing session. Our men are to undertake something of a heavy lifting job in the next couple of days, and we were advised of some special safety precautions. The task is not an enviable one, but at least our visit to HQ enabled us to get a decent breakfast in the officers' mess. We sat at a long wooden table with a colonel who was having some difficulty negotiating a slice of scrambled egg on toast; it was interfering rather badly with his mutton-chop moustache. The food was a comparative luxury for us, but alas we were not to enjoy it without disturbance. An orderly was at the door trying to fend off a group of angry and distressed French women, who seemed to think he might understand them if they shouted louder, but it was all in vain. Nowell, who speaks good French, took it upon himself to intercede, and shortly came back to relay a message to the colonel.

'They're saying, sir, that one of our men has assaulted a girl, and they would like an officer to come immediately and arrest him.'

The colonel reluctantly put his triangle of toast back on the plate. He pointed at Nowell and myself.

'You two, come with me. And the orderly can follow too.'

We marched out into the main street with a dozen or more women trying to explain themselves in nervous, angry voices, with Nowell translating as best he could. They claimed that a soldier had taken to a young woman who worked in the café. He had become excessively drunk, and tried to buy her favour with a ten-franc note, much to her disgust. It is alleged that he then followed her home, clawed at her clothes and demanded that she marry him. The girl resisted, and when he grabbed her in an attempt to kiss her, a struggle ensued in which her dress was torn. She managed to reach her house and bolt herself in, but the man stood beneath her window all night, shouting abuse, and made several clumsy attempts to climb up and break through the window.

'Le voilà!' shrieked one of the women, jabbing her finger at a man who sat sulkily on a bale of straw in the village square, sipping delicately at a water bottle. The colonel strode up to him, with Nowell and myself on either side.

'Well I never,' said the man with a nervous laugh. 'It looks as if half the British Empire is after me.'

I felt a tug of pity for him. He was a nice-looking fellow, with black hair, a strangely angelic face, and bright, clear blue eyes. He had lost his cap, and sat with his arms folded around himself in a gesture of self-protection. He briefly glanced over the gardens and fields behind the market square, weighing up his chances of escape. But there was no escape.

The colonel placed him under arrest, and the orderly tied his hands with a piece of rope, and we took him back to HQ. He was still groggy with drink, and was secured in a pig-sty while an identity parade was organised. In the meantime we went back to our breakfasts.

'What will happen to him if he's found guilty?' I asked.

'Death,' replied the colonel flatly, and he popped the final corner of toast into his mouth with military precision.

At the identity parade we saw the girl. She was a slim, pretty thing in a green dress, attractive, but not worth dying for. She looked at the line of men in front of her. Then her finger thrust out at the man we had just arrested.

'Oui, c'est l'homme.'

The man made no attempt to deny it, but looked appealingly at the girl with his bright, unblinking eyes. After that he was taken away for court-martial at the military prison in St. Omer.

'Selfish woman,' Nowell complained on the way back. 'He was a decent enough lad, wasn't he? Why shouldn't he have the pleasure of a pretty French girl's company? He was fighting for France, for God's sake.'

Part of me agreed with him, but I imagined how I would feel if any foreign soldier had molested Louisa. Frankly I would kill him, whether he was fighting for England or not.

19th September 1915
Too tired to write much. I have been part of a fatigue party, with five other officers, whose task is to transport heavy canisters to the front line. These canisters – there are around five thousand of them – have been brought up from the railway terminal at Gorre to a collecting point in Vermelles. They must now be carried by hand to the trenches, a distance of about one mile. We set off last night under cover of darkness, each canister slung on a pole between two men, and we promptly got lost in the great muddle of communication trenches. One of the canisters was dropped on the edge of a muddy sump pit and we had a devil of a job trying to get it out. While the men heaved and cursed in the mud I stood by and watched a very bright star flickering over the town of Loos, hoping it was a good omen.

'These aren't normal shells, are they sir?' one of the young chaps asked.

There was no reply I could give. The newspapers and magazines which have arrived from England are full of indignation and disgust at the Germans' use of poison gas in Flanders a few months ago. How would most English people feel, then, to know that the same illegal and immoral weapon of creeping death is about to be unleashed by the British army, and that in a few days' time the fields around Loos will choke and seethe with British-made poison? But they will not know, because we refer to the canisters only as 'the accessory'. The rest is silence.

Chapter Twelve

Joe listened, with some satisfaction, to the light scuffing noise the rotten apple made as it skimmed across Jeannette's porch and erupted on impact. He stood for a moment surveying the squishy mess he had made, and glanced furtively up and down the road. There was no sign of anyone watching. He began to walk away casually, feeling, for the first time in many years, a guilty thrill which made him want to laugh out loud. He knew there would be repercussions. If the police responded to water pistols they would certainly respond to decaying fruit. Well, good luck to the silly cow. Let her try to prove it.

His mobile phone let out a sudden quivering trill which made him jump so sharply he nearly tripped over. He wiped the worst of the sticky apple residue on the leg of his trousers and retrieved the phone from his inside pocket. He always felt self-conscious when the phone rang in a public place, even when there wasn't anyone around. He half expected it to be Jeannette, ever ranging the street with her omniscient binoculars.

'Hello?' he said in a furtive voice.

'Joe? That is you, isn't it?'

'Hello Kath, yes, it's me.'

'Your voice sounds all funny. What's the matter?'

He cleared his throat. 'Nothing. No, it's just these phones. Never get used to them. Bloody embarrassing.' He looked over his shoulder at a passing car, and imagined the driver must be staring at him. 'Any joy yet?'

'Not really. I was wondering whether I could borrow some books from your collection. The newspaper anthology thingies from the first world war. I can't concentrate on anything else at the moment, so I may as well do something useful.'

'Yes, sure. Would you like me to bring them round?'

'If you're sure it's no trouble.'

'No trouble at all, if eight o'clock's OK. Have you got a lift sorted out for tomorrow?'

'Yeah, my friend Mike says he'll take me. And he'll come in and help me look. He did some research on his family tree a year or so back, so he knows how the record office works.'

'Good. Makes it a lot easier if you've got a responsible helper to do some of the legwork.'

A snort of static came down the line.

'I don't know that I'd call Mike responsible. He once tried to poke himself in the eye with a compass because he wanted to have odd-coloured eyes like David Bowie.'

'Well, you can get him to carry your notebook and pencils if you can't trust him with anything else. Anyway, I'd better go.' He didn't know how much longer he could stand the smell of putrid apple in such proximity to his nose.

'All right. See you then.'

The phone was stuck to his hand, and his hand smelled of rancid cider; perhaps this was karma at work. He went back to the house to clean up.

He arrived at Katherine's flat a few minutes early, and listened to the sounds of frantic last-minute tidying through the closed door before she would let him in.

'I don't know why you're embarrassed about the mess,' he said, snagging his foot in the handle of a Tesco bag full of library books. 'You know I use my floor as a filing system too. And I'm not a judgemental person, am I?'

'That's not the point,' replied Katherine, anxiously slamming the cupboard door shut on a frighteningly wobbly stack of old videos.

'Well, I've brought a bit more mess for you,' he said, putting a pile of large, tatty hardback books onto the one small space on her table.

'Oh good. That'll give me something to do for a few evenings.'

Joe planted himself down in the nearest available chair, and noticed Raoul curled up on top of a cupboard, totally blissed out, wedged between a clock and a vase of flowers.

'Is that cat all right up there?' he asked dubiously.

'Oh yes, he never knocks anything over, don't worry.'

'OK. You can borrow the books for as long as you like, only don't let the cat make a nest on them because they're quite precious. I've brought all the volumes from 1914 to 1918, so that should give you all the relevant ones.'

'The *Gloucestershire Graphic*. I've never heard of it.'

85

'Not a going concern any more, but it was very popular at that time. Anything worth knowing about in Gloucestershire –' he patted the cover of one of the books, '– it'll be in here.'

'Is there an index?'

Joe laughed. 'Not bloody likely. You'll just have to trawl through the whole lot. I'm not even sure what you should be looking for. Hopefully something may stand out.'

Katherine pulled one of the huge books towards her and began to flick through it. The yellow-brown pages were full of overly inky photographs of dignitaries at garden parties, and adverts for tooth powder. There were also lots of pictures of soldiers in small fuzzy portraits with oval borders. Most of the portraits went alongside an announcement that the soldier was dead.

'That one's printed on bog paper, I'm afraid, which doesn't do a lot for the quality of the pictures,' said Joe. 'War-time paper shortages, that's the trouble. The 1914 one was much glossier.'

'Still,' said Katherine, 'it'll help me to get a feel for the time, if nothing else.' She turned the pages gently. Raoul shifted himself closer to the clock and sighed with a loud deflating noise.

'Oh yes, and I brought you a web address too.' Joe pulled a scrap of paper from his jacket pocket and showered Katherine's carpet with little shreds of crumpled and torn up paper. 'Oh bugger. Now look what I've done.'

Katherine eyed the shreds with interest. 'Been in a bit of a temper, have we?'

'Well, just a little.' Joe leaned down and carefully picked up all the bits. He saw that Katherine was hoping for some more information, so he said: 'It's the dreaded nudey-woman again.'

'Sending you *billets-doux*, is she?' said Katherine, winding him up.

'This,' said Joe, waving a fragment of ripped paper in her face, 'was a letter from Mrs Grady's solicitor, threatening to take legal action if I persist in keeping my wheelie bin outside my own back gate. She reckons it's obstructing a right of way. I've checked the land registry documents and there's no doubt I'm in the clear, but it makes me absolutely bloody boiling mad.'

'Let her do her worst then. If she wants to waste sixty odd quid on a solicitor's letter it's up to her.'

'I know,' whined Joe. 'But I'm bloody furious anyway.'

'What were you going to do with those ripped up bits?'

'Stuff them through her letterbox. At least, that was my first thought. Then I thought that might look a bit childish, so I chucked a squishy apple at her front door instead.' His eyes lit up with the memory of it. 'A really suppurated one off the compost heap.'

'Joe, you're a bloody laugh, you know that, don't you?'

She went over to the corner of her living room which doubled as an office, and booted up the ancient Mac which she had salvaged from an office clearance.

'Let's have that address, then.'

Joe handed over the paper on which he'd written the web address of the Commonwealth War Graves Commission.

'This site is a godsend to old farts like me,' he said. 'You can imagine how many hours I spend looking at people's graves on here.'

Katherine cleared her throat. 'And this has every military grave from the whole of the first world war?'

'Yep. Everything. Even the poor buggers with no known grave, it'll tell you which memorial has got their name on it.'

'So, if this Monroe chap died during the first world war, we should find him in this database? And what will that tell us?'

'Quite a lot, actually. The exact location of the grave, some details about where and when he died, and with a bit of luck it'll say who his parents were.'

'And if he's not in the database?'

'Then either he survived the war, or we're barking up the wrong tree again.'

'So if I just put in "Monroe" and do a search...'

The page came up with a list of five soldiers called Monroe. Katherine scrolled through them and huffed with disappointment.

'This isn't right. One of them was a Marine, two of them were in the artillery. Nothing from the Gloucestershire Regiment.'

'Hmm. It doesn't look too promising, does it?'

'Might he have been missed off for some reason?'

Joe shook his head. 'Not very likely. The War Graves Commission are a pretty organised lot. You don't find many mistakes.'

'Well, that's that then.' She switched off the monitor.

'What's the matter?'

'We're not going to find him, are we?'

'Rubbish. We've only been trying for two days. We've barely even started yet.'

'Not the nicest of places, Gloucester,' said Mike as he swung across the middle lane of the roundabout, cutting up a BMW which had been about to come past him. He watched the reflection of its driver mouthing obscenities in the rear-view mirror. Katherine gripped the arm-rest, and noticed that she was also holding her breath.

'Are you all right?' he asked.

'Never felt better,' she said sarcastically.

'Now, if I remember rightly, the record office is down here...' He swung the small Vauxhall round to the right and hurtled up to a red traffic light with such enthusiasm that Katherine instinctively stamped her right foot on the floor.

'Sorry,' said Mike. 'There's no brake on the passenger side.'

'I can't help it,' grumbled Katherine. 'It's a reflex.'

Mike laughed. They crawled along in a traffic jam for a while, and Mike amused himself by flicking idly at the air freshener which dangled from the steering column and scrolling through the ringtones on his mobile phone.

'You've got an attention span of about five seconds, haven't you?' complained Katherine.

'Eh?' He turned off down a residential street and began to accelerate. 'Let's have a look for a parking space then. I'm too tight to leave it in the NCP.'

They spent ten minutes getting lost down narrow terraced streets, none of which had any parking space. At one point they managed to go the wrong way down a one-way street, and had to reverse all the way back.

'Oh sod it, look, I'll pay for a ticket in the multi-storey.' Katherine began to ferret in the bottom of her handbag for some loose change.

'No, it's all right, here's a space.'

He manoeuvred the Vauxhall into an incredibly tight space while an old woman gave them a filthy look through the window of a pink-fronted house. Katherine began to wish she had taken the bus.

They found the record office, a red-brick building which had originally been a school. Katherine pushed Mike in ahead of her, and made him go and sort out a reading ticket while she sat at one of the tables. A few other people were already there, rummaging through cardboard boxes and looking very serious. Mike came back looking mortified.

'A *quid* they charge for a one-day reading ticket.'

'Oh for God's sake,' said Katherine, rolling a pound coin along the table towards him. 'Stop whingeing and tell me where to start.'

'Well, they've got baptisms, marriages and deaths. Take your pick.'

'No idea. But I suppose baptisms would be a good place to start.'

'OK. What year?'

Katherine thought for a moment. 'Well, if he served in the first world war, and wasn't all that old, I suppose he must have been born between about 1880 and 1895.' She saw that Mike was looking dubious. 'Is that a problem?'

'It'll take a while to search through all that, but OK. Now, do you know what parish he was born in?'

'Not a clue. Somewhere around Cheltenham, possibly. Or maybe not.'

'Right. We could be in for a long day. You'll have to go through them all one at a time. Don't just dip in at random, or you'll get into an awful mess.'

For three hours Katherine searched through the parish records, jotting down the details of any male children called Monroe, while Mike unbent a paper clip, played with a Wallace and Gromit figurine which he had in his pocket, and pinged a rubber band repeatedly at the ceiling tiles and caught it on the way down.

Finally Katherine threw down her pen. 'It's no good, I can't do any more. My eyes are going round in circles.'

'Any joy?'

'I don't know.' She showed him the pages of Monroes she had written down. 'He could be any of these.'

'Flipping heck. You have got your work cut out, haven't you?'

'I'll get there,' she said, with more defiance than conviction. 'Let's just get home. I feel an urgent craving for a cup of tea.' She stood up and they made their way back to the car.

'Who is this guy you're looking for, anyway?' Mike asked as he started the engine.

'Oh, just someone I came across,' said Katherine, who hadn't got round to concocting a credible story yet.

'A relative?'

'Yeah,' she lied. 'Sort of.'

'It's worth it though. When you find what you're looking for. It's like train spotting, really. Collecting information just for the hell of it. But you do get a buzz when you find something.' He wound down his window, subjecting the people of Gloucester to a loud burst of Blondie's *Atomic* from the car stereo. Katherine kept her right foot pressed firmly against the floor of the car and held it there – the only way to avoid instinctive stomps on the imaginary brake-pedal.

'Can't you give us a bit more of a clue?' Katherine said out loud in the solitude of her flat. She often sensed the soldier's presence in a vague sort of way, and it didn't seem out of place to talk to him, even if she couldn't hear a reply.

She was sitting cross-legged on the sofa in her dressing gown, nursing a cup of cocoa, with today's newspaper spread out unread in front of her. On the front page was a photo of the Queen wearing a horrendous pastel green hat and suit. It looked as though she had a strip of lasagne verdi wrapped round her head. Katherine tossed the paper aside in annoyance, unable to concentrate. Perhaps the old newspapers would be more suited to her current frame of mind. She reached for the fourth volume of Joe's stack of books. She had already had a good flick through the first three, without coming across anything of any relevance, although it was all fascinating stuff in its own way.

She loved finding old photographs of her neighbourhood. It was amazing in some ways how little had changed, since Cheltenham had managed to preserve many of its historic buildings, apart from a short period of frenzied destruction in the late sixties. There was a picture of some trainee soldiers digging a trench alongside a set of railings beside the college cricket ground. Apart from the lack of traffic, and the size of the trees in the background, the scene was completely unchanged after the best part of a century. On the next page was a picture of some boy scouts carrying huge tins of rice pudding on their bicycles outside the Rotunda, a gorgeous Regency building (now a pub) which was then a home for convalescing soldiers. In the foreground a couple of scullery maids were standing to attention in starched aprons beside a gawky man with big ears. Below the photo was an advert for Parasitox, allegedly an effective treatment for Body Vermin, available in a non-greasy and pleasant-to-use stick for one shilling.

Other pages were packed with soldiers' faces in extensive pictorial obituaries. She ran her eye over the list of names, occasionally distracted by a familiar name or an attractive face. Then she would turn over the page to find pictures of women in stiff skirts planting leeks, and adverts for sulphuric acid-flavoured bath salts. She caught sight of a small oval photograph of a dark-haired man with a smart tie, and her stomach did the same falling-down-a-liftshaft sensation which she had felt during her trance experience.

It was him.

There was no doubt.

She wasn't sure whether she had seen the caption first or the photograph, but she shouted a string of joyful expletives and went for a quick dance round the room before settling back down for another look. It was the face she had seen in her mind's eye so many times, and now here it was in black and white. His pale eyes were gazing wistfully into the middle distance, with a slightly shy and embarrassed look twitching at the corner of his mouth. He wore a military uniform, and even the texture of the fabric was clearly visible in the photo. Not the sexiest hair-do perhaps, but his face looked gentle and friendly. Underneath was a caption: 2nd-Lt. Richard Munro, 10th Glos. Regiment.

'I've got you this time, haven't I?' she said to the empty room, a delighted grin spreading across her face. There was no reply, and she couldn't be sure whether his presence was still around or not. There was a sense in which her exuberance shattered the fragile threads of perception, and chased away his vibrations. She glanced at the clock. It was getting close to midnight. Oh, what the hell, she thought, and dialled Joe's number.

He took a long time to answer, and when he did his voice was more of a dull bark than anything else.

'Joe, I've *found* him. Oh God, you won't believe this.'

'You're kidding?' His voice immediately sprang into life.

'Those *Gloucestershire Graphic* books you lent me. He's here, there's a picture of him.'

'What? You're sure it's him?'

'Positive. It looks exactly like him. I was just browsing through the 1917 edition, and there he was. His first name's Richard.'

'Do the surname and regiment match?'

'Oh yes,' she said triumphantly. 'Too right they bloody do. You know what we've been doing wrong? The fucking *spelling*. It's Munro with a U, not Monroe.'

'Oh, pants. That's my fault, isn't it? I should have been thinking of Scottish mountains instead of Marilyn.'

'I don't care whose bloody fault it is, I'm just bloody ecstatic.' She almost jerked the phone off the table.

'So what does it say about him?'

'Not a great deal. There's an article about a fund-raising bash at a local Red Cross hospital. He was a patient there, and did a lecture on astronomy.'

'Oh right. So he's not on the corpse list, then?'

'No. I haven't found any obituary for him. Do you think he survived the war?'

'Very possibly. Listen, bring that book round here tomorrow evening. I'm dying to have a look at this bloke.'

'Oh Christ,' said Katherine, her voice suddenly taking on a chill of panic.

'What?'

She swallowed hard. 'So there really is somebody talking to me inside my head. It's not just my imagination.'

Joe hesitated, confused. 'I thought we'd established that weeks ago.'

'Yes, but it's not the same, is it? I mean, up until now there was always a chance of being wrong, but now – does this mean he can see everything that's going on in my head?'

'No, of course not. Look, Kath, I'm going to put the phone down in a minute, and you're going to go into the kitchen and eat some chocolate or something, and then go to bed. And if you get any unwelcome visions, you know how to deal with them.'

'If you say so.' She swallowed with an audible gulp.

'Bummer about getting that name wrong though, eh? I'll see you tomorrow.'

As she clicked the receiver back in its cradle she wondered how she was going to tell Mike that their long day in the record office had been a waste of time.

Chapter Thirteen

~

30th September 1915

Louisa, I pray God you will never see this diary, and never ask me, at any distant point in the future, what I saw during this time. Soon I shall write you a cheerful little note to say that I've survived. At least I am fairly certain I have, but whether I am wholly the same person is another matter. I feel as though something fundamental had been irrevocably changed. I look down at my hands, and they are my own hands – familiar, but in a detached, unfamiliar kind of way. I have become a stranger to myself.

I hardly know where to start in trying to make sense of the last few days. My words scarcely serve to describe it. It is a dark phantasmagoria of madness.

I am in a casualty clearing-station near Chocques. It is unlikely that I will be here long, as I'm not wounded very badly, and apart from some blinding headaches I am well on the mend. The hospital has a garden where I can pick raspberries. All very dignified.

To pick up the missing part of the story, five days ago I marched my men to a safe spot in a place called Le Morquet Wood, where they were able to rest – which they needed after two long nights transporting 'the accessory'. On the same day our artillery began bombarding the German line with the heaviest arsenal of munitions ever unleashed. I know this because there was a 15in. howitzer belting away just behind us. In our debriefing we were told the exact purpose of this bombardment. It would cut large holes in the enemy's barbed wire defences. It would wipe out the soldiers manning the German front line. It would leave the enemy's main position undefended, allowing our men to sweep through the breach and capture their trenches with little or no resistance. That was the plan. That's what the moronic lieutenant-colonel told us, smiling with his moustache rather than his mouth. Then the rumours started to come back that the wire had not been cut. It started as a murmur among the men, and then I had it direct from a sergeant who had been on reconnaissance, who had been perched in a tree with a pair of binoculars and seen for himself that the enemy wire had been damaged in places but not breached. He was on his way down to HQ to pass on the message. We reacted with both dismay and relief, because it now seemed inevitable that the attack would be cancelled.

It wasn't. All we got in the way of a response from HQ was a memo about leakage of information, warning us that there were spies in the area, both male and female, and we were not to speak about military matters in the presence of civilians. I don't see how it would have made much odds. The Germans knew we were about to attack them, because we'd been pelting them with explosives for the last four days. Most of my men were still quite cheerful about the whole business, just wanting to get on with it, although there was a subtle feeling of melancholy hanging over the more experienced men. Nothing more.

We marched up to our jumping-off point on the 24th. The men had spent hours cleaning their rifles and equipment, but it was all filthy again by the time we arrived. And so we spent the night – tired and dirty – in a bitterly cold trench. I didn't feel able to sleep, so I walked around for a bit and then chatted with a group of men I found huddled round a brazier. They were burning a pair of old boots salvaged from a dead comrade. Not good enough to wear, they explained, and they hadn't got any other fuel, despite being only a few hundred yards from the woods. God only knows where their officer was. Busy, they said. I was half afraid they were lying, but it turned out that they were in one of the poison gas companies, and there was no doubt that the officers in charge of the gas had their work cut out. I asked them what had happened to the owner of the boots. Shot in the head, they told me, when he walked past a small gap in the sandbags which was being covered by a German sniper. Didn't even see the gap was there until he got shot through it. Now everybody remembered to duck when they went past that spot. The men were in the Royal Engineers, like Hugh. I couldn't stop thinking of Hugh. How I might get killed and never see him again. And how easily it might have been him standing out here, risking a casual bullet in the head. I wasn't happy when they sent him out to Egypt, but now I thank God with all my heart that they didn't send him here.

At around 3a.m. we were interrupted by two Special Division R.E. officers – gas engineers – who appeared to be having a blazing row, but were managing to do it with lowered voices to avoid exciting the Germans. We saw them for a few moments in the section of trench next to ours before wandering out of view. One was a grave-looking subaltern with a narrow face who kept shaking his head, the other a tall fair-haired lieutenant who used a lot of foul language.

'Did you catch what they were arguing about?' I asked a corporal beside me.

'Wind speed's dropped,' said the corporal, pointing his bayonet up at the curl of smoke rising from the brazier. It was true. The smoke rose up with barely a ripple of air to disturb it. But in my ignorance I didn't realise the significance of this.

I made my way back to my platoon, which took some time, since the quantity of men and equipment piling up along the main trench almost blocked the gangway, and whenever two people met from opposite directions they both had to squeeze themselves flat against the trench wall to get past. The communication trenches were completely blocked with troops waiting to go over at dawn, and nobody could have squeezed through them no matter what. None of them spoke, and I would hardly have known they were there if it weren't for the sound of their breathing, and the chinking of the tools they carried on their backs.

But as zero hour started to draw closer there was a lot of murmuring going on, making everyone nervous. A light drizzle was starting to fall. The appointed time for the release of the gas came and went, and nothing happened. Dawn began to break. Some field-guns just behind us started up, firing just over our heads in (presumably) a last desperate attempt to cut the German wire. Still nothing happened. It was almost broad daylight when the order was given and the gas canisters were finally opened. It went hissing down the hoses and out into No Man's Land, quickly drifting up into a forty-foot high curtain of billowing fog.

A commotion started somewhere down the line. There were lots of panicky voices, but nothing to be seen. Something clearly wasn't right. I started to walk down the trench, and met the fair-haired lieutenant from the Royal Engineers coming the other way, looking flustered.

'What's the problem?' I asked.

'Absolute fucking cockup,' he said, and swept past.

It was Lockey, my batman, who eventually told me what the problem was. The great plume we'd sent out into No Man's Land had barely even rippled. With no wind to blow it across to the German line it had just stayed where it was, looming ominously in front of our own trenches. And at any moment I would be given the order to lead my platoon over that piece of ground, whether the cloud was still there or not.

My men were assembled and waiting for the whistle when the first of the stretcher cases came past. A Scotsman, first, with his bonnet pulled tightly over his nose and mouth, wheezing. Then a cluster of four or five more, one of whom was breathing with a horrific gurgling noise. I exchanged glances with Lockey, but nobody said anything.

We went over the parapet at six thirty. At the same moment the barrage from our own guns stopped abruptly, and I led my group of men up and over the front of the trench. Not very gracefully, because I was nervous and my boots kept slipping on the greasy wood – there was nothing to give a decent foothold. As I came level with the parapet I felt – rather than heard – the rapid pat-pat-pat of machine-gun bullets hitting the front of the sandbag I was clinging to. A strange, surreal calm descended on me, and over I went. I stood for a moment on the parapet in full view of the German trenches, and nothing hit me, which seemed like a good start. Then I started to run. Lockey was there beside me, and he let out a whoop of exhilaration. It struck me as such a daft thing to do that I found myself laughing. Everything was so ridiculously unreal there was nothing else to do but laugh at it.

To be honest I could see very little. I had a good image in my mind's eye of what the area was like, but now I was running across the real thing it just looked like a muddy patch of field with a couple of slag heaps in the middle distance. We had been told to head for Lone Tree, which was a solitary blasted cherry tree on the horizon just in front of the German line, but there was no chance of seeing it through all the smoke, if indeed it was still there after the barrage. The enemy parapet floated in and out of view through the cloud of poison gas which was still drifting slowly along in front of us. It was impossible to see whether it had actually reached the German line or not. A lot of it seemed to have been blown aside by a crosswind and eddied back towards the British trenches.

A thin line of soil whipped up from the ground just in front of me as another machine-gun raked across. I leapt over it with childish glee, and began to head off to the right where I could see some men streaming through a gap in the German wire. It was around this point that I looked round again and noticed that Lockey wasn't there any more. I have no idea what happened to him. I didn't see him again.

Closer to the German line it became more treacherous. There were a lot of deep craters left by our bombardment, and some fleecy folds of gas and smoke had slipped into them and sunk to the bottom. I was shocked by the number of men who were lying in the mud, dead or wounded, but there wasn't time to stop and help them. There was a most bizarre whining noise, a combination of the German artillery shells which were now screaming overhead and the warble of bagpipes from the Scottish battalion which was advancing behind us. The most alarming discovery, however, was the scattering of dud shells, British shells, which littered the area right up to the German line. There were masses of them; it was a nightmare to avoid tripping over them. These were the shells which were fired over yesterday to cut the wire for us, and they had simply plopped down and failed to explode.

I gestured to what was left of my platoon to make their way towards the gap. There were quite a few bodies piled up on and around the wire, but I watched another group of men rush through the gap unscathed and dive down into the German trench. I followed them through and ran up to the enemy parapet, to find myself confronted by a line of bayonets pointing upwards along the edge like an ornamental picket fence. Then a soldier's head popped into view, wearing a British cap, thank God. He held a grimy hand out to me and helped me to slither down into the trench. It was swarming with British soldiers, not a German in sight. So much for my first confrontation with the enemy.

I set off straight away down a communication trench which was built in a dizzying series of zig-zags. I had never been in a German trench before and I felt quite vulnerable without Lockey. There were now a lot of shells coming over, but most of them were ranged on No Man's Land which was now safely behind us. We were lucky, I think, to get through when we did.

Then I hurtled round a traverse in the trench and came face to face with a German. I stopped abruptly and one of the men coming up behind cannoned into me, knocking me against the wall. The German was tall and stocky with wide grey eyes and a sweaty face, grubby from the battle. I didn't move and neither did he. My revolver was pointing at his chest, but I hesitated to use it and we stared at each other in silence. Then I saw that he was actually stone dead, shot through the neck. By some unfortunate quirk of death he had become stuck on some object on the side of the trench and held upright, in what looked rather like a sentry position. That, more than anything else I encountered that day, gave me a horrible fright.

'Carry on,' I called back over my shoulder, and we moved along uninterrupted for another hundred yards or so until the trench fizzled out and we were once more in the open.

It must have been somewhere around this point that I lost my bearings. It was a pretty bland landscape, and there didn't seem to be much in the way of visible landmarks. I tried in vain to recognise some similarity to the collection of housebricks and coal chunks which the general had shown to us a few days ago. There was a patch of scrubby woodland some distance away to my right and a few half-demolished buildings, but nothing else of note, and the drizzly weather reduced visibility. I looked for somebody else I might be able to follow, but everybody seemed to be running around in different directions. Then I heard a yell of "creeping barrage!" from a sergeant about ten yards away. Sure enough, the Germans were now ranging their guns with deadly accuracy on what had been their own front line, now full of British men, and were slowly moving the line of fire forwards. In another few minutes the full force of the bombardment would be on us. It is impossible to imagine how that feels, when you are stuck out in the open with nothing to shelter behind.

I decided that our best chance was to make a bolt for the woods. It seemed like a good idea at the time, anyway. The woods were impossibly far off, of course, but there was nowhere else to take cover. As I moved forward there was a thundering crash just behind me which swept me right off my feet, and I was tossed like a rag-doll in a shower of flying earth and stones. I landed hard on my face and felt a devastating crunch in my mouth. I thought I'd lost all my teeth, but when the fall-out settled and I was able to lift my head enough to investigate I found that I actually just had a mouthful of dirt. Very crunchy, gravelly dirt. The physical damage was nothing more than a cut lip. My body must have gone into some kind of shock though, because I found it very difficult to move; my limbs were heavy and aching. I reached for my water bottle and swilled out the worst of the soil and grit from my mouth, along with a tiny amount of blood.

I couldn't lift myself up far enough to see what was going on around me. There were still lots of crumps going off nearby but the worst of it seemed to have passed over. I didn't know whether the men in my platoon had been blown up or simply carried on without me, but I eventually conceded that I would have to get up and find out. As I lifted my head I sensed an uncharacteristic warmth on the back of my neck. I couldn't feel anything when I touched it, but the palm of my hand came away completely red. This was my second major shock of the day. Further investigation confirmed that I had a lump at the back of my skull and my hair was absolutely soaked with blood. It didn't hurt at all, which was very strange because the cut lip, which was rapidly swelling, hurt like hell.

I waited for my brain to clear a little, then stood up and started walking shakily towards the woods. I didn't realise then that the woods were still occupied by the Germans, and if I'd been able to walk much quicker I would probably have been cut down before I got near them. But I must have plodded on for a couple of hours like that, unable to focus on the battle at all.

I never reached the woods. I must have blacked out two or three times at least. I remember the first time, because I was still sucking particles of grit from between my teeth, and the warm crunchy texture and chalky taste became the only thing I was aware of. Then there was a loud rushing of blood in my ears, a slight sick feeling, and my eyesight faded out like an electrical valve going off. This much remains clear in my memory, but I must have been unconscious for the best part of the next 24 hours.

Several episodes stand out with remarkable clarity. I remember a young private, a lad of about eighteen, leaning over me and looking at the back of my head. He undid my water bottle and sloshed most of its freezing cold contents into my mouth. I hadn't noticed until then how much I needed the water. My throat was so dry it stuck together every time I swallowed. He put the water bottle back into my pocket and pulled my coat more snugly around me.

'I'll have to move on, sir, but don't worry. There'll be a couple of lads along in a minute to sort you out.'

He stood up, and I watched his ankles stride out of my line of vision. What bothers me now is that I can't remember if I was *compos mentis* enough to thank him.

The couple of lads failed to materialise, or if they did, they must have overlooked me. If I blacked out again they probably thought I was dead. I came to during the night, though, with an awareness of someone's presence in the dark. I saw, or at least was somehow aware of, a woman sitting close by. She didn't say anything, she was just gazing up at the stars in silence. I looked up too and saw a beautifully clear sky full of glittering constellations: Auriga, Gemini, Cassiopeia, and most notably the Pleiades. I recall seeing flashes of fire cartwheeling round the heavens. Shells, I thought, and then I started to see colours, and began to witness an amazing display of planetary splendour. Mars came up in an intense blood red fire which darted straight through the sky and was gone. After that came Mercury, burning up in a piercing orange flame. Then a rich emerald green from Venus, which whirled and throbbed, taking in a dainty back and forth orbit as the surface colours slowly intensified and radiated. I even saw Saturn, a black fire, condensing out of the darkness between the stars and pulling the fabric of the sky with it as it flared and retracted. I was captivated by this display for some while, taking delight in guessing which planet would come up next, savouring the intensity of its colour, which was like nothing I had ever seen. Then the woman who had been sitting with me in unspoken companionship was suddenly gone, and I realised I was shivering and felt a creeping awareness of how cold it was – bitterly, savagely cold – and how sick and shaky I felt. There were no colours up there. No companion either. It was all hallucination.

My most vivid memory was of a period of time during the next day. I remember I was crawling along the ground looking for some shelter. I wasn't sure why I was doing it to start with, but then I registered the fact that I was once again in the heat of battle. Soldiers were rushing past me. Explosions were going off on every side, spraying my face with more grit, which got into my eyes. I just kept crawling, though every now and then I had to veer to one side to avoid a corpse. Stepping on them is one thing, but going over them on all fours with your face only a few inches above them is another. There are some things you can't bring yourself to do, even when you're three-quarters out of your head. I also managed to cut my hand on a fragment of barbed wire which was curling out of the ground like a rusty bramble.

I thought I'd struck it lucky when I came to the edge of a deep shell-hole, plenty big enough to keep me out of the way of the guns. But it was already occupied, by three dead men and a foggy layer of chlorine gas. They had probably not considered it dangerous enough to merit putting on their gas helmets. One of them had got as far as taking his helmet out of its case; too late.

I carried on a bit further, and things started to get hotter. This was confirmed when I started to see some men running the other way, back towards the British line. Then I felt strong hands under my armpits hauling me over to one side and down a slope. I was propped, rather uncomfortably, against the edge of a shell-hole alongside some other semi-conscious human wrecks. The hole was deep, and well banked up on one side. It was also free from noxious gas, and a sergeant of the Irish Guards was valiantly bringing as many wounded men within its shelter as possible. There was no medical assistance though, and no water. My tongue felt like a lump of pumice stone, but my water bottle was now empty. I regretted being so stupid as to waste water on cleaning my mouth out, instead of saving it for when I really needed it.

Even the taste of moist gravel would have been better than what I was feeling now. I was also shivering from being out in the cold all night in damp clothes.

The sergeant came back with a very young officer who had been wounded in the mouth, most likely by a shell splinter, and whose big eyes were welling with tears which he wouldn't allow to fall. He was a dark, heavy-browed lad with a distinctly myopic appearance, and wore a pair of round spectacles with one lens missing. The sergeant dropped him down right opposite me and we stared at each other in a daze of shared misery. It crossed my mind that I'd seen him before somewhere, but my head was too fuzzy to dwell on it. His wound was nasty, it distressed me to look at it, and I could see that it was going to leave his face permanently disfigured. There was a panic in his eyes which made it clear he knew this too. He had tried to put a field dressing over it, but the blood had carried on streaming down his shirt-front undaunted.

'Kipling,' I said, as much to myself as anyone else. He looked at me in astonishment, probably not remembering me from the ten minutes of conversation I'd had with him in a café in Béthune about a month ago. He made no reply, but that was probably because he couldn't speak. He couldn't swallow either, and I noticed that he had to tilt his head slightly to let the saliva run out of the side of his mouth. I felt a tremendous pity for him.

After about five minutes a crump exploded fairly close to us. The earth shuddered underneath me, and a few seconds later a shower of dust and stones pelted down. I just lay quietly with my eyes shut and let it fall on me. The stones stung my cheeks, but there was no shrapnel, thank God. I heard a gulping noise, and when I opened my eyes I saw that Kipling was crying. Big tears were splashing down his face and into his wound, and the diluted blood dripped off the end of his chin. He was in agony, and the helplessness of our situation was unbearable to him. He wasn't going to be able to sit there all day waiting for somebody to come and get him, he was too restless. I tried to find something encouraging to say to him, but my brain was blank.

Just then a group of five or six men ran past the edge of the shell-hole, away from the German lines. They had thrown down their rifles and packs and were just fleeing for their lives. Kipling looked hard at me, with the pain and frustration ingrained on his face. The remaining lens in his spectacles had steamed up, so I'm not sure how well he could see me. He obviously wanted to say something, but couldn't use his jaw.

'We've got to get back,' he gulped. He spoke without moving his mouth, but even this much effort at speech brought a fresh glut of gore welling up at his lips. He looked terrified.

'We can't go back,' I said automatically, and quickly realised that it wasn't a good idea for me to speak either, because it made the back of my throat feel as though I had swallowed a metal rasp. The pain of it made my eyes water.

He slumped forward, and I thought for a moment that he was going to pass out, but he pulled himself upright and boldly slithered out of the shell-hole on his hands and knees. I watched the soles of his boots slide out of view, and a small clod of earth roll down into the hole where his foot had dislodged it. I kept my eyes focused on the clod for some while, aimlessly fixated.

The sergeant who had helped us didn't come back again, and the daylight started to fade. I suddenly had an intensely clear train of thought and realised that Kipling was right. If anything had happened to the sergeant and nobody knew I was here, the cold would finish me off even if the Germans didn't. It was imperative for me to get back to the British line. I saw that the man lying next to me had died, and I didn't want to be joining him just yet.

I took the man's water bottle off him, which made me feel very guilty, even though he was dead, and tipped it into my mouth. Not much in there, but the relief was like nothing I'd ever experienced. Then I turned round and lifted my head above the rim of the hole. I had actually got remarkably close to the wood, which I now saw was hardly a wood at all, just a collection of bushes and splintered trees around an old chalk quarry. The ground was strewn with the dead and dying, British and German all tangled together. There were still a lot of shells going over from both sides, but the worst of the fighting seemed to have moved to the other side of the wood. I couldn't believe how stupid I had been to keep crawling out into enemy territory when I should have just returned to base as soon as I was hit. I would be in a nice clean hospital bed by now if I'd only had the sense to go back when I had the chance.

The thought of lying on crisp white sheets – lavender scented sheets such as I would have at home – was the biggest incentive to rescue myself that I'd yet had. I aligned myself with the general direction of the British line and set off with an unprecedented determination. I had to go on hands and knees, and my body was so stiff I could hardly move it – due in no small part to the chalky mud which had soaked into my clothes and set like cement. I was absolutely filthy and I kept thinking how annoyed my mother would be if she could see me.

When I'd gone about a hundred yards I found Kipling. His wounded mouth was resting in the mud and a small pool of blood had run off and collected in a nearby bootprint. I stopped briefly to check that he was dead, even though I knew he was, and groped for the identity disc around his neck. Couldn't find one. I laid my hand on his back for a moment to pay my respects and then carried on. I had only gone another fifty yards when another crump came down. It was a faulty one which detonated late and buried itself in the ground before exploding. Lucky for me that it did. When the patter of falling debris had subsided I looked back at the area I'd just crawled across. There was nothing there except a pile of clean earth. Kipling had gone. So had four or five other bodies which had been lying near him. I watched the fronds of smoke rising up from the disturbed soil and then kept going.

This is where my memory is more fragmentary. I have no memory whatsoever of the two stretcher bearers who eventually found me crawling across the field. No recollection of an excruciating journey in a horse-drawn cart over a pocked road. No recollection of the medical orderly cutting my clothes off me and laying me on those crisp white hospital sheets. They smelled of carbolic soap actually, but I wasn't complaining.

Apparently I was out on the battlefield for two days. They told me that the Scots had taken the village of Loos, after an awful fight. They also told me that my injuries were not severe, but I would get a week or two to recover from the bang on the head. I suppose I can't expect to stay in hospital for long with a fat lip and a grazed hand. I found out from another wounded officer what had caused the panic before we went over the top. As I feared, some of the chlorine gas had been blown straight back into the British trenches, and gassed quite a number of reserve troops. A lot of them are here in the hospital; I hear their laboured coughing at night. They are also filling up an alarming amount of space in the adjacent cemetery.

A nurse came by on my first night here and asked if there was anything she could get for me to make me more comfortable.

I thought about it dreamily for a moment and a homely aroma filled my imaginary senses.

'Lavender,' I said.

Chapter Fourteen

The doorbell rang, and Joe jumped up and tossed his newspaper to Judi. 'That'll be Kath. See if you can finish that bloody crossword, will you? Seventeen down.'

Katherine was clutching a Tesco bag, glowing rosy-cheeked from a mixture of cold and exhilaration.

'So much for springtime. It's bloody freezing out there.' She followed Joe into the warmth of the living room, which made her nose run. She cuffed it discreetly with her sleeve.

'You haven't really met Judi properly, have you?' he asked.

'Hi,' said Katherine. She had barely seen Judi on her last visit, and was slightly surprised to find herself in front of a young woman with two-tone red and black hair and dark lipstick, who managed to beam a broad grin while chewing gum at the same time.

'I'll go and make the tea, shall I?' Judi said. She reached for a walking stick at the side of her chair and levered herself up with a slick manoeuvre.

Joe rubbed his hands together gleefully. 'Let's have a look at your feller, then. I've heard so much about him, I'm dying to see what he looks like.'

Katherine took the *Gloucestershire Graphic* book carefully out of the carrier bag and opened it at the page she had bookmarked, sending a musty old library aroma into the air. Joe smoothed the old paper flat with his finger.

'Oh yes,' he said, peering closely at the picture. His face broadened into a grin. 'Oh yes. What a fine chap.'

'It's quite a find isn't it? It says a little bit about him in the article underneath.'

'So it does.' Joe found the paragraph and read it out. '*In the evening the patients enjoyed a lecture on "Practical Astronomy" by Lieutenant Richard Munro of Wisteria Lodge, Cheltenham, followed by a presentation on "Things Indian" by William Crooke, the anthropologist and writer, who lives in Charlton Kings and who is also Mr Munro's uncle. Mr Munro, who is serving with "the Fighting Tenth", is a convalescing patient at the hospital, having seen action in two great British victories at Loos and the Somme, and is very much looking forward to rejoining his regiment in France.* What absolute bollocks they used to write in those days. Like hell he was looking forward to it, poor sod.'

'It's fantastic info though, isn't it?' beamed Katherine. 'I mean, it tells us his home address and where he was serving in the war. We'll be able to find out loads about him from that, won't we?'

'Yes. We certainly will.' Joe gave a delighted laugh. 'God, I'm so glad we made the effort to pursue this. All we have to do now is decide which bit to follow up first. I'd like to know who this Uncle William the Writer was. I've never heard of him.'

'Do you fancy a trip to the record office, Joe, when we've had our tea? We might be able to find his birth certificate.'

'No need. I think we can access everything we need online, I have a subscription. Suppose we find out where this Wisteria Lodge is, or was?'

'Yeah.' Katherine frowned slightly. 'I thought wisteria was some sort of horrible disease, like foot and mouth? Funny name for a house.'

'No, that's listeria. Wisteria is an enormous shrub with beautiful dangly blue flowers which last about two weeks and then looks boring for the rest of the year.'

'Is there an easy way of finding out where the house is?'

Katherine pulled excitedly at a cushion, and accidentally ripped out a small bit of stuffing. Joe hadn't seen, so she rammed it back in with her finger.

'The census is a good place,' said Joe, 'because it lists houses and streets in sequential order so it's good for finding exact locations. The 1911 census would be perfect.'

Joe's laptop sat in the middle of the coffee table, trailing wires across the sofa. He had an account with one of the searchable public records services provided for family tree researchers, which was also something of a wet dream for historians.

'Let's see how many Munros there were in Cheltenham in 1911.'

'Sounds good to me. I'll just hold the pen and look intelligent.'

There was only a handful of results in the search.

'This looks promising. Munro, Richard Montague, aged 17. That would make him about twenty-three or twenty-four at the time of the photo in 1917. Sound good so far?'

'Yeah, definitely.'

'OK, let's have a look at where he lived.'

He clicked on the link to the original census image and a scan of a yellowed document filled in with pleasantly looped handwriting slowly loaded on the screen.

'Wow, bloody hell.'

'It's good innit? The 1911 census is the only one which features the original household schedules filled in by the residents themselves in their own handwriting. Makes it expensive to subscribe to, but far more fascinating.'

'Here we go, look. Wisteria Lodge. Wellington Square.'

Joe followed the list of names with his fingernail. 'John Munro, aged 42, architect. Virginia Munro, 39, wife. And Richard Montague Munro, scholar, aged seventeen. Looks like he might have been an only child, or the youngest if there were others who had moved out by then.'

'The poor bastard.'

'What?'

'Having Montague for a middle name.'

'I've seen worse. So Wisteria Lodge was the family home where his parents lived. And he was still there when the war broke out. Let's see if we can find it on the map.'

Joe sprang to his feet and walked straight through the laptop's power cable, which fortunately was on a magnetic connector which pulled out of its socket rather than dragging the computer off the table. The screen went dark as the battery struggled to keep up.

'I've got this lovely old map,' he said, pulling out a large picture frame from behind the sofa and propping it up on a chair. 'It's 1834, so it's a bit out of date for our purposes, but it shows individual buildings. Hand coloured too. By my ex-wife.'

The map was beautiful, and showed the town of Cheltenham, considerably smaller in extent, laid out on a distinct cross axis. From west to east, the small, densely filled buildings of the High Street formed a stuttering trail along the old pre-medieval line of the town, undulating and condensed, dark clusters of buildings packed along a line that mirrored the course of the town's river. From north to south, the wide, spacious estates of the Regency property speculators swept downwards in a band across the old town and its environs, erasing old field boundaries, redefining the natural landscape; broad ribbons of ordered streets and symmetrical villas, crescents and circuses and wide green promenades. Now, the whole townscape seems blended together, its spaces filled up and its streets filtering outward like ink along cracks. But in 1834 you could still see the underlying structure of the town's evolution, obscured but fixed beneath, like the frame of a kite.

Wellington Square was near the top of the map, orderly and spacious, equal sided and defiant of the land's natural contours and old tracks, carved out from a town planner's dream. There were large houses spaced around its outer edge, while the inside was green and open, circumambulated by paths and clumps of trees. On the bottom left corner of the square was a green park marked Botanic Garden, with a twirl of paths and shrubbery, a long vanished feature now almost lost from history. Wisteria Lodge was in the middle of the northern side, its garden reaching back to the tiny service lane which ran along behind the houses.

'We have to be a bit careful,' said Joe, 'because Wellington Square was still under construction when this map was made, and some of the houses are shown here as they were originally planned, not as they were actually built. Those detached villas on the west side, for example, ended up being a solid terrace.'

'I don't know how you take in all this information. So is Wisteria Lodge still there?'

'That I don't know. The quickest way to find out is to go over and have a look.'

'Ooh, that would be fun.'

'And now we're spoiled for choice in what we look up next, because there's so much info to go on in that census return. There's the 1901 census, which should show Richard as a 7-year-old. We could try to find his birth record. Or else have a look at the marriages index to find out when John and Virginia got spliced.'

The marriages index for 1891 had an entry for John Munro, whose bride's name had been Virginia Warren. After a few more searches they had Richard's birth certificate spread across the screen.

'Tenth of November 1893. Wisteria Lodge, Wellington Square, Cheltenham. Name, Richard Montague. Father, John Percival Munro. Percival! Flipping heck, you were right, it could have been worse. Mother, Virginia Alice Munro, formerly Warren. Occupation of father: architect. God Joe, this is fantastic. It all ties up. I wish it was this easy to find his war records.'

Joe snapped his pen down on the table with a start. 'I've just thought of something. Hang on a minute, I'm just going to make a phone call. If I can get a bloody signal on my mobile.'

He wandered off into the hallway, where she could hear him talking between longish pauses. He came back ten minutes later looking decidedly pleased with himself.

'Well? Been ringing up your mates in the secret service or what?'

'Not quite. I've got this friend called Bob who's completely obsessed with the Gloucestershire Regiment. And I mean *really* obsessed, positively duffel-coat level. His pet project is a massive database of surviving service records, going right back to the Napoleonic wars. He says he hasn't finished cataloguing all the first world war stuff yet, but he thinks he ought to have something about Richard Munro in his project file somewhere, if we can just give him time to root around for it.'

'How long is that going to take?'

'Not long, if I know Bob. He'll be so delighted that anyone is taking an interest in his project, he probably just needs a few minutes to get over the shock.'

As if on cue, there was a flurry of shouting and screaming outside in the street. Joe tripped over the laptop cable again as he tried to rush towards the door. Katherine was nearer to it and got through it first. She flung the front door open, leapt over the doormat and ran out to the gate, where she was confronted with the sight of Jeannette, red-faced and spittle-lipped, holding a full size baseball bat above her head with shaking arms while Judi slapped at her frantically with her hands and fists. Judi was screaming as she pummelled. 'Leave her alone! Leave her alone you mad bitch!' It was only then that Katherine looked down at the pavement and saw Alison lying on the floor among some deflated and crumpled binbags, whose sorry remnants of orange peel and chip wrappers had spilled out and were spread gracelessly across the street and into the gutter.

111

Joe vaulted straight over the garden gate without opening it and ran at Jeannette. For a horrible moment it looked as if she was going to swing the baseball bat into him but instead she suddenly snapped into a state of taut calmness.

'It's all right. I don't need any help from you, Joe Waldron. It's all sorted out now.' She lowered the bat and dangled it casually as though it were no more than an umbrella or shopping bag.

Katherine crouched down amid the strewn detritus and put her arm around the woman on the pavement, who was trying to sit up.

'What the fuck is going on?' Joe inquired, not unreasonably.

Judi responded. 'She just hit Alison over the head with a baseball bat. She's mad.'

'Oh I'm just going in to have my breakfast,' Jeannette declared with a stiff joviality and a half-laugh, and began to walk away. 'I'll leave you all to it.'

'She's mad,' repeated Judi.

'What happened?'

'I'm all right,' said Alison, with a quaver in her voice.

'Bye,' said Jeannette, and her front door clunked shut.

'Fuck, I should have got that baseball bat off her,' said Joe. 'I'd better call the police.'

By the time the police arrived, the baseball bat had disappeared. Or at least the police hadn't been able to find it. They hadn't been able to do a full search, obviously. Judi, Joe and Katherine all sat in Alison's living room with mugs of tea while the policeman took statements with painful slowness. Judi had seen the most. She had been coming home from the corner shop and saw Jeannette and Alison in the street having a conversation. Saw Alison putting out the rubbish bags, bending over to place them by the gate. Saw Jeannette come back out with the bat and smack Alison over the head with it two or three times, red with rage. Alison would have to give her statement later as she'd been taken to hospital to be X-rayed, but she had told them the row was about binbags. About whether she was entitled to put her rubbish bags outside the gate which adjoined Jeannette's property. She had done so as a matter of principle, knowing that it would annoy Jeannette. But rather underestimating how much.

'She has a little bit of a thing about dustbins,' conceded the policeman, who had had to do the paperwork on the occasion when Jeannette had lodged formal complaints about the orientation of Joe's bin behind the back garden.

'I hope they lock her up before she kills somebody,' said Judi, bruised and shaken, but still relishing the memory of the paddy wagon drawing up outside the house, a melodramatically oversized police van with riot bumpers on the front and blacked out side windows, and watching gleefully from her bedroom window as the small wiry old woman was escorted into the back of it by two police officers, screaming curses and threats at them as she went. She had captured the whole arrest on her phone and couldn't wait to post the pictures on Facebook.

The sun was not far off going down by the time Katherine and Joe got round to visiting Wellington Square. They went in Joe's car.

'Now, I can't actually drive into Wellington Square from here because they've put those bloody annoying concrete bollards round it. We'll have to park down the lane at the side and walk back.'

Katherine wound the window down and snorted in the fresh air. There always seemed to be a fresh and moist atmosphere in this part of Cheltenham because there were so many trees. Wellington Square was still a pleasant quadrangle of 1830s villas on the edge of Pittville Park, with broad pavements and extravagant grass verges, which had retained a lot of its original prestige. Not all the buildings had survived, but all the same its grandeur was barely tainted. It still had the miniature park in the centre just like it was on the old map, fenced all around with wrought-iron railings. It had started out as a private garden for residents but now had a muddy public footpath through the middle and a red plastic bin for dog poo.

'According to this, the house should be the one in the middle, over there.'

She clutched at the street plan as she got out of the car and they strolled off down the street with an almost unbearable sense of anticipation. Katherine could imagine Richard Munro walking along the same bit of pavement, over the same wonky stone slabs, past the same railings. It would still be quite familiar to him if he were alive today, apart from the cars and television aerials and the height of the trees. Many of the houses had been divided into flats, and one of them was now an exclusive residential home for the elderly, adorned with ridiculously extravagant Austrian blinds which looked like a squidged up ice-cream dessert hanging from the window. When she reached the next house she stopped in her tracks.

'What is that fucking 1960s bungalow doing there?'

Joe stopped too. 'Oh dear.'

'The map shows Wisteria Lodge right in the centre, just here. Next door to Cranham Lodge, which is just over there, look.'

'Oh dear,' Joe said again.

'You don't think this *is* Wisteria Lodge do you? Slightly altered? I mean, there isn't any sign to say it isn't.'

'Kath, it's a pebbledashed monstrosity. Can you imagine an architect wanting to live in it? Anyway, if you look at the shape of the garden, it's in a villa-sized hole, which suggests that that's what was probably there originally. What a bummer.'

'Only two original houses demolished in the whole street,' fumed Katherine, looking round at the rest of the square, 'and one of them had to be his. Well, town planners are complete bastards, that's all I can say.'

'Nice collection of rose bushes though.' Joe twanged a branch which was sticking out over the pavement, setting the whole bush vibrating like a silent jew-harp. 'Well it's a shame but we can't have everything. Let's get out of here before the Neighbourhood Watch group gets nervous and reports us to the police. Don't want one of those old ladies coming at me with a bat.'

A trilling noise broke out from inside Joe's coat. He pulled out his phone and looked at the number on the display.

'It's Bob,' he said breathlessly. 'I'd forgotten all about him.'

Katherine began to pace anxiously on the grass verge while he took the call. She heard him saying 'Oh great,' followed by a lot of 'yes', and 'right'. She stood pressing her heel into the squashy turf, and noticed that an old man in the residential home was scowling at her suspiciously from underneath the folds of creamy Vienetta. She heard the bleep of Joe ending the phone call, and turned to him expectantly.

'Well?' she asked. He put the phone back in his pocket.

'Well,' he said, 'there is indeed a matching record in his project folder.'

'And?'

'Apparently your feller Richard was killed in Flanders in 1917, and has no known grave.'

Chapter Fifteen

3rd October 1915

Recovering. I was seen by a French doctor today who told me that I am suffering the effects of exposure as well as concussion, so I am going to have to take things easy for a bit. Pity, as there is a very interesting conjunction of Mars with the Moon tonight, which ought to be visible from here, but I don't really feel up to crawling outside for a midnight stargazing session just at the moment. It's cold enough indoors! Somebody showed me a map of the fighting area, and I found that I'd made it all the way to Chalk Pit Wood, which was quite some way off our original objective. Not a good start to my military career, but at least I can blame it on the concussion.

That very sweet V.A.D. nurse, Kathie, came back this morning and presented me with a small posy of lavender. How she managed to find anything so lovely in this hell-hole I don't know, but she said she saw it growing in the front garden of an abandoned farm cottage on her way into Chocques. Of course at this time of year the lavender is just going over, so it's really just a tuft of soggy grey stalks with some old flower-heads still clinging, but I was over the moon and very touched by her thoughtfulness. It now sits in a tin mug – nearest thing to a vase I could find – at the side of my bed. Kathie is a bright little star who lavishes us with kindness and smiles. Nurses get into awful trouble if they are caught being too friendly with the patients, no matter how innocent the attention. Most have too little time to spend with us anyway; they are always in a frightful rush, struggling to deal with the more seriously wounded men in other wards. Even so, I would swear I have fewer nightmares when Kathie is here on the wards at night.

I am in what is known as a 'light medical ward', which in this instance is a purpose-built wooden hut with ten beds and no heating, and which is reserved for officers. Nobody in this ward has any life-threatening affliction, except for one unfortunate captain in the bed next to the door, who has got a bullet irretrievably lodged in his brain and is slowly fading out. He was brought in here because there was no room for him anywhere else, and this is a quiet ward where he can die with dignity. One of the staff nurses stops by every couple of hours to ascertain whether he is still with us, and the rest of us require minimal medical attention. A nurse comes round in the mornings to do a routine check of pulses and temperatures, and apart from that there is only the daily renewal of wound dressings. These huts – there are four or five others – are built on the playing fields of a school, and the school building itself is used for the surgical wards. I have not been in there myself, but I have heard the panicky shrieks of men coming round from their anaesthetics. Officially the V.A.D.s are not supposed to carry out real medical duties because they are not qualified nurses, but Kathie tells me that this rule has gone out of the window in the wake of the recent fighting; for all the efforts that have been made to bring in extra staff, the number of casualties arriving here is far in excess of what the qualified nurses can cope with. Thus the untrained volunteers are required to flush out gangrenous wounds and heaven knows what else. It distresses me to think that Louisa may some day come out here and be confronted with this.

It distresses me even more to admit, having promised Louisa I would be thinking of her while I was in the heat of battle, that when it came to it I didn't think about her at all.

4th October 1915
During the night I was woken by the clattering of a lantern, and saw that the screens had gone up around the captain's bed. He was taken away first thing this morning. My head was quite sore today, so I spent most of the time dozing on my bed. During the evening, however, I was roused from a light sleep by the sound of more clattering from the captain's bed, and a loud, indignant voice:
    'He's got some flowers. Why don't I get any fucking flowers?'
    This was met with an outraged admonition from the nursing sister, who is a bit of a prim old girl. I shuffled over onto my side to see what was going on. The sister and two V.A.D.s were grappling with an elegant blond-haired officer whose arm was

swaddled with filthy bandages, and who wouldn't keep still as they tried to unwrap it to clean and dress the wound. He was a new arrival, still spattered with trench mud. One of the nurses had him pinned down, surprisingly firmly. The other one stood beside a trolley full of dressings and enamel trays, while the sister tugged aggressively at his bandages.

'There's no need to rip my fucking arm off,' he said.

Sister's face was getting redder and redder. He carried on.

'I know your sort. Ruddy cheeks an' all. I reckon when you were born the doctor slapped your face instead of your arse, and they've been the wrong way round ever since.'

'If you don't behave yourself I shall report you to Colonel Wemyss,' she quavered in barely controlled rage.

'Colonel Wemyss! Oh my God, not Colonel Wemyss!' He fell back against the pillow in a melodramatic swoon. The sister jerked the remains of the old dressing off his arm with unnecessarily brutal force, and began to scrub the wound with salt water and that unpleasant carbolic acid solution which seems to permeate the fabric of all hospitals. The officer cried out in pain two or three times, but had blown his chances of sympathy.

When the new dressing was finished and the nurses had rattled away with the trolley, he went very quiet. Several times during the evening I looked over and saw him gazing up at the ceiling, his eyes open and unblinking, completely submerged in his thoughts. Like many of the officers I've met in the last few weeks, he had the haunted look of a man who had seen too much.

I lay awake for some hours with the throbbing discomfort in my head, eyes closed against the glow of the lantern hanging from the rafters. It was a relatively quiet night; even the gas cases in the next ward seemed to cough less than usual. I heard the tread of a nurse on the floorboards, slowly creeping from bed to bed as quietly as possible. I didn't want to disturb anyone else, so I kept my eyes shut and pretended to be asleep. I felt the waft of cool air on my face as the nurse walked up to me; it brought the scent of her uniform, the obligatory cotton and carbolic soap smell tempered with a more feminine floral scent, which I fancied was lavender. The floorboard creaked, and I expected the sound of her walking away again but the next thing I knew was the touch, the lightest touch, of a finger pushing my hair back from my forehead, and then a soft kiss placed on my brow in its wake. Nothing flirtatious or sensual; just a gentle secret kiss like a benediction. Knowing I was not meant to be conscious of it I kept my breathing slow and deep and let her believe I was asleep. I heard her walk away towards the next bed and I dearly wanted to open my eyes to see who she was and whether she kissed all the patients or just me. But I dare not; I accepted the blessing in a grateful unknowing and let its memory tingle on my skin until I slipped into sleep.

5th October 1915
Coincidences in war seem to happen so often that I wonder why I'm still surprised by them.

Of all the officers and men who must have poured over the fields in the recent attack, I end up sharing a shell-hole with somebody I'd met in a bar weeks earlier, and the son of a famous author to boot. A second chance meeting was the last thing I expected. And yet this morning while I was lying down reading a book I became aware of somebody standing at the end of the bed staring at me. I realised it was the Royal Engineers Special Division officer I'd met in trenches; he who was fair of face and foul of tongue. It was he who now occupied the captain's old bed.

'Hello,' I said, a little self-conscious.

He carried on staring at me for a moment, then said: 'You look more intelligent than the rest of these fuckers.'

I didn't really know how to reply to this, so I just said: 'We've met before. You were one of the gas engineers, weren't you? I remember seeing you on the morning of the 25th.'

'That's right,' he said, and his face lightened slightly. 'Complete bloody waste of time that was, wasn't it? The Germans pissed all over us as usual.'

'I knew something had gone wrong before we went over. Is it true that the gas blew back into the British trenches?'

He nodded. 'Completely fucked a whole battalion of the Black Watch. We could all see it was going to happen but the brass-hatted shits wouldn't listen. They never do.'

He moved away down the ward and then hesitated, and turned back to me.

'I say, do you fancy a game of cards?'

And thus I became acquainted with Lieutenant Tate, who declined to give me his Christian name, but in many other ways laid open his soul. We played a few rounds of rummy while he told me a little about his home life in Blackfriars, London, where he is studying to be a lawyer but still hopes to take over his father's engineering business in the fullness of time. I asked him how he had wounded his arm, but he seemed rather cagey about the details.

'It happened in trenches, not on the field,' he said. Then he added: 'An accident with a bayonet.'

'Is it bad?'

'No, not really. Though it's a bit ominous that they've put me in the bed next to the door. Not a good sign, that.'

I looked at him without comprehension, and he explained: 'They always put the no-hopers next to the door. The chaps who are liable to peg out at any moment. That way they can wheel out the stiff without upsetting the other patients.'

'How do you know that?' I asked dubiously.

'Well,' he said, 'where's the chap who was in that bed before me? Gone back to his regiment, has he?'

'No,' I had to admit. 'As far as I know he's moved on to the Chapel of Rest.'

'Chapel of Rest? Don't make me laugh. They pile up the stiffs in a fucking coal bunker. I've seen them.'

I am quite accustomed to hearing the men use filthy language and coarse slang, but it sounded most peculiar in the clipped tones of an English gentleman in an officer's uniform. Once I got used to it, however, I couldn't help but like him. He was intelligent and witty, and once he got talking on a subject that interested him his eyes brightened and there was a passion in his voice; he would gaze into the middle distance and speak with great depth of understanding about the political and strategic machinations of the war, which he could see with an almost prescient detachment, as if he were looking down at the battle zone from a great height and able to see it all as a cohesive whole. I also suspected that his coarseness and contempt were masking a deep empathy and understanding of the human suffering involved, much as he didn't want to show it.

He insisted on taking me round to the back of the building to show me how Britain honours her war-dead.

There was a secluded path down the side of the old school building, muddy from regular use. It led to a small brick lean-to on the rear wall of the school, with a raggedy white door which was rotting at the bottom where the paint had peeled off. The brickwork bore scratched initials and childish doodles, a souvenir of its former purpose.

'Have a look in there, go on.' Tate had a strange glint in his eyes which gave them an almost frightening intensity.

I hesitated, not sure that we were supposed to be there at all.

'Go on,' he said. 'They don't bite.'

I pushed the door open, and it almost immediately scuffed against a heavy bundle wrapped up in hessian. Possibly the captain. He was one of seven such bundles, which had been laid tidily side by side on the floor and stacked up in two layers. The building was indeed a coal bunker; there was no coal in it now, but the hessian parcels bore a fine sprinkling of black dust in their folds and crevices, and it glittered between the stones on the floor. The stench of death is familiar enough out here, but these fellows had a very strange odour which was quite new to me. I pulled the door closed with a shudder.

'What's that smell?' I gulped.

'Eusol. It's the stuff they use to irrigate septic wounds. Nasty, isn't it? Come on, let's have a stroll up to the cemetery.'

We walked up to the plot behind some trees where the wooden crosses were starting to accumulate in dense rows. I smoked one of Tate's cigarettes; it was the first time I had wanted one since before the battle. We sat down on the low wall and watched two privates digging out a shallow trench through the grass, no doubt to accommodate the present contents of the coal bunker. They saluted us, and carried on their work in a rather slow, demoralised kind of way. On the whole it was a peaceful place. One could still hear the thumping and booming of the big guns, of course, and the occasional clattering of an ambulance train coming out of

Chocques station, but there was green grass underfoot, and rooks whirling around in the sky. I never realised until now what a luxury it is to be able to walk on soft turf with the autumn sun in your face. It is one of those things you take for granted until you experience a hellhole.

'Do you have anyone who will miss you if you end up in here?' asked Tate thoughtfully.

'My mother,' I replied. 'And my sweetheart, Louisa. And there's my cousin who's serving in Egypt with the R.E.s. He's only 18. We're more like brothers than cousins, we more or less grew up together. Both of us an only child, you see. What about you?'

He shook his head and sat gazing over the field with a glazed look, lightly drumming his heels against the wall. Then he turned and fixed me with a peculiar piercing look, and said in a matter-of-fact tone: 'Well since you ask, my father is a nut-case. My mother looks like a circus freak. Both brothers are bastards. In the figurative sense.'

'No sweetheart?'

He shook his head again. 'Women don't like me.'

I smiled inwardly at the thought of this. With his extraordinary pale eyes, toffee-blond hair, pleasant face and tall elegant bearing, he ought to have had most women falling over themselves to catch his fancy, but I could see how one line of conversation with him would probably send them screaming out of the room.

'You'll find somebody,' I said, trying not to sound patronising.

'I won't,' he said. 'I'll end up in here. Half a coal sack, a cheap union flag and a bunch of bum-fuckers puffing on bugles, that's what I shall come out of this war with.'

I laughed, not at what he said but at the way he said it. He looked a little taken aback for a minute, then started to laugh with me. The grave-diggers cast us disapproving glances.

'I was right about you,' he snorted, pleased with himself. 'You're not a bad old fucker at all, are you?'

9th October 1915

Pandemonium. Colonel Wemyss came into the ward last night and told us we had to get ready to leave, wounds or no. The Germans have counter-attacked at Loos, and the casualty clearing station has been put on alert for a fresh influx of casualties. The main building is already full beyond reasonable capacity, so they have no option but to commandeer our ward and discharge us. Four of the officers here are still unable to get about much, and they are being transferred by train to the base hospital. The rest, including Lieutenant Tate and myself, received telegrams ordering us to rejoin our regiments as soon as possible.

Tate and I decided to travel back together; as no transport has been arranged and we have to make our own way, we may as well keep each other company. I had not been out of the hospital grounds since I arrived, so it was the first time I had seen the vicinity of Chocques.

'And it bloody well *is* a shock,' Tate warned me as we walked towards the railway station just outside the village. A barbed-wire prison compound had been put up in a field behind the station, where hundreds of men in grey uniform were huddled miserably in the mud. They had been rained on during the night, having no place to shelter, and I don't think I have ever seen a more dejected and degraded collection of human beings. There were many small groups of them slumped together for warmth, with others lying flat on the ground in pain or exhaustion. One man was lying up against the fence, his facial features squashed through the wire, fast asleep. Despite my many months of active war service, it was the first time I had actually seen Germans at close hand, apart from the dead ones around Chalk Pit Wood. They looked pretty harmless in the prison compound; cold, hungry teen-aged boys most of them.

I am ashamed to say that we hurried along without looking too closely when we walked past the field beside the railway line where the wounded were laid out on stretchers on the wet ground, waiting to get a slot on a crowded ambulance train. A makeshift wooden platform had been built along the side of the railway, and the most urgent cases had been lined up in readiness. Then a motor-ambulance passed us on the road, probably containing the men for whom we had vacated our ward at the clearing station. So great are the numbers of casualties streaming down from the Front that there is only room here for those who are so badly wounded that they cannot travel any further. I looked back at the ambulance and saw only the muddy boot soles of the patients poking out from under brown army blankets, and felt grateful for my own deliverance from my first battlefield experience.

With so many emergency supplies and support troops being transported up to the Front we had little chance of catching a lift, so we walked as far as we reasonably could and then settled down for the night in a laundry room at the back of an empty farmhouse. It had a small fireplace and an undamaged roof, so we were grateful enough for it. And it smelled better than the hospital. We had to spend the last half hour of daylight grubbing around for some wood which was dry enough to burn, but it was cosy by the time the night chill set in.

'Are you going back up to the sector by Lone Tree,' I asked when we finally got settled on the brick floor by the fire, 'or have the engineers moved on by now?'

'They're still at Lone Tree,' said Tate, 'but that's not why I'm going back there.'

I looked at him in confusion. 'What do you mean?'

'I'm not in the R.E.s any more,' he explained. 'I've been transferred to the 10th Gloucesters.'

I sat up in astonishment. 'But that's my regiment,' I said.

'I know.' He chewed appreciatively on a half-boiled potato. 'That's why I befriended you, you idiot.'

'Not because I looked intelligent?' I asked, disappointed.

'Well,' he conceded, 'that as well.'

'So why have they put you with the Gloucesters?'

'It's a bit of a long story. And a sordid one.' He paused, obviously wondering how much he ought to tell me, or how much he could be bothered to explain. 'Suffice to say I was given a choice between transferring to an infantry regiment or being sent for court-martial.'

'Ah. I see.' This told me a couple of things about Tate which came as little surprise. Firstly that he was a trouble-maker, one of those officers who would not, or could not, settle into the routine and discipline of army life. And secondly that he was a brilliant soldier who was being given a fresh start because the army frankly couldn't do without him. I wondered whether it was one of his own men or another officer who had given him the bayonet wound, and what he had done to deserve it.

'How the fuck are you supposed to smoke this?' he asked suddenly.

Across the dimly lit room I saw that he had picked up my silver cigarette case, which no longer contained cigarettes but the posy of lavender from Kathie, which I had meticulously dried off and brought with me, hoping that it might serve me in some other time of distress – especially as I had not had a chance to say goodbye to her.

He sniffed at it suspiciously. 'Do you mix it with tobacco or just stick it in a pipe?'

'It's lavender, you idiot,' I said. 'Just a sentimental keepsake. You can't smoke it.'

'Well I might,' he said sharply. 'Depends how desperate I get.'

Chapter Sixteen

26th March 1916

The letter I had from Hugh this morning was not as bright and humorous as usual, and I can't help wondering whether something might be bothering him. Something is certainly bothering me: it is his birthday on April 3rd, and this may be the first time that I have ever not been able to give him a present. I have absolutely nothing worthwhile I can send to him, and no way of purchasing anything. There are no inhabited towns here any more.

Tate came waltzing into the dug-out, with a coating of mud right up to his elegant knees.

'Trod in that fucking sump pit again,' he announced, and launched himself into his hammock, which swayed and creaked under the sudden weight. I have been secretly keeping a tally of the number of times he does that, because Hugh and I have been laying bets as to how long he can keep doing it before the hammock collapses. There is already a split in the wooden board which holds the whole thing together, so I know it is only a matter of time.

He blew his nose ostentatiously, and then, without even looking at me, said: 'What's the matter?'

He can sense the subtle vibrations of my emotions as if they are beaming out as radio waves.

I told him that I was rather depressed about Hugh's birthday, and apologised that my sense of cousinly duty made me so foolish and sentimental.

'Not at all,' he said. 'I'm sure I'd feel the same way if I was in the same boat.' He lay in silence for a few moments, then asked: 'What would you most like to send him, if you could get him anything you wanted?'

'To be honest,' I replied, 'the ideal thing to send him would be a souvenir. I think he feels he's missing out a bit by not being out here. Something from a German, like a button or a regimental badge. He'd be chuffed to bits with that.'

'Well,' said Tate encouragingly, 'you might get lucky while we're on patrol tonight, and find something out in No Man's Land. Plenty of Boche stiffs out there.'

This cheered me up a little, because he was right; No Man's Land is full of all sorts of bits and pieces of clutter, so I had a fair chance of finding something worth picking up.

Patrols are not my favourite aspect of trench warfare, even when the moon is in its dark phase, as it has been these last few nights. But it is necessary. The Germans opposite us have acquired some kind of trench mortar, a miniature piece of artillery which sends quite sizeable fin-tailed bombs into our front line, to devastating effect. Fortunately, because the bombs have such a ridiculously high trajectory, it is sometimes possible to see them coming and get out of their way. But it is still a major priority for us to find a way to put this menace out of action. Hence the patrol.

After a good deal of observation, we pinpointed the most likely location for this weapon: the Germans have dug a sap – a narrow trench which extends out into No Man's Land by about twenty yards from their front line. On a good day we can just about see the line which forms the passageway, with a wide indentation at the end. We decided that this wide dip was probably the site of the mortar gun.

In theory it should be an easy target for sabotage, as the sap runs outside the main German fortification into vulnerable territory and was therefore likely to be only lightly manned. Tate has a good working knowledge of German light artillery, as he spent some time dismantling and reassembling captured guns while he was with the Engineers. So naturally enough it was he who volunteered to take out a small working party and see what could be done. I agreed to go with him, and we had four volunteers: Private Adams, a sharp-witted lad in my platoon, Sergeant Roland, and a couple of privates from Tate's platoon – Gray and Ferrers.

Even though we were going out in total darkness, with no moon, we had to sort out some camouflage in case we got caught in the light of a flare. We had to 'brown' all our visible skin. Somebody got hold of some grass seed, which we patted onto our faces to absorb the sweat; one always sweats heavily on patrol, even in the most freezing conditions, and if one isn't careful it can glisten sufficiently to draw the attention of an enemy sniper. We smeared some mud into Tate's hair too, to dull its colour. Then we filled the pockets of our great coats with Mills bombs, and Tate also carried a set of tools rolled up in a thick khaki cloth to stop them from clinking together.

We went over at eleven thirty.

It was a beautiful night, and the first thing I noticed when I crawled over the parapet on my hands and knees was Vega, which is always a very bright star, twinkling magnificently above the German trenches. The absence of any moonlight turned the whole sky into a shimmering delight, with every star along the milky way seeming to stand out individually. I must have paused for a few seconds in awe of it, because the next thing I knew Sergeant Roland knelt on my legs. He probably thought he'd knelt on a corpse, because he let out a muffled exclamation which provoked some frantic hushing sounds from the others. It really was pitch black out there, we could barely see our own hands in front of our faces. Tate found the gap in the wire, which had been made specially for us by last night's wiring party. It was a kind of slalom between two barbed-wire entanglements, so we had to crawl to the left and then to the right to get through it. This was a necessary precaution to prevent the Germans from seeing the gap – otherwise we would have been greeted with a sniper's bullet when we went through. As it was, I snagged my coat rather badly but nobody challenged us as we slipped out silently into No Man's Land.

From then on it was a long, slow crawl. We were almost flat on our stomachs, pulling ourselves along by digging our fingers into the soil and dried grass – and worse. The terrain was quite rough, and we had to crawl in a straight line over all the ridges and dips and shell craters to avoid losing our bearings. The similarity between this situation and my excursion over the Loos battlefield was not lost on me; neither was the irony that this current scenario was slightly less dangerous than a full-scale battle but infinitely more terrifying. At least on the previous occasion I had had the benefit of a knock on the head to blur my awareness of it – this time my mind was pin sharp, and the suspense was absolutely dreadful. Private Gray lifted his rifle up over a large clod of earth and I saw a glimmer of starlight on the metal. I heard Sergeant Roland whisper: 'Cover that sodding bayonet!'

and a moment later a Very light went up in the sky, exposing us all in an orange glare.

'Freeze!' hissed Tate, and we all did. Gray had got his hand over the bayonet, which was a relief. I was walking along on all fours when the flare lit up, and had to remain motionless in that position with my arms at full stretch. The tiniest movement might provoke a blaze of gunfire, and the only chance of staying alive was to keep absolutely still.

I cannot describe the feeling of exposure and helplessness in that situation. The area all around us was lit up, a spooky orange parody of daylight which made us fully visible to the dozens of German sentries who were looking out through their periscopes searching for signs of movement; all we could do was pray to God that if we kept still enough they might not notice us.

My arms began to ache, and the tension sent a searing cramp down my back. I felt myself break out in a sweat, because I knew that if my arms gave way it would mean death, probably for all six of us. The grass seed was beginning to slide very slowly over my cheeks and eyelids, and a bead of sweat hung tenaciously to the end of my nose. The temptation to cuff it or shake it off was immense. To relax myself, I tried to breathe deeply and focus my mind on Vega, the beautiful star which I knew was in the sky right above me, but which I couldn't see in the glow of the flare and with my eyes cast towards the ground. But each slow breath sent a dangerously visible plume of steam into the air around my head. I wished I could stop breathing for a few minutes.

The Very light slowly began to fade. The muscles in my arms were quivering, and eventually went into spasm. Fortunately I managed to hold out until darkness had resumed its protective cover, and then dropped onto my stomach in the dirt, stunned by the sense of relief. Sweat prickled my scalp, and quickly turned cold with exposure to the night air. We kept still for a minute or so, listening for any sign of activity in the German line.

Nothing.

Apart from a few distant rifle shots, and some crumps bursting further down the line, the enemy position was virtually silent. I could just about see Tate lifting his head and turning round to make sure everybody was all right, and then we carried on, one precarious crawling step after another.

My hand closed on something cold and rigid, like cardboard. I groped around and was disgusted to find that it was the arm of a corpse. Its sleeve had begun to stiffen with frost. I could feel a button on the cuff, but just now the idea of stopping to collect souvenirs was out of the question; the threat of imminent death was bad enough, without having to think about birthday presents.

Tate waited for me to crawl alongside him, leaned his face close to my ear and pointed at the sky.

'What's that bright bugger?' he whispered.

'Vega,' I whispered back.

'Well keep a bloody good eye on it. We may need it to find our way back.'

We crept forward, shoulder to shoulder, towards the dip in the ground where we believed the mortar gun was nesting. There is a great comfort in sticking close together. It doesn't make you any safer to have a friend alongside you but it makes an enormous difference to your courage and morale. Eventually we could make out the line of the sap trench snaking its way towards the German front line, and a circular pit at our end, now within easy crawling distance. There was a pile of twigs and dried leaves carefully arranged around the edge which was no doubt intended to make the pit invisible from the British line.

'Now hush,' whispered Tate, although none of us had actually been making any noise. He slithered forward as silently as he could, and I saw him go right up to the edge of the pit and lean over the side. My heart thudded against my ribs, and time seemed to have elongated – ultra slow, nightmare-time. Vega still twinkled above us like a distant beacon, and I tried to convince myself that it was watching over us. At last I saw him begin to shuffle backwards and make his way towards us.

'Deserted,' he whispered, 'but there's a bend just along the trench, and I can't see past it.'

We decided that one of us should crawl out and check the trench further along, and Adams volunteered. It was possibly the longest ten minutes of my life, waiting for him to shuffle down to the bend and back. We couldn't see him once he'd gone a few yards, so we couldn't be absolutely sure that he would come back at all. But he did, and he was shaking so much that beads of sweat were springing off his hands and face.

'Two Germans,' he whispered hoarsely, and pointed. 'Just the other side of that bend.'

'All right,' Tate said. 'Come on.'

I slithered up alongside him and we made our way towards the pit, while the other four stationed themselves further down towards the bend, to intercept any Germans who came round it.

Tate leaned cautiously over the edge of the pit to check that it was still deserted and then slipped quietly down. There was a gentle splosh as his feet touched the bottom, and after a short pause I followed him. I dislodged a small amount of soil as I slid down, which made an alarmingly loud pattering noise.

'For fuck's sake!' Tate hissed, and grabbed my arms in a painfully tight grip. We stood in petrified silence waiting for the sound of approaching Germans, but all I was aware of was the blood pounding inside my skull, and Tate breathing against my face. After about half a minute he loosened his grip and we cautiously got on with the job we had come for.

I had in my pocket a specially adapted flash-lamp, a very small one, just bright enough to enable us to look around, but not visible over the top of the trench as long as we kept it low to the ground. In its feeble glow we saw exactly what we had hoped to find. Right in the centre of the pit was a small and solidly ugly *Minenwerfer*, with its blunt muzzle angled upwards towards the British line.

'Bingo,' said Tate under his breath.

I held the lamp for him while he had a look at it. It was like a field gun in miniature, with a short barrel. Tiny though it was, it was far too heavy for us to shift, and firmly mounted on a concrete base. We decided on Plan B. Tate delicately unwrapped the tool-cloth and found something with which to lever the back of the gun open, while I stood listening for a footstep, or a voice, or a digging sound, or anything. He set to it quickly and calmly; I couldn't see what he was actually doing but I could tell from the steady and sure movements of his hands that he knew what he was about. I crouched over him to deflect the light downwards, and tried to calm my mind by focusing on the bright star which was still just about visible over the lip of the trench, ready to guide us. Even though the others were keeping watch further down the trench and would meet any approaching Germans before we did, it was impossible to shake off the feeling of intense danger, which probably arose from the fact that we were trespassing, fiddling about with the Germans' property. Absurd though it seems, I had a deeply unsettling feeling that I had no right to be there.

Tate brought out a canister of some sort from his coat, and briskly poured its sticky contents down the *Minenwerfer*'s barrel, taking care not to let it touch the sides. Then he packed his things away and rolled up the cloth.

'That's it,' he grunted in my ear. 'The next Hun who fires anything out of that is in for a bloody surprise.'

I switched off the flash-lamp and we made our way along the trench to where the others were standing guard, and they were quite relieved to greet us. Now we could get on with the long crawl home. Tate began to climb out of the trench, when all of a sudden the two Germans came round the corner right upon us. We didn't have time to react, because the moment they saw us – and they must have taken us to be a tidy crowd – they let out a blood-curdling yell and bolted down a large dug-out whose entrance we hadn't even seen in the dark.

'Fuck,' wheezed Tate, and signalled to us all to keep quiet. I flicked the flash-lamp briefly and saw half way down the steps of the dug-out; it was a proper one, timber-framed with a stairway which changed direction in the middle. There was a square hole above it which presumably was a ventilation shaft. We listened in terrified anticipation, in case the shouts of the Germans had attracted the attention of their comrades in the surrounding trenches. But nothing happened, nobody came, and the inside of the dug-out was absolutely quiet. I held my breath and felt the pulse beating with a bruising force inside my head.

Then suddenly a group of three or four Germans came running up the steps in fighting attitude, with fixed bayonets. Ferrers and Gray were right in front of the entrance, and both made a dive to the right. The Germans swung after them. Several shots rang out and I heard Gray screaming in terror. While their attention was diverted, Tate pulled the pin out of a Mills bomb and hurled it straight into the group of Germans. They panicked and began to fall backwards down the steps, clamouring to get back down their hole to safety. The bomb bounced once on the steps and then exploded, throwing a fiery cloud of earth and smoke out of the dug-out entrance.

'Out!' screamed Tate at the top of his voice.

Sergeant Roland was already over the parapet and making a dash for it – the hallmark of a seasoned soldier. I gave Adams a leg up out of the trench, and scrambled up after him. I thought Tate would be right behind me, but he wasn't. When I glanced back he was still standing by the mouth of the dug-out, throwing Mills bombs down the ventilation shaft one after another as if he were tossing potatoes into a cooking-pot. The explosions lit up the inside of the dug-out and cast a glow on his face.

I dived over the top of the trench and into No Man's Land, and ran about twenty yards before dropping down onto my stomach. I could hear muffled explosions mingled with the harrowing sound of men groaning and screaming. The noise had obviously reached the German front line trenches, because a few bursts of nervous gunfire broke out here and there along the line. I swivelled round on my belly and watched the lip of the trench to see if Tate was coming over it. Nothing happened. Finally the string of explosions stopped, and an eerie silence took their place. I waited. There was no sign of Tate.

I lay with my chin on the frosty mud for one, two, three minutes. Then a cold, sick feeling of dread started to stir inside me. I had to make a very difficult choice: to return to base without him, or to go back and attempt to retrieve him, at the risk getting myself killed too.

I'm not sure which option I would have taken, because just at that moment I heard a dull thud, an unmistakably English expletive, and saw a tall shadow hopping over the top of the trench. I didn't dare wave to attract his attention, but he was crawling in the right direction and I slithered over to meet him. He seemed to be in one piece, apart from a wide trickle of blood down the middle of his face. I could only see it because the blood was darker than the grass-seed.

'Are you all right?' I asked, overwhelmed with relief.

'Fine,' he murmured. 'Where are the others?'

'They skedaddled after the first shot.'

'Gray is dead.'

'I know.'

I patted him on the back and we turned our heels on the German trench and crawled stealthily across No Man's Land. Neither of us spoke another word all the way, and the restless gunfire became less frequent. Our main deed had probably not yet been discovered. I held the barbed wire aside while he crawled through, and we both slipped, exhausted, into the safety of our own trench.

We reported our return to the sentry and went back to our dugout – which I have to say was rather primitive in comparison with the luxurious German one. I looked at Tate, who was filthier and more battered than I've ever seen him, and saw that he had a rather messy nose bleed.

'How did you get that?' I asked.

He briefly put his hand to his face and looked at the red smear on his fingers.

'Oh, I did that to myself,' he said. 'Smacked my face on the side of the trench on the way out. Daft fucker.'

I fetched a bowl of water and some carbolic soap, and cleaned him up as best I could. He was very quiet, not his usual self at all. He sat there with a distant and disturbed look in his eyes while I dabbed at his face. I believe – though I wouldn't dare tell him so – that he was quite distressed by the killing he had carried out, and the screams of the Germans trapped in their hole. I was well aware that he had probably saved my life in the process, but I also knew he would be disgusted if I tried to thank him. It was easier for both of us to say nothing.

We sat on our hammocks in silence for some time without putting the lantern out. I didn't think I would be able to get to sleep, shattered though I was. After a while Tate swivelled round on his bunk and began to rummage in his pocket.

'I nearly forgot,' he said, and the smile came back into his eyes. 'I brought something back for you.'

He handed me a beautiful cigarette case of polished silver. It was exquisitely made, and was engraved on the front with a Teutonic eagle and the words *Mit Gott für Vaterland*.

He grinned at the look of astonishment on my face.

'Hugh's birthday present,' he said.

Chapter Seventeen

Not much was likely to shock Katherine after the baseball bat incident, and after all she had met a fair number of weird people over the years. But she had to do a double take when she turned into Joe's street and saw Jeannette outside the garden gate hoovering the cracks in the pavement. She had cylinder vacuum cleaner on a long extension lead which trailed through the daffodils, and she was pressing the nozzle hard against the edge of the kerb for maximum suction.

'Oh my God,' said Katherine to herself, and hastily turned in at Joe's gate. Jeannette looked up and glared with undiluted disdain. She was wearing a pale blue nylon crochet top, and rather obviously had no bra underneath, bare crabby nipples poking through the wide weave. 'Oh my God,' said Katherine again and jabbed at Joe's doorbell with some urgency.

'Let me in, quick,' she hissed, almost pushing him over as he opened the door.

'What's the matter?'

'That madwoman is out there, hoovering the bloody public highway.'

Joe wasn't particularly surprised. 'Is she wearing clothes this time?'

'Outer garments only, I suspect.'

'Well it could be worse then, couldn't it?'

He wandered through into the kitchen. Katherine followed, standing in the doorway while he rummaged about on the draining board for some clean mugs.

'I've been thinking a lot about all this psychic business,' he said, 'and why the first world war should crop up like this. I spoke to this bloke called Mark the Pagan, and it struck quite a chord with him.'

'Mark the Pagan? What kind of a name is that?'

'Well, that's what I've always called him. You'd understand it if you met him. Anyway, don't you want to know what he said?'

'Go on then.'

'He said he wasn't the least bit surprised that you'd made a contact with a soldier from the first world war, because he's been getting psychic contacts with the war dead for the last eighteen months.'

Katherine spluttered. 'Not with Richard Munro?'

'No, no, probably not. He gets images of soldiers while he's meditating, sometimes whole battalions, sometimes individuals. Do you want Earl Grey or ordinary?'

'Ordinary, please. What exactly do you mean?'

'Well,' Joe retrieved a tea-bag from a rather dusty biscuit-tin. 'It may sound a bit loony to put it like this, but he thinks there are quite a few soldiers who died in the first world war who are actively trying to get in touch with people in the here and now, anyone who's sensitive enough to pick them up.'

'Why does he think that?'

'Because they're there. Lots of them, turning up spontaneously in meditation. It's not just you.'

'And does Mark the Pagan have any idea why they might be doing that?'

Joe hesitated for a moment.

'I think you should meet him,' he said.

From the description Joe had given her, Katherine expected Mark the Pagan to be dressed like an extra from *Robin of Sherwood* and to live half way up a tree. The reality was slightly different, because he actually lived in a terraced house with a garden gnome cemented to a paving slab in the front garden. But he did look like a civilised, domesticated version of the wild man of the woods. He had slightly curly brown hair, longer than would be considered fashionable, and mottled greenish-brown eyes, the colour of tree bark. There was a slightly crumpled and slouched look about him which actually made him look rather contemporary, despite the fact that he was wearing a zip-up woolly cardigan. He had a wide and charming smile which Katherine soon noticed was a semi-permanent feature, because he smiled with his whole face, and she took an instinctive liking to him. Joe seemed to know him fairly well, because he spread himself out on the sofa and helped himself to a Malteser from a bowl on the table without waiting to be asked.

'How do you two know each other then?' Katherine asked.

'Mark and I share an interest in, um, esoteric practices,' said Joe delicately.

'Ritual magic,' beamed Mark the Pagan.

'Oh.'

As a conversation stopper it was a pretty good one.

'It's nothing to worry about,' said Joe cheerfully. 'We don't sacrifice chickens or anything. We're in a group which meets every couple of months.'

Katherine was a bit dubious. 'Is it one of those groups where you dance naked round a bonfire?'

'Not at this time of year,' said Mark regretfully.

He went off to fetch refreshments, while Joe helped himself to Maltesers. The living room was tastefully decorated, and clearly reflected Mark's interests. There were embroidered Indian cushions on the chairs and at the fireside, and several enormous plants, some with neatly twisted stems and bursts of luxurious foliage which were practically climbing the walls. The centrepiece was a large leafy shrub in a blue-glazed pot right under the window. All its growing tips had been carefully bent downward and fixed with wires so that it grew in a rosette shape, with a mass of fluffy branches in the middle like fox-tails. A black statue of an Egyptian cat, with gold earrings, occupied a space in the middle of the sideboard with a gold candle on either side. Above the fireplace was a beautiful painting of a goddess, emerging from a spiral of light against a background of darkest sea-green, surrounded by stars. Katherine found her eye drawn towards it again and again.

Mark returned and flopped heavily onto a sofa.

'I'm really interested in hearing about your experiences,' he said. 'What do you know for certain then, about this Munro bloke?'

Katherine unfolded a piece of paper from her pocket. It was the print-out which had come from Bob's project database.

'I can read you what I know of his military record,' she said, 'but it isn't very much. He joined up at the start of 1915, and first saw action in the battle of Loos in September of that year. He served in the Loos area until July 1916, when his battalion transferred to the Somme, and were among the troops who made an unsuccessful advance on High Wood on September 9th 1916. In February 1917, shortly after being gazetted a lieutenant, he was invalided home suffering from neurasthenia.'

'Shellshock,' translated Joe.

'It says "After a period of recovery in a hospital in Cheltenham, Munro went back to the front line in Flanders, shortly after the battle of Messines Ridge. He was reported missing after a trench raid on the night of 20th July 1917, and his body was never found. He is commemorated on the Menin Gate Memorial to the Missing at Ypres." '

'Wow. That's pretty good. You don't get many spooks coming through which you can corroborate to that extent.'

'Spooks?' Katherine gave Joe a nervous glance.

'Sorry,' said Mark. 'It's just my pet name for them.'

Katherine took a sip of home-made elderflower spritzer, which was surprisingly gorgeous.

'I don't know what he wants from me though. He's pleasant enough, but I wish I knew what he was here for.'

'Do you get communication from him?'

'It's not like he's trying to put across any message as such,' she explained. 'I get images of him, and a sense of him just being around, almost as if he just enjoys the company. It's like he's standing just behind my right shoulder. Yes, it always seems to be the right shoulder. When that happens I tend not to get a visual image of him, but other times I see him really clearly, either smiling at me or just sitting around gazing into space.'

'And there's the dreams as well,' prompted Joe.

'Yes, I get these recurring dreams about various battle-related situations, like being down in a cellar, and – oh God, the worst one – I had this one again the other night – standing in a pile of rubble looking down at a dead soldier with dark eyes and a smile on his face.' She described the dreams to him in as much detail as she could remember.

Mark was intrigued. 'And what makes you so sure that the dreams are connected with Richard Munro?'

'Well I'm not sure, actually. It's just a gut feeling, plus the fact that the dreams started about the same time.'

'Interesting.' Mark drew his legs up onto the sofa. 'So you've got dreams about traumatic war scenes, and a silent soldier who keeps turning up and not saying anything.'

'That's right. He just seems to like hanging around. He's kind of nice, though, I suppose.'

'I know what you mean. It's like having somebody else with you in the house, isn't it?' said Mark. 'Only they don't get in the way or leave washing up in the sink.'

'Yes,' grinned Katherine, 'I suppose it is.'

'Any ideas, Mark?' asked Joe.

He thought for a moment. 'My immediate thought is that these dream scenes are actually memories.'

'Memories?' Katherine was taken aback.

'Yes. I'm not suggesting that they're your memories. Somebody else's. Maybe Richard's.'

'How do you work that out?'

'Don't you think that makes sense? You experience them at first hand, they have a powerful emotional component, and however alien the scene may be to your everyday life it feels real and logical within its own context. I mean, it's not the erratic, distorted reality you get with most dreams.'

'I suppose so. I hadn't really thought about it, but yes, they do have a self-contained logic about them. But how does a memory get into someone else's mind fully formed? How can I see things which happened to someone else in a different time? And why is he here, why me?'

'Well,' he said, transferring his feet to the coffee table, 'as I said to Joe earlier I think these guys are very much around at the moment. There's a lot of first world war stuff very close to the surface. What I keep getting is an image of a church or chapel, really dark and dingy with heavy brown drapes over the windows, and a whole load of men in first world war uniform kneeling in the pews. It's just like they're sitting there waiting for something. There's an atmosphere of guilt, a real tension. I get a really strong urge to go and fling all the curtains open and let in some sunlight, but the curtains always seem to be stuck.'

'It does sound like it's on the same wavelength as what I've been getting.'

'It does have a common ring to it, doesn't it?' said Mark. 'Different people, same theme. So anyway, I've been doing a bit of meditation on it, see if anything happens. And the impression coming through is that these soldiers are carrying a collective burden of guilt, a truly enormous one, and they can't move on until it's dealt with.'

'Hmm.' Katherine didn't know what to say.

'Does Richard Munro have an air of guilt about him?' asked Joe.

'No, I wouldn't say guilt. It's more of a pensive, gazing-into-the-middle-distance kind of thing, as though he's waiting for a bus.'

Mark smiled. 'Now there's a thought. I'm really glad you told me about this. It'll be interesting to see how it develops.'

'I love that goddess painting over the fireplace,' said Katherine, realising that her eye had been drawn towards it for about the twenty-fifth time.

'Thank you.'

A thought struck her. 'You didn't paint it yourself, did you?'

'Yes,' he said modestly. 'I do loads of things like that. Paintings and drawings of things I see in my head.'

'I'm not surprised,' said Joe. 'Look at the way this is coming on.' He rubbed one of the fox-tails on the plant by the window, and sniffed his fingers appreciatively.

'Yes, that one's my best ever,' said Mark. 'It's the third time I've got it to flower. It's good stuff, too. You can try a bit if you like. I'll dry it for you in the oven.'

'I'd love to,' said Joe. 'But I'm driving.'

'Oh, so *that's* what it is,' said Katherine, the truth dawning on her at last. At least now she knew why she'd never seen any plants like that in a garden centre.

'Do you want to try some?' asked Mark, a little shyly.

Katherine thought for a moment. Her only previous encounter with marijuana had been a tiny choke-inducing puff behind the school bike sheds, and it hadn't really had any effect. Then again, she hadn't really tried elderflower fizz before either, and that was a pleasant surprise, so she was feeling adventurous.

'Go on, then,' she said. 'I'll try a little bit.'

Joe shoved a red and silver cushion behind his back and nestled into it appreciatively. 'I'd love to go over to the Somme,' he said wistfully. 'And Loos, and all those places.'

'Me too,' said Mark. 'And I will. This year. I've made my mind up.'

'I'll come with you then,' Joe suggested, part joking, part testing the water.

'I was hoping you'd say that,' grinned Mark.

'Oh?'

'Because I'd rather take your car.'

Katherine spluttered into a wheezy cough as she made her sixth attempt to inhale from the tiny joint Mark had given her.

'How's your head, Kath?' asked Joe, smirking.

'Nice,' beamed Katherine, no longer caring whether she made a fool of herself or not. It was having that much effect at least.

'I know what,' said Mark, who was also beginning to feel the effects of a slightly larger joint. 'Let's *all* go to the Somme.'

'OK,' said Katherine, and giggled compulsively.

'We can take Joe's car, book into a *gîte*, and drive around all the places where Richard Munro was in action.'

'Brilliant!' squawked Katherine.

'It'll have to wait till the school holidays,' said Joe.

Mark tutted. 'I wouldn't normally go on holiday while the schools are out, because everywhere is swarming with kids. But I suppose it's worth it, to get the Mazda.'

'What's so special about my blasted Mazda?'

'I think it's part of my karma to own crappy cars.'

Katherine was stuffing herself with Maltesers from the bowl on the table. Chocolate had never tasted so good. In fact the whole world had suddenly come into sharp and beautiful focus: colours were brighter, edges crisper. She felt spectacularly happy and a pleasant tingling sensation shimmied down the back of her head like a warm running stream. Her veins were running with warm honey.

'I think it's part of my karma to wear crappy T-shirts as well,' Mark went on. 'Look at this, a girl persuaded me to buy it in Glastonbury. I haven't had the nerve to wear it openly yet.'

He unzipped his cardigan and revealed a logo which said FUCK THE LAW, SMOKE THE DRAW in large letters with a small print of a marijuana leaf underneath.

'The things we do for politics, eh?'

Katherine was holding her breath trying not to laugh. She managed it until both Mark and Joe turned and looked at her at the same time. Then she exploded in giggles.

'You enjoying that spliff, then?' grinned Mark.

She clutched her side, tears of laughter blurring her vision.

'It's great,' she said at last. 'It's like eating those fizzy fruity sweets, only it's in your brain instead of your mouth.'

Mark gave a brief hoot of laughter which set Katherine off cackling again.

'Oh God, they're both stoned,' said Joe to himself.

'Don't knock it,' snorted Katherine brightly. 'I haven't felt this good for bloody years.'

Chapter Eighteen

'Come on, I haven't got all day.'

'Yes you have, you're just impatient.'

'Aren't *you*?'

'Yes of course, but I can't make this berk go any faster.'

Joe accelerated forward towards the car in front, ready to overtake, but when he rounded the corner there was a long stream of traffic coming the other way. Katherine fed Maltesers into her mouth one at a time, sucking at the honeycomb until it collapsed and then chewing up the chocolatey bit. She had developed a newfound taste for them after her evening with Mark.

'I hope you won't get into trouble taking the day off,' said Joe.

'No, I'm past caring about that. I'll probably have to take tomorrow off as well to make it convincing. It always looks a bit suspicious if you take a one-day sickie, doesn't it?'

'If you say so.'

The slow car pottered off down a side road and Joe accelerated gratefully. Katherine had the window open slightly, and felt a pleasant rush of air flood in as the speed increased.

'Do you think Mark the Pagan meant it when he suggested going to the Somme?' she asked.

'He wouldn't have said it if he hadn't already got it sussed out. He's very dynamic when it comes to following things up.'

'He seems a very nice person,' she said, feeling her cheeks flush despite the stream of cold air.

'You like him, do you?' smiled Joe. 'I thought you would.'

'Well, he's very down to earth, isn't he?'

'What else do you expect from the Pagan? But yes, he's very good company. And you'll find he's very generous with his time, if ever you need help with anything.'

'Why do you call him the Pagan?'

Joe laughed. 'You saw all those swirling goddesses and ethnic crafts, and the strange talent he has with plants. You should see his garden in the summer, bloody hell. Eighty-odd medicinal herbs all tagged with their Latin names, *and* he could tell you exactly what to use them all for. When we have meetings with our meditation group, Mark is the one who comes up with stuff about crystals and forests and flowers, or something based on ancient legends. I expect he hugs trees when nobody's looking.'

'What does he do for a living?'

'I believe he's a freelance editor, working from home. Has to, I suppose. I mean, I really can't imagine him holding down an office job, can you?'

Katherine didn't want to appear too interested, so she stuffed herself with chocolate in silence.

When they eventually reached the record office it was quiet and almost empty. Joe went over to the desk and asked to speak to the researcher he'd commissioned to search the local archives. The woman went away and came back with a younger colleague who had a blonde pony-tail, round glasses and colourful dangly parrot earrings.

'Hi, I'm Jane,' she said. 'Would you like to come through?'

She led Katherine and Joe to a private reading room, where a couple of cardboard boxes had been put on the table.

'It was only because you mentioned his uncle's surname, Crooke, that I was able to find this,' Jane said. 'It was lumped in with the Crooke family papers, because we've got quite a bit of material about them. William Crooke was a bit of a local celebrity in his time. None of this stuff has been catalogued though, so I don't know what's in there.' She picked up one of the boxes and pushed it towards Joe. 'This is the one you'll be interested in. It's got paperwork relating to Richard Munro. All these papers were given to us by a Mrs Louisa Driscoll in 1978. I don't know her connection with the family, but you may find out as you go through it.'

'Brilliant, thank you.' Joe took the lid off the box.

'Jesus wept,' gasped Katherine. The box was nearly half full with yellowed envelopes, scraps of paper and photographs.

'I'll leave you to it,' said Jane cheerfully. 'Give me a shout if you need anything.'

'Oh God Joe, this stuff is incredible.'

Katherine picked out a photograph which was sticking out from the middle of the pile. It was a sepia-tinted print of a young man on a horse, photographed in front of a white wall. The horse was small and apparently chestnut coloured, with an alert face and a white blaze, and the young man had rather a cheeky smile.

'Is that him?'

'I don't think so,' said Katherine, a bit disappointed. 'He looks too dark, and too chirpy.' She turned the print over, but there was nothing written on the back. 'Actually, he looks more like the bloke I keep seeing in that horrible dream, the one who's lying in the rubble. There's a resemblance, anyway.'

'Let's go through these systematically,' said Joe. 'Put that back where you found it and we'll start at the top.'

Katherine put the photo back and picked up a postcard from the top of the pile. It was brittle with age, and featured a rather twee picture of a girl with a hairdo like a lump of dough, leaning coquettishly towards a vase of gladioli on a table. It had been hand-tinted in gaudy, unlifelike colours.

'It's addressed to this Louisa woman,' said Katherine. 'Whoever she is. Look.'

She showed Joe the reverse of the card, which had been written on with a fountain pen in a slow, awkward script. It was addressed to Miss L. Carson of Glendale House, Tivoli Road, Cheltenham, with a green half penny stamp and a smudgy postmark which looked like *JU20 14*.

'June 20th 1914.' Joe wrote it down carefully on an A4 pad. 'Anything interesting?'

The message started off in a tidy hand which became more cramped and sprawling further down.

> Dear Louisa,
> How are you getting on, because I am a little better & I'm glad I am, because I have had about enough of it, this time, because I have never been like this before, Well I hope I see you another day, How do you like this pretty card, don't you wish it was you
> From Jocelyn
> Goodnight

There was another bit written sideways down the edge.

"Tell Lizzie I'll send her one sometime", with a double underline.

145

Katherine put the card to one side. 'Bit of a boring person to have as a pen-friend by the sound of it.'

'Well,' said Joe, 'a lot of people didn't have a proper education in those days.'

'Oh dear, here's another.' She held up a yellowing picture of Cheddar Gorge, with the same hesitant scrawl, in a deep blue ink this time.

Dear Louisa

It is a long time now since I wrote to you, But I could not during these last three weeks as I have been so very ill, because this time last week I thought I should never get over my Illness, but I am thankful to say I feel nearly myself again, My Dear don't worry about poor dear Richard, you must be having a frightful time, but don't worry, because Tom says he has most likely been found by the Germans, and taken to Safety, and you will see him when the War is finished, It will be all right you'll see, My throat is a trifle weak but I think by next week it will be stronger
Love from
Jocelyn

'Aha,' said Joe. 'We have a mention of Richard, and of him being missing. Do you think Louisa might have been his girlfriend? She couldn't be his sister, because she had a different address and surname.'

'We can't be a hundred per cent sure it's our Richard, can we?' said Katherine. 'Could be somebody else.'

'True. It's tragic though, isn't it, how people really convinced themselves that their missing loved ones had been carted off to Germany, when nine times out of ten the poor bugger had been blasted out of existence.'

'It's hardly surprising though, when you look at the crap they read in the newspapers. Those *Gloucestershire Graphic* annuals were packed with jolly jingoistic twaddle about how well everything was going. People must have believed it. Makes hypochondriac Jocelyn seem positively normal.'

She unwrapped the next item, which was a small wad of sepia-tinted photographs in fine blue tissue paper.

'It's the young lad on the horse again,' she said. There were three quite similar poses, and another one taken from further back, which revealed that the horse was standing at the front of a flat-fronted stucco'd Regency house with tall pilasters down the front and a handsome portico over the door set on Doric columns. The driveway swept round in a curve and on the left hand side was a redwood tree. Joe leaned across and stared at the photograph.

'I recognise that building,' he said. 'I don't know where or why, but I've definitely seen it. It's somewhere in Cheltenham, I'm sure of it.'

'There are loads of houses like that in Cheltenham,' said Katherine, squinting at one of the close-up pictures. 'Nice looking bloke actually. Nice dark eyes.'

'It's not Richard though?'

'I'd say definitely not.'

She unfolded a sheet of crispy yellow-brown paper.

'Bloody hell,' she said, scanning through it. 'Bloody hell, look at this.'

It was a standard form, printed but with all the personal details written in by hand, signed illegibly by the Officer in Charge of Records.

Army Form B. 104—82a.
Infantry Record Office
Warwick Station
12 January 1918

Sir,

It is my painful duty to inform you that no further news having been received relative to *Lieutenant R. M. Munro Gloucestershire Regiment*, who has been missing since *20. 7. 17*, the Army Council have been regretfully constrained to conclude that he is dead, and that his death took place on the *20. 7. 17* (or since).

I am to express to you the sympathy of the Army Council with you in your loss.

> Any articles of private property left by missing soldiers which are found are forwarded to this Office, but they cannot be disposed of until authority is received from the War Office.

'Is that what they did then, to notify the families?' Katherine was appalled. 'Just sent out a pre-printed letter like that?'

'No, they would have had a telegram first. Saying much the same thing, though.'

'I can just imagine it. "Thank you for sending us your husband/son (delete as applicable) to fight in our war. Sadly he has been blown to shit, but if you wish to complete the attached form we may send you back his wristwatch and underpants." '

'Something like that. Actually his wristwatch would probably have been nicked by the gravediggers. I'm not sure about the pants.'

'Oh wow,' exclaimed Katherine, turning over the next item in the box. 'That's him.'

It was a photograph of Richard Munro sitting on a brick wall, smiling at the camera. He was in immaculate army uniform, complete with jodhpurs which bulged out at the hips, sleek riding boots and a glossy leather Sam Browne belt across his chest. The wall curved away from the camera, and there were a few strings of ivy snaking up between the bricks.

'Groovy trousers,' said Katherine, fascinated.

'Is that picture taken in the same place as the others?' said Joe, taking it from her and looking closely at it. 'There's some kind of white building behind him, by the look of it. I reckon it could be the same house. The photo looks like it's come from the same batch.' He compared it with one of the pictures of the boy on the horse. 'It's the same size and format, same width of white border round the edge.'

'You could be right,' said Katherine. 'Oh blimey, I'd do anything to get a copy of this picture. A decent copy, not a photocopy. I wish I'd brought a camera with me. I don't suppose there's much chance of finding the negative?'

'I'm not sure they even had negatives in those days. It was probably taken straight onto a glass plate.'

Katherine stared at the photograph. It was almost like making eye contact with him, the way he was gazing straight out of the picture. He looked a lot more relaxed than he had appeared in her various dream images, but the sense of his character, and a presence building up behind the character, was intense enough to make the air tingle.

'There's more,' said Joe, nodding towards a fat envelope in the box which he was dying to look inside. Katherine reluctantly put Richard's photo to one side and picked it up.

'There's a whole load of stuff in here by the feel of it.'

She carefully tipped out the contents onto the table. There were two separate wads of smaller envelopes, plus some cards and a badly creased photograph. Katherine picked up the photograph, which was a portrait of an elegant, proud-looking officer with fair hair and bright, intense eyes.

'Phwoar, who's the Robert Redford lookalike?'

Joe looked closely at the picture.

'No idea.' The photograph was smaller than the others, printed on thicker paper, and had a distinctly metallic sheen on the emulsion. Not from the same batch as the others, evidently. The image was slightly cracked where it had been crumpled. Joe looked at one of the wads of small envelopes.

'It could be someone called Hugh Crooke,' he said.

He held up the top envelope, which was addressed to Second-Lieutenant Hugh Crooke via the Royal Engineers in France. There was no postage stamp on this one, just the letters O.A.S. hand written in the top corner. The postmark just said 'Field Post Office', and it had been rubberstamped 'Passed by Censor' in red ink.

'What's O.A.S.?' asked Katherine.

'On Active Service. It means the person who sent it was probably in the trenches.'

'Are they all like that?'

Joe flicked through them. 'They're all addressed to Hugh Crooke, but only the top four were sent to France. The rest went to Egypt. He got about a bit, didn't he?'

'This must be him then, don't you think?' Katherine carefully smoothed out the crumpled photograph.

'Well, it says second-lieutenant on the address, but the feller in the picture is a full lieutenant by the look of it.'

'How can you tell?' asked Katherine.

'Pips,' said Joe. He pointed at the officer's sleeve. 'You see those two diamond-shaped blobs on his cuff? That's his badge of rank. One pip for a second-lieutenant, two pips for a lieutenant and three for a captain. After that comes a major, who has a crown instead of the pips.'

'Well I never knew that. Probably won't remember it either.'

'It may be that this Hugh bloke was made a lieutenant later in the war, and the picture was taken after his promotion.'

'And presumably he was a relative of Richard's. If Richard had an uncle called William Crooke, maybe Hugh was another uncle, or a cousin.'

'Well, we're in exactly the right place to find out. You carry on looking through those envelopes. I'll be back in a mo.' Joe grabbed a sheet of paper off the A4 pad and scuttled out of the room.

Sitting in the room on her own, Katherine was convinced that Richard Munro was very close by. It felt as though he was in the room with her, standing just behind her, out of sight, as was his way on some occasions. So strong was the feeling that she turned round to look, just in case he was really there.

'I've caught up with you now, haven't I?' she whispered to the empty room, very quietly in case any of the record office staff were outside the door and thought she was a nutter.

The atmosphere suddenly felt a degree or two warmer. She remembered reading in a library book on paranormal phenomena that the temperature often drops when ghosts are around, hence the traditional 'chill down the spine'. Perhaps this should be classed as para-paranormal.

She delicately opened one of the envelopes addressed to Hugh in France and took out the letter, which was written on two small sheets of blue paper in an attractive, garlanded script.

'Jesus gibbering fuck,' she said out loud, not caring who heard.

30th August 1916

Dear Hugh
I'm glad we managed to have our little meeting, despite the difficulties. You seem to have adapted to trench life very well after all those months of sunshine. Perhaps I just worry

too much; you are obviously more than capable of looking after yourself. Things have been pretty hellish for the last two months but we have both come through it so far, so let's not grumble.

I met some lads from the field artillery yesterday who had spent the entire night painting the words "with compliments" on the shells in their ammunition dump, in big white letters. I don't think you can actually read them while they're flying through the air, but they said it puts joy into their hearts to see them go over.

I must keep this brief as don't have any time to spare at the moment. It is ironic that whenever anything happens which is worth writing about, I don't have enough time to actually write it. Even the diary has gone by the wayside this month, for all my bragging about the importance of regular writing.

Keep your head down, and don't let the Boches bite.

Toodle-pip,

Richard

After all this time, it was unbelievable that she was actually holding in her hands a letter which had been written by Richard Munro. The pleasantly looped handwriting was actually his. These pieces of paper had belonged to him, and it was his hand which had folded them, tidily but not quite square, and put them into this envelope. She tried to imagine his hand resting on the paper, forming the letters as he moved the fountain pen across the page. It was a vivid thought with a strong emotional charge. Having handled something that was personal to Richard made him more of a real person. But it also brought with it a strained feeling of emptiness and loss. Tears were brimming at her eyes.

The door suddenly burst open.

'Back again,' said Joe, then he saw the look on Katherine's face. 'You all right?'

She nodded, and wiped her eyes and nose on the back of her hand.

'What is it?'

She laid the letter down on the table with reverent care.

'These letters to Hugh,' she sniffed. 'They're all from Richard.' For some reason, saying his name out loud just tipped her over the edge, and she burst into tears with big, gulping sobs.

'Oh dear,' said Joe, who was always embarrassed at the sight of women crying, and wasn't sure it would be socially acceptable to put a comforting arm round her. Then again, it looked a bit heartless just to stand there and do nothing. He compromised by digging out a tissue from the bottom of his pocket.

'Here we are,' he said. 'I think it's clean.'

Katherine accepted it gratefully. It was warm from Joe's body heat, and she clutched it like a security blanket.

'I'm sorry,' she gulped. 'I'll be all right in a minute.'

Joe sat down and picked up the letter.

'Dear oh dear,' he said, feeling a slight lump forming in his throat, 'you'll have me at it in a minute. And we've only got the one tissue.' He read the letter through and then sat with his face resting on his hands, elbows on the table.

'It brings it home to you, doesn't it?'

'Yes,' squeaked Katherine. 'It bloody does.'

He sighed.

'Well, I'm not sure if this is the right time to tell you, because you may get even more choked up, but I've found Hugh Crooke as well.'

He spread out on the table a photostat from the 1901 census. 'You were right, he is Richard's cousin.'

Katherine blew her nose and leaned over to have a look.

'Langford House, London Road. I wonder if that's still there, or if it's been demolished for flats or traffic lights.'

'There were quite a few people living there, by the look of it. William Crooke, retired of the Indian Civil Service, aged 53. Evelyn Crooke, wife, aged 37. So that's the aunt and uncle. Bit of an age gap between them, but I suppose that's their business not mine. Then we've got Hugh Crooke, son, aged 4. The others are all servants. Five of them. Must have been a well-to-do family. I've had a look for Hugh's birth certificate, but he isn't listed.'

'If Hugh was only four in 1901,' pondered Katherine, 'surely he would only just have left school in 1914?'

'Yes, he'd have been seventeen when the war broke out.'

'He looks a bit older than that in the photo.' She picked up the photograph of the fair-haired officer. 'Nearer twenty-five, I should say.'

'Yes, I see what you mean. Maybe the picture was taken quite late in the war. If it is him at all.'

'Maybe.' She reached across to the other bundle of envelopes. 'Look, these are all addressed to Richard. Maybe they're from Hugh.'

'A bit odd, if they are,' said Joe.

'Why?'

'Well, you don't normally find both sides of the correspondence in one place. Hugh may have kept all Richard's letters, and Richard may have kept all of Hugh's, but they wouldn't end up all together in one box, would they?'

Katherine opened the letter. It was indeed from Hugh Crooke. Both sides of the correspondence. It was quite a coup.

'Maybe when Richard went missing they found all Hugh's letters and sent them back to him. He'd have both sets then.'

A thought suddenly struck Joe.

'There isn't a diary in that box as well, is there?'

'No,' said Katherine. She flicked through the remaining items in the box to double check. 'No, there isn't. Why?'

'It's just that Richard mentions one in his letter.'

Katherine's eyes widened. 'Christ, so he does.'

'Shame it's not here, it would have been a really interesting read. Still, if the letters have survived there's a reasonable chance the diary has too. Somewhere.'

'If it has, do we stand a chance of finding it?'

'Possibly. But I suppose we've got enough to be getting on with as it is. Are you all set?'

'What for?'

Joe scratched the back of his head with his biro.

'I can feel a mammoth photocopying job coming on.'

Chapter Nineteen

17th April 1916

A rather disturbed night. I have reached the point where I can sleep through most of the shelling, but on this occasion I was woken by the sound of Tate shuffling around in the dark with a string of panicky expletives. I struck a match and saw him crouched over his hammock with his revolver at the ready.

'What's up?' I asked, groping for the candle.

'There's a fucking great rat,' he said shakily. 'It was walking about on my chest.' He peered into the darkness in the corner of the dug-out. There was no obvious sign of any rodent, and I wondered if he had imagined it. Living in a constant state of nerves, it is not uncommon for men to dream about being molested by vermin.

'It's under my bed somewhere, the little bastard,' he declared. 'I'm going to find it and shoot its bloody head off.'

I groaned sleepily. 'It's probably gone back down its hole by now.'

'It wouldn't *fit* down any hole, the big fat bastard. I'm not getting back in that bed until I've blown its arse to kingdom come.'

'For God's sake,' I said, slithering out of my bunk with all my blankets still wrapped round me. 'You have my bed. I'm not that bothered by rats.'

This idea seemed to pacify him a little, and we duly swapped beds. He dived onto my hammock with his usual energetic leap and I heard the wooden frame crackle under the strain. I blew out the candle and settled myself carefully in Tate's rather wobbly hammock, too tired to worry about rats.

I must have dozed rather than slept, because I was dimly aware of trying to turn over onto my left side and hearing the sound of tearing wood, and then the whole hammock, with me in it, fell to the ground with a crash. After weeks of systematic abuse by Tate its frame had finally given way. We both yelled, startled by the noise.

'What the fuck is going on?' he warbled.

'Nothing,' I gasped, slightly winded from having landed on my back. I heard him lurch across the room in the darkness, and there was a horrendous clatter as he walked into what sounded like a pile of metal plates.

'Fuck bollocks!' he yelled, thrashing about in panic.

'Will you stop that,' I hissed, 'before the whole bloody German infantry come over here and tell us to keep the noise down?'

'Munro, are you all right?' He lurched forward with another clatter and I felt him grab hold of my ankles.

'I've fallen out of bed, that's all,' I moaned. 'Leave me alone.'

'It's that fucking rat again, isn't it?'

'There are no rats. Go back to sleep, Tate. Please.' I turned over and snuggled against the wall, trying to make myself comfortable on the cold earth floor. Presently I heard the creak of him jumping back onto the other bed, still muttering obscenities, and I was able to slip gratefully into oblivion.

When I woke up at dawn he was sleeping peacefully like a child, lying on his back and snoring with his mouth open. His blond hair was splayed onto the pillow, and his revolver – cocked and loaded – was still lying on his chest.

I was summoned to Company HQ today to escort some new recruits up to the front line. We have been greatly in need of them, so I couldn't complain. Although the miserable winter is now coming to an end, our ranks continue to be depleted at an alarming rate by cases of pneumonia and trench foot. It is not the enemy which is eroding our battalion, it's the weeks of standing around ankle-deep in cold puddles. Officers are supposed to carry out regular foot inspections on all their men, but we abandoned the practice a couple of months ago. The problem is that as soon as the men take off their boots their feet begin to swell, and then they can't get the boots back on again. The only practical solution is for the men to keep their boots on for weeks at a time.

Major Pershore has done quite well for himself, because he now occupies a very elaborate dug-out. Although it is only a hole in the ground, it has been shored up with a very tidy row of wooden planks placed vertically along the walls, like panelling. There is even a recess with a wash-stand and jug, and an iron-framed bed with half-decent linen, and the overall effect is of a cheap but comfortable hotel room. He sat behind a slightly battered desk with a large field telephone occupying much of its surface, and handed me instructions for deploying the new troops – only four of whom are destined for my platoon. I was just about to leave when he called me back, and sat back in his chair with his arms folded on his chest.

'I've been hearing some things about your friend Mr Tate,' he said, keeping his eyes fixed on me to observe my reaction.

'What kind of things, sir?' I asked in a casual tone.

He thought for a moment, then said: 'Tell me Munro, do you consider Tate a responsible officer?'

'Absolutely.'

'Not a little… reckless… perhaps?'

'Reckless? Oh no, sir,' I replied, bordering on untruth now.

Major Pershore smacked his chops thoughtfully. 'I've been looking at the incident a few weeks back, when I understand he led a party of men on a raid to put an enemy gun out of action?'

'Yes, sir.' The memory was still clear in my mind, not least the spectacular explosion which went up the next day when the Germans tried to use the sabotaged *Minenwerfer*.

'You don't consider that he took any – excessive risks – on that occasion?'

'Sir,' I took a defensive step towards the desk. 'I know Tate may seem a little hot-headed sometimes, but he never risked the life of anybody but himself. He is the bravest officer I have ever worked with, his integrity is absolute, and I would entrust him with my life. He *has* saved my life.'

The major smiled, and to my surprise looked pleased with my display of loyalty.

'Good,' he said, nodding his head contentedly. 'That's all I wanted to know.'

There was some sad news waiting for me when I got back. I heard that one of our officers had been hit by a shell splinter and died of wounds. Then somebody told me that it was Hubert Corke, whose father is the vicar of Holy Apostles church in Cheltenham. The splinter struck him in the lung while he was standing by a dug-out in the trench called Regent Street, and they couldn't save him. He was a good friend of Hugh's, as they were such close neighbours, with only a couple of years' age difference. Poor Hubert. Poor Hugh. I will have to write and tell him.

3rd June 1916

The post arrived early this morning, bringing me the double pleasure of a letter from my mother and one from Hugh. Tate also received a missive, which is quite a rare event since he has little affection for his family, and probably *vice versa*, and they don't write to him much. He sat on his bed with his feet up, perusing it with a blank expression.

'Fuck it,' he exclaimed suddenly.

I looked up and saw that his expression had turned to indignant disgust. He screwed the letter up into a ball and flung it across the dug-out, then stormed out without another word.

I waited until I was sure he had gone, then crept out of my hammock to retrieve the ball of paper, which had come to rest by the table leg. I couldn't imagine what awful news would send him into such a fury, and I certainly wasn't prepared for the surprise I got when I unwrapped the paper and flattened it out.

It was a brief letter on official army paper, and it said:

> To Lieutenant A. S. Tate
> The G.O.C. congratulates you on being awarded the
> Military Cross by the Commander-in-Chief.

I was astounded. The MC is no small honour, and I couldn't see any reason why Tate should not be delighted to receive it. I carefully screwed the letter up again and dropped it on the floor, knowing how cross he would be if he knew I had read it. I would have to feign ignorance until he decided to tell me about it himself.

My own letters were not entirely a bundle of joy, either. Hugh wrote to tell me that his battalion is about to be posted to France. Rumours have been building for some while about a major offensive, and quite a few movements of troops seem to be in the offing. Hugh is scheduled to leave Egypt within two weeks, and God only knows what awaits him on the western front. I dread to think.

Tate was not able to keep his secret for very long, because news spreads very quickly in the trenches. I heard it first from the sanitary corporal – or shit-house wallah, as he is more popularly known – whom I overheard talking to some of Tate's men outside the latrine. He was gleefully explaining to them how their officer had got the MC for that midnight raid because he had single-handedly held off the Jerries while his comrades escaped. That was the official story, he said, which was going to be printed in *The Times*. Suddenly the strange conversation which I'd had with Major Pershore made perfect sense. I thought he had been hinting at some disciplinary action, when in fact it was quite the opposite.

I noticed that Tate was very quiet while we were eating our lunch, and just banged the plate a lot. Eventually he put down his fork and looked at me.

'I suppose you've heard the news,' he said acidly.

'Yes,' I said, and tried a happy grin, which was not reciprocated. 'Why are you so down in the mouth about it?'

'I don't want it,' he said.

'You deserve it,' I ventured cautiously.

'Don't give me that shit,' he burst out angrily. 'I know what I deserve and what I don't, better than the fucking Commander-in-Chief. I don't want to come out of this war with any fucking gongs.'

I knew better than to argue with him, so I carried on eating in silence.

'I won't wear the bloody ribbon,' he said gruffly. 'I'm not going round with a trinket hanging off me like some great fucking Christmas fairy.'

He lacerated a potato with rhythmic, violent cuts.

'And another thing.' He jabbed his knife in the air. 'If I hear that *fucking* Tipperary song once more I'm going to throw myself out of the fucking window.'

I looked thoughtfully at the solid structure of planks, corrugated iron and hard-packed mud which surrounded us.

'Tate, we haven't got a window.'

'Then we'll have to get one of the little fuckers in the Labour Corps to *make one* for us, won't we?'

I smiled to myself, and he noticed the look on my face.

'What's funny?' he demanded.

'Nothing,' I said.

8th July 1916

We have moved a step closer to Hell.

I am writing this in a hotel room, which gives the scene a deceptive air of normality.

It is anything but normal. Four hours ago I could not have believed I would live long enough to write this.

The hotel lies in a back street of Albert, which is a small town in Picardy – where the roses come from. We travelled some way south by train yesterday morning, and are here for a few days before moving forward into the support trenches. It is a grim place, and no doubt about it. There has been a lot of shelling here, worse than any I've seen before. Buildings have neat holes punched through them. Some have their façades blown out, leaving an empty casing; others have seen their roofs tumble in with their walls still standing. The wind constantly whips up a cloud of lime dust, whose damp smell mingles with the burnt odour of explosives.

When we arrived here, Tate and I decided to go for a stroll to get used to this strange new wasteland. The town is centred around its *basilique*, a modern but flamboyantly beautiful church which has now taken quite a pelting. By far the most spectacular feature is its gold-domed tower, which bears a figure of the Virgin Mary holding the Christ child above her head, with the child reaching out in a gesture of benediction. In the course of the shelling, the dome has been all but destroyed, and the statue – which is undamaged – keels over at a bizarre angle, as if the holy mother and child had been about to dive into the rubble below, but were frozen in time just as they began to plunge. It is literally only a coil of wire which holds them in suspension over the desolate landscape.

There were several gaping holes in the tower like bite-marks in a cake, and the back part of the roof had come down. The inside of the building had tall, graceful arches decorated with a black and white checked pattern, some of which had lost their keystones and collapsed in a pile of shattered rubble around the high altar.

High-explosive shells had burst into the nave and snapped off the sturdy square pillars as though they were matchsticks. Masonry lay all over the floor, damped down by the recent heavy rain, giving off a musty smell of mildew. And every inch of the remaining walls was decorated with fantastically elaborate paintings and mosaics, the figures of saints and angels peering out dimly through a patina of brick dust and soot. The colours stood out in gaudy contrast to the scorched wreckage. Above our heads, rooks fluttered noisily between their perches in the broken vaulting.

Tate ran his finger through the layer of ash and rubble on the altar and revealed that its surface had originally been gilded. It was part of a colourful mosaic in sky blue and gold, standing on pillars of exquisite marble. The whole *basilique* was a treasure, an irreplaceable work of art. All laid waste.

'Savage business, war, isn't it?' said Tate sadly.

There wasn't a lot else to say, standing within that carcass of twinkling beauty. A rook clapped its wings in the azure-painted gallery high above us and a fragment of loose masonry tumbled down in the aisle, exploding into dust as it hit the floor. With every step we took, the crunching of rubble under our feet echoed round the arches. I couldn't bear any more of it, and we went out into the remains of the market square.

A very eerie silence lingered in the former houses and shops, in contrast to the distant rumbling and pounding which could be heard from the direction of the battle front. Some houses were nothing more than a pile of dusty bricks, with charred timbers and splintered furniture all mixed together. The iron debris of war lay scattered over the road: lumps of melted shrapnel, shell casings, crumpled sheets of corrugated iron and numerous mangled objects whose original purpose could not be guessed at. The swollen body of a dead horse lay in the gutter with its head on the pavement. I have a peculiar sensitivity to the suffering of horses and had to avert my gaze.

We went back to the hotel, where the bar was like an oasis in the desert of desolation. It was crowded with officers and men, chattering contentedly over drinks and card games. The wine was not of a good quality, but there was at least a plentiful supply. With so many administration headquarters and command posts in Albert, the powers-that-be had managed to ensure that alcoholic refreshments were brought in on the supply wagons as regularly as the munitions and medical supplies.

I was not really in the mood for socialising, however, and went up to my room on one of the upper floors. It is the first time I have had a room to myself for the best part of a year, and the luxury feels very strange. Before the war I would never have imagined that a tiny room with an iron bedstead, coffin-like wardrobe and ancient washbasin could be considered luxurious, but my perspective has changed since then. I lay down fully clothed on the bed and gazed at the floral printed wallpaper until I drifted off to sleep, which gave me an hour or so of respite. When I awoke the sun was low in the sky, a thin fragile light. I washed and went down for dinner.

Tate was already settled in the dining room with a ginger-haired officer who had a smile like the Cheshire cat and a high-pitched laugh which sounded uncannily like a machine-gun.

'Come and join us,' said Tate merrily, dragging a chair from under the table and motioning for me to take it. 'We're getting gloriously binged on this fine whisky, or whatever it is.'

He poured me a glass of the pale liquid. It didn't taste much like whisky in the usual sense of the word, but it left a pleasantly fiery tingle down my throat all the same.

We were able to enjoy a very decent meal as well, thanks to the French chef who is defying the bombs to continue plying his trade in what has become an increasingly lucrative market.

'The Golden Virgin is legendary around here,' said the ginger officer with a boozy leer. 'Been like that for the past eighteen months, hanging off the edge of the tower like that, with both sides too superstitious to shoot her down.' He dipped a chocolate biscuit in his whisky and sucked on it appreciatively. 'You're supposed to stand directly underneath it and make a wish, you know, and if the Virgin likes you it'll come true.'

'Did it work for you?' asked Tate with a sarcastic smile.

'Yes, well I actually wished for the ruddy thing not to fall down on my head, and it didn't, so that's nice isn't it?' He swigged some more whisky straight from the bottle.

'Bit of a hot part of the line round here, isn't it?' asked Tate.

'Bloody murder,' snorted the ginger officer. 'And my mother

thinks I'm out here enjoying myself!' He laughed with his bizarre high-pitched cackle.

'Better than Clacton, though, eh?'

They both cackled together.

The officer who was sitting on my left, a podgy chap with watery blue eyes, leaned across to me.

'You know what this town's motto is?' he asked.

I shook my head.

'*Vis Mea Ferrum* – "my strength is in iron".' He jerked his thumb over his shoulder. 'There used to be an iron foundry just down the road there. Then the Boche started delivering some iron of their own, and the whole place is coming to pieces.'

'Bit of an irony, that,' said Tate, and giggled. 'Iron-y. Get it?'

The ginger-haired man let out a prolonged laugh which was as disconcerting as any machine-gun enfilade.

Somebody began to play the piano in the corner of the room, cutting through the laughter with tinkling arpeggios. There were a few discordant notes too as some half-drunk men tried to join in by prodding at the keys with one finger. Then the pianist clattered out the introduction to *Mademoiselle from Armentières* and the whole room burst into song. I joined in for the first three verses, but I was not familiar with some of the variants which the others were singing, each successive verse becoming more vulgar than the last, until a rather prudish-looking colonel wearing a frown above his thick moustache flung down his napkin in disgust and walked out.

Tate leaned sideways in his chair in time to the music, to the extent that his chair tipped up and he only stopped himself from falling by grabbing hold of the tablecloth. This made him positively scream with laughter.

'Is he drunk?' the watery-eyed man inquired discreetly.

'Oh no,' I said. 'He's always like this.'

There were two ear-splitting crashes outside the front window of the hotel, one after another in quick succession. The whole building shuddered, and I felt my chair tremble beneath me. The piano and laughter ceased abruptly, and there was a loud noise of rending wood, tumbling bricks, and a cascade of splintering glass. Everybody threw themselves down on the floor, the instinct for self-preservation overriding the effects of the alcohol.

The worst of the noise subsided, but we could hear the whining of shrapnel shells overhead, and the crash of falling masonry further up the street. These were the sort of bombs we call 'furniture shifters', because each time they come down they move the entire contents of the room by about half an inch – even pianos and tables.

'They're making a bit of a mess out there,' said one officer who was crouched under the window and had a view into the street outside. 'Perhaps we ought to get away before things hot up any further.'

The room began to empty, until there was just a handful of us left, principally those who were staying in the hotel overnight. We lit up cigarettes and maintained a watchful silence, in which even the light chink of a whisky bottle against a glass was enough to make everyone jump.

'I'm going to bed,' I announced at last to a semi-conscious Tate. 'At least if I'm going to be killed I shall do it in comfort.'

I made my way up the two flights of stairs to my room and lay down on the bed, intending to go to sleep. But the whining and crashing in the street outside made it impossible. I lay in the dark visualising the metal nose of a bomb bursting through the white ceiling above me, and the room all around shattered into rubble. No matter how hard I tried to dispel the image it kept flashing into my mind with each new thump and clatter outside, and I was unable to keep my eyes closed for fear of that vision becoming a reality. Twice I got up and went to the window, where sparks of shrapnel burst in the moonlight, and shadows accumulated in the gaping holes among the houses. A couple of streets away I could see a building on fire, which cast a flickering glow across the rooftops.

I returned to bed and made another attempt to sleep, but a few minutes later there was an enormous crash, louder and closer. The bed shuddered violently and I heard a shattering explosion of glass somewhere downstairs. Then there was another fall of bricks close by. The fear which came over me was a cold, sickly dread, rather than panic. I found to my surprise that it was not death *per se* that I really feared, but the prospect of dying alone, uncared for, in a bombed-out French hotel. I wasn't ready for death. Despite the luxury of my own room after months in cramped dug-outs, my strongest instinct was to abandon it and seek the company of other human beings.

I opened the door and wandered out into the corridor as far as the top of the stairs. In the glow of moonlight I was relieved to see Tate pacing up and down in silent agitation. He perked up when he saw me.

'Bugger this,' he said in a quavering voice. The moonlight shone into his pale eyes and I could see hints of fear in them which I'd never seen in him before. 'Shall we try the cellar?'

'I don't know. What's best?'

'Clearly not the top floor if they blow the fucking roof off.'

Above the stairwell the windows had been blown out, and we crunched through the litter of broken glass as we descended the stairs. I think there were two or three cellar areas under the hotel, but we ended up in a very small one. It was tiled but had been limewashed at some stage in the past and the ceramic bricks were a dirty greyish white. We had to pick our way over heaps of wooden crates and the crouched bodies of other men who were seeking shelter down there. The ceiling was vaulted, and had a single electric light hanging from a twisted wire in the middle. Its glow was feeble, but enabled us to find our way to a small space on the opposite side, where we crouched underneath a tall window blackened with grime.

It is a common instinct during a bombardment to burrow down and find shelter within the earth, but that cellar gave us small comfort. Each explosion in the street outside rocked the hotel to its foundations, and the cellar acted as an acoustic box to amplify the noise. However unsafe I had felt upstairs in the bedroom, perched in a vulnerable position at the level of the rooftops, I certainly did not feel any safer closed into that oppressive little dungeon with the whole weight of the hotel shuddering above my head. A direct hit would have killed us either way. I tried to get comfortable with my back pressed against an empty wine crate, but there was only enough room for us to sit hunched up, and no space to move around.

The window in front of my face was more sinister than any I have ever seen. It was like a gaping mouth of hell, totally black on the inside, gummed up with many years' worth of detritus. There was a rusted metal grille over the opening, but little could be seen inside it. It had partially filled with earth and other unidentifiable debris that had slipped through from the outside, and which was banked up towards the top. I began to feel quite uneasy, sitting there staring into it. Underneath, a sticky stream of dark mud had oozed through the corner of the grille and streaked down the wall in an ugly smear. In other places it had dripped down as liquid, leaving dark lines down the bricks.

Outside, the shelling was monstrous and relentless. Most of the time it was concentrated in other parts of the town, and the noise of collapsing houses came to us as nothing more than a soft whoosh and pattering. Other bombs came down close by, screaming overhead and bursting with ferocious impact into the buildings across the street, which we could hear falling in a clatter of glass and bricks. Every now and then a burst would spit debris against the walls of the hotel, until even the stone floor beneath us shivered.

After one particularly close and nerve-jangling explosion there was a heavy rustling sound from the black recess above us, and a large piece of cloth-covered debris which must have been at the top of the arch slipped down and caught against the grille. It was a corpse. British. Mercifully it had its back to us, so we were compelled to view only the blackened tunic of its uniform, but it looked disturbing and grotesque, doubled up in a semi-recumbent pose and slumped against the rusty bars. God only knows how long it had been stuck in the window recess, because it was certainly not a recent casualty. It was not a great comfort to reflect that this poor soul had probably crawled into the recess in an attempt to shelter from an earlier bombardment.

The shelling continued for most of the night with varying degrees of intensity, until my whole body ached from confinement in the cramped space. As soon as daylight began to trickle down into the filthy recess Tate struggled to his feet.

'I can't stand this any more. I'm going for a walk.'

I got up to follow him, although the onset of agonising pins and needles made walking difficult. There were still a few bangs and crashes as we went out through the hotel doors into the street, but in all honesty we were no more likely to be hit out in the open than we were in the cellar, although it was quite a different matter psychologically. Three or four houses on the other side of the street were utterly wrecked; the roadway was strewn with rubble and splintered roof timbers. A fog of thin smoke wafted through the dawn air from burning buildings in other streets.

Neither of us spoke as we made our way towards the market square, scrunching over broken glass and smoking our cigarettes with nervous fingers. Whenever the scream of a shell came overhead we retreated into doorways, making slow progress up the street with a door to door dash when necessary, while bricks tumbled down onto the pavement. Some stretcher-bearers came past us with a casualty wrapped up in a blanket, but otherwise the town appeared deserted. The *basilique* had lost another bit of its roof but I was astonished to see that the madonna still lurched out from the top of the tower, unscathed.

'Are you going to make a wish?' asked Tate as we came level with the tip of the leaning statue.

I stared up at the outstretched arms of the Christ child against the new light of the summer dawn, and wished, silently, that wherever and whenever my turn comes to die, that I will be in the presence of someone I love.

Chapter Twenty

The doorbell buzzed.

Katherine disliked unexpected visitors. Friends who turned up without phoning first rarely got a welcome, and she always made a point of chasing off salesmen. When it was Jehovah's Witnesses and politicians, she just shut the door in their faces.

She grudgingly went out into the lobby to the front door, and was greeted by the cheerful smile of Mark the Pagan.

'Oh, hello,' she said, pleasantly surprised but also rather embarrassed, because the doormat under her feet stank of cat pee.

'I'm really sorry to barge in on you like this,' said Mark, 'but it's good news. I want to show you something.'

'Oh right. What is it?' She was nervous of inviting him in because of the untidiness.

'It's best if you see it for yourself. Only it means going over to my place, because that's where it is.' He stood for a moment looking sheepish. There was a momentary, awkward pause.

'Did you want me to come round straight away?'

Mark made a shrugging gesture. 'If you're not doing anything. I don't want to interrupt you if you're busy.'

'Um, well, yes, why not. I'll just grab my coat.'

Mark's car was an ancient VW Polo with a Greenpeace sticker in the back window. There was a certain saggy, comfortable feel to it, which fitted well with his personality. Katherine looked out through the rain-streaked front window and wondered what on earth she was letting herself in for.

'Joe told me you'd found all that stuff in the local record office,' said Mark. 'That's really brilliant.'

'Yeah. It took a couple of evenings to wade through it all. It's quite spooky the way all the dreams and hunches have connected up with real events.'

Mark gave her a quick glance as he accelerated away from a traffic light. 'You're not entirely happy with this psychic business, are you?'

'No, not really. I don't want to believe in it, but Richard Munro has become so real lately, I can't get away from it.'

'Ah well,' Mark said pleasantly. 'I expect you'll get used to it.'

'So why have you got a gnome cemented to your garden path?' she couldn't resist asking as she settled into an ethnic beanbag.

'He's not a gnome, he's an elemental guardian.' Mark smiled, and she couldn't tell whether he was joking or not. She began to notice that he did this a lot. 'He's been talismanically charged to channel earth energy into the garden.'

'Does it work?'

'You come back in the summer and see my plants, then you tell me. Mind you, I do put horse shit on them as well, so that might be a factor.'

He lit a joss-stick with a cigarette lighter, and stuck the bottom into a blob of blu-tack on the sideboard.

'Anyway, I'd like to know what you found in those letters.'

'Right. Yes. It seems that Richard and Hugh wrote to each other pretty regularly, apart from a few gaps when one or other of them was in action, but the letters only go as far as the end of 1916. If there are any others after that date they weren't in the box.'

'Do you know what happened to Hugh?'

She shook her head. 'That's next on the list. We've already got quite a lot of details about him. His father was a bloke called William Crooke, who worked in the Indian Civil Service, moved to Cheltenham when he retired, and wrote a few books about India. And there was a picture in the box which we think was of Hugh. A tall bloke with blond hair. Quite different from Richard.'

Mark frowned and shook his head. 'Hugh wasn't blond. He was dark.'

'How do you know?' asked Katherine, slightly alarmed. She had a horrible feeling that he was going to tell her he'd had mediumistic contact with Richard's deceased relatives, a psychic form of social networking.

'You'll have to handle this by the edges, it's still a bit damp.' He reached a large photographic print down off a shelf and handed it to her. It was a crystal clear photograph of a young soldier.

'That's Hugh,' he said.

She looked at the picture. It was a formal portrait of a boy in first world war officer's uniform, aged about eighteen and good looking. He had a rounded face, full lips which curved up on one side into a half smile, and had one eyebrow slightly raised, which gave him a slightly cheeky appearance. His hair and eyes were very dark, almost black. It dawned on her, somewhat belatedly, that she had seen the face before. She was looking at a close up photograph of the boy who appeared in the other photos in the record office, the one on the horse.

'Where did you get this?' she gasped.

'I just printed it in my darkroom.'

'No, I mean, how do you know it's Hugh?'

'Oh, it's Hugh all right.' He took a sip of elderflower cordial. 'I've been doing some detective work. There's a bloke I know at Cheltenham College, which is where all the well off chaps went in those days, so I asked him to do a check to see if either Richard Munro or Hugh Crooke had been pupils there.'

'And?'

'They had. Both of them. So I asked very nicely if I could come and have a look at their archive, and they said yes.'

'And that's where you found the picture?'

'Yep. They keep pictures of most of their old boys. It's not a complete collection, but I found this brilliant photo of Hugh. The quality is stunning, considering it was taken such a long time ago. And the college staff were really helpful, they let me bring my camera in and photograph the pictures. So that's how I got it. It's a second generation copy, obviously, but the detail is beautiful.'

'And this is what you brought me here to see?'

'Part of it.' He got up and opened a door under the staircase which led down into the basement. 'Have you ever been in a darkroom before?'

'No.'

'Not many people still use conventional film, I know. But I find the image quality nicer than digital.'

She made her way down the steps into a windowless room with a wide worktop and a sink, and a chemical smell which was not altogether pleasant. There was an enlarger in the corner, which looked like a miniature slide-projector mounted on a vertical pole, and a row of trays half filled with chemicals.

'I found something else in the college archive,' said Mark. He flicked a switch to put the overhead light out, and a dim red lamp came on simultaneously on the wall above the enlarger.

'Do you recognise this man?'

He switched on the enlarger, and a man's face was projected, in negative, on the baseboard underneath.

Katherine drew in a sharp breath. 'It's Richard.'

Mark smiled. 'I thought you'd like to come and watch me make the first print.'

'You thought right.' A broad grin spread across her face.

'OK, well the paper is light-sensitive, so I have to put a red filter over the image while I set it up.' He pushed a slider under the enlarger and Richard's negative face turned an eerie black and red. Mark took a sheet of paper out of what looked like a black binliner in a cardboard box, and put it down on the baseboard. When he'd got it lined up with the red projected image and checked the focus he switched the enlarger off. Richard's face vanished.

'Why is it OK to use a red light, if the paper is light-sensitive?'

'It's only sensitive to blue and green light. Not to red. Though red light would fog the paper too if it was very bright, but it's safe to work with at low levels.' He pushed the paper down on some blu-tac to keep it flat. 'Mind you, all this only applies to black and white photography. If you want to do colour you have to do it in complete darkness, because the paper is sensitive to all types of light.'

He pressed a button on a small control panel and the enlarger lit up for a few seconds and then flicked off again.

'I cheated a bit,' he said. 'I have a gadget to work out the exposure. We'd have been here ages otherwise trying to get it right. Anyway. Now we get to the exciting bit.'

He looked at his watch, and then deftly shoved the sheet of paper into one of the trays of chemical. Katherine leaned over for a closer look.

'You're not supposed to put your hands in this stuff,' said Mark, putting his hands into it. 'But I always do.'

He rocked the tray backwards and forwards a few times to slosh the chemical over the surface of the paper. The sheet was still blank, and shone scarlet under the red light. Mark kept rocking it patiently, keeping the liquid moving. A faint shadow flushed across the surface of the paper, so faint that she thought at first it was just her eyes going funny in the low light. But it gradually intensified to a nebulous grey, and slowly, as if from nowhere, the

170

shadows of a human face emerged. She watched, transfixed, as the image deepened and sharpened and became the face of Richard Munro, gazing benevolently at her from the bottom of the tray of chemical.

'Magic, isn't it?' said Mark. 'It doesn't matter how many years you've been doing it, you never get bored of watching the image come through in the developer. I've got a digital camera which doesn't need all this palaver, but I love doing it the old-fashioned way.'

'Brilliant. I love how it looked like a blank sheet of paper until you put it in there.'

'It's called a latent image before it's developed. Funny thing to get your head round, actually. The paper had Richard Munro's face on it before it went into the chemical, but it was outside our range of perception, only visible on a molecular level. It was there all the time, and we saw nothing.'

Katherine stared into the tray in awe. The paper now had a fully developed portrait of Richard, very similar to the picture of Hugh. He was in his military uniform, gazing straight into the camera, and the quality was beautiful. It was by far the best picture she had seen of him so far.

'That's about two minutes now,' said Mark, dipping his fingers into the chemical again. He pulled the sheet out and held it up by one corner to let it drip.

'I know it looks finished, but if we put the light on now it would be ruined, it would just turn black.' He dropped the sheet into the next tray and sloshed it about. 'This is a stop bath, which is like an antidote to the developer. It stops it from developing any further, because it might make it look a bit manky if it overdevelops. Then it goes in the fixer for four minutes.'

'You do all your own photography like this?'

'God, no. Only special things, it's a right old rigmarole. Imagine doing all your holiday snaps one at a time like this? No thanks. I only use this set-up for black and white arty prints.'

She leaned over the tray of fixer, unable to take her eyes off the photograph.

'I'll put the light on,' said Mark. 'It should be safe now.'

The fluorescent tube flicked a few times and came on. Katherine was momentarily dazzled, but under the bright light the photograph stood out in all its detail. The quality really was astonishing.

Mark took it out of the tray and held it up to drain. 'I quite like the fixer chemical,' he said. 'It smells of salt and vinegar crisps.'

'That's not quite how I would describe it,' said Katherine.

She watched while he put the photo in the sink and blasted it with water from both taps.

'Now the boring bit. You have to wash it and wash it for ages, to get all the chemicals out of it.'

He let the water run over it for a couple of minutes, then picked it up and slapped it against the wall, where it stuck with a wet splat on the ceramic tiles. Then he switched on a hairdryer and began to blast warm air over it.

'Sorry this isn't very hi-tech,' he said, 'but at least it'll be dry enough for you to take home.'

'Ooh, can I really have it?' exclaimed Katherine.

'Yeah. Why do you think I brought you over here to see all this?' He grinned. 'It's for you.'

'Positive I.D. on Langford House,' shouted Joe gleefully, and brought the car to an abrupt halt with two wheels up the pavement. The car behind had to brake sharply, and as it cruised past the passenger gave him a filthy look through the window.

Katherine looked at the photocopied picture of Hugh on his horse, with the white house in the background.

'Yep, I'll second that.'

'So, it's now a pub and family restaurant. And the A40 is swarming with cars. But at least it's still here.'

He waited for a gap in the traffic and then drove into the car park entrance between two Victorian brick walls. The pub was even called the Langford, so it was unmistakably the right place.

'I suppose this car park used to be part of Hugh's garden,' said Katherine.

'Oh yes. Until quite recently, actually. I told you I recognised this place. It used to be a convent school years ago, when I was a kid. I used to ride past it on my bike every day on the way to school. Then it was derelict for a long time. About ten years ago a pub chain bought it and did it up. I expect they've ruined it to some extent, but at least it's safe from the bulldozers.'

'It must have been fantastic to live here when it was a private house,' she said. 'It's absolutely beautiful. Much bigger than it looks in the picture.'

'And bloody draughty in the winter, I don't doubt.'

They wandered round to the front, which had hardly been tampered with in the pub conversion and still had its pilasters and small portico. All along the front were Regency sash windows, with one tiny round window stuck incongruously at one end. The redwood tree in the photograph had thrust itself into a massive column which eclipsed the front of the house, and three beeches flanked the semi-circular driveway. The drive had been tarmacked, but was still unmistakably the same one that Hugh's horse stood on in the photograph.

'I think Hugh would still recognise it, don't you?' said Katherine, stooping to pick up a cone from the patch of earth under the redwood tree. It smelled pleasantly medicinal. 'There was a bit more of a garden here in his time, but they haven't messed with the actual house.'

'They can't, can they? It must be a listed building, surely.'

The main entrance to the pub was round at the back, and the sight which greeted them there was not so encouraging. The house had obviously been built with extensive gardens, but they had now been landscaped in a very clinical way which owed more to a JCB than to the loving hands of a gardener. Whatever beauteous things may have grown there in the past, the bulk of the garden had been flattened and tarmacked to accommodate a large overflow car park, which was almost empty. A token effort had been made to make it blend in by adding a few shrubs and a weed-suppressing woodchip mulch, but the bottom end of the garden was fenced off and now sported a bungalow. Between the car park and the back of Langford House was a lawn, with a steep artificial bank rising up to the patio area, possibly the remains of a ha-ha or simply the residue of machine-landscaping. The patio was laid with modern concrete slabs, and set with outdoor pub tables, and a new conservatory had been built on which made a gesture towards blending in with the rest of the house but didn't quite pull it off. The only original features left in the garden were the high brick wall and one or two more senior trees.

Katherine looked through the doors into the house itself.

'I don't think I'm going to like this,' she said.

The interior of the house had been completely ripped out. Plastered beams ran across the ceiling where walls had been taken down to make it into one giant lounge area. Any Regency features which had been there had been replaced, ironically, with mock-Victorian wood panels and stained glass. It was tasteful in a generic kind of way, but it did look exactly the same as all the other pub-restaurants Katherine had been to. It had the same mirror-backed bar, the same deep-pile red carpet, the same slot machine with flashing coloured lights making a moronic electronic burbling. She noticed, glancing at a menu on the wall, that it served the same over-priced plasticky scampi and chips as well.

'I don't think I can face staying in here,' she shouted over the noise of the juke-box.

'Me neither,' Joe shouted back. 'If you want to go back outside I'll get the drinks and bring them out to you.'

'Good idea.'

She wandered outside and settled down on one of the outdoor benches, and presently Joe came out with two half pints of Guinness. It was really far too cold for sitting outside, but at least that meant they had the place to themselves. Katherine gazed out thoughtfully over the ex-garden.

'I'm trying to imagine what it must have looked like,' she said, 'but it's hard to visualise it.'

Joe took a swig of his drink and grimaced. 'Horrible Guinness. Tastes of cleaning fluid.' He ran his tongue round the inside of his mouth distastefully. 'And bloody expensive, too.'

'When do you think the Crooke family moved out?'

'I don't know. Before my time, probably. The nuns were certainly here by the early sixties. It was a girls' school, to go with the Catholic boys' school up the road.'

'Wait a minute.' Katherine stood up, and peered towards the path that led from the car park.

'What is it?'

'That wall over there.' She pointed to a low brick wall, curved with a limestone coping along the top, which they had walked past on their way round from the front. 'It looks very like the one Richard was sitting on in that picture in the record office.'

Joe turned round and looked. 'Mm, it does a bit.'

She flicked through the folder of photocopies which she had brought with her, and found the picture in question.

'Come on, it's got my curiosity stirred up now.'

They grabbed their drinks and walked over to where the old wall was joined to the main part of the house, in front of a small patch of lawn.

'It bloody well is, too.' Katherine had to stand in a rose bed to find the exact spot, but it was almost certainly the same wall as in the photograph, minus the ivy.

'Well I'll be jiggered. You're right.' Joe went over to the wall and ran his hand over the crumbling Cotswold stone blocks along the top. 'It hasn't changed much.'

Katherine extricated herself from the rose bush, coming away with several thorns in her jeans and coat. 'We'll have to come back here with a camera, and you can take a picture of me sitting on that wall.'

'If you like. Perhaps by then we might have found out what actually happened to Hugh Crooke.'

Chapter Twenty-One

⁓

11th July 1916

We deserted the shattered town yesterday and marched up to the support trenches near a village called Fricourt. Before we left, Tate and I paid a final visit to the *basilique* where the rooks were circling in a rain-grizzled sky and flapping through the torn brickwork to perch in the remains of the tower. They looked like so many miniature aircraft, gliding on black outstretched wings, diving around and above the golden virgin and screeching with a noise like cynical laughter, as though mocking the stupidity of those below who were fighting and dying in the mud.

'I was thinking,' said Tate, 'about your little encounter with Rudyard Kipling's son at Loos.' It was something I had told him about on one of the long winter evenings in the dug-out.

'What about it?'

'Did you know the old man is frantically trying to track him down? He was listed wounded and missing and they're trying to find out what happened. Even sent a fucking aeroplane over the German lines to do a leaflet drop, asking for information. That pissed chap in the hotel told me about it. He said Kipling has actually got Queen Mary to intercede on his behalf with the American Embassy in Berlin, to find out if darling boy is a prisoner in Germany. Bloody incredible, isn't it?'

'Bloody selfish,' I said. 'There's time for that sort of carry-on after the war has finished.'

Tate looked at me. 'You're not going to do anything about it, then? Put Mr K. out of his misery?'

'Not while there are thousands of other boys dying out here, whose fathers can't afford private aircraft and leaflets.'

His eyes narrowed with a mischievous delight.

'You cynical bastard!' he said gleefully. 'You've been spending too much time under my bad influence.'

We took a short-cut back through the rubble. One of the streets has been so badly bombed it is no longer necessary to walk along the pavement to turn the corner; you can cut straight across the flat heap of masonry that was once a row of houses and their long gardens. I walked through the parlour of a house whose walls were now no more than three feet high, and was about to step over the wall into what looked like a kitchen when I had a nasty shock.

Stretched out on a bed of rubble in front of me was the body of a young boy, recently killed. It was not entirely clear how he had died, because there was no wound, no blood. I have seen enough human wreckage over the past year that I am pretty well desensitised to all but the most grisly remnants, but two things about this corpse made it peculiarly disturbing.

To start with, I thought it was Hugh. My cousin has a distinctive face, rounded and friendly, and this boy looked exactly like him. The eyes were wide open: dark, dark, glazed eyes. In this he shared Hugh's most distinctive feature – common among the French but rare in an Englishman – of brown eyes so deep in colour that they appear almost black. He also had the same near-black hair, the same arched eyebrows. The resemblance was striking. The other disturbing factor was the expression on his face. He was smiling. Although his eyes were blank and sightless, his mouth was curved into an expression of joy, and had frozen there in *rigor mortis*. Men here die in grotesque, distorted positions, limbs folded, shoulders creased, the horror of their mode of death ingrained on their faces. But this was the most graceful corpse I'd ever seen. He lay flat on his back, smiling joyfully into the sky as if he were expecting at any moment to be assumed into heaven.

My legs almost gave way under me. I really believed at first that it must be Hugh, because I know he is now somewhere in France, and with the recent concentration of British troops in the Somme area it was possible that he was not far away from here. But then I saw that the boy wore the uniform of a lance corporal, not a second lieutenant. It wasn't Hugh, it couldn't be, but I found it profoundly shocking.

I heard Tate come up behind me.

'I say, old man, are you all right?'

I must have been very pale because he took one look at me, one look at the dead boy, and then reached forward and grabbed my arms. He caught me just as I started to go down, and held me up with his elbows under my arms. I lurched against him in a frenzy of panic.

'Get me away!' I screamed at him, and pummelled at his chest with my fists. I wanted to scrabble forward but my legs wouldn't take my weight, and thrashed uselessly on the surface of the rubble.

'All right, all right,' he shouted, dragging me with some difficulty over a pile of bricks while I clawed frantically at him, desperate to get away from that smiling dead face. Finally he pulled me into a small dip in the ground and held onto me while I gasped and retched. It was the first time I had lost control of myself since I arrived in France, and I would have died of shame if anyone else had witnessed it, but Tate seemed to take it in his stride.

'There now, it was only a stiff.' His voice was soft, as if he were comforting a child.

'I thought it was Hugh,' I said hoarsely. My heart was thudding at a frightening rate and I felt weak and sick, but the moment of panic was over.

'It wasn't him, though?'

'No,' I said. 'Sorry if I've behaved like an idiot.'

'Not at all,' he said brightly. 'It happens to the worst of us too, you know.'

Two hours later we were marching towards the battle front, the column of men stretching out in front of us and behind us in large numbers. All that was visible of most of them was the ubiquitous tin helmet, which has become such an indispensable part of the British uniform that we can't imagine being without it. It seems odd now to think that only last year we were going into battle with nothing more than our cloth caps to protect us.

The contrast between this area and the Loos sector is striking. Gone are the coal heaps and industrial towers. This is a region of gently undulating farmland, but it bears hideous scars of war. The main thrust of the fighting has moved on from the area which we now occupy, which lies about half way between the villages of Fricourt and Mametz. It has left behind it a wide, sterile swath of desolation. Our map shows Fricourt as a little cluster of farms and cottages and a sprinkling of woodlands. The reality is a little cluster of tumbled piles of brick and a sprinkling of fire-blasted tree-stumps. Mametz, on the other hand, has virtually been blown off the map, with barely a blasted tree-stump to show for itself. Part of its church is still recognisable, having one sad, shell-pocked tower wall still standing, but it is difficult to imagine the heaps of debris and stinging-nettles ever being a site of human habitation. Both villages were in German hands until a few days ago, and I'm afraid to say the worst of the damage has been wrought by our own guns, which bombarded the area with great ferocity prior to the British advance. The mud here is unbelievable. Although it is summer, and the nights are warm, a long spell of very heavy rain has left some of the trenches almost impassable. We are wading around in the shlop and the shluck wherever we go, and men clump along with ludicrously oversized feet where an accumulation of mud has stuck to their boots. It is dashed slippery too, which makes for a generally unpleasant place to live and work.

Now that the fighting line has squelched by into the next village, our given task is to shovel up the dead, and bury them.

28th August 1916
Today I met Hugh, in an old trench behind the lines.

He came with a refined, striding gait, sploshing gracefully through the puddles as if he were traversing the lawn at Cheltenham races. It was by this familiar stride that I recognised him, in the first instance, not by his face. In the many long months since I saw him last, an air of maturity has set into his features and he looked rather older than his nineteen years. He is now quite handsome, and has a deeply tanned complexion from many months under the Egyptian sun; I could see why he had found it easy to pass himself off as a native. It was a tremendous relief to see him, because my mind has never stopped dwelling on the possibility that my finding the corpse in the ruins of Albert might be an omen, and every now and then the feeling wells up as a cold dread of losing him. As soon as he saw me his face broke into the familiar lop-sided smile.

'You don't know any spells for invoking the sun god, do you?' he asked. 'It's damned cold over here.'

'Cold? This is the height of summer.'

'Well it feels cold to me.'

He had brought two small dixie cans with him, and a flask of wine. We sat on a couple of upturned ammunition crates and watched the sun slowly making its way overhead from the direction of the German trenches.

'If I'd known you were only two miles up the road I'd have arranged to meet earlier,' I said.

He shook his head. 'We've been all over the place. And so busy I would probably never have managed to get away.'

He poured some wine into a can and handed it to me.

'Cheers,' I said.

We clinked cans. I don't know where he got the wine from but it was surprisingly good. Very different from the stuff which one normally buys from the French civilians, the flavour of which varies on a scale from dilute pond-water to fermented battery acid. In some ways I was shocked at how quickly Hugh had grown up: this was a man who was now sitting opposite me, not the adolescent I last saw. On the other hand he still had a round, innocent face, a child-like charm, and a habit of fidgeting with the strap on his Sam Browne belt, which had caused the leather to curl at the end. However mature he might have become it's not been very many years since he was playing at Red Indians in Pittville Park and crying his eyes out when he fell off his pony.

He was scrutinising me, too, probably thinking very similar thoughts. After all, war makes us all into old men.

'You look as though you're surviving all right, Richard.' He prodded me in the stomach. 'Have you put on weight?'

'Out here? You must be joking.'

'Oh well. Must be my imagination.' He looked at my stomach again with a sly smirk.

'So what have they got you doing out here?' I asked.

'Building gun emplacements,' he said. 'Or should I say digging holes in the ground and dropping big bits of machinery in them. Very dull.'

'Field artillery?'

'No. Toc-emmas.'

He was referring to trench-mortars.

'Does that mean you're up in the front line trenches?'

He caught the note of anxiety in my voice and looked at me with a twinkle of amusement. 'Somebody's got to do it,' he said.

I suddenly had a mental picture of him during one of our many food fights at school, fearless and carefree, bunging sprouts and bread rolls across the oak-panelled dining hall with the same ebullient, boyish smile on his face that he had now.

'Would you like to see something interesting?' he asked.

'Yes, if you like.'

His face fell slightly. 'Actually, you might not think it's interesting. You might find it a frightful bore and wonder why I bothered to mention it.'

I sighed impatiently. 'Well, show me anyway.'

'It's a couple of minutes' walk. Do you mind?'

We took up our wine tins and he led me down a series of trenches until we came to a rather shabby looking straight trench with a high parapet.

'This used to be the front line,' he explained, 'when the French held this sector. And look what they left behind.'

He pointed to a niche in the trench wall with an arched top, like a Gothic window, and a border of dried wild flowers woven together round the edge. The niche contained a dark, hand-made clay statue of a female figure, bulbous and ugly like a prehistoric goddess. A painted sign set into the trench wall said *Notre Dame des Tranchées* – Our Lady of the Trenches.

'Isn't she sweet?' he said, and his face lit up with a beaming smile.

'Sweet, in a manner of speaking,' I replied dubiously. The figure looked very dark and pagan, but I had to admit it had a certain air of sanctity about it. There was a little ledge underneath which had been decorated like an altar, with gaudy candlesticks and a red glass votive jar which had burned out.

'She's made from trench mud,' explained Hugh. 'So she's very fragile.'

He took a stub of candle from his pocket, melted the bottom of it with a cigarette lighter, and stuck it into the votive jar. I noticed that his lighter was home-made, expertly adapted from a brass bullet casing with a copper cap, and polished to a sheen worthy of any jeweller's window.

'Where did you get that?' I asked with a hint of jealousy.

'One of my lance-corporals made it,' he said, handing it to me so that I could have a closer look. 'He was a silversmith in civvy life and likes to keep his hand in. Why, do you like it?'

'Like it? It's beautiful.'

It had a brass sleeve around the outer casing which was cleverly connected to the cap by a series of pins and wires, so that when you slid the sleeve upwards it automatically lifted the cap off, revealing a little brass wheel and a wick ready for lighting; the raised-up sleeve provided a wind-shield around the flame at the same time. The ingenuity was amazing, and it was so beautifully made that the mechanism slipped up and down with perfect smoothness.

'You can keep it,' said Hugh.

'Are you sure?'

'Yes, of course. It's got some petrol-soaked wadding inside which you have to keep topped up or it doesn't work. I find it a bit of a nuisance trying to get hold of petrol for it, to be honest, so if you can be bothered then you're welcome to it.'

I flicked the brass wheel and a small blue flame sprang up from the wick. I used it to light the votive candle and we both stood looking at the crude madonna or goddess or whatever it was.

'I have to say, she doesn't look much like the Mother of God by the usual standards,' I admitted.

'Oh, I don't know,' said Hugh buoyantly. 'She has a certain whatsit about her.'

'I suppose so. But not really in the same league as the golden virgin at Albert, I'm afraid.'

'Nonsense. Golden virgin, black madonna. They're different aspects of the same thing, that's all.'

10th September 1916

After two months in the Somme sector we finally got our slice of the action – almost.

We moved up to a position just beyond a place known as Crucifix Corner. There are many Crucifix Corners on the trench maps, but this one is particularly notorious. The crucifix itself is of fine wrought-iron fretwork, with the forged Christ figure perched high up on its narrow frame. The sun shines with glittering rays through the iron curlicues on the cross head, and the body of Christ is pocked and scarred by gunfire.

Our troops were making another advance across the murderous valley towards High Wood, which the Germans have hung on to with formidable tenacity during these last few weeks. It is no longer a wood in the proper sense, merely a stretch of woody stubble littered with torn off tree trunks, and the only thing that seems to grow there are hedges of barbed wire. But our commanders have decreed that the wood must be taken at all costs. No doubt the German commanders have decreed that it must be held at all costs too.

We were in the support line, allotted the task of following the main assault troops if required. Some jumping-off trenches had been dug during the night in No Man's Land, and these were occupied by the first wave troops. Meanwhile we waited in the front line trenches, ready to consolidate any ground which they were able to capture. Looking through the periscope at the wide, open plain in front of the German fortress, I wondered if the staff officers had any concept of what this place was really like as they swilled their fine brandy and made arbitrary decisions about which blob on the map we should capture next.

I stood at the junction of two trenches, listening to a chap called Sergeant Russell who was spouting off about his own merit and invincibility. The men were only half-listening, tense with a combination of nerves and boredom.

'I'm not worried. I shall come out of the fight without a scratch,' he said confidently, 'because I am actually immune to gunfire.'

He was young for a sergeant, a stocky, red-faced man with pouting lips and pudgy cheeks. An archetypal playground bully, dressed up in khaki.

'Arrogant little shit,' muttered Tate quietly. 'He'd better bloody hope he *is* immune to guns, because he's going to get my revolver up his arse in a minute.'

The heavy guns had been pounding High Wood for many hours, and we took it in turns to watch through the periscope as plumes of smoke rose out from the tree stumps and great gouts of earth shot up into the air. Sometimes human figures were visible in the flying earth, the dead left over from the last push for High Wood, tossed into the air, resettling, and tossing again as if they

183

were taking part in some bizarre circus display. Rumour has it that the only men who came back alive from that push were gibbering and mad. And now it was our turn. When our guns went quiet, we surged forward.

The men in the first wave came out of their trenches in neat rows and began to advance across the scorched grass towards the wood. Our back-up troops made their way forward through the sap lines which stretched out into the valley, but these narrow trenches turned out to be waterlogged. Some of the men tried to run straight through the water, but it was thigh-deep in places and most of them simply fell over in it. The only way to get past the worst parts was to straddle the bottom of the ditch, with one foot on the trench wall on either side. I was gratified to see Sergeant Russell lose his footing and splosh heavily into the slough of soggy despond, his pudgy hands flailing in the air. Not immune to stinking slop, obviously. The muddy conditions made progress slow, as the men in front of me squelched and side-slipped round the edges of the water, clutching at the tufts of couch-grass which grew on the sides of the trench. Somme mud is truly the stuff of legend.

After some distance there was a fork where the trench branched off in two directions. Tate and I and a handful of men went to the right, down the narrower of the two paths. A captain who was coming along behind called out to us.

'Don't advance until you hear the signal.'

The signal never came.

We ended up, Tate and I, in an old jumping-off trench from an earlier battle. Into this mere scrape in the ground the wounded had piled for shelter, and had died there, beyond the reach of any rescuers. The bodies were heaped up in a grotesque stinking pile, one on top of the other. The only way we could occupy the trench would be to crouch down on top of that seething, fly-blown mess.

'I'm damned if I'm going to walk across that lot,' said Tate with genteel revulsion. 'Rather risk a bullet instead.'

We climbed cautiously up the side of the trench and out into the open field. Looking back towards the British line we found we had come a long way forward, but were still some distance from High Wood, mercifully outside the range of machine-gunners. A few shells thundered overhead with a noise like the slamming of metal doors. Luckily for us there was a pair of trees nearby with a patch of stinging-nettles at the bottom, which provided us with some very welcome cover.

And so we watched through our field-glasses as the first wave of troops made their attack on High Wood. They were tiny on the horizon, a band of khaki formed by hundreds of men striding forward shoulder to shoulder. Another similar band rose up behind them, and then a third. A few German shells were dropping onto the plain, surrounding them with a fine mist of smoke, and we could hear the crack of their rifles making tiny smoke-puffs. They must have known that they were going to their deaths, but none of them faltered. Behind us the British guns were conspicuous by their absence; nothing now seemed to be falling on High Wood from our side, and the infantry were carrying out the attack alone.

'Where the fuck is our artillery?' asked Tate incredulously.

'I expect that's the order from top brass,' I said, repeating something I'd heard two other officers discussing. 'The staff officers don't believe the Germans are still holding the wood. They have intelligence which suggests there's nothing more than a few isolated pockets of resistance which the infantry can quickly flush out.'

I trained my field-glasses on the tangle of splintered trees, where nothing seemed to be stirring. The first solid band of khaki was getting closer to the southern tip of the wood, approaching stealthily. Then above the noise of rifle shots we heard the tutting of machine-gun fire, which broke out in a rash along the edge of the wood. Through the waving nettles I saw the right-hand edge of the khaki band begin to fritter away, slowly at first and then in an increasing sweep from right to left. Within half a minute the whole line had dropped down into the grass. The second and third lines kept advancing, undeterred, into the clatter of machine-gun bullets until they too began to fray on the right-hand edge, again dissolving in a tidy pattern from right to left. The machine-guns kept up their angry stutter even when there was nothing left except the smoke rising from the plain.

'Those stupid brass-hat fuckers,' said Tate bitterly. I looked round and saw that there were tears running down his face. 'What the fuck have they done?'

I put my field-glasses aside and lowered my head onto my sleeve.

Presently we were ordered to withdraw. There was no point in our following up the assault troops to consolidate the position. There was nothing to consolidate.

Chapter Twenty-Two

12th October 1916

We are not in a pleasant situation. I am in charge of twelve men in a listening post within forty yards of the German line. In fact, the trench I am occupying is an old German one, hastily adapted to switch its fire-step and sandbags to the opposite side; a narrow communication trench still connects it to a German outpost a few yards away. There is a good-sized tangle of barbed wire separating us from the Germans, but nothing more. On clear nights we can see their sentries quite plainly on the other side of the wire – and of course they can see ours. They know we are here, and they could blow the whole lot of us sky high at any moment. But we could just as easily do the same to them. And so we live uneasily face to face, tolerating each other.

Another thing which is not pleasant is that my second-in-command is that obnoxious man Russell; he who believes he is leading a charmed bullet-proof life. We have little respect for one another. He has a smelly air of self-importance about him, and I get the impression that he thinks he should rightfully be a second lieutenant with me as his sergeant. He is a thick-set young fellow with a wide neck which always seems to be an angry red colour, and pale-coloured hair. Rather like a ferret. Tough and disciplined he may be, but he hasn't a shred of sentiment or imagination. And aside from this, I am currently without the comfort of Tate's company; he is commanding another similar post about a hundred yards further up the line.

I have with me a newly arrived recruit, Private Boulter, not exactly the cream of British stock. He made the mistake of admitting to Sergeant Russell that he was afraid of the guns.

'You should be like me,' blagged Russell, with a rather vulgar and self-satisfied snort. 'I don't get frightened, because I know the bombs and bullets aren't going to hit me.'

Boulter gazed at Russell in absolute wonderment, and from that moment treated him like a demi-god. Russell, for his part, treated the boy like a pile of horse manure.

Boulter is barely eighteen and is mentally and constitutionally unfit for active service. In an ideal world he should never have had to enlist, but the new Military Service Act has forcibly sucked him up into the machine of war to which he is so ill-suited. Physically there is little the matter with him; he is a stocky, apple-cheeked chap with very pale blond hair – much lighter than Tate's – which is the subject of ridicule among the other men because they consider that he looks like a German. Mentally, however, he has too little presence of mind to be of much use, and is deeply and genuinely distressed by the putrescence and ruin all around him. He has only just arrived at the Front, having been plucked from his mother only three months ago and given minimal training, and has not got used to the experience of being under fire. I doubt that he ever will.

Yesterday I noticed that the boy was distressed during breakfast, and the sly glances he was getting from Sergeant Russell made me suspect foul play. Eventually I pressed the truth out of one of the other men. Some bread had been sent up to us that morning, and Russell had given Boulter a butter tin which had been filled with dubbin – grease for rubbing on boots. He spread his breakfast with it and ate it without complaint because he was afraid of offending Russell by making any comment.

I took Russell aside after the evening stand-to and put his back unceremoniously against the trench wall.

'If I catch you playing a prank like that again you'll get five days' field punishment,' I said.

He curled his lip slightly, and flushed an even brighter red. I could tell he was slightly afraid of me, but had so little respect for me that he wouldn't accept my authority, no matter what I threatened him with. He was becoming insolent, and the longer I avoided doing anything about it the more brazen he became.

Subsequently a rather sticky incident occurred, while I was up on top of the parapet late last night listening for signs of activity in the enemy trenches. I was unable to go any further out because the moon was full – although mercifully its brightness was tempered by a veil of cloud. So close were the Germans that I could hear the sound of their low voices and guttural accents, and the occasional chuckle of laughter. I even watched, in the dark, the glow of two lighted cigarette ends flitting about by the barbed wire. A quiet night in the German trenches. I heard a soft shuffle behind me and felt somebody tug at the bottom of my coat. It was Private Adams.

'Sir,' he whispered, and I could see his arm gesturing back towards our trench. I turned round as quickly as I dared – bearing in mind that the slightest noise would provoke a volley of rifle fire – and slithered back into the trench. Boulter was pressed up against the fire-step, half covered with a blanket, and held down by two other men. He was shivering all over, absolutely terrified.

'We can't settle him, sir,' said Adams in a low voice.

I looked around at the faces of the other men, dimly visible in the light of the small trench lantern, and saw the fear in their eyes. Boulter was making little whimpering noises, half way between a howl and a sob, and in such proximity to the enemy he was putting all our lives in danger.

I knelt down in front of him and made a reassuring noise. His eyes looked straight through me, registering nothing. I had never witnessed such blind, all-consuming terror in my life.

'Now look, old man,' I said softly. 'You're perfectly safe here, but you really must stop that noise.'

He showed no sign of having heard or understood.

'Would you like me to have you sent down from the line tomorrow, get you away from here for a while?' It was an insincere offer. Of course there was no way I could get him excused from trench service. Not without a good reason, and fear is not considered to be one.

'Where's my mother?' he whined in a loud voice. The rest of us cringed, expecting at any moment to have a rifle grenade land in our midst from the German trenches.

This was not the first time I have heard young boys – and sometimes even mature men – crying for their mothers. In its own way it is one of the most harrowing of war experiences. I am normally quite sympathetic to those who find themselves in such a state, but there is little room for pity when one is crouched in an outpost in No Man's Land, within earshot of the enemy line.

A Very light went up from the German trenches, filling the sky with a harsh light which whitewashed the moon.

'That's it,' said one of the men in cold panic. 'The Jerries have heard him.'

'I want to go home,' the boy wailed, and made a frantic lunge forward to get on his feet, almost knocking me over. Sergeant Russell caught him by the lapels as he got up and belted him hard across the face. The boy swayed like a drunkard and sat down with a heavy thud on the firestep. Then he slowly pulled the blanket up around himself, like a snail retracting into its shell. We all held our breath waiting for the reaction, but he didn't make another sound.

Neither did the Germans fire on us.

With the Very light over the trench almost as bright as daylight I could not avoid seeing the look of smug contempt on Russell's face. He was breathing heavily, excited by his own violence. I could see what he was thinking: that I had been too soft and sentimental to handle the situation. That I had put the lives of my men at risk by trying to soft-talk the boy when I should have dealt with him sharply.

The awful thing is, he was right.

14th October 1916
Things came to a head today. Inevitably. And I have had to prove my mettle in a way I would not have thought myself capable.

It might be expected that somebody would notify us if any localised attack were to take place in our immediate vicinity, but no, somehow the message did not get through.

Therefore I was greatly surprised this morning, as I lay curled up in my cubby-hole in the wall of the trench, trying to breath through my mouth to evade the smell, to be woken by a great noise of gunfire some distance over to our right. It was far enough away that I could only just see what was going on through the periscope. I watched a bombing party swinging their way over No Man's Land with their Mills bombs and their light machine-guns. They met with little direct resistance from the German trenches, but the artillery responded by pounding the British front line just behind us. Shells screamed by quite close to us, which was utterly terrifying; but they were ranged on the front line trenches, not on our little outpost in No Man's Land. All of them skimmed over our heads with a whining noise like a frenetic tom-cat.

Then there was another, more alarming scream. It rose in pitch like a kettle steaming on the hob, and then broke into a series of rhythmic wails which were an absolute torment to listen to. I stepped back from the periscope and was almost knocked over by Boulter, who was running down the trench in a frenzy of panic. He reached the far end, and for a horrible moment I thought he was going to scale the trench wall and run out into No Man's Land. But he hovered in fear and desperation like a cornered animal before turning and running back past me down to the other end of the trench. The other men recoiled from him nervously as he went past, as if he were possessed by some demonic spirit.

In some ways the situation was not quite as bad as the previous night. In daylight, and with shells flying overhead, there was not so great a risk of the Germans hearing him and firing on us. But there was a new danger this time: panic is contagious. All men, however brave and experienced, get the wind up when they're under bombardment. If one of them loses control and goes beserk, it is seldom very long before the others lose it too.

I could see the panic beginning to rise in the faces all around me. The boy's cries had something unworldly about them that was utterly unnerving, like a scream from a nightmare.

As he ran back down to my end of the trench I grabbed him and pressed his face into the shoulder of my coat, hard, stifling that dreadful noise into silence. He didn't struggle. I held him as tightly as I could until the screams subsided into great gulping sobs. He was shaking, the spasms of panic running right through him. I saw his hand come up and try to grasp my lapel, but he was shaking so much that the cloth kept slipping through his fingers. I just kept hold of him, and God knows how long I sat there. The other men just looked down at the ground.

I'd got it into my head that if I comforted him for a while he might calm down, he might get a grip on himself and stop having these panic attacks. But while I sat there with my face pressed against the top of his head I knew without a doubt that he was as good as dead, and it was beyond any powers I had to save him.

He was guilty of the worst crime any soldier can commit. He had shown cowardice in the face of the enemy. It didn't matter that he was a farmboy barely intelligent enough to understand what was happening around him, and had never been away from home before. It didn't matter that his inability to face up to the horror of trench warfare was genuine. He was guilty. And now he'd done it twice.

I tried to be compassionate the first time, but I couldn't now. I looked at Sergeant Russell, who was sitting with his back to me sucking nervously on an unlit cigarette, and I knew exactly what he was thinking. The realisation spread through me with a chilling, sick feeling in my stomach, that if I succeeded in calming the boy down, in saving him from these immediate horrors, he would simply be led off to court martial and shot by his own compatriots.

And he wasn't calming down. The moment I started to loosen my grip on him he began to shudder more violently, and let out a gasping cough. He was choking on his own screams. I pulled him closer to me and began to stroke his hair. Through my own jaw I felt the hollow vibrations of his teeth chattering, echoing through his skull and mine. Still he wouldn't settle down. It was unbearable. He clung to me in absolute desperation, as if he were afraid that he would fall off the face of the earth if I let go of him. I stroked his head and felt the warm dampness where my tears had run into his hair.

He made a sudden convulsive twist of panic and I only just managed to stop him slipping out of my grasp. I kept hold of his head and pushed his face hard into my coat to stop him screaming. My right hand was on his chest. I could feel his heartbeat, which was thumping hard and fast, even above the constant shivering. I noticed that my own hand was shivering too. His heartbeat seemed to vibrate right through him, through both of us, pulsing up my arm. Too intense. I put my hand through the gap between his tunic buttons and ran my fingertips across the rough fabric of his shirt, feeling for the spot where the heartbeat was strongest. He began to sob, and his body jerked with the most awful convulsions; I just kept still, reading his heart with my fingers. I will never know whether or not he heard the sound of me cocking my revolver, but he certainly put up no resistance when I gently guided the barrel to the spot my fingers had found. I took three deep breaths to steady my hand and then shot him. The recoil slammed me back against the wall of the trench and I felt his blood spray across my face, stinging my eyes. Strangely, we both stopped shivering.

The next thing I recall was Adams crouching beside me with a mug of tea. Some dark clouds overhead had thrown the trench into shadow, and he had to put his face quite close to mine before I noticed him.

'You can let go now, sir, if you want,' he said.

I saw that I was still holding on to the boy. My right hand still gripped the revolver; both were bloodied. Adams saw the confused look on my face, put down the mug of tea and pulled the boy's body off me. I looked at the shoulder of my trench coat where his head had rested and saw that it was stained with snot, dribble and blood. Not much compared to the blood which had seeped into the lower part of the coat, but somehow far more distressing.

'Do you want me to get him buried, sir?' asked Adams.

I nodded, and we both looked down at the boy, whose blond hair was slowly soaking into the mud.

He did at least have the grace to die with his eyes shut, so I didn't have to look at them.

15th October 1916

I was still awake at 2 o'clock in the morning when a Very light flared up and I noticed that the sentry on duty was getting jittery. He looked towards my cubby-hole several times, obviously weighing up whether he should come and wake me or not. To put him out of his dilemma I got up and went over to see if everything was all right. He was monitoring the area of No Man's Land over to our right through the periscope. It was almost as bright as daylight out there, with the flare blazing above us.

'Over there, sir, straight ahead. Something that looks like a wooden post. Only there weren't no wooden post there an hour ago.'

I looked into the eyepiece and saw what he meant. Only someone who was familiar with the lie of the land would have noticed it, but there was a tall upright strut of some sort in the middle of the quagmire which hadn't been there before.

'Should I fire at it, sir?'

I thought about it for a moment, then shook my head.

'Not worth upsetting the Germans just for that. Better keep an eye on it though, see if it moves.'

It is not uncommon, when a flare goes up at night, for a sentry to spot a human disguised as a post. This often occurs when somebody in a wiring party or a trench raid is walking across No Man's Land in the dark, and is caught in the sudden flare of a Very light. To throw himself into a shell-hole would bring certain death, as the snipers on both sides would spot the movement. But by standing bolt upright and absolutely still, he has a sporting chance of blending in with the landscape.

We stood on guard as the light faded out and waited for the next one to flare up, as it was one of those nights when the flares were bursting regularly left right and centre like a firework display in slow motion. It was about three minutes later that the next one lit up.

The sentry peered into the viewfinder and then turned to me with a look of alarm.

'It's a man, sir. Shall I shoot?'

I looked through the periscope at the 'post', which had moved towards us by a good few yards and was now clearly recognisable as a human-shaped object. My heart lurched in alarm, but then I realised – or at least was fairly sure – that the uniform on the figure was khaki, not grey.

'British patrol,' I whispered to the sentry, and motioned him to draw his rifle back from the firing slot. 'Probably a wirer. Don't shoot at him. Just be vigilant, that's all.'

It stayed dark for the next five minutes or so. Then there was a soft shuffling noise close to our trench, and a faint splosh. Somebody was coming straight towards us, and in the absence of any flares we couldn't see a thing. I heard a loud sucking noise, as of a foot being retracted from a particularly viscous patch of mud, and a whispered voice muttered 'Fuck.'

The sentry had his rifle back in the slot in a flash, and challenged the visitor as loudly as he dared.

'Halt! Who goes there?'

There was a brief but electrifying pause.

'Don't be ridiculous,' came the reply. 'I'm a friend. *Anglais.*'

I thought perhaps I was hallucinating, but a moment later Tate's head appeared above the top of the trench, startling us both.

'Munro, old man. There you are. I was afraid I might have come to the wrong trench.' He slithered down the wall onto the firestep, and I could smell something alcoholic on his breath.

I was not impressed.

'You bloody idiot! You nearly had your backside shot off.'

'Oh, don't be like that,' he said in an ingratiating tone. 'I thought you'd be pleased to see me.'

'What are you doing here?'

'I was on a fact-finding mission over in the Jerry trench. Thought I'd drop by and see you on the way back. I can always pretend I got lost.'

He wasn't drunk, although he had obviously taken a sup of something. It was just as though he didn't care about the danger he had put himself in.

We settled down on the firestep, and the relieved sentry resumed his vigil. Tate showed me a German trench map, hand drawn, which marked the position of their front line in our immediate vicinity and the names of the battalions which held it. A very precious resource for our intelligence officers.

'Now you know who your neighbours are,' he said proudly. 'A Fritz officer gave me this. After a little persuasion.'

A shadow suddenly appeared at the other end of the trench. Sergeant Russell, doing his rounds. Checking that the sentries were still awake.

He was naturally rather taken aback to find another officer present in the trench, especially as he had been sitting in the one and only pathway leading from the British lines and had not seen anyone come past. I saw him squinting through the semi-darkness at the number of pips on Tate's sleeve, and seeing that he was a lieutenant, i.e. one rank higher than me, saluted ostentatiously.

'Sir.'

This display of shallow military etiquette was about the worst thing he could have done in front of Tate, who remembered him from the previous occasion.

'You're young for a sergeant,' said Tate cheerily, mentally taking the measure of his prey. 'Decent soldier, are you?'

195

'Oh yes sir. I like to think so, sir.' Russell's head was rigid, his hands stiffly at his sides, standing to attention.

'All balls and no personality, that's the spirit, eh old chap?'

Russell's eyes bulged in astonishment, but he didn't waver from his parade-ground poise. Besides, Tate's voice was reassuringly friendly.

'Sir, yes sir,' said Russell.

'That's what I like to see in a young soldier,' Tate said approvingly. 'A stiff-arsed salute and a face like a constipated bull trying to have a shit. Don't you agree, sergeant?'

'Sir, yes sir,' said Russell, a worried look starting to twitch at his face.

'Yes, I can see you're one of those little ticks who thinks military discipline is a badge of worth. You'd hand over your mother to the Germans if you were told to by somebody with two fucking pips, wouldn't you old chap?'

'I like to think I have an independent mind, sir,' said Russell with a note of polite desperation.

'Independent mind? Seems to me it's so fucking independent it's upped and left you.' He didn't give Russell a chance to respond. 'I expect you'd prefer it if officers wore their badge of rank on their arses, wouldn't you, so you'd know how hard to lick without having to look at their fucking sleeves? You're a disgrace to your fucking country, do you know that? A disgrace. Now fuck off, before I put you on a charge for insubordination to an officer.'

'Yes sir.' Russell saluted with clean precision, turned on his heel and strode very swiftly away down the trench.

I looked at Tate and Tate looked at me.

'I enjoyed that,' he said.

Chapter Twenty-Three

Captain G. Stockwell
67th Field Company
Royal Engineers

Beaumont-Hamel
14th December 1916

Dear Mr Munro,

I am replying to your request for information about the events of 10th December, as detailed in your letter. I shall endeavour to supply you with as much detail as I can, and hope that it will be of some help to you.

On the morning of the 10th I visited an artillery position behind the lines, accompanied by Lieutenant Philip Greenroyd, Second-Lieutenant Hugh Crooke, and ten other ranks. We had been sent for by the officer commanding the battery, to make some repairs to their 'super-heavy' – a 12 inch howitzer mounted on rails. I presume you know the general nature of these weapons: they are fixed onto specially adapted railway carriages, and set upon a length of portable rail track. The carriage is stabilised by dampers on either side, and the rails allow the howitzer to move backwards some considerable distance during the recoil from firing. This particular gun had shaken its mountings loose, and the stabilisers, which are held together with metal rivets, were no longer in a fit state to prevent the gun from throwing itself off the rails. Hugh personally oversaw the engineers who attended to the mountings, while Greenroyd and myself carried out a check on the other guns. When the work was complete the gun was tested successfully, and we returned to our base near Beaumont-Hamel at around five-thirty in the afternoon.

The village of Beaumont-Hamel is, as I am sure you can appreciate, in rather a sorry state after the recent fighting, and has only been in British hands for two weeks. Most of the facilities here are recycled from whatever the Germans left behind, and our camp is no exception. Officers of the Royal Engineers have the use of three low wooden huts, draughty but secure, which had been constructed as officers' accommodation by the Germans. When the line of battle advanced beyond Beaumont-Hamel in late November, the area became somewhat less 'hot', and our officers have been living a comparatively comfortable life during these few weeks – at least relatively safe from enemy action.

Hugh took dinner in the officers' mess at around eight o'clock. I remember this distinctly, because he gave me a fair copy of a humorous poem which he said he had composed last month when we were having some disturbance from the enemy's long-range artillery. I still have the copy and it runs as follows:

> I hate all Huns, yet most I hate that surly-livered blighter
> Who with persistence breaks my sleep with his ten-times-
> a-nighter;
> When fast asleep, and in the arms of Morpheus or some
> other,
> The rotter looses off and then — oh damn it, there's another.

He was pleased with the ditty and was in the process of making more copies of it to send out to his family and friends. I suggested to him that he ought to collect together some more of his work and submit it somewhere for publication, but he jovially dismissed the idea on the grounds that 'Father would never speak to me again'. At around eight-thirty, or just after, he returned to his billet in the officers' quarters to rest.

Let me reiterate that Hugh cannot have had any awareness of the shell which killed him. He probably did not even hear its approach. I was still in the mess hut when it fell, and was caught completely off my guard when the windows blew out. I received nothing more than a few cuts to my hands, and immediately rushed outside to see what had happened. It was, of course, dark by then, but there was a bright full moon overhead. There was a fresh shell crater in the grass only a few yards from one of the timber huts. The damage to the hut was slight; it had part of its end wall smashed in, nothing more. Unfortunately, however, this wall was directly next to the bed in which Hugh was resting. I could see very little from the outside because of the smoke, so I rushed in to check that everybody was all right. I found three or four officers crouched behind a cupboard, some with minor injuries. At the far end of the hut I saw Hugh lying face down on the floor with his bed overturned on top of him, and the blankets strewn around. I saw that he had been hit by a shell splinter, as there was a large exit wound in his back. I turned him over and wrapped him up in a blanket to try to keep him warm, but he was already dead. He looked very peaceful. A chaplain from the RAMC came in and made a brief effort to revive him, but there was nothing which could be done. The chaplain agreed that he could not have suffered any pain, as he was killed instantaneously.

I hope these few details of his last moments will be of some comfort to you in your loss, which I fully understand, having lost my own brother last year in the Dardanelles. It is customary in letters such as this to praise the deceased in glowing terms, but as a fellow officer I would not insult your intelligence by saying such things if they were not so. I can truthfully report that Hugh was a most gallant boy, always keen, and undoubtedly one of our best subalterns. He was dearly loved by his men for his chirpy demeanour and his irrepressible sense of fun. One of my most enduring memories of him is a spontaneous impersonation of Harry Lauder with which he entertained us during a spell in the trenches, complete with silly costume made from a couple of empty sandbags. One of the men laughed so much that we feared he had stopped breathing.

With regard to your question about the source of the fatal shell, I am unable to give a conclusive answer. I would call it a 'stray' shell in that we are some distance behind the lines and currently receive very little enemy attention. Whether it was a British shell or not is open to conjecture. I have heard several witnesses state that it came from one of our own guns, and certainly the position of the impact – facing away from the enemy lines – would seem to suggest that this is the case, but I cannot confirm it one way or the other.

I am returning a few small items which were found among Hugh's personal possessions, including your own letters to him, which he had carefully preserved. The rest of his effects have been forwarded to the War Office in the usual way.

Please accept my deepest sympathy at this distressing turn of events. I can only hope that you will take comfort in the knowledge that, however tragic the circumstances, Hugh died with a smile on his face.

Yours sincerely

George Stockwell (Capn.)

Chapter Twenty-Four

Katherine dumped her bags down beside one of the scuffed metal benches, and removed a crumpled french fries carton – which somebody had evidently sat on – from the seat. The seat was spectacularly cold, and she felt its perforated surface pressing a dappled imprint into her backside. She turned to Mark, who had decided against sitting down at all, even though he was standing beside an empty seat.

'I hate Victoria coach station,' she said grumpily. 'Actually I hate all coach stations, but this one just about takes the sodding biscuit.'

He nodded sympathetically. 'Do you think they lay on special staff to make the place as dirty and depressing as possible? As a deterrent to people coming in here for a sit down and a fag?'

'If so, I think that kid over there might be on the payroll.' She made a discreet gesture towards a snotty-nosed child which had spilled some bright purple sugary drink all over the floor and was now running up and down trying to slide in it. Its mother sat nearby in spreadeagled indifference, flicking through a magazine.

'It does make you despair for the future of the human race, doesn't it?' said Mark.

'Especially in the light of all this first world war stuff. I mean, is this really what all those men died for? To give our generation the freedom to eat polystyrene hamburgers and get pissed in bus stations?'

'We should have come down with Joe. I'm really jealous of him, spending three days in the Public Record Office. He'll have found lots of interesting things to gloat about.'

Katherine made a dismissive gesture. 'I could never have justified taking the extra time off work. It's bad enough as it is. Anyway, I'm fed up with doing research. I'd just as soon let somebody else get on with it and just tell me the results.'

Mark looked at his watch. Joe was late, but that wasn't altogether surprising when he was trying to manoeuvre a car up Buckingham Palace Road and find somewhere to decant it temporarily while he came to meet them. He leaned his back against a telephone kiosk and watched a tramp sniffing at a piece of sandwich from one of the bins.

Katherine couldn't settle. She disliked waiting for people, and the noisy bus station made her edgy. She crossed and uncrossed her legs a couple of times, trying to gauge the status of her bladder and its prospects for continuing a long journey without recourse to a lavatory.

'I think I'd better nip to the loo again, to be on the safe side,' she decided. 'It's twenty pence to get in, and I think that's all I've got.'

She rummaged in her purse, but it contained only one twenty pence coin and an enormous number of pennies.

'I've got another ten you can have,' said Mark, handing her a coin. 'If it's any more than that I'll have to buy a bar of chocolate to change a ten-pound note.'

'If it's any more than that,' she muttered, 'I shall nick a couple of bog rolls to get my money's worth.'

She managed to get into the toilets, after a brief struggle with the automatic turnstile, and found herself in a vast room full of cubicles, so many that there was a constant chorus of flushing, all cascading together like an indoor waterfall. Ironically, it seemed to be the cleanest part of the bus station. In fact it might have been worth the twenty pence for anyone who did just want a sit down and a fag.

She picked an empty cubicle in a long row of empty cubicles, but almost as soon as she had gone in and locked the door she heard someone go into the one on her immediate left. This made her feel nervous, so she had to wait until they had gone, which took ages. Then she worried that Mark would notice that she had been a long time in the toilet and might think she had something wrong with her, and that in itself made her tense enough to clam up, which wasted even more time. The psychology of public toilet behaviour would surely make a fascinating topic for research, she reflected, gazing idly at the paper holder where somebody had scratched the word 'cunt' into the plastic casing.

When she came out, Joe had arrived. He looked decidedly radiant, which probably meant he had found something fruitful at the record office.

Mark smiled. 'Any joy with the bog roll?' he asked loudly.

She shook her head. 'Rough stuff. Not worth nicking.'

Joe looked concerned. 'What's all this? I leave you to your own devices for three days and you set up a crime partnership?'

'Something like that. Here, Mark, you can have your 10p back. Lavatory admission charges obviously aren't rising in line with inflation.'

'Sorry I'm a few minutes late,' Joe said. 'I left the car down a very busy side street, so I hope it's still in one piece.'

'So do I,' said Katherine. 'Because you've got to get me out of London as quickly as possible. It's doing my head in.'

'Katherine doesn't like London,' Mark said. 'In case you hadn't noticed.'

They retrieved Joe's car and headed out of the city towards the south. It was a fairly leisurely journey once they were clear of the urban bits, and it soon became a straightforward cruise through the Kent countryside on the motorway. Joe had a preference for the channel tunnel, because, he said, he got a childish pleasure from driving his car onto a train.

He refused to talk in any detail about the things he'd found in his researches until they were settled into their digs and he was able to spread out all the relevant bits of paper. Otherwise he would get confused, he insisted. And so it had to wait until after they had found the *gîte* which was to be their base – a weatherboarded house with bare wooden floors and geraniums erupting from every window-sill, and whose garden sloped down to the bank of the Somme canal. It also had to wait until after they had had an incomprehensible conversation with the non-English-speaking landlord about *poubelles*, and found enough utensils to make a cup of metallic-tasting tea and some cheese sandwiches. Then Joe opened his briefcase and began to organise his note cards and print-outs across the long, narrow dining table in the back room.

'I've been everywhere looking for all this,' he said. 'Woolwich Academy, the Royal Engineers Museum, the India Office records in the British Library. A right old goose chase.'

'India Office?'

'Yes. That's why we couldn't find Hugh Crooke's birth certificate. He was born in India, while his dad was serving in the Indian Civil Service. It's all here, a great wad of it.'

'You have been busy.'

'Yes. I went through the list of civil service officers and found one called William Crooke, who was Irish, as it happens, came from Macroom in County Cork. He went out to India in about 1869 and was based in Bengal.'

'Is that what's now Bangladesh?' asked Katherine.

'I think so. Anyway, they didn't have an official register of births and marriages in India at that time, but they kept quite good parish records in the numerous Anglican churches which sprang up over there. I found an entry for William Crooke's marriage to Evelyn Warren in 1884. It looks as though Evelyn was a sister of Richard Munro's mum, which we'd guessed anyway. I couldn't find any children during the early years of the marriage, but I did find a record of Hugh's birth on 3rd April 1897. Either he was an only child or his siblings weren't recorded. The family must have left India shortly afterwards, because we already know they were living in Cheltenham by 1901. After that –' Joe shuffled some papers, '– it ties up with Mark's research, which already told us that Hugh went to Cheltenham College between 1905 and 1914. After that he seems to have moved on to Woolwich Military Academy, and been commissioned into the Royal Engineers the following year. April 1915, according to this.'

'Is there a military record for him?' asked Mark.

'Not a complete one. He was in the 67th Field Company, and they were deployed in Egypt for a time, but I couldn't find out much more than that. Then they went to France in 1916 to help in the build-up to the Battle of the Somme. The battle lasted from July to the end of September, but I don't yet know what part he played in it. And now we've got Katherine's research on the Commonwealth War Graves website, so we know that Hugh was killed on the 10th December 1916 at Beaumont-Hamel and is buried in Hamel Military Cemetery. It's a bit ironic really, surviving the carnage of the Somme and then being killed when everything had calmed down. Trench wastage, they call it. Very unlucky.'

'And that's why his letters to Richard stop at the end of 1916,' said Katherine. 'Poor Richard, it must have been a hell of a blow. It's obvious from the letters that they were really close.'

'Yes. Well this is where it gets really interesting, because I did find a full military record for Richard. Couldn't find out anything much about his early life, but his war service – no problem.'

Katherine leaned over the table, impatient to lap up the details of whatever he had found.

'Here we go, I've got a copy of his attestation papers. Five foot nine, medium build, with brown hair and grey eyes. Enlisted at the recruiting office in Great Western Road, Cheltenham. It's all here.'

'Grey eyes, eh? Yes, I suppose that is how I see him.'

'And we can trace his movements through most of the war. I've had to put together information from several different sources, but it goes something like this. He was commissioned as a 2nd-lieutenant in the 10th Battalion of the Gloucestershire Regiment, which was pretty much made up of Cheltenham men, and during his training he would probably have lived in officers' quarters in Lansdown Crescent.'

'I used to have a flat in Lansdown Crescent,' said Mark.

'Really? I've always wanted to know, is it curved on the inside as well as the outside?'

'No. The inside the walls are straight. I never could get over the way I could push my sofa up against the front wall and not have a gap down the back.'

'According to the regimental records he would have gone out to France in August 1915, just in time for the Battle of Loos, and that's confirmed in his letters as well. The 10th Gloucesters had a really terrible time at Loos and a lot of them were killed. There isn't any specific mention of Richard, but he wrote to Hugh afterwards from a dressing station – which of course he wasn't allowed to name – saying he had been lightly wounded in the head. As far as I can tell he was still in hospital when the battalion made a second deadly assault at Loos, so he was lucky to miss that. I don't know when he was actually discharged, but the 10th Gloucesters held the line at Loos right up until the following July.'

'Presumably it wouldn't have been so nasty there once the battle had finished?' asked Mark.

'No, probably not. The battle lasted till October, and for the next eight months or so it would have been much quieter. Then there was the Battle of the Somme, which started on the 1st July 1916. They weren't in the main attack on the fateful first day, though, because they didn't go down there until 10th July. Apparently they were based in the village of Fricourt, which is just up the road from here, and gradually moved forward through Contalmaison, Bazentin-le-petit and Bazentin-le-grand, and ended up in an attack on High Wood in September 1916, near the village of Martinpuich.'

'Funny name, isn't it?' said Katherine.

'From this point it gets a bit vague. I haven't been able to establish where Richard was based towards the end of 1916, although I guess it must have been somewhere on the Somme. And of course Hugh was also here at the same time, a couple of villages away, and according to the letters they met up at least once. Then Richard seems to have been sent home with neurasthenia at the beginning of 1917, not long after Hugh's death, so there could be a connection there.'

He spread out a photocopy of a Cheltenham street plan from 1917, and two stacks of photographs.

'So now we're back in Cheltenham again. We know that Richard spent several months at a Red Cross hospital called the Priory, which was a big Regency house on London Road, on the corner of Priory Street. Unfortunately it was demolished in 1968 and replaced by a hideous concrete and glass office block.'

'Oh yes,' said Katherine. 'I know the one you mean. It was derelict for most of the 1990s. And then they knocked it down and rebuilt a pseudo-Regency house there. I remember.'

Joe laid out a sepia photograph of the original Priory building, with another picture he had taken himself of the newly rebuilt version. It was quite similar, with the same wide two-storey bow window at the front and tall decorative pilasters. Only similar on the outside though, because the new building was constructed as luxury flats with an underground car park.

'They haven't done a bad job at all,' said Joe, 'but it would have been a lot better if they'd left the bloody thing alone in the first place. There was a localised outbreak of demolition mania on the Borough Council in the late sixties, mainly down to members of the planning department with a personal financial incentive to wreck the town's heritage.'

'Not that we're bloody bitter about it,' fumed Katherine.

'So,' Mark picked up the old photograph and scrutinised it. 'If the Priory was in London Road then it wasn't all that far from Hugh Crooke's house, because that was in London Road as well.'

'Yes. About half a mile further up the hill, so it falls within the neighbouring parish of Charlton Kings. You wouldn't be able to see Langford House from the Priory, but it would only be five or ten minutes' walk.'

He reverently laid out a row of photographs which he'd taken during the last couple of months. Langford House, square and beautiful in its bulldozed garden, restored in two-tone cream and white, with close ups of the voile-curtained windows, the white panelled French doors beside the lawn, and an antique porcelain gadget attached to the front of the roof which had once carried a telegraph wire. He had also taken some pictures of Holy Apostles church, which he had established was Hugh's local church, built on what had originally been part of the garden of Langford House and still its closest neighbour. Its knobbly rusticated Cotswold stone bulk stood at the junction of two main roads and he had carefully photographed all its carved features; the black and gold Victorian clock above the porch, the ornamental lamp post at the front, and, round at the back, a delicate iron gate leading to a green bank rippled with daffodils.

'Unfortunately there isn't much to tell us what happened after Richard went back to the fighting line, because he was dead by July 1917, at some unspecified location near Ypres. The battalion war diary for 20th July just states that "Lieutenant Munro and five other ranks were missing following a night raid on the enemy line." Not much help, really.'

'Is there any way of finding out where he died?' asked Katherine, disappointed.

'Not really.' Joe grinned. 'Unless you're feeling extra specially psychic.'

It was a pleasant, warm evening, and Katherine was feeling extremely energetic after being cooped up in a car for several hours. Now that she had arrived on the Somme she wanted to rush out and drink it all in straight away. Joe was too tired to do anything except slump in an armchair – 'old farts' prerogative', he claimed – but Mark agreed to go with her on a walk through the village. There wasn't time to explore much before nightfall, but it seemed a shame to waste the bright evening.

They strolled down the narrow main street, which mostly comprised modern chalet houses with wooden shutters, and a few old brick walls. There was a very strange looking church of red brick with a pitched roof, which had a rather apologetic tower at one end, rising to four triangular gables with a miniature spire stuck on the top. It looked as though it had been built with a full-sized spire which had slipped down and shunted itself through the roof until only the top bit was showing. The whole village was luxuriously padded with hedges and trees, and every garden had at least one rose bush.

'I used to think that *Roses of Picardy* was just the title of an old song,' said Mark, delicately fingering a velvety globe which nodded over a fence along the path. 'But there must be some tradition behind it. I mean, since we arrived in Picardy I don't think I've ever seen so many roses in so many gardens. Really nice old-fashioned ones, too.'

'It's a lovely area here,' said Katherine. 'Very like England actually. Or like England should be.'

They walked down to the centre of the village, where the road split into two and crossed the Somme canal on a small road bridge. The canal was fairly wide, with grass banks and a near smooth surface with no more than a trace of a ripple. Apart from a signpost, and a telephone box on the bank, it had probably changed very little since 1916.

The other road, leading away from the canal, made a steep ascent onto a ridge, and they decided to go that way so as to get a view of the former battlefields. The area was very quiet, with no sign of human life except for the occasional Peugeot whirring past. Katherine struggled to get up the hill in one go without stopping, and tried to imagine what it would feel like to climb up there with a heavy rifle and pack. Then they crested the ridge and a wide vista opened up to the north. Nothing much to see except green farmland, but they both stood and used their imaginations to recreate the scene.

'Do you know where we are?' asked Katherine. 'I mean in relation to where Richard was?'

Mark gazed around at the scenery to get his bearings. 'Well, if that's Eclusier down there on the right, then we're looking towards Fricourt, which is one of the places Richard was posted. That might be its church tower over there in the distance.'

Katherine leaned on a fence post and let her mind drift, until she became aware that a cluster of pale-coloured Charolais cattle had accumulated in a semi-circle in the field just in front of her, watching. One of them came up quite close and was blinking at her curiously, darting its tongue alternately up each of its wide pink nostrils and puffing breath that smelled of seaweed.

'Hello cow,' said Katherine, stretching out a hand towards the animal, inviting it to sniff her. The cow swung its head sideways, trailing a ribbon of snot, and began to snuffle coyly at a patch of nettles.

'Ah, antisocial bovines,' said Mark. 'Look, there's a cemetery just up here. 'I thought it was a civilian one, but there are some war graves as well.'

Katherine dragged herself on up the slope to the cemetery, where a very strange collection of monuments clustered together. The most impressive was a large stone mausoleum beside the path, carved with attractive circular patterns like a miniature temple. On the side was a panel which had been carved to look like an arched window with a rather stylised image of a flower inside it, and the pitched roof sported a headless terracotta statue.

'Nice,' said Mark, wandering round the structure with an appreciative eye. 'Wouldn't mind ending up in one o' them.'

They stood for a moment surveying the great obelisks and slabs of black, pink and grey granite, and their offerings of brightly coloured plastic flowers and horrible vases, which filled much of the cemetery. Some of the graves just had a pile of loose stones on them instead of a headstone, but were still adorned with gaudy plastic tributes.

'You can tell this is a Catholic country by the way they pile up extravagant tributes to their dead. In plastic. Can you imagine seeing a display like this in a British cemetery?'

'It wouldn't be allowed in a British cemetery, that's the point,' said Katherine. 'There are conservative rules about what you can put on graves and what you can't.'

On the right hand side was a large plot of French military graves set into beds of red rose bushes. All the headstones were identical; a concrete cross with a small metal plaque on the front, giving only the barest details of the men buried there. A little way behind was a triple row of British graves. Their shape was familiar from the many examples Katherine had seen in cemeteries at home, but it made her feel quite uneasy and sad to see the English names on display – out of place and isolated – in France. She wandered along the row until she saw one that caught her eye, poking through a beautiful spray of mauve irises.

'Gloucestershire Regiment!' she exclaimed excitedly. 'Look, it's the only one in the whole cemetery.'

'I wouldn't get too excited,' said Mark in a sombre tone. 'You'll see plenty more of those before the week is out.'

Chapter Twenty-Five

'This is a great place to come for a holiday if you want to be really depressed and miserable, whatever the weather,' said Katherine. She leaned towards the car window so that the breeze streamed into her face and blew her hair into a fluttering plume. It was a refreshingly warm day for early summer.

'Are you not enjoying it, then?' asked Mark, concerned.

'Oh yes. I love it. But I've had a permanent lump in my throat for the past forty-eight hours and it's beginning to ache a bit.'

During those forty-eight hours they had walked down the street in Flers where the first tanks had gone into battle, and which had a set of medieval zodiac carvings over the church door; stood in the base of a stone tower dedicated to the Ulster Division (with the cleanest toilets in France), and gazed out over the Belvedere de Vaux, where the River Somme and Canal de la Somme, flowing side by side, meandered into a network of miniature islands and jetties thick with trees and clusters of swamp grasses.

They had seen crumbling concrete bunkers, curves of corrugated iron poking out of the ground in fields, religious statues tucked away in old shrines of red brick on isolated roads, and prolific clusters of cemeteries. They had also seen, just about everywhere they went, the small piles of rusty shell canisters stacked beside farm walls and gates; some tied round with red and white plastic tape, some still live with their fuses intact. They even found, on the grass verge close to the Irish monument, a live Mills bomb with its brass pin rusted in place and folded over neatly at the end. It pained Katherine to leave such a fascinating souvenir lying in the grass, but even she had to concede that it would be extremely unwise to pick it up.

They stopped to visit a truly stupendous mine crater at La Boisselle, which had a sign in front of it warning that you might still be blown to smithereens by buried ordnance if you strayed from the footpath. Another sign requested that the crater be treated with respect as it was effectively a giant grave, since most of the German soldiers killed by its 1916 eruption were still buried in it. Consequently Katherine didn't feel inclined to follow

Mark when he slithered down its chalky bramble-tangled slope. The sides were treacherously steep and it went down to a depth of about ninety feet, which made her doubt that she would ever be able to get out again. For her it was enough to walk round the edge and look out over the fields of oilseed rape which still showed patchy lines running through the crop where the trenches had once been.

'Would you believe there used to be two of these,' said Joe. 'One each side of the village, both blown at the same time on the first day of the Somme. The other one has been filled in.'

He had been a teacher for too long, and found it impossible to switch off the automated guidebook mode.

'I feel sorry for whoever was sitting on it, that's all I can say.' Katherine stood for a moment, contemplating the rearranged terrain.

'I think,' said Joe, 'unless I'm much mistaken, that the church spire on the horizon over there is Beaumont Hamel.'

'The place where Hugh died?'

'Yes. I guess he would have heard this mine go up, now I come to think of it, because he wasn't far away at the time.'

'And Richard?'

Joe thought for a moment.

'No, he would still have been in Loos then. In fact he must have come to the Somme ten days after the crater was blown. He probably wouldn't ever have been here, but he was only a mile or so away, at Fricourt over there.'

'Oh no,' she said, distracted. 'Mark's embarrassing us again.'

Joe looked down into the pit. There was a small knobbly hump in the ground at the bottom, the fossilised epicentre of the explosion, and Mark was perched on it cross-legged with his eyes closed, meditating.

'What does he want to meditate down there for?' asked Joe. 'He'll give himself nightmares.'

'There's some people coming,' she said. 'We'll have to pretend we don't know him.'

'We'll wander off and pretend we're going to drive off without him,' said Joe. 'That'll get him shifted.'

They only got half way back to the car before the sound of jogging footsteps could be heard behind them.

'God, what a freak-out,' enthused Mark, wheezing from the effort of trying to catch them up. 'I thought my mind was going to go bang.'

'Why?' asked Katherine. 'What's down there?'

'Nothing really. Just some bloody depressing vibes.'

'It was depressing enough walking round the rim,' she said. 'I'll be glad to get away from here.'

They piled into Joe's car, with Mark driving. Joe was nervous about driving in France because he couldn't deal with the concept of being on the right-hand side of the road. But it also made him nervous to let somebody else drive his car, so he suffered either way.

The afternoon sun was making them feel quite sleepy, but it was necessary to find a town with some food provisions before turning back, so they drove into Albert, a couple of miles up the road. It wasn't a very big place but it had a supermarket and a car park. It wasn't until they were shoving the bags of groceries into the boot of the car that Katherine noticed the shining golden figure on top of the church, just visible over the rooftops of the adjacent street, throwing off a dazzling light from the low slung sun.

'Cor, look at that,' she said.

'Oh yes,' said Joe. 'They've stuck her back up.'

Katherine gave him a crumpled look. 'What are you talking about?'

'The golden virgin. It was famous in the first world war, because it spent two or three years hanging off the top of the tower like it was on an ejector seat.'

'Oh yes,' said Katherine, suddenly comprehending. 'Yes, I've seen pictures of it.'

'I think it fell off in the end,' Joe added.

'Can we go and have a look?' asked Mark. 'If we haven't got anything in the shopping bags that will melt into a stodgy mess.'

They walked down a gently sloping street, past a public urinal and a shop selling geraniums, and came out in the market square where a tricolor fluttered sedately in front of a striking red-brick basilica. The market square had become a large roundabout with a car park in the middle, and the basilica looked like a giant chocolate cake with a golden fairy on the top.

'Bloody hell,' said Joe. 'I've never seen anything like it.'

'It's certainly – flamboyant,' added Mark.

The building had three large arches at ground level with a bigger one just above, and was built from contrasting layers of brown and white bricks. Its tower, which was striped around the middle, had a complicated series of pinnacles at the tip which culminated in the gilded statue of the Virgin Mary holding a rather chubby Jesus at arm's length. It totally dominated the street beneath it and caught a dazzling flash of sunlight which made it almost painful to look at.

'It looks a bit different from how it was in 1916,' said Joe. He pointed through the window of the card shop they were standing next to, displaying a poster print of an old war photograph. It showed a sepia-tinted basilica with its roof smashed in, gaping chunks blown out of its tower, and heaps of rubble banked up against every surface. *'La basilique après les premiers bombardements allemands.'* The market square was a mess of scrubby grass and iron debris, and the blackened virgin was hanging sideways off the top of the tower, like the head of a splintered matchstick.

Katherine felt a lurching somersault in her stomach which shuddered upwards between her shoulder blades.

'Richard was here,' she said. 'He was, wasn't he?'

Joe looked surprised. 'I don't know. Not that I'm aware of.'

A momentary twinge of doubt came in but failed to take root in her mind. The inner conviction was stronger.

'He was, I'm certain of it. I've got such a clear image of looking up at that leaning virgin with all the heaps of bricks and corrugated iron all around me. It's a memory. His memory.'

She began to stride forward towards the basilica, feeling strangely drawn to it. Mark stopped to take a photograph, and slipped into the shop.

The basilica's décor wouldn't be everyone's cup of tea, but it was certainly elaborate. All along the nave were arches bearing a black and white chequer pattern, and the wall above was painted with a richly coloured frieze. All of the walls, ceiling and floor seemed to radiate colour, but there was an general theme of sky blue and gold. It appeared everywhere, from the winking metallic squares in the mosaic floor to the painted slats above the roof timbers, and its crowning glory was the high altar with a fantastic mosaic of gilt and azure tiles. The overall effect was quite overwhelming to the senses. It was an incredible feat of reconstruction, and the sense of renewal and hope was everywhere.

'Picking up anything?' asked Mark, swinging out from behind a red marble pillar.

'No,' said Katherine, a little frustrated. 'But I really like the feel of this place. It's not like any of the other sites we've visited.'

'Interesting. There's some sort of buzz in the air here, I think you're right.'

'I don't feel quite so confident about it being to do with Richard now, though.' She paused, reading the atmosphere. 'It's more of a general thing.'

She set off on a third circumambulation of the building.

'I'd like to get the inside of my house done up like this,' said Mark. 'With a replica of that high altar in the middle of the living room.'

'And a golden statue on the chimney pot?'

'Yes, why not? I've got a papier mâché figure of the goddess Isis at home, and a tub of masonry adhesive. I think it would look quite good. In fact,' his eyes lit up, 'I could make a golden virgin weathercock. One that would spin round, and point the baby Jesus in whichever direction the wind was blowing.'

He stared upwards through the rainbow-chequered stained glass, lost in thought, then turned and fixed his gaze on Katherine.

'I wonder if I can do that without planning permission?'

When she reluctantly left the sanctuary of the basilica and wandered back outside, she found Joe hovering around a pair of field guns, one British, one German, which were on display beside the front steps of the church. The British one had a brass plate giving instructions for how to fill it with buffer oil.

'Apparently it's not the original virgin up there,' said Joe, glad to have someone to lecture at. 'The original fell off in the end and nobody ever found it. I expect it's standing in someone's garden pond in Germany, if some officer was able to get it stuffed up his jumper. Probably been covered in clematis for the last ninety years.'

'Some jumper, to shove a thing like that up it.'

'Well anyway, it went walkies and they had to make a new one.'

'Mark wants to make one out of papier mâché and stick it on the roof of his house. I wish I could work out when he's joking and when he's being serious. It's impossible to tell sometimes.'

'I'm not sure if he knows himself half the time,' said Joe.

It was a warm evening, and after dinner Katherine sat out on the verandah at the back of the house – which was actually more of a lean-to shack with a corrugated plastic roof, but pleasant enough to sit under, and watched the slow glide of the Somme canal, its movement heavy as treacle. A luxurious clump of waist-high stinging-nettles separated the end of the garden from the canal bank, but the green water was easily visible, carrying on its surface a sprinkling of leaves and willow blossoms.

'Mind if I join you?' Mark asked, dropping an armful of art pencils on the table. 'I was going to try a bit of sketching.'

'What are you going to draw? The canal, or the patch of stingies?'

He tapped his forehead. 'Things I see with the inner eye. Work straight off my subconscious.'

'Fair enough.' Katherine thought it sounded like an utterly loony thing to do, but he seemed to be able to come up with the goods.

'It's not so different from your synaesthesia,' he explained. 'Same crossing over and blending of senses.'

'Tea, anyone?' Joe was leaning out of the kitchen window.

'Yes please,' said Katherine. 'I wondered where you'd got to. What are you doing?'

'I'll come and join you in a minute. I'm having another look through Richard's service records.'

Katherine sat and watched Mark flitting lightly over the surface of the watercolour paper with a soft pencil, spreading out nebulous lines and whirls which might, if he was lucky, form themselves into some meaningful image plucked from the ether. She let her gaze transfer to his face, which was set with serene concentration, and noticed the way his hair caught on the neck of his sweater. There was no doubt that he was pleasant to look at. She didn't want to admit it even to herself, but she always felt really good in his presence. He was a bit mad, but it had increasingly become a matter of some importance to her that she was able to spend as much time with him as possible.

Three tea-bags came flying out of the window. They swished past Katherine's head and landed with a triple splak in the middle of the lawn.

'Joe, will you stop *doing* that!' yelled Katherine. 'This isn't a bloody medieval midden heap, you know.'

Joe's head came out of the window. 'It's good for the garden,' he said indignantly.

'Not when it misses the garden and lands on the lawn it isn't.' Joe came outside with a tray, and settled himself in a nearby seat with his pile of notes and papers. He never seemed to be happy unless he was sticking his head into some books or papers.

'It all goes full circle,' said Mark. 'For centuries people just threw their food scraps out of the window, until society got more civilised and went "Eurgh, yuk, that's disgusting," and stopped doing it. Then we suddenly realise that throwing organic matter onto the garden and recycling food scraps is actually quite a good idea after all, so we start doing it again.'

'It's not the same though, surely?' argued Katherine. 'People didn't sling stuff out of the window just so that their rose bushes would bloom better. It was because they hadn't invented dustmen.'

'Bugger me,' said Joe suddenly.

Mark gave him a glance. 'Is that the best offer I'm going to get this evening, I ask myself?'

'I've just found something, look.' Joe waved a photocopy of the battalion war diary for the 10th Gloucesters. 'You're right, Kath, Richard did spend time in Albert.'

'Oh wow,' said Katherine.

'His battalion was sent to Fricourt, I knew that, but I hadn't taken much notice of how they got there. They travelled down by train on July 7th – this would be 1916, of course – and disembarked at Albert station. It wasn't until July 10th that they marched onward to Fricourt. They spent three days resting in Albert, though they had a slightly rough time by the look of it. "Enemy artillery active throughout the night. Two casualties." So there you go. Richard would have seen the golden virgin leaning over the town exactly as it appeared in that photograph in the shop.'

'You mean this one?' said Mark, and whisked out a framed 10x8 print of the image from a paper bag beside his chair.

'Oh Lordy,' said Katherine, feeling the shivery sensation between her shoulders again. 'It's all starting up again. Psychic stuff. I don't think I'm ready for this.'

'Is it upsetting you?' Mark asked, hastily shoving the photograph back in its bag.

'Not upsetting. I just feel I'm on the edge of something a bit too heavy and I'd like to put a stop to it for the moment. It's not just Richard who's building up now, it's a whole load of them.'

Joe put the photocopy on the bottom of his pile of papers. 'That's fine, just give it a break for a while. Take her out into the kitchen, Mark, and stuff her with chocolate. She'll be all right.'

Chapter Twenty-Six

12th June 1917

How can I hope to chronicle these last few months? I let the diary slip. I have been ill; far too ill to write of my experiences, although in many ways this has been my most significant war experience so far. Despite my good intentions regarding the constant maintenance of this diary, I find that I must catch up on the six months' worth of semi-dream life which passed in shadowy blushes while this book lay untouched in my valise.

I don't think anybody could have predicted that I was about to snap. I felt perfectly fine until the moment I lost myself. Indeed, I was preoccupied with worrying about Tate, whose emotional state seemed to become more intense – and his behaviour more reckless – by the day. He is technically due to move up to the rank of Captain now, but has been told that he cannot be promoted yet due to "irresponsible behaviour while under fire". Not that he seems in any way chastised by this.

Of course, the shroud of gut-wrenching agony which envelopes me whenever I think of Hugh, or write his name, or imagine his face, has been with me from the moment I first received the news last December. It was too late to attend the funeral; they buried him without knowing that he had a close relative only a couple of miles away. Full military honours though. They say.

Christmas came and went. New Year came and went. My promotion to Lieutenant came and went and was duly gazetted. The battle-slain of the Somme melted into the midwinter mud, and life went on as 'normal'.

During the first week of January we took part in a minor skirmish. In his "irresponsible" way, Tate was the first officer over the top, and – foolish though it sounds – I followed right behind him so that, in the event of his being hit, the bullet might go through me too. But he was too fast for me, charging towards the enemy lines like a beserker, until I lost him in the smoke. I began to see why he didn't feel comfortable about being awarded the MC. It wasn't gallantry that made him run straight into the path of the guns. It was indifference. He just didn't care.

As it turned out we both got back safely. He was tired but exhilarated when he came back, like a horse which has just won a race. The Germans counter-attacked, but got nowhere near our trenches. The whole business was over in half an hour.

After another ten minutes the Germans came out of their trenches under the cover of a red cross flag, and began to gather in some of the wounded – both their own and ours.

'Leave them be,' I told the sentries. It's beyond my personal morals to shoot at those engaged in acts of mercy.

Sergeant Russell was hovering close by (yes, he did once more uphold his immunity to gunfire), ready to raise an eyebrow at the first available opportunity. But I would not be bullied into eliminating a party of stretcher-bearers and wounded men, German or not. Perhaps he did get the last laugh, because I noticed, as I watched the rescue teams scuttling back to base, that some of the 'wounded' on the stretchers were shaped suspiciously like Lewis guns. However, being in the mood for clemency, I gave them the benefit of the doubt.

The first hint of things to come occurred on that same night. It is natural enough for men to feel dazed and disturbed after a battle, but it is not so usual in the way that I experienced it. A nebulous feeling of unease which had been plaguing me since December snapped into focus with startling clarity. I was lying on my bunk in my dug-out trying to get some rest, and with an sudden jolt I knew that Hugh had suffered in his death. I just knew.

I'm not sure whether it was some kind of psychic telepathy, or the onset of my illness, or just that my unconscious mind had picked up on a tiny discrepancy in the letter I received from Captain Stockwell, which I had previously overlooked. Something had been bothering me about that letter, and now I knew what. Stockwell claims that Hugh felt no pain, on the basis that he was 'already dead' when he found him. Yet he said that an RAMC chaplain who arrived a few minutes later tried to revive him. Why? If he was dead then wouldn't that be obvious to an officer of the Royal Army Medical Corps? Especially a priest, who spends much of his useful life in the company of corpses, even in peace time. If the priest thought that Hugh was alive, I'm inclined to believe he was.

There are good, traditional reasons why Stockwell might have lied in his letter. Almost all such letters contain lies. It is the only way we can deal with the awfulness of it. After I shot that boy, Private Boulter, I wrote a chivvying letter to his mother assuring her that he had been one of the most gallant and promising new men in my platoon and that he died 'in action'. All lies, but if I told her that her dear boy had howled like a mad, fear-stricken animal before he even got near any action, and that I had despatched him as one would a horse with a broken leg, it would have destroyed her. Having made the greatest sacrifice a mother can ever make, where is the harm in allowing her to believe that he had done his bit for his country, and died an honourable and painless death? At least that's what I thought, until I began to suspect that Captain Stockwell had done the same thing to me. And now I find I don't want the cheerful and sanitised version. I want the truth.

Ironically that same dreadful and oft-repeated phrase, 'he was killed instantaneously', was one of the few statements in my letter to Mrs Boulter which was actually true.

I confided my anxieties to Tate, as always. He listened carefully, and pondered for a moment.

'You're getting the jim-jams,' he said. 'Don't let yourself think about it. Worst thing you can do.' And we left it at that.

But this absolute conviction that Hugh's death was not straightforward and painless remained with me during the following week, and finally manifested in a horrifying dream. It wasn't a dream about Hugh, at least not obviously so. But its meaning was quite clear to me on the intuitive level.

I half woke during the night with a very lucid, very disabling sensation and a frightening shortness of breath. There was a cold feeling at the top of my legs, from knee to thigh, ice cold, as if some heavy weight were pressing down on them. I tried to sit up to see what was wrong with them, but found my upper body almost paralysed. It was an enormous effort to draw breath, and so distressing was this effort that I found myself letting out a small cry of fear on each outgoing breath. My lungs did not seem to be working. There was also a searing pain in my left arm, and I couldn't move that either. I was paralysed and unable to breathe.

221

I began to panic. My legs were frozen, as if held down by steel bars, and even my face and jaw felt stiff.

I began to cry, and tried to shout for help. I'm not sure whether any sound came out or not. Saliva ran from the corner of my mouth because I was unable to swallow. I felt the creeping certainty of death crawling up my body in a slow, cold wave, starting from my feet and working upwards. I wanted to howl in protest against it, but my lungs couldn't take in enough air. Then I felt something pulling at me. Warm hands, trying to turn me over.

'Munro? Are you all right?'

I couldn't tell where the words were coming from.

'Munro, what the fuck is the matter?'

Pale grey eyes came into focus, intense and anxious; Tate leaning over me, breathing against my face.

I tried to speak to him, but it came out as an anguished wail. He grabbed my shoulders and began to shake me violently.

'That's enough,' he demanded. 'Just fucking well wake up.'

That seemed to do the trick. The warmth surged back into my legs, and my lungs drew a deep merciful draught of dank trench air.

'Thank God for that,' said Tate, kneeling down on the floor beside the bunk. 'I wasn't sure if it was a dream or you were having a seizure.'

'Both,' I croaked.

He looked very strange, sitting on the floor gazing up at me with the glow from the paraffin lamp casting unfamiliar shadows on his face. His eyes, which are his most striking feature at the best of times, bored right into me. His pupils were dilated in the low light, blacker than darkness, like a tunnel into another dimension.

'This is about Hugh again, isn't it?' he said.

I nodded.

He looked down at the floor for a moment, then fixed his eyes on mine again.

'He hasn't moved on yet, has he?'

I swallowed. 'What do you mean?'

I knew exactly what he meant, but I wanted to hear him say it.

He cleared his throat. 'Sometimes the war dead seem to take a bit of time to go wherever it is they're going. You can sense them hanging around.'

I wasn't going to pretend that I didn't know what he meant. There are shadows and presences all around us out here, and we're always aware of them even if we choose not to acknowledge them. One of the most vivid ones for me is the presence of a woman, who I first saw on the Loos battlefield and then in many other places since. Sometimes I think it's Kathie the nurse, other times it seems like someone different, but with the same presence. I have never spoken of these things to anyone; it just isn't done.

'Do you mean you can sense Hugh hanging around?' I asked.

He hesitated, then nodded. 'Can't you?'

'I wasn't sure,' I said. 'I didn't want to assume it was anything other than my imagination.'

The truth was that I could feel Hugh's presence as strongly as if he were in the room with us. I could 'see' him kneeling on the floor staring up at me, exactly as Tate was doing. The lamplight was reflecting bright points of light in his near-black eyes, in contrast to the pale moon colour of Tate's, and his face had its usual lop-sided half-smile. I could see in my mind's eye exactly how he had looked the last time I saw him, loping along the trench with the kind of long stride which is normally the reserve of much taller men, smiling, with a stray strand of dark hair slipping down onto his forehead. Then another memory of his face in profile, sipping a cup of tea and gazing into the distance, lost in thought. Everybody has memories of their loved ones who have died in this war, and mine struck at the very core of my soul. He was amusing, sweet-natured, intelligent. He was loved and appreciated and given every encouragement to do something worthwhile with his life. For such a spark to have been snuffed out at nineteen was too cruel to bear.

I looked at Tate, who had been intently watching my face as the kaleidoscope of images twirled past my inner vision.

'I don't know why this is so important to me,' I said, with a lump swelling in my throat, 'but I must find out what really happened.'

'All right,' he nodded. 'If you feel it's the right thing to do.'

The next morning I trawled through Hugh's letters, desperately searching for a half-remembered reference to an army chaplain whom he'd met during his time on the Somme. It tore at my heart to see his familiar handwriting, which until recently I had perused without a second thought but which now seemed like a treasured relic of the utmost sanctity; the preciousness of a fluid and ongoing thing suddenly made finite. This had to be endured, though. I eventually found the passage in question; it referred to an RAMC priest called Vickers who had 'slipped over on his backside in the mud' while administering the Blessed Sacrament in a trench-side Mass. It was very like Hugh to find this sort of incident amusing. Of course there was nothing to suggest that this was the same priest who had attended him in his last few minutes, but at least it was a start.

I dashed off a letter to Vickers, asking him if he had been present on the night of December 10th and begging him for any information he might be able to give. The letter probably sounded a little frantic and over-emotional, but it reflected the way I was feeling.

That night I had a dream while fully awake. I was sitting on my bunk gazing into the lamp flame, not ready to attempt sleep, although Tate was already in the arms of Morpheus and snoring open-mouthed on the other side of the room. I wasn't even particularly thinking about anything, just studying the delicate ripples in the flame and the way it dipped and resumed each time a crump came down outside, filtering the vibration of the explosion. As I stared I became aware of a curious tingling sensation between my shoulder blades, and then suddenly the room seemed to tilt somewhat – or perhaps it was me, because it was as if the whole room had condensed in a tunnel-like manner and the bed beneath me was levitating a few inches above the floor and at a slight angle. And then I saw with startling clarity the face of a woman on the other side of the lamp. Her hair was loose over her shoulders but disappeared into the blackness of the shadows, and her clear green eyes were staring straight into mine. I knew her at once; I have seen her many times in moments of stress. But always as a vague presence, a half-seen companion. This was the first time I had engaged with her face to face and made eye contact. The jolt it brought was like a bullet through me. I was not even sure whether I saw her with my physical vision or an inner dream vision, but she was as clear as day, and I didn't imagine it. She had a nice aura about her, a kindness and understanding. It was as if she *knew*, and was trying to reach out to me, though the reaching out was mind-to-mind, not physical. Then the vision vanished in another disorientating jolt as another muffled boom went off outside and somebody dropped a clatter of metallic objects in the trench right outside my door.

From then on, the feeling of disorientation was impossible to shake off. It was as if I was now partially detached from reality, seeing it all like the overlapping but not quite matched image in a pair of unfocused binoculars.

The last thing I remember – and it must have been about three days after sending off my letter to the Reverend Vickers – was walking down a straight section of a trench in what felt like a slow, dream-like motion, like walking through treacle, with men staring at me as I passed. I recall that one of my puttees had come loose and unwound, and trailed absurdly behind me like a streamer from a maypole. It dragged in the mud and slowed my movement so that one leg struggled to keep up with the other. But I don't recall anything at all after that point.

What they told me afterwards was that I had been found wandering in a dazed state, trembling and twitching. I do have a peculiarly lucid memory of being in a wooden compartment on a train, like a coffin, rocking gently from side to side with the motion, and of a medical orderly with a black moustache leaning over me and saying to an unseen colleague 'His nerves are shot to hell.' I don't remember being loaded onto the ship, but I do recall being unloaded; a man came and looked at the cardboard label that was attached to my uniform and then carted me off to a train which was waiting beside a large compound full of wounded men. I then endured what seemed like an unending journey in another wooden coffin. I could hear one man screaming almost non-stop the whole way. The nurses just ignored him after a while. Then, to my utter astonishment, I found myself being deposited on the platform of the Great Western station in Cheltenham.

'You've got lucky, sir,' said the corporal who held onto my arm on the way from the platform to the motor ambulance, with a hint of resentment. 'You've got a place close to home.'

It was indeed lucky, in that it is comparatively rare to be sent to a hospital in one's home town. But to me it was an absolute torment – all my grief and pain in my memories now manifested in physical reality. And I wasn't able to go to my actual home, so close and yet so unattainable. I was placed – and stayed for the next five months – in a grand stone-fronted Regency house called the Priory. Or, to give it its War name, Glos. 30 V.A. Hospital. Having been built originally as a luxurious residential house it had bright, airy rooms and plenty of space, and I was given a bed right next to one of the front windows on the upper floor, with views over the Sandford fields where the River Chelt races under the line of trees towards the old mill. Unfortunately for me the house stands on London Road, which happens to be where Hugh lived – where my aunt and uncle live. Of course I couldn't actually see their house from my ward, as they are some way further up the road in Charlton Kings, but a hundred thousand memories seemed to come flooding through my brain every time I glanced out of that wretched window. Everything – the lime trees lining the road, the Cotswold-stone terrace in Oxford Parade set back from the street with black railings and dainty lead canopies and square communal lawns, the big white house at the far end with the brick wall running along the side, even the black and white cast iron street sign outside and the detail of a slightly discoloured slab in the pavement – all of it brought Hugh back to me in a rush of images from the recent and not-so-recent past. Unavoidable, when I walked with him so many times along that bloody street.

The war has brought many changes to Cheltenham. The grandstand at the racecourse is now a Red Cross temporary hospital. The playing fields at our old school have been ploughed up and the boys who used to play rugby there are now tilling rows of carrots. But every street, every ivy-clad house-front, every gatepost, portico, curtain, railing and kerbstone seems to be woven into my bereaved memory somewhere along the line.

I can hardly face the prospect of describing my existence at the Priory. The place was run entirely by Red Cross volunteers, who did an exemplary job in keeping everything going swiftly, comfortably, and vigorously scrubbed. But the state of some of my fellow officers – and I suppose, to some extent, myself – was absolutely pitiful. I was technically admitted with neurasthenia, but it was essentially a combination of exhaustion and grief. Much of the time I felt quite well but was plagued with an

226

uncontrollable shaking, which so upset my mother when she came to visit that I had to ask the nurses to deter her from coming. At other times I would shake less, but be disturbed instead by voices in my head and great surges of confusion and fear, which caused me to fidget and twitch almost as badly as the shaking phases anyway.

Another officer on my ward, Jenkins, was terrified to go to sleep because of the 'bits of dead bodies and splashes of blood' which haunted every non-waking moment. He begged the night nurse to wake him up whenever she saw him dozing, but she rarely did – he needed the sleep. So he would nod off, and within a few minutes he was thrashing around under the blanket, muttering or whimpering or letting out a trembling sigh, until something turned up in his dream which was shocking enough to jerk him back to consciousness, often with a shout of fear which woke up everybody else. The night nurse was always on hand with soothing words and a glass of milk, but nothing would stop the dreams – not even the sedative drugs which were frequently put in his night-time drink. Some nights when I lay awake myself I would see the flare of a match light up the darkness like a star shell, and then the orange glow of a cigarette end. Sometimes it helped me to get to sleep, watching the small fiery tip of light above Jenkins' bed and seeing it fizz and brighten each time he took a drag. This ritual would be repeated over and over again and for me it had a relaxing, soporific effect. But Jenkins would go on smoking through the night in a desperate attempt to keep himself awake, until his face was an ashen grey, his vision fragmented and his senses blurred and grainy. In the end the physician told him that they could no longer tell which symptoms belonged to the shellshock and which were brought on by lack of sleep.

'I see bits of severed limbs walking about on their own,' he told me in a soft, slightly Welsh voice, his eyes retracting into the horrors that were constantly played out inside his head. 'I see blood sprayed on walls, clotted up on fabric, smeared across flesh, collecting in puddles on the ground. Blood splashed over everything. It's dreadful. I can't bear it.'

He was by no means the only victim of this torment. Another man in our ward spent every night desperately trying to un-jam the mechanism of an imaginary Lewis gun in his sleep. He kept replaying this scene because it was what he had been doing when his friend was blown up by a grenade right next to him, blasting him with a shower of gore. 'I even had it in my mouth,' he told me, trying not to throw up at the memory of it. A small, quiet man at the far end of the ward would routinely – and silently – wrap himself up cocoon-like in his blanket and roll from side to side in his sleep until he slipped off the edge of the bed. The night nurse often didn't have the heart to disturb him, as the fall rarely woke him up, and he would still be there in the morning, snugly wrapped up under the bed.

Only two things of great note happened during those months in the V.A. Hospital. Firstly, a letter arrived from Tate enclosing a reply from the Reverend Vickers, who, much to my disappointment, turned out to have had no more than a fleeting connection with the Royal Engineers, and had been elsewhere by December last year. However, my letter had touched his heart, and he had taken the trouble to do a little research on my behalf. He had found that, of the dozen or so medical officers serving behind the lines at Beaumont-Hamel on December 10th, only one was a clergyman: a chap called Captain Morrell. He had not been able to verify the details, but believed it to be very probable that Morrell was the 'chaplain' who had attempted to resuscitate Hugh.

The other significant event shortly after my return to Cheltenham was my first meeting with Louisa. Of course she visited me frequently during those months, but it was that first meeting which sticks in my mind. I was extremely nervous about it, since I had not seen her for over a year, and I was not exactly looking my best. I feared that she would be put off me when she saw how weatherbeaten and fidgety I had become, not to mention my new-found tendency to get upset about the slightest thing. For this reason I did not want her to come and see me at the Priory, and begged the commandant to allow me to leave the hospital for a few hours, so that I might meet with Louisa in a café in Montpellier. The meeting had to be a little formal, because there are still rules regarding social conduct between nurses and patients – even when they are not from the same hospital. 'Fraternising' is strictly banned. But at least if she was disgusted by the sight of me she managed not to show it. She looked beautiful; war experience had matured her, as it had me, but her lovely green eyes were brighter than mine, and her smile made all my apprehensions recede the moment she entered the room.

'I'm so relieved to see you, Richard, you've no idea.' Her eyes welled up as she struggled to hold up the public façade.

I immediately flouted the military rules by kissing her hand. It smelled of carbolic soap.

'Sorry if I'm a bit twitchy,' I said.

She made a dismissive gesture. 'Don't worry about that. I have seen shellshock before, you know.'

'Of course.'

She was working full-time as a voluntary nurse at New Court hospital, another private house donated to the Red Cross for the duration of the war, and I suppose she had seen enough of the twisted wrecks scooped off the battlefields not to have any illusions about what the war was all about.

'It could be worse,' she said. 'At least you're alive.'

I don't think she intended any reference to my recent loss, but it was obvious by the way her face suddenly fell that she realised it was a sore point.

'I heard about Hugh.' She shook her head sadly. 'The poor darling. I can hardly believe it.'

'No. Neither can I.'

'William and Evelyn are absolutely distracted. Have you been to see them yet?'

The prospect of visiting Hugh's parents was too great an anxiety for me, something I had psyched myself up to dread. How could I bear to see them? How could they bear to see me? Knowing how easily it could have been Hugh lying here in a Red Cross hospital and me lying in a Somme grave? War chooses its victims so randomly.

We talked for some while about our mutual friends and acquaintances, and what they were up to. She was full of sparkle, and it was infectious. But there was also a distance between us, something more than the physical space across the table. It was as though a pane of glass was separating us. She understood perfectly well how dreadful the war could be – in her nursing work she frequently had to deal with men who had come straight from the battlefields, complete with muddy uniforms and stinking four-day-old field dressings – but somehow I couldn't make her see my experiences the way I saw them; she couldn't relate to them. She was also disturbed at how casually I talked of horrors and accepted the possibility of my own death.

I handed her a package which I had carefully wrapped up in several layers of brown paper.

'Would you be able to look after these few things for me? Until the end of the war?'

'Of course,' she said, taking the package. 'What are they?'

'My letters to Hugh,' I said. 'And his to me. They were all returned to me by his commanding officer.'

She nodded, and clutched them protectively. All my instincts screamed in anguish at the thought of allowing such precious items out of my possession, but to keep them with me would be folly; they might so easily be lost or damaged when I went back to the Front. And I knew I could trust her to look after them.

As an afterthought I pulled out a photograph of Tate which he gave me after his last visit to his parents – they like taking photographs of him in his uniform and handing them out like sweets; it makes them feel patriotic. I had been carrying the picture around with me for a few months and it had become somewhat creased. I wanted to be sure to preserve it, a keepsake after the war.

I saw the instinctive reaction on Louisa's face when I gave her the photograph.

'Very dashing fellow,' she said, slightly embarrassed.

'He's handsome, yes,' I conceded, 'but you wouldn't like him.' I laughed. 'Believe me my dear, you wouldn't like him.'

We walked back towards the Priory through Imperial Gardens. I wanted to avoid the obvious route along Montpellier Terrace, as it came out almost opposite my old College. Too many memories.

I yearned for some sort of token contact with Louisa, just for comfort, but she insisted that she would get into awful trouble if she even linked arms with me in public. It didn't matter that we were practically engaged and had been so since before the war; affection between a nurse and an officer is taboo.

After this initial meeting I was happy to let her visit me at the hospital, where I was very proud to show her off, but the glass wall between us persisted. I slowly began to realise that, one way or another, it was very unlikely that I would ever marry her.

Chapter Twenty-Seven

⌒

4th July 1917

I tracked down Captain Morrell to a village called Wytschaete, generally known as White-sheet to the troops (though Tate naturally has an alternative name for it), which is just south of Ypres. Lucky for me, because it isn't far from where my own regiment is now stationed. I wrote to him while I was on the train up to the front line, without going into detail, merely enquiring whether he had come into any contact with the Royal Engineers' 67th Field Company, and if so, would I possibly be able to meet him. I posted the letter as soon as I arrived.

I found most things unchanged after my five months away from the line, except that we are in a new location. Indeed we are in another country, as our village of Ploegsteert (Plug Street, inevitably) is just over the Belgian border. The mud here is completely different from the Somme; it is thick with a sticky texture, like heavily sugared porridge. I imagine it is a lot more sloppy in the winter months, but at this moment in time it is dry enough to stick to anything and everything in great gobbets. It is also quite stony – lots of small flint-like pebbles, as opposed to the fine silky chalk on the Somme. Though of course it is the powdered chalk residue in Somme mud which makes it so slippery, like walking around on banana skins all the time.

I believe after the war I shall be able to make my fortune as the writer of an authoritative *Field Guide to the Mud Textures of Northern Europe*.

Tate's loyalty is touching. He has not allowed anybody else to share a dug-out with him since I left. I'm not entirely sure that anyone would want to, but that's beside the point. I found a celebratory meal of jam and biscuits awaiting me in my new quarters (viz. hole scraped out of side of hill) when I arrived, and on the table (or upside-down ammunition crate, to be more accurate) a few tufts of yarrow and ragwort artfully arranged in an old corned beef tin.

'Flowers?' I exclaimed in surprise. 'I thought I was supposed to be the sentimental wet blanket around here?'

'Exactly,' said Tate. 'That's why I thought you'd like some flowers.'

I sniffed them appreciatively. They stank of damp earth and cordite.

'I suppose you managed all right while I was away?'

'I didn't have a lot of choice, did I?'

'Well, perhaps it's your turn next for a Blighty ticket.'

He threw his head back haughtily. 'Going crackers is a luxury I cannot afford, as you well know.'

We munched our way through the jam and biscuits, which was rather poor fare compared to what I had become used to in hospital, but I felt far happier than I had done at any time during my stay in England. The feeling of inner joy at being in the company of a good friend was greatly preferable to that hollow ache of loss which plagued me in Hugh's home town. Even Louisa had reminded me of Hugh in a roundabout way, to the extent that I sometimes felt disturbed and irritable in her presence, although it was hardly her fault.

It was just beginning to get dark, and I was searching in my baggage for a fresh candle, when Tate suddenly yelled out 'Christ!' A religious conversion was somehow unlikely, so I jumped up to see what had prompted the outburst.

He was standing at the entrance of the dug-out, pointing at the sky over to our left.

'What the fuck has happened to the moon?'

Just above the southern horizon was a large red-brown orb, a dark and murky full moon the colour of stale blood.

'Good Lord,' I said. 'It's the total eclipse. I forgot all about it.'

'What the fuck has it gone like that for?'

'It's the earth's shadow falling across the moon, you idiot,' I said. 'Perfectly natural phenomenon. It still reflects some light from the sun even when it's eclipsed, that's why it looks red.'

'Well that sounds damned silly to me. But still, I'm glad I'm sharing a dug-out with an astronomer, not a coal miner or whatever, otherwise I wouldn't have known what the fuck it was.'

'No, but you'd know a thing or two about coal instead.'

'I've never seen the moon look like that. It's vile.'

'It is rather sinister, isn't it? The ancients believed it was an omen of death, and you can see why.'

Tate looked at me with one eyebrow raised.

'It's a bit late out here, isn't it, for an omen of death? If it had come up with it three years ago I would have been impressed.'

5th July 1917

Tate shook me awake in the middle of the night. I had not heard him get up and light the lamp, but he obviously had done so. His face was grim but calm, and his eyes were lit with an intense, pale stare which was highly disconcerting.

'I've had enough of it, Richard,' he said. 'I've absolutely had enough.'

It wasn't what he said that rang my alarm bells, it was the fact that he'd called me by my Christian name, for the first time ever. I sat up abruptly in bed.

'What's up?' I asked.

'I don't want to do this any more.' His pupils were dilated and he looked quite unlike his normal self, but it wasn't fear – or shellshock – which gripped him. He was perfectly calm and rational.

'Don't want to do what any more? You mean the war?'

He nodded.

'Richard, will you shoot me?'

I gave a snort of morbid amusement. I didn't think he was serious.

He held out his revolver to me, holding it by the barrel so that the butt was towards my hand.

'Please,' he said. 'You did that boy last year, didn't you? So I know you can do it.'

'That was completely different.'

'Why was it different?'

'It was a last resort.'

'What, because he went beserk? If I go beserk, will you shoot me then?'

'Tate, you've got to stop this right now.' I threw my blankets aside and put my feet down to the floor but he backed away from me, still holding the revolver.

'You don't get it, do you?' he said. The glow from the lamp lit up one side of his face and made his eyes sparkle every time he moved his head. 'I'm not mad. Not at all. I'm just sick of it. Sick of all this bloody nonsense. I mean, what are we all out here for? What are we fighting for? For England and St. George, or some such fuck-brained drivel. It's a fucking waste of time, so why do we do it?'

I was stumped. I'd never been faced with a situation like this before and it was frightening. I tried to take a step towards him but he backed off again.

'Tate, you really don't want me to do this.' It sounded corny, but I didn't know what else to say. 'It's the coward's way out. You're worth far more than that and you know it.'

'I'm worth more than this stupid bloody war, I know that,' he spluttered. 'But a coward I am not. Look here, I'll do it myself if you won't help me.'

He put the gun up to his head and I heard an awful double click as he cocked the trigger. I have no doubt that he meant to do it, but there was something slightly theatrical in his manner, almost as if it was all being laid on for my benefit.

'Why are you doing this?' I asked, afraid to make any move towards him now. 'You don't want to kill yourself. You don't want to die, I know you don't.'

He was staring straight into my eyes with a strange intense look, as if trying to read my soul. It was almost as if he was waiting for me to dare him to do it. After a long drawn-out moment he slung the revolver down in disgust and it spun across the dug-out floor.

'Oh, what's the bloody point? Even death is a waste of fucking space.'

I swallowed heavily, wondering whether or not I should make a grab for the gun, which had come to rest beside the upturned crate.

'If I died now, nobody would even remember me,' he said bitterly. 'That's what really pisses me off. If I thought anybody would give a sod about my passing then I would do it.'

I was annoyed now. 'Oh, and you think I don't give a sod? Is that what this is about? Seeking attention?'

'No, of course not. Just forget it. It's not important.'

'Not important?' I raged. 'You ask me to blow your brains out and then say it's not important?'

'It wasn't loaded,' he said slowly, as if spelling it out to an imbecile. He saw the doubt on my face and made a shrugging gesture in the direction of the gun. 'See for yourself if you don't believe me.'

I didn't doubt his word, I just couldn't believe he had put on this show for nothing.

'Have a look,' he insisted.

I reluctantly picked up his revolver and carefully opened it. Six empty chambers gaped back at me. I put it down wearily.

'Why did you do this to me?' I moaned, suddenly feeling heavy and tearful.

'Sorry,' he said. 'I just had to find out how you would react.'

'You're a complete and utter bastard,' I said, with some feeling.

'Thank you,' he said pleasantly. 'That's all I needed to know.'

He settled down on his bed and blew out the lamp, and I heard him snuggling down under the blankets. I remained for some while sitting on my bed in the darkness. He'd put paid to my chances of getting any more sleep.

In the morning – and I should point out that Tate behaved as though absolutely nothing had happened – we received our orders to move further forward, to the village of Messines. It was not far away, and was one step closer to Wytschaete, which at least gave me a sporting chance of being able to meet up with this chap Morrell.

These days every town and village on the Western Front seems to have been totally pulverised, so it is no longer any great shock to see the scale of the devastation. Messines, at least on the surface, exists only in name. It was a German stronghold right from the beginning of the war, perched up on a long ridge, and so the British guns have been pounding it non-stop since 1914. Then last month, while I was still in hospital (lucky me), the mining division blew the whole of the ridge absolutely sky-high – the culmination of months of tunnelling beneath the earth, secretly packing it with tons of high explosives, a task carried out with amazing skill and audacity. When the mines were detonated, all in one go, the shockwaves were felt as far away as the south of England; it was in all the papers. Now the fighting has moved on. Having successfully taken the whole of the ridge, a further push was made to consolidate the land on the other side of it, to make the ridge easier to defend. Consequently it isn't quite as frisky around here as it was on the Somme. Even so, it *is* pretty exposed, and a high enough vantage point that you can see as far as Lille on a clear day. And no doubt the Germans have a good view of us too.

The village of Messines is now a series of low humps; humps of rubble, sporting a fabulous crop of stinging-nettles. Not a single building stands above ground level, and you can only find your way around by following the line of the trenches, with the aid of a trench map. In order to distinguish it as something more than a rubbish tip, the name 'Messines' has been painted on a wooden signpost in front of the debris, and some wag has painted an extra 's' on the end, which just about sums it up. If it weren't for the signpost, one would not be able to recognise it as a village at all.

Under the ground, however, there is more going on. Firstly a veritable network of cellars, still intact after the houses above them have been knocked to pieces, and which have been linked together and fortified by the Germans. And the Germans certainly know how to build good defences, far better than anything our lot could have done. It was like walking around in one of London's underground stations; a little damp, a little echoey, but very solidly built. Even some of the trenches themselves were lined with brick walls, having been constructed around the foundations of bombed houses. This was quite a luxury, as it helped to keep the trench clean and dry as well as giving better resistance to enemy shelling. I found an excellent dug-out in the form of an old coal cellar, brick-built, with a low arched roof. It had green algae growing up the walls and smelled like the inside of a wellington boot, but Tate and I considered it very grand.

No further mention was made of his behaviour during the night. I am not sure what was going through his mind, but he looked perfectly all right now. Indeed I knew he was back to his old self when a letter arrived for him from one of his brothers – not a common event – which basically comprised a four page invective about some real or imagined misdemeanour on Tate's part which had caused offence to the family. Tate read it through once without emotion, then folded it crisply and tore it into strips for lavatory paper.

'Next time I write to my brother,' he said cheerfully, 'I must ask him to use better quality paper. This stuff is frightfully scratchy, and I'm not getting a sore arse on his account.'

7th July 1917
This afternoon I was attending to a dispute between two men about the correct way to fill a sandbag (this is what happens when there is not enough strife to keep them occupied), when Sergeant Russell came up and saluted me with what looked suspiciously like sarcasm.

'There's somebody here to see you, sir.'

'Who?'

'I'm not sure, sir. He's a captain though.'

There was something about the way he used the word 'captain' which set my teeth on edge.

'I asked him to wait in your dug-out.'

I made my way quickly back through the tangles of nettles, which were interspersed quite attractively with nodding scarlet poppies, and found a tall stranger sitting on my bed in the dug-out, wearing a white dog collar at the neck of his uniform.

He immediately stood up and shook my hand.

'Lieutenant Munro?' he said politely. 'I'm Captain Morrell. I got your letter yesterday.'

A strange tingle ran through my arms and stomach. He was in his late thirties, a dark-haired man with a kind face, a toweringly tall stature, and a very soft, low voice. I felt immediately that he was someone I ought to trust.

'I'm so sorry to spring myself on you out of the blue like this,' he said, 'but I had a feeling from your letter that it might be quite urgent. And since my vocation gives me more freedom of movement than most officers I thought it would be easier if I came to see you.'

'I'm very grateful,' I said. 'I'm awfully sorry I haven't got anything to offer you in the way of refreshment –'

'No no no, it's all right,' he said, making a stilling gesture with the palm of his hand. 'I don't think that's what this is about, is it?'

I sat down on Tate's bed, and Morrell sat opposite me with his hands lightly clasped, as if he were about to hear my confession. In some ways he was.

237

'I hope I haven't dragged you here under false pretences,' I began, with an audible quiver of nerves in my voice, 'but I wondered whether – from your service at Beaumont-Hamel last year – you know of a young man called Hugh Crooke.'

'Hugh Crooke?' He pondered carefully, with his face lowered towards his hands, then looked up at me. 'No, I don't believe I do.'

My heart sank, but I tried again.

'Or you might possibly remember attending to a young man in a wooden hut, who died after being hit by a shell splinter? Around December the tenth.'

There was still no sign of recognition on his face, and he began to shake his head.

'Under Captain Stockwell's command,' I ventured.

His head stopped in mid-shake.

'Oh God,' he said, and I saw his eyes glaze over as he replayed a dreadful memory in his mind. 'Oh God. A dark-haired boy, with very dark eyes?'

'That's him,' I gulped. 'You tried to revive him?'

'That's right. I never knew his name. Oh God, I'd been trying so hard to forget that.' He leaned towards me solicitously, his brow furrowed. 'Is he a relative of yours?'

I nodded. 'He was my cousin. We grew up together. In fact he was pretty much everything.' I felt several burning hot tears suddenly dash down my face, and Morrell put a comforting hand on my arm.

'I'm so sorry,' he said. And I believe he meant it.

I discreetly mopped my nose on the sleeve of my tunic and fixed him firmly in the eye.

'I have got to know what happened to Hugh,' I said, no longer caring how foolish I looked. 'Please, it's so important to me. I have to know everything.'

'I understand.'

'Captain Stockwell wrote to me, very kindly, but I don't believe he told me everything. I don't blame him for that, he was just trying to spare my feelings. But I must have the truth.' I kept my gaze on his face, unblinking. 'Hugh died in pain, didn't he?'

Morrell stared back at me, his gaze flitting from one eye to the other. Then he nodded slowly.

I waited for him to begin his account, but it was obviously something which had affected him deeply, and it was hard for him to talk about it.

'I do understand,' he said softly, 'how important it is for you to know this, so I'll tell you. I'll tell you all of it. I was billeted with the Royal Engineers during the first two weeks of December, as you already know. I heard a shell come down. I don't recall what I was doing at the time, but I heard it come down. It was a British shell. I've heard enough of them that I can tell the difference in the sound as they come over. This had the wrong noise for a German shell. It came down in a patch of grass beside the officers' huts.'

He paused, and swallowed heavily.

'I saw that the hut was blown in on one side, so I rushed in through the front door. I didn't have time to fetch my medical bag, I just went straight in. It was light inside, as they had a lot of lamps lit up. A lot of furniture strewn around the room. There was a small fire underneath a table where a lamp had been knocked over, and two men were beating it out with blankets.

'I heard an awful sound of weeping from the far end of the hut, and I found Captain Stockwell leaning over an officer who lay crying on the floor. A baby officer, not more than eighteen or nineteen. He'd got a piece of shrapnel right through his chest, poor thing, and he was so frightened. He was trying to speak but he was crying so much I couldn't understand a word he said, and he was gasping for breath. Stockwell had tried to turn him over, because he had fallen face down, but his legs were trapped by the metal bed frame which had fallen on top of him. He was completely pinned down, so we could only move him a little. I remember Stockwell said something about trying to lift the frame off him but I didn't think it was a good idea. We wrapped him up in a blanket and I shouted to one of the men nearby to go and fetch my medical bag. I didn't have anything with me that I could use.

'I tore a pillowcase in half and pushed it into the wound on the front side, and tried to slow down the bleeding by pressing my fingers down on the artery. It wasn't any use though. His lungs were filling up with blood until he could hardly breathe. So I gave that up and just tried to comfort him. He was absolutely conscious, that was the awful thing. I don't think he fully realised what was happening – he was in deep shock – but he looked straight at me. God help me, I shall never forget that face and the way he looked at me.'

Morrell fell silent for a moment. My throat had seized up, but I had to ask one question.

'His wounds,' I croaked. 'Did he have a wound in his left arm too?'

Morrell looked at me with wide eyes and nodded.

'Yes, I believe he did.'

I indicated a point just above my left elbow. 'A small wound, just here?'

'That's right.'

I think he guessed that I'd had some kind of psychic experience, but passed no further comment. He cleared his throat quietly and continued his story.

'I didn't have anything I could give him. No morphine, without my medical bag. I put my hands on either side of his face and prayed with all my heart that God would take away his suffering. He was still crying. He was terrified. I must have stayed with him like that for another minute or so, and then he began to go down. It was as though he had purposely let go, because he went very fast. His breathing slowed down and a peaceful look came over his face. That was the thing that haunted me the most. He died with his eyes open, with an odd sort of half-smile. Very graceful. Not the sort of death you witness every day.'

I felt a wave of dizziness pass over me, with a sickening memory of the corpse I'd seen in the ruined house at Albert. I'd used the word 'graceful' when I described it at the time. For a moment I almost passed out, and put one hand down on the mattress to steady myself.

Morrell dabbed his eyes with a crisply laundered handkerchief, and shook his head sadly.

'Such a nice, sweet-looking boy, too. It was heartbreaking. Such a waste.'

'I'm truly grateful,' I said sincerely. 'For your honesty.'

'I must emphasise that I couldn't have saved him even if I'd had a whole crate of medical supplies. It was a very serious wound, quite untreatable. I might have been able to give him something for the pain but I couldn't have saved him. By the time the man came in with my medical bag he'd already left us. He must have suffered for three or four minutes, nothing more. And that really is the truth.'

'Thank you,' I said, and gripped his hand.

'That's all right. It was only fair that you should know.'

'I mean thank you for being there. For looking after him at a time when I couldn't do anything for him myself.'

His eyes were brimming. 'If I ever performed any true service to God or humanity in this war, then I believe it was on that night. And I can assure you I'll never forget him.'

Chapter Twenty-Eight

8th July 1917
I'm writing this in an interesting place which I found today. Down a hole between some clumps of nettles. It is the crypt of Messines church, which is the only part of the building which is still intact. Indeed I only recognised it as a church because its nettle-clad hump was bigger than all the other nettle-clad humps, which implied that it had once been a larger than average building. There wasn't anything else in the rubble to suggest an ecclesiastical structure; everything had long since been looted. Down the hole was a set of ancient steps which led into a low stone chamber, probably medieval. The walls down here are formed from a series of arched recesses, built from very small stones, along with several stone pillars in the middle of the room holding up the vaulted ceiling. I assume the Germans used it as a dressing station, because there are bits and pieces of hospital debris lying around; glass bottles with German writing and an empty box of bandages.

I have spent a lot of time in cellars and other subterranean structures recently, but the atmosphere in this one is extraordinarily different. It has a fantastic aura of optimism and hope. Perhaps that sounds a little fanciful, but in all honesty it would be impossible to feel any kind of anxiety or despair in this place. You could sit in here and feel the devastation all around suddenly beginning to knit together and mend itself, a centrifugal regeneration from around this magical centre. It absolutely radiates peace.

Perhaps the power of this subterranean temple emanates from the black madonna which stands on an altar in the central recess. This shrine has been respected through all the disturbances, and still bears a white cloth (albeit rather dirty) and two candlesticks. The madonna reminds me very strongly of the one Hugh showed to me last year in the Somme sector, although she is carved from dark wood, and painted. A deep blue veil has been set on her head, held in place by a bright metal crown of stars. Once again there is something decidedly pagan about it, but I get the same feeling from it as I did from the golden virgin at Albert, the same nurturing, transformative feminine benevolence. Hugh was right, they are just aspects of the same thing. Dark and Bright Isis.

9th July 1917
It is a strange thing living one's life underground. This is a war within the earth, and so being immersed in the earth (in one way or another) is part of our lot. Trenches are a half-way house, in which one lives *in* the ground rather than under it; open to the elements, open to shelling, open to ear-shuddering noise, as the sound of a bursting shell in the open air is like the sudden slamming of an iron door. Underground all is calmer; the explosions are more muffled, the rain is kept out, and the solidity of the surrounding earth and brick brings a sense of being safe. Perhaps it is the orderliness of bricks, all identical and laid neatly in regular rows, which gives the impression that life within them is contained and controlled. It is an illusory safety, as the walls would be shallow comfort if you got 'crumped' in your little dungeon and couldn't ever get out again. The Germans made a wise decision in networking all these basements together, as it provides for a greater range of escape routes. What is not so comfortable is the jangling headache one inevitably ends up with after a day of constantly smashing one's metal helmet against the low roof beams, and the cramps of standing around in the tunnels which are only between four and five feet high in places, and the damp, smelly air which makes everyone cough and feel stifled. In such circumstances, it is easy to find oneself longing for a gasp of 'fresh' trench air.

One of the more fascinating features down here though is the relic of the German mine tunnels. Before the audacity of our tunnelling operation enabled the ridge to be blown up and captured, the Germans had been in the process of doing the same thing, burrowing their way towards our line through the secret substance of the earth, and had got some way with it. And then at some point they chose to abandon the effort. Their engineering and craftsmanship survives as a work of wonder, and it is possible to walk some considerable distance into the side of the hill through a dry, neatly lined corridor, before coming out into a gallery which is high enough to stand up in, with spaces for electricity generators (now looted) and the wiring for electric lights all still intact. I didn't fancy going any further when I reached a point in the tunnel where the roof timbers had split and allowed a tumble of earth into the pathway. It was those smashed beams which brought home to me more than anything else what an immense explosion occurred here last month, to rupture timber so deep in the earth, and so decisively curtail the Germans' occupation of these crafted ant-holes.

There is always respite, however, even in war, and it was our men's lot today to be commandeered for a spot of road repair work, so we were able to emerge, Tate, Nowell and myself, blinded and gulping, into the daylight and fresh air. I'm not sure whose idea it was that our men should attend to the road mending, but presumably not someone who was close to the vicinity, because frankly, we couldn't find the damned road. There were chalky tracks, and ruts, and short portions of roadway interrupted by thick-spread piles of pulverised bricks, so you couldn't tell which direction the road was supposed to go in. In the absense of surviving houses, the layout of streets shown on our out-of-date maps was insultingly irrelevant. Is this undulation of rubble the line of the Rue de Lille, or just a random scattering of bricks? Who can tell? We had to clamber across about four hundred yards of wreckage before we found the main road into the village, which was already being cleared and mended by a half dozen other platoons working in small teams. We sent our platoons to join in and help them, rather than try to make any headway on the ridiculous rubble heaps in the village centre.

'How different the terrain is out here now, compared with two years ago,' said Nowell as we picked our way back over the mess. He wasn't wrong. I had been upset in 1915 when I'd first seen shellpocked houses with burned out windows and sagging roofs, and barb-wire gardens; spilling over with the fresh civilian objects of everyday life newly and rudely interrupted, cooking pots, food packets, hairbrushes and vanity mirrors, cheap books full of made-up adventures. Now the landscape is utterly dehumanised, with no trace of personal belongings, no discernible outline of hearth or home. It is impossible to imagine that anyone ever lived here, when all the eye can see is the undulating dunes of anonymous devastation. And not only that – the landscape has adjusted to this and become settled in its new shape. The freshness of newly-spilled bricks has given way to a sense of permanence, as moss forms along the broken edges and weeds spring up in robust clusters among the black and dirty ruins; nettles and rosebay willowherb knotting their roots firmly around heaps of broken bricks, and nets of coarse-textured grass embracing the rubble and forming fibrous mats over it. As far as the weeds are concerned, the rearranged landscape is here to stay.

We came across a well, which presumably had once been located in someone's back garden, but was now gaping open in the featureless environment. We only found it because someone had thoughtfully heaped up a tangle of barbed wire over it, weighted with bricks, to prevent any hapless soul from falling down it. Through the middle someone had shoved a plank of wood on which was chalked 'Napoo'.

Nowell leaned over the hole and sniffed.

'Ewww,' he said. 'That's pretty poisonous. Corpses or worse down there.'

'I can smell something else,' said Tate suspiciously. 'Something floral.'

'Not violets?' I said. The sweet violet smell of poison gas is all too familiar a scent out here.

'No. Proper flowers.'

And no sooner had he said it when we both caught sight of a tumbling mass of green behind a heap of bricks, laden with pink blossoms. It was a briar rose – a wild, dog rose – which must have survived in somebody's garden even after its accompanying house had been blasted away. Rising above the nettles and the clutter, it was blooming for all it was worth, and the scent was delicious.

A short way beyond it two officers were sat on a salvaged bench, and, in a scene so surreal I could hardly believe I was seeing it, were about to take tea. They had spread a tablecloth over something resembling a table, and on it were spread their genteel items of crockery; a dainty little china teapot, and matching willow-patterned cups and saucers, and only slightly incongruous, a tin mug full of sugar.

'Hallo there. Won't you join us?' asked one of them, who was wearing a chaplain's collar. I seem endlessly to bump into church types out here now.

So the three of us sat down and joined the little tea party. The weather was glorious; a heat haze shimmered off the fallen bricks into a blue sky, the dog rose was radiantly fragrant, and apart from the semi-regular flight of high-velocity shells screaming towards Ypres, you would hardly know there was a war on. We sipped our commendably palatable tea and made very English chit chat, perched among the smashed and mildewed bricks of ruined Messines.

'You need dowsing rods these days to find the road through this place,' said the other officer, a lean and lanky chap from the medical corps. 'There's a fierce bend in the middle of the village, but you may as well take the short way straight over the rubble.'

'And yet look at this, a china tea set that survived completely unscathed in all this devastation,' said the chaplain, shaking his head. 'There's no sense at all under the hammer of war.'

'Too true,' said Nowell, extricating his finger from the teacup's dainty handle with some difficulty.

'It's just as random with the boys I deal with,' said the lanky officer. 'You see the most frightful injuries and the chap just heals up as if nothing had happened. Whereas another lad will barely even sneeze and fall down dead. No sense to it. But in either case you just have to chivvy them along. Even when they're dying you just tell them that if they keep smiling they'll be right as rain.'

'Lying seems to be an occupational hazard out here,' said the chaplain with a bitterness, and the lanky man laughed a wheezy, smoke-and-asthma laugh.

'Brother Maythorpe here has lost his faith,' he said to us by way of explanation. The chaplain looked dejectedly down at the tablecloth.

'That must be hard,' I said.

'It is,' he said, as if addressing the teapot. 'Never a moment's doubt in forty years. And now – men come to me wanting answers – why their comrades died, why it was right for them to stick a bayonet through a man who was pleading with his hands up – and I have no answers. Only lies.'

We all sat around in silence. He carried on.

'They want some kind of redemption. Something to make everything all right. And I say, eat this piece of wafer and say your prayers. And what I really want to say is, run away, go home. There's nothing here that can save you. God died on the Somme.'

We all stared at the teapot. We all knew exactly what he meant and there was nothing any of us could say. It was Tate who finally broke the awkwardness.

'I take your point, but it's not really fair to blame God.'

'It's not blame exactly,' protested the chaplain. 'I just can't see how it could be allowed to continue, if there were a God. We would surely have won by now if there were any divine mercy involved.'

'But the trouble is, God is not commanding the Fifth Army,' insisted Tate. 'The Fifth Army is commanded by a bunch of fucking useless wank-buckets.'

The chaplain reeled slightly in his seat and I saw Nowell stifle a small laugh under his handkerchief.

'I have seen,' said the churchman in a slightly tremulous voice, 'young boys bayonetted even as they knelt in prayer. Wounded men shot even as they begged for mercy.'

'And what the fuck do you expect God to do about it?'

'Oh come now, Tate, you know the man speaks the truth,' interceded Nowell. 'We've all seen these things.'

'My point being,' continued Tate, 'that if you preach a doctrine of hate, if you inspire blood-lust in the minds of the gentle and the foolish alike, if you teach boys that the committing of dreadful crimes is their duty in the pursuit of justice, then things are bound to get a little out of hand. And if you plaster a veneer of godliness over it, and pretend that the love of Christ *demands* that you murder your fellow human beings on the basis that somebody born in Munich rather than Scunthorpe must be somehow less than human, then don't be surprised if God disowns you and leaves you to it.'

'It is a righteous war though, however brutal the day to day business,' said the chaplain. 'It was necessary for us to come into it when the Germans violated Belgium.'

'This war has nothing to do with the sovereignty of Belgium, and you know it. It was brought about by military jealousy, pure and simple. My army's bigger than yours. No it isn't. Well we've got bigger guns than you have. And look, we've got two-thirds more warships than you have, and they've got bigger flagpoles with shiny knobs on the end, so yah boo and sucks to you.'

'Yes you're right there,' said lanky. 'Old men and their empires. That's what we're here for.'

'This whole bloody mess could have been avoided,' continued Tate, 'this whole bloody war averted, if the Kaiser and King George had simply been allowed to strut up and down on a podium and show off who had the biggest cock. So don't tell me that it's a righteous war or that divine mercy should have stopped it.'

The chaplain put out his hands in supplication. 'Lieutenant, I do understand that God would never have stopped it, it is rooted in the folly of men. But why does He not help us to break through, when it would bring an end to so much unnecessary suffering? Why will He not let us push the Germans back to their own territory and restore France and Belgium to their rightful people? It is the Germans who are being greedy, invading lands and taking what doesn't belong to them. They are in the wrong, fairly and squarely.'

Lanky nodded in agreement.

'Ideologically yes, they are in the wrong,' said Tate. 'Their leaders are in the wrong, which is no help to the poor fuckers crouched in the mud. And the same is true of our side. We may have the moral high ground, but we have the intellectual low ground when it comes to those fuck-witted brass-arse stiffs who cook up these fucking ludicrous schemes to break through the line by making silly localised attacks on obscenely difficult objectives.'

The chaplain shrugged and nodded. 'You mean the Somme. Yes, it was a poor show.'

'The Somme is exactly what I mean. See here.' He began to line up chunks of brick on the table. He always had an almost prescient ability to see the battlefield as a whole, as if his spirit projected itself up there in the middle of the night and took in the lay of everything. He quickly and knowingly constructed his tabletop Somme out of splintered fragments of Flanders. 'You have all these modest defences running along here in a line, and every now and then there's big one, a fortress.' He stuck a big half-brick on the table. 'If they'd just got their act together and pushed forward against the whole line at once, with resources balanced and united, it would probably have yielded, and they could have pushed it back, all in one go. But no. Cooperative effort and united armies don't enter the brain of General Brass Fuckwit. He just looks at his map and says "ooh look! There's a fucking great concrete bunker full of machine-guns. Let's go and bang our heads against it and show the Germans what for." And so in we go, thousands of brave men obeying their orders, thumping at the impenetrable gate with their battering rams uselessly over and over again, when the walls either side of the gate are thin enough that they could just run straight through them. But oh no, it wouldn't do to break through in the weaker parts of the line. We have to focus all the firepower of the British Empire on taking these monstrous and impossible objectives. And when our men and our weapons are spent, the plan is screwed up into a paper ball and it's back to the map to see what other impenetrable fortress we can bang our head on.'

'I completely agree,' said Nowell. 'The Somme was a collection of costly and pointless minor battles, when if it had been more coordinated it might have got us somewhere.'

'Arrogance bordering on indifference,' said the lanky officer. 'I don't know how the brass-hats sleep in their beds at night.'

'They have no conscience, no responsibility, and they don't learn,' said Tate. 'They are fucking fossilised sticks of subhuman shit.'

The chaplain shivered. 'You're right, of course. But the fact remains. It's not shellshock which is the biggest problem out here. It's soulshock.'

10th July 1917
When I woke up this morning I had a curious feeling of solitude. I looked over to Tate's bed on the other side of the dug-out and it was empty. It was most unlike him to rise so early; it normally takes a lot of effort to induce him to get up in the mornings. More to the point, he seems innately incapable of getting up at any time of day or night without knocking things over and making an infernal racket.

I got up, and found there was a note on the table in Tate's handwriting, though it was unsigned and not addressed to anybody. It just said: *Last one home is a fuck-face.*

Well, wherever he had got to he certainly couldn't have gone home, so I put the note to one side and got on with the morning chores. I shaved and had breakfast, and asked Adams if he had seen him anywhere this morning. He hadn't.

Then a runner from HQ turned up, a young lad who I hadn't seen before, and who looked me up and down briefly before saluting.

I knew as soon as I saw him that something dreadful had happened. It was written all over his face.

'Yes?' I snapped nervously.

'Are you Alastair Tate's friend?' he asked.

This made me pause stupidly for a moment, unsure. I hadn't known that Tate's first name was Alastair.

'Yes, I am,' I said. 'What's happened?'

The lad swallowed anxiously. 'I'm afraid he's topped himself, sir.'

I stood and looked at the lad, and he looked back at me, and neither of us moved or spoke. I wanted to ask 'Is he dead?' but it was a stupid question. Stupid question.

He shuffled uneasily from one foot to the other. 'We found him this morning, sir, with the revolver still in his mouth.' He paused. 'If it's any consolation –'

'Don't tell me,' I butted in. 'He was killed instantaneously.'

The young lad looked embarrassed. 'That's right, sir.'

I caught sight of the note on the table, and a cold weight plummeted in my stomach. This was not the silly jest I had first taken it for. Neither was it a throwaway comment. True to form, Tate had left me the world's most improbable suicide note.

Apparently he went up to company headquarters early this morning, brusquely handed an envelope to the adjutant who was on duty, and requested that it be sent on to his family in the event of his death. Then he casually walked outside and shot himself. Major Pershore had personally heard the shot fired as he reclined in his bath.

I had an awful dilemma over whether I should go to see him or not. I was warned that it was not a pretty sight, but all the same I felt that I had to go and say goodbye to him.

I was taken to a brick enclosure – rather like a coal bunker, but without a roof – where Major Pershore shook my hand gravely, and left me to spend a few minutes alone with him. He was lying under a blanket on the grass; it covered him completely from head to foot, but there was no mistaking his familiar elegant frame. I felt very, very dizzy and sick, but surprisingly devoid of emotion. It all seemed so unreal, I expected him to get up at any moment and start swearing cheerfully at me. He was very still, but apart from that he looked no different from the countless occasions when I'd seen him sleeping.

Whatever lay underneath the top part of the blanket, however, was not going to be the Tate I knew. I decided not to look after all. It was far better that I remember him as I'd always known him, and not have the memory displaced by whatever mess he had now become. I could see some knots of clotted blood at the top of the blanket, and also, just visible around the top edge, a lock of familiar toffee-blond hair. If I had had any doubts at all that it was really him under the blanket, that one strand and its distinctive colour would have dispelled them.

I must have stood for some time, wondering what to do. What on earth can you do? It was heartbreaking to think that I would just have to turn round and walk away from him, but that was the brutal reality of it. Life goes on, for me, for a while. I knelt down beside him and stroked the blond lock once, twice, three times, drawing it slowly between my fingers. Then I steeled myself, and did it. I walked away.

Major Pershore was waiting for me discreetly behind a nearby blockhouse. Considering the amount of slaughter taking place all around us, he was surprisingly sympathetic and caring about the incident, and about the gravity of my loss.

'I just want to reassure you,' he said, 'that we will give him a decent burial. He was a terrific officer, I recognise that. But I will have to put him on the casualty returns as an S.I.W., I'm afraid. It's the rules.'

So that was the epitaph for the dearest friend I ever had.

S.I.W.

Self-Inflicted Wound.

Indeed if there was any compassion or justice in this war the enemy guns would blot us out before we came to this.

Chapter Twenty-Nine

'Well it was your idea to come here.'

'I know. I'll be all right in a minute.' Katherine sniffled into the final shred of the toilet paper she had stuffed into her pocket at Victoria Coach Station, which was not terribly absorbent, leaving her with no option but to wipe her nose on the back of her hand and dry it off on her jeans when Joe wasn't looking.

'Actually I suppose it was my fault as well,' said Joe. 'I should have realised that you might get upset.'

'It's not anybody's fault. I will be all right in a minute, honestly.'

She sat on the platform of white stone along the top of the wall and gazed across the tidy field of white headstones. There were about five hundred of them. Meanwhile Mark had wandered off down a footpath at the side of the cemetery, no doubt preferring to be alone with his visions.

'We should have visited some other cemeteries first,' reflected Joe. 'It would have helped to desensitize you a little bit.'

'No, I prefer not to be desensitized actually. It may sound perverse, but I want to experience the full impact of it.'

'If you say so.'

The atmosphere of the cemetery was bearing in on him and making him uncomfortable. It wasn't just because Katherine was upset that he felt awkward. It was something in the air.

Katherine mopped her face and gave him an appealing look. 'Actually, Joe, would you mind if I just spent a few minutes alone with him?'

'No, of course not,' he said, glad of an excuse to get away. 'I'll go and wait in the car.'

She walked across the grass, following the line of the main aisle between the stones. On the whole it wasn't a bad place to spend eternity. The cemetery had been laid out like a garden, with each row of graves made into a long flower bed packed with pink roses and columbines. The grass was meticulously mown and there wasn't a weed in sight. Beyond the walls, the French fields undulated in a sedate manner as far as the horizon, green with young corn. It could almost be called idyllic. But there was a humming tension, a taut wave of grief which resonated right through her head. She wanted to howl and rage out loud, but the silence was unbreakable; the urge stuck in a tense ache at the back of her throat. It surprised her to find her own reaction so intense. Perhaps it was because she was now doing what Richard Munro probably hadn't been able to do.

She found Row B and paced out the distance to the twenty-eighth headstone, and there he was: Second Lieutenant H. N. Crooke, Royal Engineers, 10th December 1916 age 19. That was all it said. The memory of his individual personality had died out with all the people who had known and loved him. None were now left alive. All that could be retained of him was a tantalising imaginary snapshot of his character, gleaned from his letters to Richard, his lively handwriting, the photograph of his slightly smiling face.

Katherine opened a plastic film canister she had in her pocket and took out the redwood cone that she had picked up in the driveway at Langford House. She sniffed it, savouring one last time its sharp resinous smell, and nestled it gently into the earth on Hugh's grave. It was strange to think that he would have been familiar with those very same cones, still growing in his garden nine decades later. The self-same tree, Hugh's tree.

She ran her hand along the curved top of the gravestone and persuaded herself that there was no point in standing there any longer. She caught sight of Mark pacing back along the footpath with his head down, and made her way in the same direction so that she would meet him when he got to the gate.

'Funny vibes, here,' he said, without looking up. 'There's a bit over there which really freaks me out.' He pointed to a spot at the edge of the cornfield which had no discernible features.

'But there's nothing there,' observed Katherine.

'Oh no? You try standing there and tell me that.'

She walked slowly towards the place he had indicated and felt nothing at all until suddenly a violent shiver of fear snapped through her. It was like an electric shock, but from the inside out.

'Fuck, I don't like that,' she quailed, but took a cautious step further forward anyway. It was horrible, as if dozens of hostile eyes were watching her from every direction, and a cold, sour smell of fear cramped the air.

'You see?' said Mark smugly.

'Yes, the only way I can describe it is like there's some globule of fear that's been imprinted on the atmosphere. I feel this irrational need to *hurry* when I stand here. It's not one person's fear, though, it's more of a general, collective thing.'

'That's exactly what I felt,' he said. 'And why not? All those men, feeling all that fear for all those months – they've left behind some emotional trace. Something tangible and permanent which has attached itself to the atmosphere.'

'Well, there may be nothing to it. I mean, I did walk into that spot *expecting* to feel something nasty, because you said you'd been freaked out by it.'

Mark shook his head. 'God, I hate sceptics. You always have to try to spoil everything, don't you?'

During the night she woke from an incredibly strange dream. She couldn't actually remember most of it, but the image that stayed with her was that of Richard Munro, very real and alive, trying to persuade her to go somewhere she didn't really want to go. It was some kind of war-torn citadel, closed in, absolutely choked with dead souls. It was perfectly all right to go in there, he assured her; it might seem at first that it was too much for her to cope with, but she would be able to do an enormous amount of good by braving it.

She trusted him, and wanted to help. Her last recollection before going into deep unconsciousness was walking through a stone gateway, terrified, pressed against him and tightly gripping the leather strap of the Sam Browne belt across his chest.

How long the experience lasted she couldn't remember. But at around two in the morning she came back to consciousness, dizzy and sweating. She was still aware of her fingers holding on to the cross-belt, and of her inner voice telling Richard that she was really sorry, she just couldn't handle it. And his hand guiding her back, allowing her to escape to normal consciousness. The image faded out, but left her very shaken and made her feel sick.

She made a determined effort to get up and go into the bathroom adjacent to her room and splash some cold water on her face. Then she spent half an hour with the light on, gazing at the dark blue floral wallpaper, a heavy, deadening colour, classically French.

'I hope I didn't disturb you, tramping about in the middle of the night,' she said apologetically the next day.

'No, not at all,' said Mark. 'I sleep like a corpse anyway.'

They had travelled a short distance north, beyond the fields of the Somme, and were hoping to pinpoint quite closely the ground over which Richard advanced during the battle of Loos. The countryside here was less pretty than the Somme area, and the fields were dotted with grey slag-heaps. Joe hadn't come; he had a stonking headache which he insisted was caused by excessive psychic activity, although the quarter bottle of single malt he'd put away the night before was another possible factor.

They were strolling down a wide footpath in the middle of nowhere which would have been in No Man's Land at the time of the battle, so they knew that Richard Munro must have passed over this track at some point.

'I feel a bit of a failure about that vision last night,' admitted Katherine. 'Richard wanted me to go with him and I bottled out. I wasn't up to it.'

She cast her gaze downward, keeping half an eye out for interesting objects in the newly turned soil beside the path.

'You mustn't think of it like that,' said Mark. 'I'm sure if there's anything important to communicate then it will crop up again.'

'I'm not sure I'll ever be up to it though. That's the trouble with all this first world war stuff. It's like diving into a deep, black, frightening sea. Every now and then you just have to come back up for some air. You can't just go on taking the full force of it, or you'll drown.'

'Yes, I'm beginning to notice it myself this week. There's always the risk of having your mind blown by constant immersion in these shadows. I don't envy you, having a dream vision like that.'

Katherine noticed something a bit different lying in the soil on the field margin.

'Oh God. Oh, tell me that isn't what I think it is.'

She pointed at the thing, which looked like a sizeable portion of human leg bone.

'Might be an animal bone,' Mark said reasonably. 'Cow or something.'

'Oh Mark, it's human isn't it?'

'I wouldn't know. I haven't read any pathology books lately.'

She sloshed him with the IGN map. '*Don't* be flippant. You're insulting the war dead. I shall ask Richard to come and kick you up the bum on the etheric plane.'

'Now you're being flippant.'

'Oh come on, what do you really think?'

He peered closely at the bone and touched its surface.

'My hunch is that it is human, to be honest.'

'What are we going to do?'

'Do? What do you mean?'

'Well I'm not bloody leaving it there.'

'Katherine –'

She eased the bone out of its resting place in the compacted mud and respectfully wiped the worst of the dirt off. It was a brown ochre colour and horribly splintered at one end.

'Come on,' she said. 'Which way's the nearest cemetery?'

As it happened they had three cemeteries to choose from, in a triangle, only a matter of yards apart. They decided on the biggest one, which was just beyond the track on the edge of the Vermelles road.

'I've heard of this place,' said Mark, as they went through the gate. 'St. Mary's Advanced Dressing Station Cemetery. Where have I come across that name before?'

'Doesn't mean anything to me I'm afraid.' Katherine looked at the array of white graves in front of her, intersected by a narrow aisle every ten stones. 'How about over there, on that bank at the back?'

There wasn't a great deal of spare space in the cemetery, but finding room to accommodate a bone was not too big a problem. She didn't want to bury it on anybody else's grave; it seemed impolite. In the back corner, sheltered under a hedge, was a row of gravestones set apart from the others, in a little group. She made her way over to it.

'Blimey, look at this lot. There's a whole load of them from the Gloucestershire Regiment.'

There was something different about these stones. They had the usual names and dates, but at the top was an inscription which read: *Believed to be buried in this cemetery.*

'How did they manage to lose a load of graves?' asked Mark incredulously.

'Don't ask.' She reverently laid the bone on the ground. 'I'm going to bury him here, next to Captain I. R. Gibbs, whoever he may be.'

Mark began to dig a hole, using a variety of available tools including his fingers, a bit of dry stick and a supermarket loyalty card. Katherine kept watch, because the digging of holes in cemeteries was not something you want to get caught at.

There wasn't really much they could do in the way of a funeral service, so they just patted the earth down over the piece of bone and stuck a twig upright in the soil as a monument.

'It's better than nothing,' said Katherine grimly.

'Yeah. It'll have to do.'

'I wonder how they made all these headstones? Presumably they're formed out of some sort of concrete or reconstituted stuff, to get them all the same size and shape. With the lettering pressed in when they cast the mould.'

'You're wrong there. Every bit of it was done by hand, even the regimental logo.'

'I don't believe you.'

'It's true. They were carved from Portland stone and the bevel on the lettering had to be exactly sixty degrees. The government sent inspectors round to check that the masons had got the angle right. And if they cocked it up they had to start again.'

'How do you know all that? I thought Joe was supposed to be the resident nerd?'

'Ah well, it's amazing what you learn being a copy editor. I worked on a book about stonemasonry last month. Very good, it was.'

'I see. Then I'll know where to come if I need to know about tombstones.'

'I've also edited a book about sewage, if you ever want to know anything about that.'

They were on their way back to the car when Mark noticed a grave which had more tributes and plastic poppies on it than the others.

'That's it!' he cried out, pointing. 'I knew I'd heard of this cemetery.'

The grave belonged to Lieutenant J. Kipling of the Irish Guards. Someone had put a small log at the base of the stone, adorned with a wilted posy of wild flowers and the words: *In remembrance of that wind blowing and that tide.*

'What's all that about?' asked Katherine.

'Rudyard Kipling's son. I had a lecture about this from Joe last week. He'll be pissed off that he missed coming with us to see it.'

'Aged eighteen, eh?'

'Yes, it was another depressing story. He only got into the army through the old-boy network, because his eyesight was so bad he failed the medical. And then he went missing at the battle of Loos. Just disappeared. His body was never found.'

'So what's this grave doing here then?'

'Well, it was originally marked as an unknown officer, and someone identified it a few years ago. A bit unfortunate really, because Rudyard Kipling spent the last twenty years of his life frantically searching for his son's grave, and he never found it. Poor old bastard.'

'How do they know this is him?'

'Ah, that's the other irony. It's now reckoned that the identification was actually a mistake, and it's somebody else buried here, not Kipling. The body was lying on the battlefield for about four years before they had a chance to bury it, so I suppose it's a bit hard to tell.'

She just felt herself saying 'oh no, not again,' as she drifted off to sleep, with the image of Richard Munro reaching out towards her. But the feel of it was different this time. She dreamed that she was standing in a war cemetery, but instead of the usual 'cross of sacrifice' monument, there was the figure of the golden virgin which she'd seen in Albert. She stood silently holding on to Richard while the figure of the virgin appeared to grow taller, until it was towering over the rows of graves. And then it turned into a kind of resurrection scene, where the men were coming up out of their graves, walking towards the virgin figure through a sunny mist. Even in the dream, she was aware that something important was going on and she was going to have to remember it.

She woke up with an extraordinary feeling of peace. Through the window came the flutey tones of the dawn chorus, although it was actually more of a dawn monologue, with a solitary blackbird strutting its stuff on the telegraph wire outside. Even the drab blue wallpaper seemed livelier. She padded across the bare floorboards to the window and opened the shutters. Light came streaming into the room like a swirl of fresh air. At the end of the garden there were great puffs and ribbons of mist billowing over the surface of the Somme, alight in the morning sun.

Chapter Thirty

'Actually I am exceedingly pissed off at missing the chance to see John Kipling's grave,' said Joe. 'Even if it isn't really him.'

'We could stop off on the way to Ypres,' suggested Katherine.

'No, it's far enough to travel in one day as it is. Don't want to have to rush around fitting anything else in. Rudyard Kipling was quite a dynamic force in getting the war graves organised in the first place, you know. He chose all the inscriptions you see in the cemeteries.'

'Really?'

'And he founded a masonic lodge for the blokes who carved the gravestones. The Lodge of the Builders of the Silent Cities.'

Mark was gazing out of the open window, distracted, idly toying with a reddening leaf on one of the geranium plants. Katherine watched him solicitously.

'Are you OK, Mark? You look a bit groggy. Been on the pop last night?'

'I'm teetotal,' said Mark.

'Really? I didn't know that.'

'Nothing's wrong, honestly. I just had a bit of a weird dream last night, and it's lingered with me.'

'Oh?' Katherine wasn't sure if she wanted to hear about it or not.

'It was odd. I was standing in a graveyard and there was a towering figure of a woman standing over it, like the golden virgin but made out of pure light –'

'Mark –'

'What?'

'I feel all tingly and funny. Can we change the subject please?'

There was nothing in the way of signposts to indicate where France turned into Belgium. It was apparent only in the crunch of the car suspension as the immaculate French tarmac gave way to a rather knobbly prefabricated concrete. At one point, according to the map, the border ran right along the middle of the road. It created a bizarre scene where all the driveways of the houses on the left had cars with French number plates, while their immediate neighbours on the opposite side of the street had red and white Belgian number plates. There didn't seem to be any exceptions.

They approached Ypres along a Roman road on top of a ridge, which gave Joe ample opportunity to lecture his captive audience with edited highlights of the battle of Messines, which had involved blowing up most of the area they were driving along with a phenomenal amount of explosive. Katherine mentally switched off, not particularly interested in anything which didn't directly involve Richard. He had been in this area though, even if he wasn't in the actual battle, so she took a keen interest in the concrete bunkers and blockhouses which flashed past the window from time to time.

'Now remember you mustn't speak French to anybody here,' ordered Joe as he eased into a parking space in the cobbled market square in the centre of Ypres. 'They can get a bit funny about it.'

'I don't really speak French anyway,' said Katherine, internally cringing at the memory of a recent incident in a café in which she had made an unbelievable fist of trying to order a gruyère-topped crêpe. 'And I certainly don't speak Flemish. I'll just have to not talk to anybody.'

'I can't believe this is actually a city,' said Mark. 'It's about the size of Tewkesbury.'

They wandered around for a while, trying to imagine what the pokey ancient streets must have looked like during the war. A lot of the buildings had had chips and chunks knocked out of them. The city had been hammered unceasingly for more than four years, and the scars were still there to be seen, if you looked around you.

'Where's this Menin Gate thing, then?' asked Katherine. 'It's no good, I can't bear the suspense any longer.'

'All right then. It's down here.'

Joe turned down a street just off the market square, where the shops were a bit more touristy. After a few yards the road went under an enormous bridge which spanned the whole street and loomed high above the surrounding buildings. It had been incorporated into some tall ramparts, which were much older.

'Here we are,' said Joe. 'This is it.'

At first Katherine couldn't see anything other than the bridge, which was ridiculously oversized – almost long enough to be a tunnel. Then she saw that the bridge itself was the memorial. It was inscribed with names from pavement level up to the point where the arch began, high enough that you would need binoculars to read it, and where pigeons fluttered to find perches. It didn't even look like a memorial – more like a telephone directory carved in stone. And no matter which way she turned, there always seemed to be more of it. There were steps leading upwards, with names carved right the way up the walls all along, leading out onto another level which had more names, wall after wall, slab after slab of inscriptions. These were the names of the fifty thousand British men who disappeared without trace on the fields of Ypres. And Richard Munro was one of them.

It was perhaps fitting that it was Katherine who found him first. She came across the Gloucestershire Regiment on a couple of the upstairs panels, and was glad there was nobody else around to interfere with this long-awaited moment. The names were listed in order of rank, and then in alphabetical order. Her heart was thumping uncomfortably hard, and she briefly struggled to remember where 'M' comes in the alphabet.

He was there, in stone, the only tangible trace of him that she had seen since she came to the battlefields, proof that he was there. It made him much more real, to see his name chipped out in stone. She pushed her finger into the lettering and traced it, slowly, drawing her whole mind into its lines and turns.

'Please,' she whispered. 'Please be here.' The tears flooded down her cheeks. 'I want to feel your presence now.'

There was nothing to disturb the physical atmosphere except a gentle cross-wind, but internally there was a deep sense of connection, of having touched a mind from across a vast divide.

A movement appeared blearily at the corner of her eye. Somebody else had come up onto the platform further along. She could tell it was Mark, without needing to look round.

He didn't speak a word. He walked straight over and put both arms around her.

Silently, she pushed her face into his cardigan and held on to him for dear life.

'And that's another thing Rudyard Kipling started,' explained Joe effusively as he accelerated out on to the road south. 'The last post, played on a bugle, every day at eight o'clock on the Menin Gate.'

Katherine sighed and carried on staring out of the car window, trying to drink in as much of the scenery as possible. Somewhere in one of these fields was the spot where Richard Munro had been killed, and where perhaps his body still lay. Perhaps there was a fragment of unidentifiable bone, like the one she'd found at Loos. Somebody might come across it one day and wonder whose it was. It was dreadful to think that a human being could just be blotted out of existence like that.

'Are we going to stop off somewhere to eat?' she asked, trying to make an excuse for them to spend a bit more time here. 'I'm starving.'

'There's a biggish village coming up,' said Mark, grappling with the folds of the map.

'Do you want to stop here then?' asked Joe.

'Yes,' said Mark, knowing there would be an argument unless somebody made an instant decision.

They had passed through the village of Messines – or Mesen as it was now called, its Flemish name – on the way up. It was instantly memorable by a horribly sharp S-bend, which was a bit of a strange thing to find in the middle of a Roman road and had no doubt caught many other drivers unawares. They probably had to rebuild the houses on either side of the bend on a regular basis.

Joe turned off into a quiet side street which opened out into a mini square with a church at the far end. The houses were mostly of the old-fashioned Flemish type, lined with twee little window boxes full of busy-lizzies.

'This place hasn't changed much since Richard's time, by the look of it,' said Katherine.

Joe snorted. 'Don't you believe it. The whole village was blown to buggery in 1917. Nothing left. Everything you see, it's all rebuilt.'

There was not a great deal to choose from in the way of eateries, but they found a restaurant called Vivaldi's on the corner of the main road. It looked shut, and they couldn't see through its delicate little net curtains, but when Joe tried the door it was open. There was nobody else in there.

Katherine chose a table next to the window, where she was able to get a thrill from watching lorries hurtling straight towards them as they came round the mad S-bend. It was a friendly place run by a French woman – contrary to Joe's theory about the area being entirely Flemish-speakers – and, for reasons that weren't altogether clear, had a collection of antique Singer sewing-machines in the washroom adjoining the toilet.

'Well?' said Joe while they waited. 'How does it feel now that we've covered just about every known place where Richard was in action?'

'I don't know,' said Katherine. 'I'm really glad to have been to all these places, especially the Menin Gate, but I can't help feeling we've overlooked the important bits. Inevitable really, when he's got no known grave and we don't even know exactly where he died.'

She watched a sleepy wasp bashing its head idly against the window with a noise like a Sopwith Camel.

'I wish we'd been able to find his diary,' said Mark. He popped a sugar lump into his mouth and crunched it up. 'It would probably have given us a much better idea of where he was in the last few months of his life.'

'It may still turn up,' said Joe optimistically. 'Things like that have a habit of surfacing in museums and record offices if you search patiently enough.'

'I'd do anything to get hold of that diary,' sighed Katherine. 'Just think how much detail we'd get from it. All the things he got up to, the places he went, the names of his friends, everything.'

'And then we'd have to come out here again and spend another week visiting them all,' said Joe.

'Would you mind if I went and had a look round that church?' asked Mark as they wandered back to the car.

Katherine was glad he'd suggested it. The church looked a bit modern and unexciting, but she had felt strangely drawn towards it as well, although she wasn't sure why.

The front door was unlocked, and they found themselves standing in an aisle which led straight up to the high altar, with a row of international flags lined up at the far end. It was a bright place with a pleasant atmosphere. Katherine was rather grateful to find a guide leaflet written in English.

'They're using the place as a world centre for religious and political reconciliation,' she explained. 'That's why all those flags are up there. And they've got one of those carillon things. Musical bells.'

'Does it say anything about what's down here?' asked Mark, peering through a doorway which seemed to lead down into darkness.

'Hang on. Oh yeah, it does actually. There's an 11th century crypt under the church, which the Germans used as a dressing station and a command centre during the first world war. Adolf Hitler was given first aid there. And William the Conqueror's mum is buried down there too.'

'I hope nobody will mind if I take a look,' said Mark, sticking his head over the banister at the top of the shadowy staircase. 'I sort of feel the need to go down here for some reason.'

'There's a light switch on the wall here,' said Joe, flicking it on and flooding the stone steps with light. 'Mind how you go.'

They climbed down the narrow stairs in single file. Katherine noticed a peculiar feeling creeping over her, the sort of coldness in her legs which always seemed to precede a powerful psychic encounter. She put her hand on the wall to steady herself. Mark grunted as he bumped into another door at the bottom, and had to spend a moment groping for the next light switch. With a click, the small stone room was illuminated.

'Oh fuck,' exclaimed Katherine, staggering back against the wall. Joe and Mark both turned round in alarm. She blinked around the crypt, taking in its knobbly stone walls, its arched niches, and above all the blue-veiled madonna on its little stone altar. There was absolutely no doubt about it.

'This is the place,' she said, hyperventilating slightly with the shock. 'This is the place where Richard Munro used to sit and write his diary. I recognise it.'

Neither of her companions looked all that surprised.

'Is this what you saw during the trance session?' asked Joe.

'Yes. And in all the other bloody sessions. I've not been able to get this place out of my head. *Fuck.*'

The room had changed only slightly from the vision she had so clearly in her head. It was less dark and dusty, there was no straw or rubbish on the floor, and a couple of military gravestones and other interesting artefacts had been arranged in some of the niches.

'I'm not imagining it, am I? Do you know, were the 10th Gloucesters here at any time?'

'They were certainly in this area, yes,' said Joe. 'It's plausible that Richard could have come here.'

The madonna statue was startlingly familiar, even though she hadn't seen it before.

'It's so powerful-looking, that figure.'

'A black madonna,' said Mark. 'They turn up a lot in crypts on the continent. They're fab aren't they?'

'The Christian equivalent of the Dark Isis,' added Joe.

She peered closely into the virgin's black face and lightly stroked the edge of the veil. She could still feel that ice-cold, slightly shivery sensation. The presence of Richard Munro was building up so strongly that she thought she could sense him standing right next to her, benevolently gazing past her towards the statue. It was real enough to set the tears off for the second time that day, although this time they were tears of joy.

'I don't think I shall ever feel sad about Richard's death again,' she snuffled, cuffing her nose on the back of her hand. 'I don't know where he is now. But I know he's all right.'

Chapter Thirty-One

There was a cool breeze moving over the ridge, and a graduated blue tint in the sky which was interrupted only by a single puff of elongated cloud. Over on the horizon a dull thump was followed by a fat plume of smoke, which dissipated slowly. The breeze caught at the edges of the chaplain's white surplice as he squinted at his text through thick spectacles.

'I am the resurrection and the life, said the Lord. He that believeth in me, yea, though he were dead, yet shall he live. And whosoever liveth and believeth in me shall never die.'

Richard, standing at the head of the shallow pit, could almost hear Tate's voice saying 'Fuck that.'

He looked over towards the distant firing line, watching the shrapnel shells bursting in mid-air, smoke puffs appearing out of nowhere among the thin, slashed trees. Anything to avoid having to look at the hessian-wrapped bundle, tied up with baling twine, which sagged ungraciously towards the bottom of the pit. Death was such an undignified business. It didn't suit Tate at all.

In some ways he was saddened that nobody had come along except the burial party and a couple of privates from Tate's platoon, but at the same time he wanted to keep things low key and have a bit of privacy. His mind went back to the occasion – many moons ago – when they had sat on a cemetery wall and discussed funerals. As it turned out, Tate had to do without the union flags and bugles which he had scorned so much. The burial facilities here only stretched to a piece of sack and a wooden cross.

Even now, even as he stood watching his companion being committed to the earth, Richard felt no emotion. He had blubbed and lamented endlessly over Hugh, but this second dose of grief did not penetrate his heart at all. It was almost as though his heart had been removed altogether, for his own good, and replaced with a stone. He had gone so far down into the depths of grief that he had come out the other side and was no longer capable of feeling anything.

Two men hopped down into the pit and tried to arrange the bundle tidily along the bottom. Unfortunately, because Tate was so tall, the pit hadn't been dug quite big enough for him, and the men had to make a rather undignified effort to shove his feet down. This wasn't particularly successful, and in the end they had to leave him folded at the waist, with his legs stuck half way up the side of the pit. It looked utterly preposterous, and Richard stifled a perverse impulse to laugh. The chaplain looked embarrassed and got on with the job hastily.

Before they filled in the pit, Richard took the silver cigarette case from his pocket in which he still kept the remnants of lavender which Kathie had given him at the hospital. It was now no more than a bunch of dried brown sticks, but it retained an extraordinarily strong aroma. He gathered up most of it and scattered it into the pit. If nothing else, he thought, it would give his friend something to smoke in the afterlife.

Without waiting for the sordid business of shovelling in the earth, he made his way back to the church crypt in Messines village. He wanted to spend some time alone, which was not always easy in a war zone, and the crypt was probably his best chance of finding it. He lit the bedraggled pair of candles on the altar and sat down on the floor in front of the black madonna, and tried to clear his mind of all the 'if' thoughts which plagued him. If he had noticed the disturbance in Tate's behaviour, and taken his earlier suicide threat seriously, it might have been treatable. If he had woken up when Tate got up and left the dug-out on the fateful morning, he may have been able to stop him. If he'd known how bad things had got, he could have been a more supportive friend. But there was no point in dwelling on these things. How could he have known? He understood well enough what shellshock was like, but Tate did not have it. Shellshocked men shiver and twitch and claw at themselves. Tate was the exact opposite – he got calmer and calmer. Nobody who had seen him striding across the battlefield, bright-eyed with his trenchcoat flapping in the wind, could ever believe he was fearful or weak under duress. Hadn't his 'reckless' disregard for safety prevented him from becoming a captain? His suicide was not, in any respect, an act of desperation. It was just as though he had simply got bored with it all and decided to call it a day.

Major Pershore had shown great concern for Richard and was making an effort to secure his well-being. He was well aware that

Richard's collapse, from which he had still not fully recovered, was a direct result of Hugh's death. To lose his closest friend – from whom he had become inseparable – might be one tragedy too many. The major was keen to send him back home on whatever pretext he could, even if it was just for a couple of weeks' leave. He offered to 'pull some strings' among senior officers, but Richard coolly declined. With or without Tate, he felt his place was here now, looking after his men. What he didn't tell Pershore was that he had already decided in his mind that he would not be returning home at all. Home no longer existed in the true sense, only as a phantasmagoria of painful memories. The bridges which connected him to that world were already burning.

He reached out mentally to the madonna in front of him, whose black face was nothing more than a shadow in the candlelight. In a flicker of his eye he thought he saw the face become animated, looking back at him. The vision evaporated quickly, but the presence lingered, and the sense that he was being watched over by someone who really cared for him. He smeared away the tear that had formed at the corner of his eye.

*   *   *   *   *   *

The sun was starting to dip below the level of the trees in the distance, staining the sky orange. Mark steered the Mazda out onto the N365 and turned its nose towards Ploegsteert.

'We must be mad,' he said. 'Coming all this way at this time of the afternoon. It might even be dark by the time we get there.'

'It had to be done,' replied Katherine. 'I couldn't have gone back to England without setting my mind at rest about Messines. Just as well Joe was so understanding, really.'

'Yes. He might not be if he could see me revving the guts out of his car.'

The first of the sharp bends unfolded as they came to the edge of Messines.

'OK boss, where would you like me to stop?'

Katherine thought for a moment.

'Just carry on a bit, would you? I think I'll know when it's right.'

He drove slowly through the village and out the other side.

'And keep going?' He was starting to look a bit uneasy.

'There!' she said. 'Turn right at the crossroads.'

He turned into a smaller road which had a few houses alongside it but quickly became rural, with nothing but fields on either side. Katherine swivelled round in her seat, surveying the area on both sides.

'Pull over just here. If you wouldn't mind.'

Mark shunted the car over onto the grass verge and switched off the engine. The silence seemed to close in on them. They both gazed out over the fields.

'I know it looks like there's bugger all here,' Katherine explained, 'but I really think we're near the right spot.'

The evening was warm and pleasant, with nothing disturbing the quiet fields except the occasional tick of the cooling engine. The sun was almost down, but it was still reasonably light.

'Don't worry,' she said. 'I've brought a torch.'

She got out of the car, bringing a small rucksack with her. They strolled along the edge of the road in silence for a short distance, Katherine's inner senses reaching outwards and around like a radar. And then Mark spotted something in the ditch.

'Is it my imagination, or is there some sort of wooden structure in the ground there? Or rems of?'

'Yes. I'm not sure what, but there's something there.'

He went a bit closer to investigate. It was nothing more than a few rotting planks of wood with traces of very old green paint, but there was a lot of it. There was also a lot of rusty barbed wire, and a couple of shell canisters. It was very well embedded in the ground and had obviously been there for a long time.

Mark pulled out one of Joe's hand-made trench maps, and held it up to the remains of the light.

'Oh yes,' he said. 'I think there is something here. The old British front line trenches intersected the road at around this point, by the look of it.'

'Wow. So this bit of mouldy wood probably lined the front of the trench where Richard Munro spent his last few weeks. What a sobering thought.'

They rooted around in the margins of the adjacent field and found quite a few bits and pieces: bent bullets, shrapnel balls, a webbing buckle, a soldier's shirt button, and loads and loads of nails. They carried on until it got too dark to see.

'I suppose, logically, that if Richard was killed during a patrol from these trenches here, and the German trenches were over that way, then the actual site of his death must be somewhere in that field on the right.'

'Very possibly. There's no way of knowing for sure.'

They strolled across the field in the twilight and stopped by a concrete block with a rusty strut sticking up in the middle, probably an old machine-gun post. Katherine sat down on the grass at its base.

'I'm just going to stay here for a bit. Meditate.'

It was strangely tranquil, sitting in the middle of the former battle zone with the stars coming out overhead. They must have sat there for about an hour, mostly without speaking, while the sky darkened and the multitude of winking points of light came up brighter and brighter.

'I can see why people used to think the stars were the abode of gods,' said Katherine, breaking the silence. 'They're so beautiful on a clear night.'

'The ancient Egyptians reckoned that stars were the souls of the dead. That's where you go when you snuff it. If you've behaved yourself. You become one of the *Akhu*, the Shining Ones.'

'Quite a nice idea really.'

'I like looking at the stars when I'm stoned. You see all kinds of colours that you wouldn't normally see. Wish I'd brought some with me.'

'It would have been a nightmare to take it through Customs.'

'I'll have to try something else. Like whacking myself over the back of the head with a French stick.'

'What?' she laughed.

'Seriously. The visual cortex in your brain is just there at the back of your head. If you whack it in the right place you can jig it up and give yourself hallucinations.'

'With a baguette?'

'Well, a stale one.'

'And you've tried this, have you?'

A big grin spread across his face.

They sat in silent companionship for a moment. Katherine's mind kept drifting back to Richard Munro, and how he must have felt when he was here in these fields. His presence never seemed to be far away now. But since her visit to Messines church there was no feeling of sadness about it. An epiphany had been reached, a gulf bridged, in her connection with him. She had come to the place where awful things must have happened to him, but she could no longer find it within herself to feel sad.

The familiar icy chill across her knees and along her arms made it clear that he wasn't far away. Things were stirring on a psychic level. The icy feeling shivered its way up between her shoulder blades.

'Are you cold?' asked Mark, noticing the small shudder. Without waiting for a reply he discreetly moved along the edge of the machine-gun post until his arm was snuggled against her.

She wasn't cold at all, but didn't want to spoil the moment. His warmth and proximity gave her an overwhelming sense of contentment. She would not have believed, a few months ago, that she would ever fall in love with a man who talked to his rosebushes and kept a concrete gnome dedicated to the elemental lord Paralda, but there you go. Times change.

Eventually he said: 'Thank you for bringing me here. On this quest, I mean. I've really enjoyed meeting Richard Munro.'

'I can't take all the credit for it. It was your intuition which took us to the golden virgin, wasn't it? And made us stop at Messines, and then you found the crypt when we got there. I think you're more in tune with it than I am in some ways.'

'I feel attuned.'

She turned and tried to make out the shape of his face in the low light.

'I believe you. So tell me what you're picking up from it now.'

He tipped his head back to look at the stars overhead. 'I was just thinking that this is more or less the same time of year that Richard disappeared. Give or take a couple of weeks. So these constellations are probably not far off what he would have seen if he'd bothered to look up.'

She thought about it for a moment.

'That's brilliant. Do you realise what an interesting thing you've just said?'

272

'What?'

'Richard was a keen astronomer. Of course he looked at the stars.'

'Buggery, you're right.'

'So what do you think went through his head when he was here, here in this very field, looking at these same stars?'

'He'd probably think that it doesn't make any odds what changes go on down here. The sky is eternal. Whether it's us sitting here wishing we were stoned, or him and the Germans crawling around throwing bombs at each other. The stars don't change. Not within a human timescale, anyway.'

His inner senses were alight now with the sense of alignment between the stars and the earth.

'The stars are what connects us to Richard. He was here at a different time, when the land was in flux, but the sky pattern is the same.'

She gazed up at it with new-found wonder, and laughed out loud. 'It bloody well is, isn't it? It's the same sky.'

Chapter Thirty-Two

Richard stayed in the crypt for some time, thinking.

The diary was open on a blank page, where he had intended to write up the story of the funeral, but hadn't been able to find the words, and the unwritten pages held only a pale glow from the light of the altar candles. The book sat between him and the black madonna as if it were an offering. From the moment of Tate's death, its voice had become mute.

He turned back to the first page. The handwriting looked strangely naïve and immature, written when he was somebody else. In the top left hand corner was Hugh's name and address, with a light-hearted request that the diary be forwarded to him if anything should happen to its writer. Bloody stupid of him, he reflected, not to have contemplated the possibility of it being the other way around.

If anything happened to him now it would probably be Louisa who got possession of the diary, and then what? Who would ever read it who would understand it?

An uncharacteristic urge to pray suddenly came upon him. He had never forged a connection with the religion whose empty motions were repeated, rote-learned and unthinking, by pretty much everyone in England – reciting their lines dutifully on a Sunday morning while in their heads they were thinking about their dinner or their laundry or about shagging the person in the next pew. Now, for pretty much the first time, he felt the presence of something genuinely holy. And it emanated from this black-faced goddess set into the wall before him.

He knelt on the floor in the straw and gazed into the face of the statue, drawn into its darkness. None of her features were visible in the low light, only the blue robe whose folds hung around her, and the winking points of light on the stars around her head.

'Take me,' he said in his mind to the goddess. 'Absorb me.'

He closed his eyes and felt himself yield to the gravitational pull. A disorientating lurch came over him, a sense of not quite being the right way up. It seemed to him then that the madonna was drawing all the agonies and flames and secrets from the surrounding battlefields and taking them up within herself, like the dark places in space which draw off surrounding star matter. All his memories and sufferings were being pulled away from him.

At that moment he became aware of somebody behind him. Nobody had come in physically, but he could feel the presence of the woman who had always been there for him on the battlefield and the other times. His inner vision could see her standing by the back wall, watching over him. The air in the crypt felt warmer. So strong was her presence that he was quite convinced that if he turned around he would actually see her there, physically. But he didn't turn; he didn't want to break the stasis and lose the vision. He wrapped her presence around himself gratefully.

In his mind he was slipping down a shaft, though which way up it was he couldn't tell; so fast he could only let go and allow it to take him. He felt the etheric pull, drawing him into the black face of the goddess and the tangle of bright stars about her head. As he plummeted he could see the detritus of war whirling towards the vortex before him. Bodies, barbed wire, broken guns, all hurtling into transformation. He knew what he had to do.

He opened his eyes and offered the diary to the goddess.

'Take this, and all that's within it.'

He took Hugh's brass cigarette lighter out of his pocket, flicked the blue flame into life and applied it to the top corner of the book. It flared briefly and the bar of orange spread slowly from the cover to the pages, consuming, transforming. He flicked the lighter again and held it for slightly longer, underneath the middle of the back cover. It caught in a rippling flame which sent shadows pulsing into the corners of the crypt. The room began to fill with smoke. He watched the figure of the dark virgin through the haze, much as he had watched the golden virgin in the post-bombardment haze of Albert. Smoke tumbled round the room and into that potent black space, taking with it the memories of all the sufferings he had committed to the book, the sweat and spume of war. All consumed and redeemed. He gave himself up to the goddess and maintained his vigil until all the paper was ash.

*　　　　*　　　　*　　　　*　　　　*　　　　*

When he returned to the front line, he found he no longer felt any fear when he heard the zing of bullets glancing off the wire, or the shuddering impact of a crump. It all seemed to go by in the same way, and he felt freed from it all. Perhaps this was what Tate had experienced; a form of redemption which raised him above the whole business.

It was in that spirit of liberation that he volunteered to go out alone into No Man's Land to reconnoitre the ground on behalf of a raiding party which had fallen to the command of Sergeant Russell. They had used this arrangement on a number of occasions; Richard would crawl over to the enemy wire, find a spot where the wire was broken or damaged, and then relay the information to Russell, who was showing some skill in getting small parties of men in and out of the German trenches at lightning speed, just long enough to throw some bombs or snatch a prisoner. It was good teamwork, which no doubt owed a lot to the fact that they didn't actually have to work together.

There was a low hedge running most of the way to the German line, an old field boundary, just visible by being darker than the darkness, which gave Richard a reasonable amount of cover. He crouched behind it whenever a flare lit up overhead, and then scurried on when darkness returned.

The situation at the other side turned out to be more favourable than usual; about ten yards to the left of the hedge was a narrow but cleanly cut hole in the barbed wire entanglement. He spent some minutes examining it by feel in the darkness, unsure whether it might have been cut deliberately by the Germans to facilitate a deadly excursion of their own. Much as he disliked Russell, it would be very unfortunate if his group encountered a German raiding party coming out just as he was going in. But the broken ends of barbed wire were twisted and rough, which suggested it had been broken up randomly by shrapnel. At any rate, the hole was big enough for men to pass through easily in single file, and that was good enough.

He made his way back to the British line and relayed the details to Russell, who noted it all down carefully in his notebook. Within fifteen minutes Russell had gathered together his team of four men and slipped over the parapet.

They didn't come back.

It was always hard to know when it was appropriate to start getting worried. Raids were never predictable, all down to prevailing conditions. Only gut feeling can judge when something is wrong.

'Shall I go out and look for them?' he asked Lieutenant Nowell, who was nominally overseeing the raiding party and was pacing nervously back and forth along the trench.

'Not likely,' Nowell said, tearing at the top of a fingernail with his teeth. 'You might startle them and end up shooting each other. I don't doubt that the bullets would just bounce off Mr Russell, but you'd darn well cop it.'

By two o'clock in the morning it was clear that something was wrong, whether Russell was immortal or not. There was no sign at all of the raiding party.

'I'm going over,' said Richard.

'You're bloody not,' retorted Nowell.

'I am too. I'll see you later.'

He hopped up onto the parapet and slithered down into the wet ditch on the other side. As he squelched to his feet he could still hear Nowell's whispered protestations, but there wasn't much he could do to stop him. If Nowell had been a senior officer it would have been harder to disobey him, but as they were both lieutenants he felt he could chance it.

The darkness was absolute. There was no moon. Richard groped his way through the barbed wire, which snagged sharply at his coat, breaking threads. High above him in the sky the shells whined past, invisible, falling some way behind the front line. No immediate danger.

He made his way to the end of the hedge and followed it along towards the German line. The soil under his feet was soggy in places and made a sploshing noise as he shuffled along. Even in July the mud clung at every step, dough-like, building up in heavy clots around his boots. It was about a hundred yards to the German line, and it couldn't be hurried.

After a while he found the gap in the wire and crouched in silence, listening. It was difficult to hear anything clearly against the faint, erratic rumble of far-off shells, but every now and then he caught the sound of the German sentry clumping softly over duckboards as he slowly paced about, the occasional clatter of a rifle touching the wooden boards at the front of the trench. Richard drew his revolver and eased himself forward through the wire with meticulous poise. The slightest cough or sploshy footstep would be the finish of him.

He stalked over to the left, to the point where the trench bent round in a sharp traverse. The bend would screen him from the sentry while he slipped noiselessly up to the parapet and clambered over into the trench. He waited, cringing, for the pattering of soil to subside as he scraped his feet down the trench wall on the other side. Nothing.

He dropped down from the firestep and cautiously felt his way around. It was almost pitch black, and he could only see the outlines of pale shapes, unidentifiable. There might even be sleeping Germans there, for all he knew. Something caught the corner of his eye further along on the firestep, something unmistakable in shape even in the dark. He listened both ways to check he was still alone, and then flicked on the tiny flash-lamp he carried with him. It was indeed what it had appeared to be: a man's body, dumped unceremoniously to one side, limbs akimbo. Indeed there were two bodies, stacked up together and draped with a grey sheet. Both wore khaki uniforms, and both had been killed with bayonets.

Richard swore silently and snapped out the light. He didn't have time to look at their faces and identify them, but if these two had ended up this way then the others were not likely to have fared much better. The sentry cleared his throat on the other side of the traverse. He sounded incredibly close. Richard slipped over into the densest shadow, under the front wall of the trench. Now that he had found the British corpses he felt that he had achieved his objective, and his priority now was to get out as quickly as possible.

He only got as far as climbing the firestep when an extra set of footsteps started to approach, and to his right he saw the glimmer of a lighted cigarette. In a stupid act of desperation he made a lunge for the top of the trench and got half way – gripping the sandbags on the far side of the parapet, with his legs still dangling in the trench above the firestep. He held his breath and felt a hot flush of sweat run down his forehead and into his eyes, stinging his eyelids into spasms. It was a German officer doing his rounds, as Richard himself had done countless times. The officer passed by with a long, ambling stride, and his trenchcoat brushed against Richard's feet. For a full ten seconds Richard hung in complete silence, half in and half out of the trench, beads of sweat running down his face like tears. But the officer passed by. Richard licked his top lip where the sweat had accumulated and a felt a certain joy at the salty taste. He was alive to taste it, that was the main thing.

He hopped forward and slid head first down the bank on the other side, using his hands to pull himself along, then crouched for a few moments just inside the barbed wire entanglements. It felt much better to be clear of the trench. He listened for any sign of activity, but the only sound from the other side of the parapet was the sentry whistling as he clumped softly up and down. Nothing else stirred. He gazed up at the sky through the barbed wire which stood out against it in spirals of spiky black. It was a lovely night for star-gazing. Or it would be, if he were anywhere else.

Slowly he got to his feet, not daring to walk upright, creeping along bent double, with his revolver at the ready. The gap in the wire was only a few yards away and he could see where a broken thread of it trailed out from the general fuzz of spikes. He took a step forward and his left foot caught in a loop of old wire which was half buried in the ground. It jerked his foot out from underneath him and he stumbled heavily, coming down on his knees with an audible squelch. The sentry stopped whistling. Richard felt another wave of sweat break out on his face, and sheer, cold terror in his solar plexus. There was nothing he could do. He waited for a second or two, still on his knees in the mud, and saw a small black object come over the parapet a short distance in front of him.

'Oh bugger it,' he whispered to himself, momentarily seized with despair, and then dropped forward on his stomach and flattened himself against the ground. He felt the force of the explosion like a blow to the small of his back, and heard the fragments of the grenade pelt the side of the trench just behind him. He was holding his breath, and was astonished to find, when he lifted his face from the mud and took the next lungful of air, that he was still alive. The grenade had been damped a little by the soggy ground.

He could now hear two or three German voices conversing urgently from the inside of the trench. He had a basic knowledge of German, having learned it for a while at school, but he found the rapid speech quite unintelligible.

There was a thud just above him and something rolled down the slope and came to rest just in front of his face. It was just visible in the dark; a black egg-shaped object. He didn't have a chance to weigh up the risk. He lurched forward, grabbed the grenade and hurled it as far away as he could. Not into the German trench, which would be asking for trouble, but into the barbed wire further along. It exploded almost immediately and flared through the wire with a fierce flash. Before he had a chance to reflect on his narrow miss he saw two or three more bombs flip over the top and roll down into the wire further along. The Germans were obviously unsure of his exact position, and were now throwing the grenades a little way off target, mainly towards the gap in the wire. He drew a sharp breath and fled some distance in the opposite direction without bothering about the consequences of making a noise. It was a chance he had to take. There were three explosions behind him in rapid succession, and he saw the barbed wire momentarily illuminated as he ran. Another explosion went off, closer, making him drop to his knees and then stumble on again. There was no way out. He was trapped. All he could do was run along in the ditch between the German trench and the German wire, and hope to God there was a gap somewhere. If he couldn't get back out into No Man's Land he was truly stuffed.

He discovered a slight kink in the line of the trench which curved inward slightly, giving him some slight protection from flying shards of metal. He stood upright and pressed himself flat against the front wall of the trench. It didn't feel very safe, knowing that there could be a German peering out just above his head, but it was his best option. The explosions stopped. He kept very quiet, knowing that the Germans would be listening out for him, trying to work out if he was still alive. Several minutes passed. There was not another sound from the German trenches.

For a few moments he was at a loss as to what he should do. It looked as though he had escaped being blown to pieces, at least for the time being, but he was still stuck behind the enemy wire and they knew he was there. What could he do? He had to get out of it before daybreak at the very least.

A little further along he could see a dark patch in the wire. It could be a gap; he wasn't sure. He stood and looked at it for several minutes, then took a few tentative steps towards it. He hadn't gone far when a flare went up above the British lines. It was some way off, but it cast a thin, insipid light over the whole area. Richard pressed himself closer to the trench wall, trying to keep himself out of the line of vision of any German sentries who might be watching. When he found the courage to turn his head and look again at the dark patch in the wire, which was now illuminated in the milky glow, he saw that it was not a gap after all. It was Sergeant Russell, curled over backwards in an arc and caught across the barbed wire with his arms flailed over his head, stiff and dead. He had a bonny bunch of roses across his chest, Richard observed, and the blood had run down the wires behind him and formed into sticky clots around each barb. Evidently the machine-guns had finally grown tired of his bragging.

He had no desire to stay where he was any longer than necessary, and as soon as the flare faded out he began to shuffle with extreme caution back the way he had come. Russell had obviously been caught in the same rat-trap as him and he didn't want to end up the same way. He tried to still the sound of his breathing and take tiny, noiseless steps. It seemed like an endless, impossible journey. There was no whistling or clumping footsteps from any sentry now; the Germans had got the wind up, and were listening out. It took him the best part of half an hour to shuffle back to the point where he had earlier entered the German trench. And having reached that point, he somehow had to break away from the shadows and make a bee-line for the hole in the wire without being seen.

There was very little to it really, he told himself. He could see the gap, it wasn't very far away. All he had to do was creep through it without making any noise. Easier said than done, perhaps, but nothing he hadn't done before.

He got down on his hands and knees and crawled a little way out from the trench wall. Nobody fired at him, which was a good start. He took another couple of short steps. Still nothing. With his own heartbeat the loudest sound in his head he made his way forward into the wire. The gap was actually slightly bigger than when he had come through it earlier, because one of the wooden frames which held the entanglement together had been splintered and churned up by the grenades. He was aware that if he was shot now he would get a bullet in the backside, but there wasn't much he could do about it.

Without a sound he crawled, still on his hands and knees, right through the hole in the wire. He wanted to weep with fear. This time the sweat was dripping off his face, falling from his nose and brow, and occasionally landing as a lukewarm splash on the back of his hand. But remarkably, mercifully, he found himself safely on the other side.

He kept going for a few yards to make sure he was clear of the gap, then stopped and turned round. The dark hulk of the enemy trench stood out from the blackness, but there was no sound or movement from behind it. Everything was still. Even the shells passing overhead had subsided.

Very slowly, Richard straightened himself out and got up on his feet, still watching the German line. A sharp burst of machine-gun fire spattered out from the darkness right in front of him. He saw the flitting, elongated flashes and felt a stinging slap across his left shoulder and chest. He turned and began to run back towards the British line but the muscles in his legs had turned to jelly. They gave way under his weight, though he tried to get in as many strides as possible before they collapsed altogether. He went down on his left side, and found his right hand grasping at the shoulder of his coat, which was already soaked. He felt no pain as such, but he was terrified to feel how rapidly the blood ran over his fingers, pulsing relentlessly with each heartbeat. His left arm was totally numb. As far as he could tell as his fingers probed nervously, there were two wounds. It was the one just below his breast-bone which worried him the most.

He had a field dressing in his pocket which he dragged out and tore open with his teeth. But it wasn't enough; the dressing soon became soaked and turned into a useless sponge, and the effort of pressing it against his chest sent his right arm into spasm. He had to lean down on the ground to let his own weight press the pad against the wound. Still the blood coursed over his fingers, unstoppable.

'This is it,' he thought. 'I've had it.'

There was no way Nowell would be able to send anybody else out to look for him. He was here for the duration. Suddenly there didn't seem to be much point in worrying about it any more. He heaved himself up and flung the bloodied dressing away. It was a good hundred yards to the British line; no point even attempting it.

He let himself slip down onto his back so that he could look up at the sky. Vega was very prominent again, he noticed, just as it had been on the night Tate had won his Military Cross. That was very comforting. The constellation of Cygnus was spread out high overhead, a dot-to-dot figure of a flying swan, with Hercules just below. It really was a lovely night for star-gazing. He felt the blood begin to run down over his shoulder and collect in a pool under his neck. The stars winked gloriously. His life seeped away into the soil. There would be a different sky breaking over him by the morning.

Coda

~

Richard blinked slowly three, four, five times, trying to clear the haze that had come over his vision. It was a fantastic sight, with the milky way arcing across the middle of the sky, a sprinkling of celestial dust. In the absence of the moon it all stood out magnificently, silver-white, lightly shimmering. If only he could keep it in focus. His mind was swimming slightly, buoyed up on the dark sea between consciousness and oblivion. Vega was still blazing above him, a little blurry now, but standing out as a beacon which would outlast him and this silly war. A few shells still flew over with a noise like a tram-car passing overhead, but he couldn't see them. They did nothing to interrupt his view of the sky, and the whole business of war had shrivelled into insignificance. It was just him now, and the stars.

He saw a ribbon of light emanate from Vega and attach itself to his mind, as if a beam had come down and fixed him between the eyes with a pleasant tingling sensation. Part of him knew that it was just an optical illusion brought on by loss of blood, but he allowed his mind to drift and go with it. Somehow he didn't need to keep looking at it; his physical eyes were wandering out of focus and he could see it more clearly when he closed them and looked at it with his inner eye. He felt very light-headed, as if his mind had become slightly detached from his body and was floating just fractionally above it, where it was free to expand. With his inner eye he could see a woman sitting close beside him gazing up at the stars, and with her came a sudden sense of wellbeing. He could let go now. It was safe to let go. He wouldn't fall.

A noise close to his head attracted his attention. A noise of boots trampling past. He opened his eyes and blinked a few times. It was almost light now and there was a pair of army boots in his immediate line of vision, walking purposefully in the direction of the British line. His vision was bleary but he could still see perfectly clearly the way the mud was caked up around the thick soles of the boots and squeezed through the eyelets around loosely tied laces. With a sudden expansion of awareness he realised that it was not just one pair of boots. There were dozens of men walking past him, a whole field full of men. Most of them were covered in mud; some were wounded and being propped up by others. He could see them rising up out of the mud, men appearing as if from nowhere, coming up off the chopped surface of the earth and taking human shape, whole battalions of them. They were all heading the same way, to a point in the west behind the British line. Richard was lying with his head towards the west so he couldn't see what was behind him, but he was aware that something magnificent was happening.

Then one of the passing figures stopped, and he looked up and saw that it was Tate leaning over him, standing in his usual elegant pose with his cap pulled down slightly over his eyes. Richard grinned sheepishly, and Tate knelt down beside him and prodded irreverently at his bullet wounds.

'What *have* you done to yourself, you silly arse?'

'It wasn't me,' Richard protested. 'It was the Germans.'

'They don't like British officers poking about in front of their trenches, Richard, you should know that.' He looked his friend up and down with mock disapproval. 'Honestly, I leave you on your own for five minutes and you go straight out and get yourself plugged by some little squirt of a Fritz. You daft fucker.'

Richard felt himself slipping into a deeper state of detachment. When he closed his eyes and opened them again he was aware of his own body lying out in the middle of No Man's Land, alone, with his mind sliding back and forth, in and out of consciousness like a ship listing on a rough sea. The stars had changed in some subtle way. He was aware of them as ancient lights, evolving over millions of years, tiny intense points of light. His consciousness condensed into something quite separate from his body. The only thing he was aware of was his right hand trying to reach into his inside pocket, where he had kept Tate's suicide note. But the effort of trying to retrieve it was too much, and he found he really couldn't be bothered.

'Fuck-face,' he shouted out, and giggled childishly. 'Fuck-face, fuck-face, fuck-face.'

The stars in his field of vision wheeled their way slowly towards the west.

Author's acknowledgements

In any historical novel the sources of research are numerous, but among those I owe credit to are Robert Graves' *Goodbye to All That*, the various works of Lyn Macdonald, and above all the incredible and largely forgotten work *Realities of War* by Philip Gibbs, from which several of the incidents in this book are drawn. Additionally, some of the poems and ditties were written in trenches by soldiers of the Gloucestershire Regiment.

I owe much gratitude to my parents Basil and Roma Wilby who walked the Somme and Ypres battlefields with me, and my deepest thanks to Daniel Staniforth, the kindest and most supportive of muses.

Lightning Source UK Ltd.
Milton Keynes UK
UKOW051222090113

204634UK00008B/156/P

9 781908 011022